Once before and had yielded to the fire in her blood and to the passionate power of a strong and skillful lover.

That first time, she was a university student in Berlin, and the dashing, domineering radical Kurt Stein sought to mold her mind—even as he made her body an instrument of his pleasure.

Anna vowed that never again would a man manipulate her mind or enslave her senses.

But facing Jim Parnell *in public,* in a crowded Chicago courtroom, *and in private,* in an intimate rendezvous, she felt again the sweet temptation to surrender to a desire she could not deny.

Anna was a beautiful, brave, and brilliant woman driven by a dream—yet hungering for love—in a world that made it so hard to have both.

Honor the Dream

Honor
the Dream

Joyce Carlow

A SIGNET BOOK

SIGNET
Published by the Penguin Group
Penguin Books USA Inc., 375 Hudson Street,
New York, New York 10014, U.S.A.
Penguin Books Ltd, 27 Wrights Lane,
London W8 5TZ, England
Penguin Books Australia Ltd, Ringwood,
Victoria, Australia
Penguin Books Canada Ltd, 10 Alcorn Avenue,
Toronto, Ontario, Canada M4V 3B2
Penguin Books (N.Z.) Ltd, 182-190 Wairau Road,
Auckland 10, New Zealand

Penguin Books Ltd, Registered Offices:
Harmondsworth, Middlesex, England

First published by Signet, an imprint of New American Library,
a division of Penguin Books USA Inc.

First Printing, January, 1992
10 9 8 7 6 5 4 3 2 1

 REGISTERED TRADEMARK—MARCA REGISTRADA

Printed in the United States of America

PUBLISHER'S NOTE
This is a work of fiction. Names, characters, places, and incidents either are the product of the author's imagination or are used fictitiously, and any resemblance to actual persons, living or dead, events, or locales is entirely coincidental.

BOOKS ARE AVAILABLE AT QUANTITY DISCOUNTS WHEN USED TO PROMOTE PRODUCTS OR SERVICES. FOR INFORMATION PLEASE WRITE TO PREMIUM MARKETING DIVISION, PENGUIN BOOKS USA INC., 375 HUDSON STREET, NEW YORK, NEW YORK 10014.

I

Contrasts
1910–1914

1

A cold damp wind swept down the platform of Lehrte Station, causing many of the better-dressed women to lift their arms to their heads in order to hold down their elaborate broad-brimmed hats. Those who were dressed for the inclement weather, rather than as fashion plates, did not wear hats, but instead chose hoods or woolen scarves.

Anna's intent blue eyes fastened on a robust woman who stood nearby. She wore a long sealskin coat and a huge felt hat trimmed with gray egret feathers and wide black satin bows. The plumage shuddered in the wind, and for a moment it seemed the soul of the bird from which the feathers had come might triumph over death and take flight. That fleeting thought caused Anna to imagine that all the women's hats would, if caught by such a gust, take wing in the early-morning air and lift from the station like a flock of dark crows startled while feeding in a field of grain. But the woman's hat, indeed all the hats, held fast, though some were a bit askew.

Anna's mother, Gisela von Bock, was wearing a large black felt hat bound with black satin and trimmed with velvet ribbon. It had no feathers, but instead was decorated with a large sterling-silver buckle which caught the flickering light from the lamps that illuminated the platform in the predawn darkness.

Anna's mother turned up the high wide collar of her full-length black astrakhan coat and buried her gloved hands deeper in her smart black fur muff.

Anna studied her mother's expression and concluded that her mother was as miserable as she. Gisela von Bock was certainly the most elegantly dressed woman in sight, but in spite of that fact, she looked neither happy nor comfortable. Her lovely heart-shaped face was tense and she spoke through almost closed lips, a certain sign that she was holding in her emotions. And when she spoke, her voice was higher than usual, as if she were speaking to a child rather than to another adult.

"Look at you, Karla . . . you'll freeze. You'll catch a terrible cold and be sick for the whole dreadful voyage!"

The last part of her mother's admonition to Tante Karla was nearly lost as she swallowed the word "voyage," unable to utter it.

Anna looked from her mother to her aunt and then back again. They were nothing alike: there was no feature or even a mannerism that would indicate they were sisters. Gisela, her mother, was only just over five feet. She was petite and had an aura of delicacy. Her complexion was pale and flawless, her blue eyes huge for her tiny face, and her hair, when uncovered and loosened, was a mass of silver and gold waves. On this morning her mother's tiny blond demeanor was emphasized by her black hat and coat.

Tante Karla, by contrast, was over five feet, six inches and seemed taller still because her felt button-up boots had a two-inch heel. And while Tante Karla did have a fair complexion, her hair was brown and her eyes were hazel. She was not fat, but she was broad-shouldered, and standing next to her older sister, she seemed like a giantess.

No, no one observing these two women would think them sisters, Anna decided. And certainly no one would guess that Gisela, her mother, was twelve years older than Karla, her aunt. At least no one would guess their relative ages unless one listened to them. In conversation, Gisela sounded very much the older sister, used to exercising her maternal role. Not that Karla needed mothering; in fact she paid no attention to Gisela's advice. Karla, unlike her mother, was a rebellious soul. Her father, in fact, called Karla a "liberal reformer" and Anna knew full well that that phrase, coming from her father, was far from a compliment.

Karla and her mother were different in other ways too. Karla was quite plainly dressed. Her coat was wool, had a tailored military collar, and large roomy pockets. It was what her mother called "serviceable." And Karla didn't have a hat either. Instead her hair was covered with a "fascinator," a warm molded crocheted wrap.

In response to her mother's scolding about warm clothes, Karla only laughed. She had a sincere, hearty laugh that reflected her true cheerfulness and optimistic personality. "I'm wearing my long woolen drawers and a warm vest, Gisela. I'm quite as warm as you. I won't catch cold, I never do."

"Sh! Goodness . . . for heaven's sake, don't discuss undergarments in public," her mother hissed.

"You *are* a prude," Karla scoffed. "It's Klaus . . . you married a much too proper man, Gisela. Much too proper."

Her mother pressed her lips tightly and furrowed her brow, then asked ever so softly, "Are we to fight during our last few minutes together, Karla? God knows when we'll see each other again . . . maybe never."

"No, we won't fight. And don't be so maudlin. Klaus has money. Tell him you want to visit America."

"He won't leave Germany."

"I suppose not, he hardly leaves Berlin," Karla responded, shaking her head.

"He works too hard, but he's a good husband. A wonderful provider, Karla."

"And the very definition of the word 'stability,' " Karla laughed. Spontaneously she hugged her sister. "Ah, we may be sisters, but we're opposites—perhaps because we're almost of different generations. I would never marry a man like Klaus, but I suppose he's good *for you*. Yes, Gisela, we're different, I know that. You want the things Klaus has to give . . . I . . . I want something else. I want adventure, I want to reinvent myself, Gisela."

Again Anna looked from her aunt to her mother. Her mother had tears in her eyes now.

"Oh, Karla, I'm going to miss you so."

"I'll write. I promise."

"You didn't write when you went to Bavaria for the summer."

"That was years ago. I will write."

"You must."

The train belched steam and a loud tooting sound warned the milling passengers on the platform to board.

Karla turned to look at Anna, and Anna looked back steadily, trying not to cry but wanting to cry. Perhaps if she did not cry, Karla wouldn't think she cared. And I do care, she declared silently. She wanted to throw her arms around Karla and beg her to stay . . . but she knew that Karla had to go to the man she loved, and perhaps just as important, Karla had to escape the stifling German autocracy and her only family, Gisela's family, who for the most part were the perfect representatives of that autocracy.

But knowing that Karla wanted to leave, in fact had to leave, did not change the fact that she wanted to tell Karla how very much she cared for her, but she knew she couldn't verbalize her feelings in front of her mother, who, in her strange neurotic way, would take such a declaration badly, would in fact interpret it to mean she loved Karla more. As she had grown older, Anna had learned to be careful around her mother, especially where her own deep affection for Karla was concerned.

Anna's thought fled to the previous summer . . . to long warm summer days spent walking in the park with Karla.

"Have you finished reading *Nana?*" Karla asked as they sat down by the pond where, by the distant shore, a pair of elegant white swans glided across the calm water.

"Yes, but I had to hide it from Father. I mentioned the title to him and he said Zola was a communist—or worse."

Karla had laughed. "Oh, God! Really?" Then urgently, confidentially, "You didn't tell him I lent it to you, did you?"

"No. But Father did ask where I heard of Zola. He said, 'I suppose Karla talked about that book. She's a bad influence on you.' " Anna smiled at her own imitation of her father's authoritarian voice and manner. "But I told him I saw it in the bookshop."

Karla had smiled. "You're quick; nonetheless, you shouldn't lie. I must admit, Zola isn't considered quite proper reading for sixteen-year-olds, but you're more mature than most, and certainly smarter."

"It's not a lie that would hurt anyone," Anna remembered saying. Then, enthusiastically, "Discuss the book with me, I have some questions."

"You have questions?" Karla had asked. "Anna, you are ten times more intelligent than I."

"I do well on examinations, but being smart involves more than reading and remembering. You've experienced life."

They had stayed by the pond for hours and talked, but not just about the book. They had talked about Karla's lover, Josef Baer. He was a writer, a journalist who had emigrated to America. Karla had talked then about leaving Germany to join him, and Anna had begun to fear she'd lose Karla, who, she realized, was truly important to her.

Karla is more a sister to me than an aunt, far more a sister than my real sister, Gerda, Anna acknowledged. Like her mother and aunt, she and Gerda were separated by years—seven, to be exact—and Gerda, now twenty-three, had been married since Anna was twelve. Gerda had a child of her own, she and Anna shared few, if any, interests. Karla, now thirty-three, had remained single long after most women wedded, and being single, she had always found time for Anna.

"You're a beautiful and very intelligent young woman," Karla's voice brought Anna back to the present. Karla hugged her and took her hands. Then, whispering in her ear, "You study hard, Anna. And most important, you be what you want to be. Don't let those brothers of yours earn all the glory . . . you can shine, Anna. You can shine brightly. And follow your heart as well as your head, Anna. Remember, my darling, life is a grand adventure."

Anna nodded and tears flooded her eyes.

Karla squeezed her hands tightly and then kissed her

on the cheek. Again she whispered in her ear, "You go to college, you hear? You insist on it!"

Anna nodded and returned her aunt's kiss, hugging her fiercely, and already feeling the loss of her only real confidant.

"Oh, it's such a long trip and it's so far away! Why couldn't you fall in love with a man who wanted to stay in Germany?" her mother wailed.

"Oh, Gisela! Even if Josef had wanted to stay in Germany, he would probably have been driven away . . . I might add, by men like your Klaus. Oh, Gisela, Gisela, we would be driven apart by our politics, don't you see that?"

"I have no politics," Gisela replied curtly, her lower lip visibly hardening.

"Ah, but Klaus does, and Josef does . . . and I do too, Gisela."

"It is Klaus who gave you the money for your passage to America as a wedding present."

Again Karla laughed. "Doubtless glad to be rid of me before I become a public embarrassment or totally corrupt Anna."

"That's a dreadful thing to say."

"But true," Karla insisted. "I don't imagine Klaus was overjoyed that you insisted on coming to see me off this morning."

Gisela avoided her sister's penetrating gaze and looked down. "He said we should have said our farewells last night. It's true, he didn't want us to come to the station . . . but only because it's so early in the morning, practically still night."

"And of course ladies do not go out at night unescorted, is that it?"

Gisela nodded, then looked up. "But I insisted. I said I had to see you off and so he relented and sent us in the carriage with a driver."

Karla smiled. "*You* insisted? Oh, Gisela; that is a small victory!"

Anna smiled to herself as she watched Karla's eyes dance with amusement. "A small victory" was one of Karla's favorite phrases and she used it whenever a woman did something of importance. "Women," Karla prophesied, "will never have a proper revolution," but she predicted, "we'll chip away at male power and there will be small victories and little triumphs until one day we wake up and find out we have achieved equality."

Her mother ignored Karla's comment about small victories. "Milwaukee . . . it's so far," she lamented.

"Josef says it is quite wonderful. He's waiting and I do love him, Gisela. After all, isn't this what you wanted? You've been lecturing me about the evils of being an old maid for years."

Gisela nodded. "Be happy, Karla. Have children and be happy."

"You be happy too. And see to Anna, Gisela. Having two brothers is bad enough, but having a sister like Gerda makes life even more difficult."

"Gerda's a good girl. You're playing favorites."

"Oh, I admit it. Gerda makes fine streusel and plays family games to perfection. But Anna reads and formulates arguments. Anna is more my type and she *is* the only one of your children who is like *our* side of the family, Gisela. Anna is like our father. She takes after him, and she needs to be nurtured. Anyway, Gerda has gone to raise her own family."

Anna thought for a moment of her maternal grandfather. He had been a brilliant philosopher, a humanist. But he was all but lost to her. Her sole memory was of a bespectacled man with a fringe of white hair—a man who spoke with almost painful slowness, a man whom she remembered as being acutely aware, but imprisoned in a decaying physical body.

Anna heard her mother's voice, soft, faraway, acknowledging Karla's observation. "It's true, we had each other," Gisela whispered, and all the control in the world crumbled. Tears ran down her cheeks and Anna watched, surprised, but glad that her mother was crying.

Karla hugged Gisela and then picked up her tapestry bag and turned suddenly and climbed the steel steps that led to the railway carriage. She turned once at the top and waved. *"Aufwiedersehen,* my darlings," she called as she disappeared, only to reappear moments later, her smiling face framed by the window.

The train jerked forward and amid billows of steam it began to move slowly away from the station.

For a few minutes after Karla disappeared from sight, Anna and her mother stood in silence on the frosty wind-blown platform. Anna watched silently as her mother withdrew an embroidered handkerchief and dabbed at her cheeks. Then resolutely her mother looked at her. "We should go home now," she said firmly. "It's only seven. If we hurry we'll be able to have breakfast with your father."

Anna didn't ask why her father hadn't come to the station to say good-bye to her aunt. She had concluded long ago that her father was none too fond of Tante Karla, though he never actually said that he didn't like her. Instead he called her "immature," a "liberal reformer," and on occasion he accused her of being "unladylike." But Karla thwarted his attempts to insult her. She considered all his labels compliments.

Anna and her mother walked briskly through the cavernous station. At the curb their carriage and driver awaited them. Anna could not help thinking that if her father had come, they would have driven in his long, shiny new Mercedes. But "ladies" did not drive and if her father was not with them, they took the carriage instead of the car and a servant drove the team of two matched brown mares.

As their carriage bumped along the Kurfurstendamm, keeping to one side of the tram tracks, Anna looked out the window and noticed that wet snowflakes had begun to fall. Soon it would be Christmas. Vaguely Anna wondered what Christmas without Tante Karla would be like . . . it will be quiet, she thought. Yes, it would be quiet because Tante Karla always argued with her father after Christmas dinner. Yes, Christmas without Karla would be serene; it might also, she thought unhappily, be quite dull.

"You miss her already," her mother said abruptly.

Anna turned toward her mother, whose lips were pressed together. "Yes," she answered truthfully.

"You love her more than you love me," her mother pouted.

Anna looked at her mother's hands. They were outside her muff and they still held her handkerchief. She was knotting the hankie, pulling the little knots tighter and tighter.

"You don't deny it. I know you love her more than you love me. You wish she were your mother."

Anna closed her eyes, 'No, Mother. That's not true. I love you." She hoped she sounded sincere. She did love her mother, but when her mother behaved this way, it was hard for her to express her feelings.

"Mother thinks if I love you, I love her less," she had once confided to Karla.

Karla had held her tightly. "Your mother is insecure, Anna. She has problems, you are the youngest of her children, and she's getting older and changing. Be patient with her."

But Anna never learned what her mother's problems were and her mother's moods remained a dark mystery.

Her mother turned and looked out the window. But Anna noted, her expression did not relax and she continued to twist and knot her handkerchief.

"Our last meal of the year!" General Klaus von Bock announced in a hearty voice. "And we are all together! Let's toast the new year . . . it will be a very special year! Germany is growing more and more powerful. Soon our army will be larger than England's."

Anna studied her father's face. He was uncharacteristically rosy-cheeked this evening, and in contrast to his usual reserve, was quite gregarious. Perhaps it was the liquor. He had drunk whiskey before dinner, consumed more wine than usual with the meal, and now he was enjoying a warm cognac.

"To the new year!" her brother Andreas toasted. He lifted his own glass, and the men around the table all stood up in military fashion, straight and tall, their heels together. They held their glasses toward the center of the table and in unison repeated Andreas' toast. The women remained seated, smiling and silent.

They had just finished a long formal dinner, and for once the great table that filled the dining salon was almost fully occupied. Usually Anna and her parents sat alone in the dining room, and even with the leaves which extended the size of the table removed, the three of them were lost and seemingly isolated as they ate their daily meals. Her father always sat at the head of the table, her mother at the foot, and she was relegated a chair on her father's right halfway down the long table. But tonight all the chairs in between were occupied.

Andreas, Anna's elder brother, who was now twenty-seven, sat on her father's right. Else, Andreas' twenty-two-year-old wife, sat next to him. Andreas and Else lived in Essen, and this holiday season was the first time in many months they had come to Berlin.

Andreas was an executive at one of the many Krupp plants in Essen. Else belonged to the huge influential Krupp family, albeit not to the main line, though her roots were still aristocratic. Upstairs, in the nursery, Else and Andreas' children, three-year-old Klaus von Bock IV, his two-year-old brother, Hermann, and his four-month-old sister, Emma, all slept peacefully.

Anna glanced at Else, whose great milk-swollen breasts made her chest resemble those of the swans which graced the pond. This was, Anna realized, the first time since the wedding five years ago, when Else was seventeen, that Else had not been pregnant. And yet, Anna thought with a sigh, it was impossible to tell that Else wasn't with child. Three pregnancies, one after another, had left Else plump with soft rounded edges. Even her once angular face was round. But Else dressed fashionably in spite of her figure, and the empire-style gown she wore emphasized her expanse of milk-white skin and deep cleavage. Her blond curls swirled around her face, making it seem smaller, and her thick waist and ample hips were obscured by the generous folds of her skirt.

Markus von Bock, Anna's younger brother, was twenty-five. He sat on her father's left. Markus' fiancée, Dorcas Strassner, sat primly next to him. She was eighteen and the very proper daughter of a Lutheran minister. Unlike Else, whose breasts had been large even before they'd filled with milk, Dorcas was flat-chested and trim. She too was blond and blue-eyed, but Dorcas' eyes were not deep blue like her mother's and Else's, they were a watery blue and her eyebrows and lashes were white blond like her thin straight hair. Markus, Anna decided, was strangely ambivalent toward this girl who was only two years her senior. She, on the other hand, spoke happily of the home she and Markus would have and the large family they would rear.

"I hope we'll have many sons," Dorcas ventured. She smiled weakly at her father-in-law-to-be. "We would have loved to name our first for you." Her father beamed and continued to beam even though everyone knew that his name, Klaus, belonged to the first male child of the eldest son and was already taken.

Else leaned across Andreas to speak to General von Bock and said softly, "Our little Klaus even looks like you, Father." Anna knew from experience that Else could hold her own, and Dorcas, who would be the newest of the von Bock women, would have to learn her place in the ferocious pecking order her father so happily cultivated.

And certainly her elder sister, twenty-three-year-old Gerda, was not to be usurped by her sisters-in-law. Her husband, Ernst von Raeder, belonged to an eminent German military family and her three-year-old son, Rudolf, boasted not one, but two grandfathers who were generals, as well as a host of other famous relatives. Gerda was well-known as the mistress of family intrigue. She played her own father's ego against that of her father-in-law, and using one ego against the other, achieved a prominent position for herself and her husband in both families. It was not an easy task. Gerda was the third of four children and traditionally a daughter was not as valued as a son. And poor Ernst von Raeder! He was the fifth of seven sons and three daughters as well as a relative to *the* von Raeders. But Ernst had chosen well. Gerda made certain Ernst figured in all his own father's plans just as she made certain her little Rudolf figured in the von Bock future by telling her own father what her father-in-law planned for the child. When old von Raeder gave little Rudolf a gift of riding lessons, her father gave Rudolf a fine horse. Then when Gerda showed old von Raeder her father's gift, he immediately offered the gift of a lifelong membership in the Berlin Riding Academy for the small boy. And so it went. When Gerda smiled indulgently at young Dorcas' attempt to curry favor with her future father-in-law, Anna knew Gerda smiled from a position of unqualified strength. In her own domestic way, Gerda was a master politician, a far better politician than their father, who certainly had ambitions in that area. Karla had once said that with the proper redirection, Gerda could have become chancellor, and Anna did not for a moment doubt her aunt's observation. She herself smiled kindly at poor Dorcas, who seemed so desperately to need support.

"To the new year!" Andreas said, repeating his toast. Again the men spoke in unison. Then her father withdrew his pocket watch.

"One minute to midnight! One minute to the year 1911!"

"Sixty, fifty-nine, fifty-eight . . ." In unison they began to count.

Anna looked from one to the other. Andreas was tall and broad-shouldered. His expression was like his father's—stern and for the most part humorless.

Markus was shorter and less muscular, but he stood straight as a stick and he looked quite handsome in the full dress uniform he wore tonight. Markus, like her father, had chosen to make the army his career. Like their father, Markus had gone to the Militarakademie and had pleased his father immensely by graduating fifth in his class, five places above his brother-in-law Ernst von Raeder.

The men were alike, yet they had chosen different paths. Andreas sought power through money, Markus sought it through the military, as did Ernst, and her father represented the power and influence they all wanted in their own right. He had it all, but now he wanted more; he yearned for political power as well.

"One! It is the new year!" her father announced. Again they toasted, then they drained their glasses and sat down waiting to have them refilled by a servant who waited silently by the door that led to the kitchen.

But once again her father stood up. He looked about him and nodded as if satisfied with his brood. "I have an announcement."

Everyone looked up at him dutifully.

"In a few months I will be leaving the army to seek a seat in the Reichstag."

Anna did not blink because she had heard her father telling her mother his "news." But the others stared at him in silence.

Anna's eyes looked toward the one empty seat at the table. It was the place where Karla would have sat had she been present instead of on her way to America. Karla might have laughed and said, "Oh, Klaus! Really!" but Karla wasn't there so no one said a word until Gerda gushed, "Oh, Father, I'm sure you'll be elected president!"

"God knows the country needs a man like you," Ernst breathed, and everyone seemed to mumble agreement.

Her father nodded silently and smiled. Clearly he was happy with their reaction. He laughed, albeit a bit nervously, then, "And first off I'll see to the defeat of this threatened inheritance tax!"

Andreas grinned. "An important issue." He followed his statement with a nervous laugh, and then added, "Especially to us."

Suddenly her father turned to her. "Have you nothing to say, Anna?"

From the far end of the table her father's eyes seemed to bore through her. Anna thought for a moment. "I'm not certain an inheritance tax is such a bad idea. Shouldn't everyone pay his fair share?"

Her father's face clouded over and he frowned; then he suddenly guffawed loudly. "I see I can practice my debates at home!"

Anna felt her face flush. If Andreas had said what she had just said, her father would have argued hotly. But she had said it and he dismissed her with a laugh. Nor would he debate her in spite of his comment. Her views, she knew full well, were of no concern to her father.

"One last brandy and Else and I must get some rest," Andreas announced. "I have a full day tomorrow even though it is New Year's Day."

There was general agreement and one last brandy was poured.

Anna stood up. "May I be excused?" she asked.

"Certainly," her father agreed too readily.

Anna lifted her long velvet skirt and fled the room, going directly to the library. She found the book she had begun yesterday, and she sat down in the large leather chair that faced the fireplace.

An hour had elapsed when Anna finally closed the book. It must be nearly one-thirty, she thought. Still, the long late meal and the conversation had served to stimulate her and she did not feel like sleeping even now. But she was about to pull herself from the chair and go to her room anyway, when the door to the library opened.

"In here," she heard Markus whisper.

His whisper had an urgent tone. Anna started to make her presence known . . . Markus couldn't see her because the chair faced away from the door.

"Someone will see us."

Anna didn't move. The voice was a woman's . . . it wasn't Dorcas' voice. It was Else's.

"You're right, I suppose. Look, meet me on Tuesday in front of Wertheim's Department Store . . . can you manage that?"

"All right . . . let go of my arm, Markus. I must go. Andreas will wonder where I am."

Anna frowned and waited silently, feeling both guilty for eavesdropping and intrigued at the same time. To her relief she heard the library door close and Markus and Else leave without coming fully inside the room and discovering her.

She waited a few moments and then she herself left to go up to her room, still puzzling over what she had heard.

It was one of the early spring's magnificent days; a day when puffy snow-white clouds moved lazily across a deep blue sky; a day when the sun shone warm enough that winter jackets and gloves were discarded. It was a wondrous day filled with sights and smells that evoked feelings and thoughts that Anna fought to sort out, to understand.

"Stand right there!" Gerda demanded. Then, "No, move a little to the right . . . as close as you can get to little Rudolf. Perhaps you should bend down so I'll be sure . . . Yes . . . Yes, that's just right."

Gerda stared intently into the glass viewfinder of her box camera and in a moment snapped the picture. "There, it will be perfect," she predicted with confidence. "And Rudolf looks so adorable in his new little outfit."

Anna nodded and reached down for Rudolf's small hand. He was dressed in a little blue serge suit with short pants, and underneath his jacket he wore a stiff white shirt and a little tie. His legs were bare from knees to pant cuffs, but below the knees he wore long dark stockings that disappeared into his high button shoes. Whenever Anna saw or thought of Rudolf, she thought of Mrs. Burnett's book *Little Lord Fauntleroy*.

And if Rudolf was dressed impeccably, Gerda was chic and looked every inch the young matron. She was lavishly adorned in a light blue voile suit, a high-collared white blouse trimmed in lace, and a huge hat with enormous blue plumes.

Anna herself wore a plain white blouse and a long skirt made of green gabardine. Her skirt had a multitude of long narrow pleats and was known as a "Panama skirt," though she had been unable to discover just why this style was so labeled.

"I want to see the elephants now!" Rudolf demanded. "And I want a balloon and a flavored ice too!"

"We'll go to the elephants and you may have a balloon if you are a good boy, but I think you should wait and have your ice after lunch," Gerda told her son crisply, then turned to Anna. "Off to the elephants, then."

Anna laughed. "You make it sound like a safari." She leaned down to little Rudolf, "You're lucky to live in Berlin. This is one of the finest zoos in all Europe."

Before them in the pathway a white-faced clown in gay costume held a fist full of colored balloons, beyond the clown a man sold ices of different flavors from a hand-pulled cart, and from somewhere the tantalizing smell of sausages mingled with the other pleasant aromas of a spring day.

This place, the zoo in the Tiergarten, brought back Anna's childhood . . . not that at seventeen such memories were hard to retrieve. Still, there was something, a sense perhaps that the carefree days, which had grown fewer when she entered the gymnasium four years ago, were now about to cease altogether. Yes, that was it. Anna had the definite feeling today that she was standing in a doorway. Behind her were the rooms of childhood, before her the unknown dark corridor that led to the rooms of adulthood. The sight of the clown, the mouth-watering aroma of sausages, and the old man with his ices on a warm spring day in the Tiergarten all combined to heighten her awareness of this mysterious passage. At the same time, Anna was aware of a sadness, a kind of longing for experiences she felt she would not again have. Oh, she might come to the zoo, but somehow she knew it would be different.

Rudolf dropped Anna's hand and skipped to his mother. Gerda forged ahead toward the zoo while little Rudolf clutched his mother's hand and ran to keep up with her longer strides.

Anna walked more slowly, her eyes lingering on the flowerbeds and the graceful trees. The Tiergarten was huge, over six hundred acres of woodland and gardens, with secluded paths and walkways, fountains and statues, and of course the zoo.

Gerda stopped abruptly and turned toward her sister. "You're slow today, and I must say you're solemn . . . no, not solemn, pensive."

Anna smiled. Rarely was Gerda observant of the moods of others; the accuracy of her observation surprised Anna. "I suppose I am," she admitted.

"We've not been together alone for a long while, Anna. I was surprised when you agreed to come with us today."

"I love the zoo. I thought it would be fun to help show Rudolf the zoo."

"I want an ice!" Rudolf tugged on Gerda's hand and

pulled at her skirt. "I don't want to wait till after lunch! I want it now!"

Gerda sighed impatiently. She fished quickly in her purse for a coin, then pressed it in his hand. "Here," she said. "Go and get your ice and sit on that bench and eat it. We'll sit on the other bench, over there under the linden tree."

Rudolf clenched the coin greedily and then dropped his mother's hand and whirled away toward the ice vendor.

"He'll get grape," Gerda said, shrugging. "And it will be all over him."

"Let him enjoy himself," Anna replied as they strolled toward the old linden tree and the bench beneath it.

"Well, whatever your reasons, I'm glad you came with me," Gerda said, returning to their conversation. "You know the age difference between us prevented our being close. But now, Anna, you're older . . . we can talk, we'll have more in common."

Anna nodded, though she wasn't sure just what they would have in common.

"I suppose you'll look down on me if you do go to university. I'll just be a hausfrau," Gerda suggested in a tone of mock self-depreciation. It was the kind of thing Gerda had said before. She wanted to be reassured, she wanted Anna to say, "You'll never be *just* a hausfrau."

"I won't look down on you," Anna answered. "How can you think such a thing?"

"Oh, I don't know. You think I don't understand. But I do. I understand that you want to go to university, and you've been thinking about how your life is going to change. I was like that before I got married. You're full of questions, Anna."

Anna looked into Gerda's blue eyes. They were different from her mother's eyes. They were narrower and they moved quickly. Gerda always seemed to be taking someone's measure, seemed often to be plotting. Anna nodded slowly, more surprised than she had been initially that Gerda seemed to understand her mood. "Can you answer my questions?" she asked.

"I might be able to answer some, but no, I don't think

I could answer most of them. I suspect your questions are vague because you are questioning experiences you haven't had yet . . . or something like that. I can't imagine what your life will be like, Anna. I suppose you'll tie your hair in a knot and wear those dreadful plain clothes that all those 'intellectual' women wear. Yes, I suppose you'll dress badly and spend all your time in a konditorei drinking coffee, eating little pastries, and discussing politics.''

Anna laughed. "Oh, I shouldn't think so!''

"You'll turn out like Tante Karla. You'll not marry till you're old, and then you'll marry a writer or a painter. You'll live in some garret, and if you have children they'll all grow up to be naturalists or perhaps even Gypsies.''

"Oh, for heaven's sake!'' Anna laughed good-naturedly at her sister's prediction. "Tante Karla is not old, she was only thirty-three when she left to marry the man she loved. And he's a publisher.'' Anna stopped there because she knew that Karla did not intend to have children, though in fact Karla had never told her why. She had simply stated, "No, we won't have any children.''

Anna paused and then said defensively, "In any case, Gerda, Tante Karla did not go to university.''

Gerda frowned. Then her face lit up. "Precisely. She was different without university. You take after her and you'll probably go to university, so you will turn out even stranger than Karla.''

"She is not strange,'' Anna persisted, though she knew full well that compared to most women her age, Karla was far from the norm.

Gerda ignored her defense of Karla. "You might not marry at all. It's hard for an educated woman to find the right sort of husband.''

Ah, that was it, Anna thought. Gerda, the master family politician, was trying to find out her plans . . . her hopes and dreams. Gerda did not care if she married or not. Gerda only cared that if she *did* marry, it would be to a man less important than her own husband. "You may be right,'' Anna agreed, though in fact she did not agree at all because she knew when her sister used the phrase "the right kind of husband" she meant a military man, a well-placed businessman, or a high-ranking member of the bureaucracy.

Relaxed now because she decided that her younger sister would offer no competition or threaten in any way her own hard-fought-for position, Gerda nodded in satisfaction at Anna's answer. "Then perhaps you will be a teacher," Gerda said with evident relief. She smiled a little smile and leaned over. "It would be nice if we could talk more, Anna. You know, become friends."

"We can talk anytime," Anna told her sister.

"Can we gossip?" Gerda leaned even closer and a genuine smile crossed her face. "Tell me, what do you think of that Dorcas? I mean, she and Markus can have a big wedding in the church because her father is a minister, but who will pay for the reception? Her family's as poor as church mice. She doesn't even know how to dress in good taste . . . and she's so . . . so pallid."

"Markus loves her," Anna replied.

"I don't think so!" Gerda lifted her brow . . . she had eyebrows like their father, they arched magnificently.

"If he doesn't love her, why is he marrying her?"

"It is expected. You are so naive, Anna . . . really, I thought you would have noticed long ago that Markus is totally—I mean totally—smitten with Else." Gerda gave a sweeping wave of her hands and her eyes twinkled with delight. She adored gossip.

Anna looked at her sister in utter amazement. "Andreas' Else?"

Gerda leaned back and threw out her arms in a gesture of exasperation. "Of course, Andreas' Else . . . what other Else do we know? Oh, I know she's a bit of a cow, but she has breasts as big as down pillows. Some men like that! Markus likes it! He leers at her."

"I'm sure you're mistaken, Gerda. He's marrying Dorcas in less than a month."

"Dorcas, Dorcas . . . what a name! And such a prude. Never mind, she'll probably only have relations with him when the lights are out. If he puts a pillow on her chest he can pretend it's Else." She clapped her hands and giggled.

"You're terrible," Anna said, and although she didn't sound serious, she meant it. Gerda was already preparing to make certain Dorcas was ignored and Else shunned. She would no doubt tell her little story to their mother and to their cousins and their aunts. In no time the fiction would take on the power of fact and it would be elaborated on too. People would say that Else had seduced Markus and that she had cuckolded Andreas. In some funny way it would all become Dorcas' fault because Dorcas could not fulfill her husband's desires. Gerda, of course, would triumph; with Else disgraced and Dorcas labeled a fool, she alone would emerge strong and virtuous. Worst of all, the glimmer of truth would make Gerda's vicious gossip believable. Anna had denied it, but she had noticed Markus looking at Else with a certain longing and there was the conversation in the library which she had overheard. Yes, the success of Gerda's intimations was inevitable. Now even in her own thoughts Anna began to question her brother's intentions, to believe the conversation in the library was not at all innocent . . . oh, damn Gerda! Anna thought, and she stood up abruptly. "I think I'll get an ice myself," she announced as she walked away. It was both a real and symbolic act . . . she wanted nothing more than to put distance between her and Gerda . . . as much distance as possible even if for only a few minutes. Anna sighed deeply. Soon she, her parents, Gerda, and her children would be going to the Schwarzwald—the Black Forest—together for the summer holidays, and during their month-long stay, other members of the family would visit. There would be no escape from Gerda's insinuations. Anna could only hope Gerda would not somehow involve her in this new intrigue.

2

"This is such a comfortable way to travel," Gisela said. She was sitting on a sofa, and in front of her there was a tea table covered with expensive china teacups. "I always look forward to it. Remember last summer when we went to the Black Forest? Remember, Anna?"

Anna nodded absently. No one could deny the pleasure of train travel, especially in an expensive private car. The walls of the carriage were made of highly polished wood, and over each window there were red tapestry shades with fringe. The shades could be opened wide or lowered with the pinch of a brass clip. It was all very Victorian, very subdued and elegant. The furniture in the rail car was of the type found in living rooms and the lamps on the walls were gaslights enclosed in pretty smoked chimney tubes. In all, the railway carriage was richly appointed, and were it not for the German countryside speeding past the window, Anna might not have been aware of leaving their comfortable family home. Last summer they had gone to the Black Forest in a car like this. This summer they were traveling to Essen for the celebrations at Krupp A.G.

"Krupp A.G. is not just *any* corporation, it's *the* corporation, one of the largest—perhaps the largest—company in the world!" her father pontificated. "And the Krupp family isn't just *any* family. They're the most important family in Germany and one of the most important families in Europe—even in the world!" He rubbed his chin, "They're like royalty"—he grinned—"but they can afford to buy their own crown jewels."

Her father's words came close to understatement. The Krupps owned Essen in the rich Ruhr Valley, and in Essen alone they had eighty factories. Beyond Essen they owned eight other gigantic steel plants. The Krupps also owned shipyards, foundries, coal mines, ore fields, clay pits, and limestone quarries. "A giant," Markus had told Anna when they were preparing to leave. "Every single day, in addition to what is produced at the eighty factories in Essen, Krupp produces two million tons of coal, eight hundred thousand tons of coke, one hundred thousand tons of iron ore, and eight hundred thousand tons of pig iron. Krupp is the largest munitions and armaments company in the entire world, Anna."

Anna had leaned back in her chair and stared out the window. Markus' description of the company Andreas worked for had been given with undisguised admiration—even awe. Both Markus and her father were enamored of the firm, and certainly had Andreas been present, he would have added his own words of praise. But had Karla been here there would have been an argument. "Blood money—they make millions in blood money," she would have said. In fact that was what she had said when Andreas married Else. But Karla was not here, and Anna, for once, did not seek the moral high ground. She chose not to argue because she was outnumbered and knew it, and because no one in the private railway car her father had rented for the trip to Essen could possibly be convinced to change his opinion of the giant firm. Dorcas, Gerda, and her mother never mentioned politics, nor did they participate in arguments. They professed to believe what their husbands believed.

"I'm so excited," Dorcas said in her mouselike voice.

Anna glanced at her and felt a wave of sympathy for Markus' wife. She tried to be a real member of the family inner circle, but Gerda kept her at arm's length and thwarted her every attempt.

"It should be quite a show," General von Bock enthusiastically predicted. "The one hundredth anniversary of the Great Krupp! This will be the Reich's equivalent of Victoria's Diamond Jubilee! Better, I imagine. Just think, one hundred years ago when Alfred Krupp was born, Germany was just throwing off Napoleon. Krupp's growth and expansion parallels the growth and expansion of our nation. Krupp *is* Germany, and is the greatest maker of war materials in the world.''

Anna turned away as her father continued to wallow in the glories of arms production. Soon he would begin talking about Krupp's plans to become the world's biggest producer of diesel engines, and the plans to put those diesels into Krupp-made U-boats. "A great anniversary," he breathed, folding his hands over his stomach. "And all owned by such a rich woman . . . Bertha Krupp's income is the largest in Germany—283 million marks a year—over six million American dollars. She makes more than the Jew Rothschild!''

"Our Andreas has married into such an important family,'' Gisela gushed with evident pride.

"He should have married Bertha instead of a cousin,'' Markus suggested sardonically. "Then the kaiser would have changed *his* last name to Krupp.''

Markus was referring to the fact that Bertha's husband's name had been officially changed by the kaiser so that it would not die out with her marriage.

"Anna is about to point out that the workers are poor,'' Gerda said, laughing. "Look at her, simmering with her desire to expound on matters of social justice.''

Anna looked up. "Well, aren't they poor?''

"Not as poor as they were. Gustav and Bertha Krupp began the company's centennial by distributing fourteen million marks among the workers.''

"That's only two weeks of Bertha's annual income,'' Anna said, doing a quick computation. "If the workers are smart, they'll use it to buy passage to America, where at least they can have some say about the government.''

"Ah, the voice of the oppressed masses speaks,'' Markus joked.

"Better it comes from a daughter than from a son,'' her father said in a tone that was far from jest. "Listen to her,'' he added, "listen, Gisela, see what an influence your sister had on the girl.''

Anna pressed her lips together and returned her gaze to the window. She was accustomed to her family's barbs and used to her father's diminishing comments. Not for a moment did he think she had a mind of her own. No matter what she said, he credited someone else for her thought. Even if he agreed with her, which was rare, he credited her brothers or himself. When he disagreed, it was Karla who thought for her, even though Karla had been gone now for over a year. Sometimes he blamed a friend, or perhaps a writer she had read. It was hateful and she focused on it. Why didn't her father see that she could think for herself?

"I'm going to refresh myself," Gerda announced.

"Yes," Gisela said, rising to join her elder daughter. "Time to powder our noses, we're not far from Essen."

Dorcas too stood up, and when she did, Markus moved next to the window. "I can see the smoke from here," he said, pointing to the horizon. "Fifteen, twenty minutes at the most."

Hedda Schnell was unlike any woman Andreas von Bock had ever met. Her physical appearance was stunning. She was tall and slim, with a long patrician neck and an angular face. Her wonderful high cheekbones and very slightly slanted almond eyes hinted at some remote tartar ancestry, while her full lips seemed to promise erotic encounters. Her long thick hair was red, not the golden red of the Scots, but a deep rich red-brown like fine, highly polished cherrywood.

The first time Andreas had seen Hedda, she had been wearing a prim high-collared white blouse with long sleeves that covered her wrists. Her tiny waist had been cinched in with a wide belt, and her skirt—a dark tweed skirt—clung to her hips and then flared out, falling a trifle shorter than the fashion and revealing her trim, well-shaped black-stockinged ankles. Her shoes were leather with little heels which made her seem even taller and more willowy than she was, and in their center a large gold buckle caught the eye. On that day six months ago, Hedda had been wearing her magnificent hair down, and though it was pulled back, he could clearly see it was thick and wavy. He had felt instantly drawn to her; indeed he had felt almost helpless in her presence.

But Hedda was more than simply beautiful. She was also mysterious—or at least she appeared mysterious to

Andreas. Among other things, Hedda lived alone and worked to support herself. That was, in fact, how he had come to meet her. She was a secretary, albeit a very knowledgeable one. Her employer was Herr Schute, a well-known banker in the Rothschild Bank in Frankfurt am Main, where Andreas traveled on business three times a month. Once Andreas had hated his trips to Frankfurt, but now, since he had made Hedda his mistress, he looked forward to them greatly and found it difficult to look appropriately unhappy when bidding Else farewell.

He lay now amid the crumpled bedsheets and watched Hedda as she went about the business of making coffee. Her apartment was more of a studio—a huge room with a skylight. The bed was at one end of the room, at the other a makeshift kitchen, in the middle, sofas and chairs and tables. Still, the room was uncluttered. He inhaled deeply and sighed with satisfaction. The room, the sheets on which he lay, Hedda's silky gown, which was spread out next to him—they all had the aroma of Hedda's distinctive perfume. It was a pungent sexual scent and its odor instantly made him feel sensuous because he associated it with her damp, excited body.

At this moment Hedda, much to his pleasure, took advantage of the warm summer sun shining through the skylight. She had not put on her bathrobe when she'd gotten up from bed, but instead wandered about naked, so that now, as she bent to take the coffee from the cupboard, he could admire the rounded perfection of her derriere and the shapeliness of her long bare legs. When she turned, he could see her breasts. They were high and firm, small but wonderfully shaped, with extraordinary nipples which were inverted and did not appear until touched. Then, like magic, they appeared hard and erect, a clear display of her sexual excitement.

"Put in an extra measure," Andreas called out. "I need strong coffee this morning."

Hedda turned and smiled teasingly. "Did I exhaust you, my darling?"

He sat up and stretched, then fell back against the pillows. "Yes, but it's a very pleasurable exhaustion."

She left the coffee to steam into the top of the maker

and returned to the bed, sitting down on the side of it. She leaned over and pressed her naked torso against his broad hairy chest. "I could further exhaust you," she said in a throaty whisper as she slipped her hand downward and breathed, "Oh, Andreas . . . you are naughty, and so early in the morning . . ."

His face flushed. There was no need for her to touch him. He was fully aroused simply from having watched her walk about nude. His hands flew to fondle her breasts, and she in turn squeezed him gently and then began marvelous taunting movements of her fingers on his penis.

"Are you insatiable?" he asked, breathing more heavily as his excitement increased. She had an incredible effect on him—partly because she was so beautiful, partly because she knew how to touch him so that his arousal was almost instant.

"Not insatiable," she purred as she laid her head on his chest and continued her toying movement. "But after all, darling, I do only see you three times a month . . . and this weekend you have to cut our time together short. How should I behave?"

She wiggled slightly—it was unbearable, the sheet was between them from the waist down. Still, feeling her movements through the thin veil of cloth heightened the erotic quality of her teasing. He groaned, and she slipped her hand beneath the sheet and continued to play upon his flesh.

"Don't move your hands from my breasts," she told him. His eyes were closed now and he shivered with anticipation. He felt truly as if he would burst. "I can't stand it," he panted.

"Keep your eyes closed, darling."

He nodded and he felt her shift her position. Then he felt her moist and warm flesh and, her movements continued till he almost screamed with delight, and then reared, shaking with satisfaction. He panted and then collapsed again against the puffy pillows.

"The coffee will burn," she said, pulling away.

He groaned and watched as she ran across the room to turn off the burner.

"Come back," he pleaded.

She laughed. "Oh, not now, Andreas. See, it is you who are insatiable. Darling, your family is already in Essen and you told me yesterday you had to catch the noon train." She turned, her eyes dancing, her smile radiant. "What is that saying in the theater? Yes, 'Leave them wanting more.' I want you to want more, so you will come back to me sooner. In any case, if I completely tire you, your wife will become suspicious."

Andreas stared at her longingly. But he knew she was right, he had to catch the noon train. In his mind's eye he could see his father's stern face and hear his mother's whining and his wife's pleading. His sexual desire and excitement fled in the face of this imagined confrontation. This was going to be a horrible three days and he would need Hedda more after it was over than he did now, he decided.

"There," Hedda said, pouring the coffee. Then, as an afterthought, she picked up her robe from the chair and covered her exquisite body.

He pulled himself from the bed. After coffee he would wash, brush his teeth, shave and trim his mustache, comb his hair. Then, God willing, he would catch the train for Essen and arrive in time for the opening of the celebrations.

For once the factories of Essen did not belch smoke and fire. The doors of the eighty Krupp factories were closed, allowing the smoke and dust that usually hung over the city to dissipate in the warm August breeze. By noon the sky above was a clear blue, and the warm sun shone brightly.

The royal train arrived promptly at ten and was greeted by swarms of workers and their families. All Krupp employees had been given a three-day holiday in order to fully participate in the grand centennial celebrations.

Kaiser Wilhelm alighted from the train and taking long purposeful strides walked down the long red carpet laid especially to greet the feet of the All Highest.

Anna's eyes widened and she found she had to fight for control. Was she mad? Or was everyone else? The kaiser was dressed as she had never seen him dressed

before, and she fought desperately to suppress her desire
to laugh because he looked like a toy soldier costumed
as All-Highest Warlord—*des allerhochsten Kriegsherrn.*
The kaiser had a fondness for uniforms, ornate uniforms
with plumage and gold braid, but this one was silly and
excessive even by his previous standards. His chest puffed
out like a mating cobra as he strode forward, his entourage following in his wake. The kaiser had brought the
entire cabinet and all the princes of Prussia as well as
Chancellor von Bethmann-Hollweg. And there were three
extraordinarily dressed women present too: the kaiserin,
Marga Krupp, and her daughter, Bertha, the Krupp heiress. Gustav, Bertha's husband, was also dressed absurdly. He stood stiffly at attention surrounded by the
women. All three women wore absolutely huge hats, hats
so large and so ornate that they looked as if they might
topple over from being topheavy.

Royalty and guests took their seats and Gustav Krupp
stepped forward to speak. Anna shifted uncomfortably in
her chair; her only real thought was how long the
speeches might last. From the look of things she feared
Gustav and Kaiser Wilhelm, both of whom loved talking,
might well go on unabated for several hours while their
audience withered in the hot sun.

A furtive glance told Anna that she alone feared boredom. Her father was sitting straight and attentive, his
eyes glued on Gustav Krupp. Her mother stared straight
ahead, lost in that unknown place to which she now mentally retreated more and more often. Else sat among her
relatives, and Andreas, who had arrived only minutes
before the royal entourage, sat at her side. Else looked
utterly and completely preposterous. Dressed in costume
for some entertainment to follow the speeches, she wore
a gold lamé gown designed to make her look like some
medieval princess. It was trimmed in velvet and had a
low, low neck. Else was all white cleavage and glim-
mering wide hips.

Gerda sat next to Ernst, who was decked out in full
military regalia. He held little Rudolf on his knee so the
overdressed tot would miss nothing of the ceremony.

Dorcas' mouth was slightly open in obvious awe—or

perhaps distress—and Markus too sat with his back straight, the stiff collar of his uniform seemingly holding his head up.

Anna pressed her lips together, and as usual, felt the alien in a strange land.

Once, several years ago, she had overheard a conversation between her parents, and at times like this it came back to her. Her mother had been sobbing and her father was speaking in a low, mean voice. "I know she's your daughter but am I her real father?" he questioned.

"Of course you are . . . you know there is no one else!" Her mother's response was shrill, hysterical. "You're the only man who has ever touched me," her mother had whispered. Her father had only grunted and left the room.

And over the years there had been other stinging comments. "She isn't like the other children," her father insisted. "She's different."

"It's because she's the youngest—it's almost as if she were an only child, Klaus."

"We haven't spoiled her . . . though perhaps you have."

Anna had listened to them in absolute wonder. Certainly her mother had not spoiled her . . . and didn't they love her? They talked about her as if she were some sort of intruder. And did her father really wonder if he *were* her father? She had cried for hours, and when she'd told Tante Karla, Karla had been outraged.

"Your father is an insensitive dolt," she had said coldly, "and your mother has her own problems."

But Karla never defined those problems and Anna always found herself wondering what they were. Regardless, she had begun then to pull even further away from her family and to keep her own counsel. However insensitive her father, and however selfish and problem-ridden her mother, they were right about one thing. She *was* different, and each day that passed she sensed it more and more. The key to her sanity and disposition was simple. While once she had felt badly about being different, now she reveled in it, indeed she strove for it.

And never more than now, she thought as suddenly

Gustav finished his speech and the crowd rose in unison and shouted, *"Das Haus und die Firma Krupp: hurra hurra!"* Then, *"Heil Kaiser und Reich! Hurra hurra!"*

She could barely mouth the words, but she did because her father was staring at her. I do not belong here. I don't want to be here, Anna thought. Her father again turned to look at the kaiser, and Anna looked at Markus, who was staring at Else even though his wife, Dorcas, clung to him. Intrigue and pettiness were the descriptive words that came to her mind as he eyes moved from one family member to another.

This family of hers did not understand her and she did not understand them. It will get worse too, she silently admitted. Next week the head of the gymnasium was coming to speak to her father about her academic performance, and that, she feared, would lead to another conflict. Women, her father was convinced, had only one role—to marry and have children.

The late-afternoon sun sank behind the far hills beyond the Ruhr Valley, bringing a less-than-successful day to conclusion.

The von Bock women gathered in the sitting room of Andreas von Bock's comfortable home some miles up-river from Essen's smoke-belching factories. The von Bock men—Klaus, Andreas, and Markus—and Ernst von Raeder, Gerda's husband, were off to the beer hall to celebrate, and Anna could easily imagine them lifting their steins and singing in an atmosphere of smoke and stale beer.

Anna sat cross-legged on the floor wondering how long before she could politely excuse herself and go to the library to read. Neither the conversation nor the company interested her.

Dorcas, Markus' thin and nervous wife, sat on the very edge of a large comfortable chair. She appeared to be listening attentively to every word spoken.

Gerda sat relaxed on the sofa next to Gisela, their mother, while Else, their hostess, sat in another chair, her hands folded placidly in her lap.

"What a scene!" Gerda sneered, referring to the preparations for the feudal tournament that had been planned as part of the day's festivities.

"I was looking forward to it," Else pouted. She was still wearing her ornate gold lamé costume. Since she was sitting, the hoop beneath the skirt had lifted slightly.

"It was terrible that the tournament had to be called off. I heard there were hundreds of people involved and they'd all rehearsed for days," Dorcas interjected. She always tried to agree with Else, and it was obvious she was trying to forge an alliance with her sister-in-law in order to obtain an ally against Gerda. Dorcas had not heard the rumor Gerda had spread, so she didn't realize that befriending Else, her alleged rival for Markus' affection, made her appear to be even more of a simpleton.

Gerda laughed. "I for one am glad it was canceled. What a bore! And tasteless! All those fat women dressed up like Valkyries, ridiculous!"

Else blushed crimson and whispered, "I was enjoying it."

"You look foolish," Gerda said sharply. "Absolutely silly."

Else looked up like a wounded bird. Tears filled her huge blue eyes, and the mascara she had put on her lashes for her stage appearance during the tournament began to run. It left great dark smudges under her eyes, making her resemble one of the raccoons in the Tiergarten zoo.

"Gerda means your costume looks foolish," Gisela interpreted. "Don't be so soft-skinned, Else. We all love you, you're one of the family."

Gerda did not apologize. "What do you think, Anna? You hardly said a word all day."

"I think the tournament was a bad idea, but none of you seem to care that it was called off because a tragedy occurred. Good heavens, over a hundred people were killed."

Gerda tossed her head. "You seem to think you have a monopoly on concern for others."

"I just think it was silly to cancel the tournament. After all, the explosion was in Bochum," Else whined.

Anna looked at her sister-in-law harshly. "For years there have been warnings about the buildup of coal dust in the shafts. Krupp never heeded the warnings because cleaning things up would have cut their profits. Now one of their stacks has blown up and killed over a hundred workers. How could they go on with those expensive, elaborate, and I may say useless celebrations?''

"I don't care about coal dust or explosions. I just wanted to act, to be part of the glorious pageant,'' Else said, thrusting her lower lip out. "You just don't like me, Gerda. And now you've influenced Anna too.'' Her eyes darted from Gerda to Anna.

Anna stared at Else. Did no one think she had a mind of her own? And who was Else to make such an accusation? She vaguely wondered when Else had last had an original idea, or any idea for that matter. Anger filled her . . . anger and the desire to get away from all of them.

"No one influenced me, Else,'' Anna replied. She stopped short of telling her sister-in-law that she was vapid. Else was, after all vulnerable. She was almost as vulnerable as Dorcas. Anna held her tongue and silently blamed Gerda for this tiff. At the same time she felt angry with herself for becoming involved in it.

"Anna doesn't dislike you,'' Gisela suddenly said. "Anna's the voice of social justice . . . she's been influenced by my sister. Sometimes I wonder where she came from, she's so unlike the rest of us.''

Anna stared at her mother, whose voice had grown cold and brittle. She felt empty inside as she looked at her mother, whose narrow lips were pressed together and whose eyes looked almost hate-filled. Why was her mother so sharp? Again she asked herself why her parents had had her; it seemed clear they hadn't wanted her. Unlike Else, she did not allow tears to flood her eyes, though she had to fight to keep them back as her mother's mood swept over her, and she fought her natural revulsion for all of them. She left the room quickly and fairly ran upstairs to the room where she was to spend the night. She sat on the edge of the bed thinking. Two more days, she thought, finally letting her tears flow. Two more days with her unrelenting family and then back to Berlin. I wish I hadn't come, she thought. But then, she had not been given a choice.

"Anna . . . Anna . . ."

Anna looked up through tear-filled eyes. The door to her room had been opened just a crack, and Dorcas peered in cautiously.

Anna felt her face redden. She didn't want to be caught crying. She crushed the tears away. "I'm all right," she sniffed.

To her surprise, Dorcas pushed into the room and closed the door behind her. She walked to the bed and sat down. "Please don't cry, Anna. I know how you feel, I do."

Anna looked into Dorcas' face and silently nodded. Dorcas probably did know, she thought as she studied her sister-in-law's expression.

"You're not exactly friendly toward me," Dorcas said slowly, "but you've never been mean either."

"I've no reason to be mean to you," Anna replied, feeling again the sympathy she so often felt for Dorcas. She reached out and took her hand, "And I apologize for not being friendlier . . . you know, I try to keep my distance from the others."

"I wish I could," Dorcas ventured.

Anna squeezed her hand. "Try to avoid them," Anna advised. Then, "If you don't, they'll eat you alive."

Dorcas forced a smile. "Perhaps you would come and visit me one day."

Anna looked at her for a long moment, "I'll try," she promised.

After Dorcas left, Anna sat for a long while in the fading light of the summer evening, watching as the growing darkness slowly changed the room. Then, feeling a sort of lonely melancholy, she turned on the lamp and took Karla's most recent letter from her purse:

My darling Anna,
    How I miss you! And how I look forward to your letters. I'm so glad your studies are going well. When will you know about university? You must write and tell me everything—of course you *must* tell me about the bellicose celebrations in Essen. I'm certain the All Highest

Grand Pooh-Bah will appear in knightly armor or some such ghastly attire. He is, I discover, something of laughingstock in America . . . in fact everywhere.

And now for my stupendous news. We've bought a house! Can you imagine? It's in the heart of Germantown. It has three bedrooms upstairs (yes, it has two stories), and downstairs there is a small library, a living room, a dining room, and a kitchen. The bathroom and toilet are upstairs. Did I mention that in America the sink, tub, and toilet are all in the same room? Isn't that peculiar? Well, I'm used to it now.

There's a small pantry off the kitchen and I plan to convert it into a little office for myself.

Josef and his paper are doing wonderfully well here and we have dozens of friends. Anna, you would love it here.

Well, I must end this letter now because it's almost time for our regular Saturday Night Discussion Group to meet.

All my love, Anna. Write to me soon.

Karla

Anna smiled and pressed the letter to her. Even at such a great distance Karla was a comfort to her. Anna pulled the chain on the lamp and plunged the room again into darkness. In her mind, she conjured up Karla's Saturday Night Discussion Group. It sounded interesting and stimulating.

No two men in the world could differ more than Dr. Schnieder, my tutor, and my father, General Klaus von Bock, Anna concluded. Not only were they physically different, but their souls seemed to spring from opposite poles of the universe.

Dr. Schnieder was hardly five feet, two inches, and his circumference appeared to equal his height. His little round head was bald and surrounded only by a thin gray fringe of hair. His glasses were thick, for he was quite myopic and he smiled readily, often giggling nervously when in her presence. She was the only female student he took a personal interest in, and tutored individually, and she assumed that her sex had something to do with Dr. Schnieder's more or less chronic embarrassment. He was, nonetheless, a stimulating teacher, and while he was intellectually demanding, he also had a sense of humor that transcended his embarrassment now and again. Perhaps, Anna thought, the only thing her father and Dr. Schnieder had in common was their age. Her father was fifty-five, light years older than her mother, and Dr. Schnieder was most certainly about her father's age, though because of his bald head and his ponderous heavy-set body, he appeared older. Still, in mind and spirit he seemed younger.

Physically, her father, by contrast, was over six feet, two inches in height. He had a rigid military bearing and stood as straight as could be. He was broad-shouldered and lean, and he had a full head of iron-gray hair and clear piercing blue eyes punctuated by thick dark brows which arched sharply, giving him an expression of permanent surprise. But when he frowned his dark brows furrowed deeply and he looked, and indeed could be, fierce. Her father also had little or no sense of humor. Or, if he did, Anna had never seen much evidence of it.

How utterly unalike these two men were had not really occurred to Anna till she had seen them together for the first time this afternoon. She had personally admitted Dr. Schnieder to the long front hall, received his coat, his gloves, his scarf, and umbrella. Then ushered him down the corridor to her father's oak-paneled study. There she had introduced the two, and it struck her that in the four years she had been at the gymnasium her father and Dr. Schnieder had never before met. Their reasons for not meeting were threefold. First, her father had not asked to meet Dr. Schnieder. Second, since she was a daughter rather than a son, her father felt her education was in her mother's domain, and third, her father had been busy when any occasion to meet the doctor presented itself. Her mother had meet Dr. Schnieder at several teas which her father had not attended. But if her father expressed no curiosity about the head of the gymnasium, the head of the gymnasium had expressed none about her father until a few weeks ago. Then Dr. Schnieder had called her into his office and requested this meeting.

When the introduction was complete, her father held out his hand to Dr. Schnieder. "Good to meet you," he muttered. And Anna thought he looked a trifle uncomfortable.

"A pleasure," Dr. Schnieder returned, looking equally ill-at-ease.

"Please sit down, Doctor. May I offer you a cognac?"

At this point Dr. Schnieder checked his watch, then replied, "I think it is not too early in the day. Yes, a cognac would be pleasant."

Her father's eyes settled on her. "Go ask Heinz to bring a bottle of cognac and two goblets, and you are excused unless Dr. Schnieder wishes you to be present."

"No, I wish to speak with you alone," Dr. Schnieder quickly injected.

"I will speak with you later," her father promised.

Anna bowed slightly and edged out of the room. What did her father think the doctor wanted? Naturally she knew, but she wondered if her father thought she was doing badly in her studies. His voice seemed to offer the promise of a reprimand. She smiled to herself. He would be surprised, especially surprised considering the academic record of his friends' sons.

"Do you smoke, Doctor?"

Klaus von Bock fumbled in his desk drawer for his pipe. The ritual of cleaning the bowl, filling it with fresh tobacco, and finally lighting it would relax him. *God, how I hate academics,* he thought as he glanced for a second at the doctor.

"No, no, I don't."

"But you don't mind?" General von Bock waved his pipe in the air and looked toward it as he asked the question.

"No, no, not at all."

"Ah, good, good." Klaus von Bock leaned back with satisfaction, and with the small metal tool he kept for such purposes, he began to clean his pipe. In a moment

Heinz entered with a silver tray. It bore two large crystal cognac goblets and a bottle of the finest French cognac.

"So, Anna has been at the gymnasium for four years now . . ." Klaus said as soon as Heinz had left the room and closed the door.

"Yes, this is her final year. She is quite my most promising student."

The general's brows arched higher than usual; then they lowered and he seemed to frown. "Do you not have several sons of other generals as students . . . General Halder's son? He's already been accepted to the academy. Is he not in Anna's class?"

"Yes."

"Well, certainly he is more promising than Anna." He laughed, and then sobered when Dr. Schnieder did not even smile.

"Anna is far more intelligent than young Halder, and she is brighter than young Groener too. He is also my student."

General Klaus von Bock pressed his lips together and twirled the end of his stiff gray mustache. He then shook his head. "Halder and Groener would not be pleased to hear that a mere slip of a girl is more intelligent than their sons."

"I do not intend to tell them. I depend on your discretion in this matter, General. But I am prepared to defend my statement with the results of countless examinations and many independent papers . . . papers I've had judged by others. There is no question in my mind, General, Anna is quite extraordinary."

The general responded only with a nod. "And that is why you have come? To tell me my daughter is extraordinarily intelligent?"

"Not entirely, General." Dr. Schnieder took a gulp of cognac. It was far better than the brandy he usually drank and he immediately realized he should have sipped and not gulped. Military men made him nervous. They were, and this one was no different, an impatient lot, unused to the subtleties of argument and the benefits of discussion. *Yes* this and *no* that was what they all wanted to hear.

"Well, then?" the general said, leaning forward in his chair.

"I've come to ask your permission to recommend your daughter sit examinations for the university. She will have an *Abitur*—the diploma from the gymnasium—the only credential acceptable for entrance, and I know she will pass the examinations. She wants to go to university and I believe she should go."

The general's frown deepened. Then he asked, "What would a woman do with a university education?"

"I believe she might be qualified to go into law . . . but of course she could always teach law."

Again Klaus von Bock hummed, then gradually he seemed to untense, and finally he leaned back. "She has always been an odd girl," he allowed. Then, thinking aloud, "it is difficult to find proper husbands for intelligent educated women. Gerda, my elder daughter, is quite normal. She married well and has already produced children. Andreas too has produced heirs, and soon so will Markus. I don't suppose it matters if Anna marries when she's older, or at all for that matter." He paused and set down his pipe. After a moment he shook his head. "Prepare her, then," he said with resignation. "Let's see if she is so smart."

Dr. Schnieder wanted to smile, but he restrained himself. Fortunate Anna! She was obviously free to attend university because her sister and brothers had already fulfilled her father's dreams. Well, no matter, he thought. The important thing was getting her father's permission to allow her to fulfill her destiny.

He finished off his brandy in silence, then stood up awkwardly. "Thank you, General, for your permission to prepare Anna, and thank you for a fine cognac."

General Klaus von Bock stood up stiffly and clicked his heels together formally. He towered over Dr. Schnieder and it made him feel comfortable to look down on the professor. "Well, I hope she doesn't disappoint you," he said without expression.

Dr. Schnieder nodded and then turned and left. Anna stood silently in the alcove near the front door. Dr. Schnieder grinned and winked at her. Anna smiled back, but sobered instantly when she heard her father's bellow from the study. "Anna! Anna! Come in here immediately."

She turned and ran toward the study, knowing only that Dr. Schnieder had let himself out of the front door.

The days of August turned quickly into September, and on September 3 Anna's father summoned her to his study, where, to her surprise, she also found her mother.

Her father sat behind his large desk and her mother sat in a big leather chair. For a moment Anna stood in the doorway; then, unsmiling, her father motioned her to the straight-backed chair by his desk.

Silently her father made a show of shuffling through various papers on his desk; then from the pile he withdrew a long white envelope which had been opened. He waved it as he spoke. "It seems you have been accepted by the University of Berlin," he stated unemotionally. "You seem to have scored very well on your examinations."

There was no admiration in his voice. He was utterly and completely matter-of-fact. "I have decided you will attend and that you will study law. Is that acceptable to you?"

Anna's heart pounded with excitement. "Yes," she managed.

"You can continue living here," her mother suggested. "It's not so far."

Anna turned and looked at her mother, and her heart sank. She did not want to remain at home. She wanted to leave now and never return. Why was her mother constantly critical of her and at the same time so possessive?

"She'll have to study long hours and be near the library and her tutors," her father intoned as he looked at her mother. "I think it would be best if a room were found for her in a reputable student house near the university."

Anna turned quickly toward her father. She had never dreamed *he* would take her side, though in fact she had not as yet expressed herself. "Yes," she said, "I will have to study long hours."

''You want to leave!'' her mother interjected in a shrill voice. ''I knew you would want to leave! Klaus, I knew she would want to leave! How can you allow such a thing? She's only a child!''

Anna watched as her father turned toward her mother. She knew that thrust of the chin, that sternness of the lower jaw. Her father was not happy that her mother had contradicted him in front of her, or that she was making what he would call ''a scene.''

''Anna is no longer a child, Gisela. She's eighteen and in January she'll be nineteen. If she's to attend university then she must live near the university.''

''She'll get into trouble. She won't meet the right type of men. She should be getting engaged.''

''Gerda is married and has produced children. Andreas has produced heirs to the family name and title. Markus will soon be a father too. There is no need for Anna to marry. She can become a teacher of law. I understand she has the ability.''

Her mother covered her face with her hands. Then suddenly she sprang up and and fairly ran from the room.

''Your mother is high-strung,'' her father explained. ''She's having a spell, but she'll recover and next week she will go with you to find a room.''

''Thank you, Father.''

Her father did not smile. ''Just prove that my faith in your good sense is merited,'' he muttered. Then, thrusting his jaw out, ''I am running for political office. It looks progressive if I have a daughter in university. See to it that our family name is upheld, Anna. Make me proud of you.''

3

September 1912

Frau Fischer was the widow of Dr. Hans Fischer, a once-renowned professor of physics at Berlin University and the son of a prominent German manufacturer. The last years of the 1860's were especially rewarding for Dr. Fischer, who found himself with both academic fame and money from a generous inheritance.

One of Dr. Fischer's first acts after receiving his inheritance was to purchase a large rambling house in Sigismundstrasse in Berlin's Tiergarten District. The house was near the splendid park for which the district was named, and it was exactly thirty minutes' walk from the university, providing him with a vigorous daily constitutional.

At first Dr. Fischer filled his house with students—mostly his protégés—men and women gifted in physics. In those days the house was alive with laughter and conversation. At the table, in the good doctor's study, in the library, and in the living room and bedrooms, students huddled together to discuss lectures, postulate theories, offer hypotheses, and sometimes even to gossip. As the good doctor approached fifty in the year 1870, the house gossip centered on his frequent meetings with an attractive blond twenty-year-old shop assistant named Frieda.

The professor, it seemed, had two passions; one was physics and the other was his burgeoning collection of handmade cuckoo clocks. Frieda worked in a clock shop and it developed they had met while the professor was buying a quite special clock which featured not one cuckoo, but a family of cuckoos who appeared in an intricately carved block to announce each and every hour. Shortly after their meeting it became obvious that the professor had three passions—physics, cuckoo clocks, and Frieda.

In 1871 Dr. Fischer married Frieda Schmidt, who was an orphan. In 1880, nine years later, Dr. Fischer died, leaving thirty-year-old Frieda with a five-bedroom house near the Tiergarten, sufficient money to live on, and 1,437 cuckoo clocks of all sizes and types.

Frieda was not a woman of great intelligence or ambition. She rented out all the rooms to students, for whom she happily cooked, and devoted herself to tending the clocks, for which it seemed she had no less fondness than her late husband. Among the students at the University of Berlin, Frau Fischer's house became known as *Der Kucknuckhause,* the Cuckoo House.

Over the years Frau Fischer had changed a great deal. Now sixty years of age, she was an oddly shaped woman who appeared quite topheavy. She had broad shoulders and huge arms. Her breasts were utterly immense, and her waist was thick. It appeared that her measurements from bust to buttocks did not vary so much as one inch, but all of this unseemly bulk was held upright by tiny spindly legs.

Her hair was a halo of white-blond frizz with a childish red bow set amid her untidy corkscrew curls. Her eyes were brown, she squinted as if she needed eyeglasses, and her skin was sallow because she seldom ventured outside. Frau Fischer's great portly figure was adorned in a massive red silk print dress that fell nearly to the floor, and sitting, as she was, in a large brown overstuffed chair, she would have looked like a huge bouquet thrust into an ill shaped vase had it not been for her hands. Her hands were constantly animated and it seemed she wore a sparkling ring on each of her fat little fingers.

Anna looked around the clock-filled room and tried desperately to suppress her smile. Frau Fischer was extraordinary-looking, and the room was a kind of Black Forest nightmare, filled, as it was, with hundreds of carved cuckoo clocks. And suddenly it happened. All of the little doors sprang open . . . not exactly at the same second, but all within two minutes. From attic to basement all 1,437 cuckoos popped out and in various tones and pitches announced the hour of three P.M.

Anna's mother sat up, stunned and at first alarmed. After a moment she whispered, "Good heavens," and then she sank back among the cushions, looking about apprehensively.

Frau Fischer grinned and with a wave of her hand dismissed the cacophony of sound. "You get used to them." Then she turned to Anna. "Yes, you'll get used to them . . . after a few days you hardly notice. Anyway, there is only one in the small room which would be yours."

"It will make it hard to study," Gisela, Anna's mother, said with a frown.

"I shall have to study in the library anyway," Anna replied.

"And to sleep . . . how will you sleep among so many cuckoos?"

"There's only one in my room. I'll get used to it. What do students in Worms do? There are hundreds of churches and their chimes ring every hour on the hour. Remember when we went there—remember? I was sick and I had a fever and I kept waking up when the bells rang. I thought I was in heaven."

"Bells are bells and cuckoos are cuckoos," her mother answered, as if that explained her objections.

Gisela returned her eyes to Frau Fischer, and Anna could see that her mother was trying to understand this rather odd woman.

"What do you think?" Frau Fischer asked, ignoring her mother and looking at Anna.

"I think it's a lovely room."

Gisela pressed her lips tight. "I don't know why you can't live at home. It's not so far."

"Mother, it's already been decided. I must leave and live where other students live."

Her mother did not answer. Then she stood up. "Excuse me, Frau Fischer, could I use your toilet?"

Frau Fischer nodded. "It's down the hall, Frau von Bock. The third door on the left."

Anna watched as her mother disappeared. Frau Fi

scher too stood up. "I think I shall prepare some tea for us."

Anna smiled. "That would be nice."

Frau Fischer disappeared and Anna looked around the cluttered, overdecorated room. She moved her foot slightly and was aware that underneath the ruffle of the settee, her heel had touched something hard. She leaned over and ran her hand under the settee, withdrawing an empty bottle—a schnapps bottle. Anna looked at it, then quickly replaced it, pushing it further beneath the settee. Ah, so Frau Fischer tippled schnapps! Anna smiled. Her mother would not let her live at Frau Fischer's if she knew. "But I'm not going to tell her," Anna whispered. Yes, Frau Fischer most certainly was kept busy between her clocks and her schnapps—far too busy to bother me, Anna thought. Oh, what would it be like to be on her own? To come and go as she wished, to plan her own time . . . oh there were a million things she wanted to do, things she had not been able to do as long as she lived at home, things she could do if she lived here.

Frau Fischer returned carrying a large tray. On it were a fancy pink-and-gold porcelain teapot, matching cups and saucers, and silver teaspoons. At the same time Frau Fischer returned, her mother returned from the toilet. "Oh, tea," she murmured, sounding surprised.

"What would happen if I had to study and could not get here for dinner?" Anna asked.

"I would just put it away and you could have it when you came. I know students are busy, I'm not fussy."

Anna nodded in satisfaction. "I do like the room, Mama."

Her mother looked defeated. Then softly, "As good as any other room, I suppose."

Anna smiled. "Then I guess I shall be moving in a week from now."

Frau Fischer smiled and handed Anna's mother a cup tea. "I usually drink coffee myself," she confessed.

agine when I'm studying late and arising early fee too." And she thought silently: I shall shall drink coffee in a *konditorei* near-
a *konditorei* was a coffee house

HONOR THE DREAM • 51

which also sold and served sweets. Anna lapsed into a daydream. *I shall sit there for hours and hours and talk politics and philosophy and law. I shall have conversations uninterrupted by family and I'll go home when I please. Freedom . . .* it was only a week away and even now Anna could taste it and she found its flavor sweet.

Anna focused on the image of her Aunt Karla. *How I wish you were here so I could share this with you . . .* and then Anna thought, *but I'll meet others like Karla. I'll meet people my own age with whom I can talk.* The promise of friends and conversation was as exhilarating as the expectation of freedom was exciting.

"You seem very happy to be leaving home," her mother said, still looking distressed.

She had said it a hundred times now and Anna's response was always the same. "I'm just looking forward to school," Anna lied. And taking a sip of her tea, she vowed to write to Karla at once and tell her all the wonderful news.

Anna signed her name at the bottom of the letter with a flourish, and then held it up, waving it to dry the ink before rereading what she had written.

She wasn't alone in the writing room of the post office, but still it seemed a more private place to write a very personal letter than her bedroom at home. At home one of her parents might well barge into her room and, leaning over her shoulder, read all or part of what she had written to Tante Karla. And if not her parents, the maid, Johanna, or the manservant, Emmerich, might steal a look, or even read her letter before it was mailed. Her parents, her father in particular, would not be happy with her letter, and the servants turned all information into idle gossip. No, it was better to write the letter here and then mail it right away. In any case, the writing room was pleasant as well as impersonal.

Anna glanced around the room. It was a large room with windows along one wall. There were a total of five curved writing tables, and each one sat five people. The chairs were padded and comfortable, and at each place there was a desk blotter, a pen, an inkwell, and on a raised shelf, a large round lamp to provide good light.

The post office writing room was most crowded in the early evening, after working hours. It was now midafternoon, and Anna was the only one at the writing table she had selected. In fact, there was only one other person in the room. She glanced quickly at him, then returned her eyes to her own letter.

The man at the table nearest the window looked a little disheveled, but, she concluded, he was certainly intent. Again she stole a glance to confirm her first impression. Yes, he was intense. She could see that his hand gripped the pen tightly, and that he seemed to be concentrating on every word he wrote. He was a good-looking man, she thought, albeit not well-dressed and certainly unkempt. His hair was dark, thick, and curly. His face needed a shave, but his profile was intriguing. Perhaps he was a factory worker, she mused. Then she looked at him once again . . . no, perhaps not. More likely he was a student at one of the technical schools. Guessing about people was her hobby, though she rarely, if ever, discovered if her guesses were correct.

Anna looked once more at the male enigma and then focused her eyes on her letter.

September 5, 1912

Dear Tante Karla,

It's been over a year since you left Berlin and I still imagine I will meet you in a few days and we'll talk about everything that has happened to me and is happening at this very moment. Letters are a poor substitute for our long conversations. I enjoyed your last letter so much. I try to picture Milwaukee in my mind, I try to picture your house from your descriptions. Please, can you send me some pictures?

In a few weeks I will begin the study of law at the University of Berlin and in only one week I will move into the house of Frau Fischer. Frau Fischer is the widow of Dr. Fischer, who once taught physics at the university. She rents rooms to students. On the outside of this envelope is her address; you may write to me there. Also, and most important, you can write to me privately. I don't think Frau Fischer will open my mail—always a danger at home.

I think if Mama knew much about Frau Fischer she would have her doubts about my living there—in fact, I don't think she would let me live there at all. Frau Fischer, I think, is into the schnapps. When no one was in the living room I found an empty bottle under the flounce of the settee. And she is such a character! I think she bleaches her hair blond and she wears a lot of powders. White powder for her face and I think a pink-tinted powder on her cheeks. Mama would have noticed that too— and the cuckoo clocks. Frau Fischer has over a thousand . . . all the students know of her. Anyway, the important thing is I shall be on my own and Frau Fischer does not seem strict. The truth is, I doubt she could remember any infraction of her house rules long enough to complain about them.

Oh, Karla, I am so longing to get started! Longing to spend time of my own at the *konditorei* even though I don't yet know which *konditorei* is frequented by students of the law. Imagine having friends with whom I can discuss politics. Imagine being able to argue without having a family fight! I'll be able to say anything I please without Papa's censure or sarcasm. Yes, since you left I have been terribly lonely. Please do write to me. I want to hear everything about your life.

Love,
Anna

Anna paused for a moment, then folded the letter and put it into the envelope, which she had already addressed. She then gathered up her purse and the bundle she had picked up at the dressmaker's for her mother, and went to the postal window to mail her letter. She glanced one more time at the young man . . . no, not a worker and perhaps not a student at the technical school either. In either case he wouldn't be here at this time of day unless he was an unemployed worker. She shrugged and turned to watch the postal employee stamp her letter and then drop it into a large box.

"Everyone," he said with a smile, "has a relative in Milwaukee."

Ludwig Schwartz was a tall gangly sort of fellow with a long narrow face, straight black hair, and a bad complexion. But it was his throat that fascinated Anna. Ludwig had an unusually long neck as well as an unusually large Adam's apple which moved up and down as he spoke, and which moved faster and faster if he talked rapidly—which he did whenever he was nervous or agitated. Just now it moved slowly, in keeping with the professorial tone of his voice.

"This *konditorei* has an interesting history," Ludwig revealed as he leaned across the marble-topped table toward Anna. Ludwig was her own age, and he had sat by her during their first lecture. After the lecture he had followed her to the library, and seeking her out, had befriended her. She was, he thought to himself, quite the prettiest girl who had ever agreed to have coffee with him. But she was more than pretty; Anna von Bock was astoundingly bright. She was the most well-read girl he had ever met, and she was, happily, also extremely friendly and just plain nice.

Anna thought about Ludwig's comment. Ludwig did not appeal to her as a man might appeal to a woman, but Anna admitted she found him interesting. He was privy to the world of male knowledge, and unlike many young men, he seemed willing to share that knowledge.

"Mind you, this *konditorei* has a similar background. None of them are what they were before 1848. They were introduced to Berlin by some Swiss entrepreneurs, you know. In those days—the days before the revolution—the *konditorei* was the only forum for unorganized political factions. Naturally, the coffee was always the best and the sweets were the finest." He cut a piece of cake with his fork and lifted it to his mouth, as if to emphasize his words, and when he had swallowed it, he continued, "But it wasn't the quality of the sweets that drew men to the coffeehouses daily. They went to read foreign newspapers and to discuss politics. In the *konditorei* they could light their cigars, lean back, and freely speak their minds.

Of course some *konditorei* were frequented by bureaucrats and others by the officers of the guard.'' He lowered his voice almost to a whisper, ''Others—this one, as a matter-of-fact—were frequented by enemies of the state. Their customers came to read *Rheinische Zeitung*, for which Marx was writing.''

Anna frowned. She appreciated the information Ludwig was providing on the history of the *konditorei*, but she had fastened on his statement about 1848, and she leaned toward him. ''You think that what happened in 1848 was a revolution?'' she questioned. Then, expounding on her own query, ''I'd say it was more of a historic turning point at which history failed to turn.''

Ludwig screwed up his face. ''It was a revolt! And furthermore, it had far-reaching implications for Prussia, for Germany, and for Berlin. How can you argue otherwise?''

''A revolt is not necessarily a revolution,'' Anna replied coolly. ''The problems that existed before 1848 still exist.''

''Are you a communist?'' Ludwig whispered as he leaned even closer. His eyes were large and his Adam's apple seemed suspended in the very middle of its usual vertical path. And at the same time he asked her the question, he pondered her statement. Yes, no matter what her politics, she had a clarity of thought.

Anna laughed. ''Oh, of course not! To recognize social problems is not to suggest that communism is the solution. How can you ask such a silly question!''

''Because there are communists at the university. Lots of them,'' he answered, relieved that she had stated her position.

''It is not a disease which one catches,'' Anna retorted good-naturedly.

Ludwig grinned. ''Your father is a general. I imagine he thinks it's a disease.''

Anna laughed again. ''My views are not the same as my father's.''

''Are you in a revolt against your parents?'' he again leaned toward her, thinking what beautiful eyes she had and wondering vaguely if she would accompany him to a matinee at the theater.

"Perhaps I am revolting against my parents," Anna hedged, deciding not to discuss her feelings toward her parents with Ludwig, whom, after all, she had not known that long and did not yet know well. "This conversation is a long way from the history of the *konditorei*," she reminded him.

"Ah, yes, well, anyway, after 1848 the importance of the *konditorei* faded and now they are only coffeehouses frequented by students and writers. Das Romanische Kaffee is filled with political writers—they depress each other by reading their rejected manuscripts aloud. And this one is for students and professors."

"Well, even if it's not the same, I think it's fun. I love coming here and I love being able to express my views freely and discuss things we're learning and even argue. Besides," she said with a wave of her hand, "I adore the almond cake."

"This is not the place for truly good arguments," a strong male voice suggested.

Anna turned because the voice came from a table behind them, and from someone who had not been there when she and Ludwig had come into the coffeehouse. She looked up at the stranger, who had left his seat and was standing. He looked familiar; then with surprise she realized it was the fellow from the writing room in the post office—the man about whom she had mused.

"Kurt Stein," he said, bowing toward Anna and smiling.

In the reading room she had seen him only in profile and from a distance. Up close and from the front he looked quite different, though, she admitted to herself, no less disheveled. He was taller than she had originally thought, but not as slim as Ludwig. His shoulders were broader, his arms clearly muscular, his chest wide. His hair was as she remembered it, a mass of black curls, and his face was absolutely clear, almost pallid. He wore rimless glasses, and behind his glasses were large, heavily lashed dark eyes, eyes so dark they seemed almost black. They were the kind of eyes that seemed to invite you to dive into the depths of the soul, they were eyes that held you. He looked at her intently and she felt uncomfortable, as if he could see right through her and read her every thought. She felt her face flush slightly, but she met his bold compelling eyes with hers. "And where should one go to argue?" she asked.

He straddled the empty chair at their table and without invitation sat down.

Ludwig scowled at Kurt Stein angrily. He was older—perhaps twenty-nine or thirty. He was a tutor and he was a communist rabble-rouser in Ludwig's opinion. Worse than that, Kurt Stein had a volatile temper and a reputation as a ladies' man. He openly talked about his conquests and even about free love.

"One goes to the Social Democratic School," Kurt replied without the slightest hesitation. "To listen to lectures and to debate social issues." He never took his eyes off Anna, and he never even acknowledged Ludwig.

"They're all communists," Ludwig hissed. "And anarchists," he added, finding his voice.

Kurt's dark eyes flashed at Ludwig. "Are you a student?"

Ludwig nodded and was aware of feeling like an insect caught in the web of a wily spider.

"Students should want to learn . . . they should be willing to listen and to evaluate before they resort to name-calling. Do I call you an 'imperialist pig' or an 'imperialist murderer'? You may attend the university, but you are no student, my friend, you couldn't be, your mind is as closed as your mouth is open."

Anna moved uncomfortably. She felt she should say something to defend poor Ludwig, but she herself felt Ludwig's comments were too quickly offered. She heard Ludwig's chair scrape as he stood up. His face was red and his Adam's apple quivered.

"We should go, Anna." He was afraid to look at her, and even as he stood there stupidly, he knew she wouldn't come.

"Perhaps Anna doesn't want to go. Perhaps she wants to stay and to learn."

Ludwig continued to avoid her eyes. Instead he looked to one side of her. "Are you coming?"

"I think I'll stay for a while," she replied. Then, finally thinking of how to defend Ludwig without going with him, she added, "I should like to learn more about a person this impolite."

Ludwig screwed up his face. Her defense was not enough to make him stay. He turned, muttering, "I'll see you tomorrow, Anna," walked rapidly toward the door, afraid to turn back. Now, he thought miserably, she won't go out with me and I probably won't see her tomorrow. Kurt was a giant, and willingly Ludwig admitted to himself that he was no giant killer.

Kurt smiled warmly at Anna and raised a dark brow. "The truth is not impolite," he said, moving his chair still closer to hers.

"It's always impolite to hurt someone's feelings."

"Your friend does not seem so sensitive to the feelings of communists and anarchists."

"I doubt if he really knows any," she answered.

"Do you?" he asked.

"I don't think so," she answered carefully.

"Ah, you do now. How about it? Will you come with me to the Social Democratic School? Will you hear Rosa Luxemburg? Will you argue with me afterward?"

Rosa Luxemburg . . . her aunt had mentioned Rosa Luxemburg and so had her father, though hardly in the same tone. Karla had found Rosa Luxemburg fascinating, her father thought she should be shot. Anna did not hesitate long. "I'll come," she replied.

"And what is your name?"

"Anna . . . Anna von Bock. I'm a law student."

His dark eyes moved vertically as he examined her from toe to head, his eyes lingering on her breasts and on her ankles. Then he grinned. "And you're beautiful too . . . perhaps a little bourgeois . . . but none the less beautiful."

"And you," she answered evenly, "are good-looking, but unkempt and egotistical."

He laughed and stood up. "Shall we go?"

"Now?" Anna asked, surprised.

Again he grinned as if they shared some enormous secret. "If not now, when?" he replied.

"Der Berliner," Kurt said solemnly. "I am a Berliner." Kurt seemed to almost sneer the famous phrase. "Do you know what that means, Anna?" He turned his head toward her momentarily, though they kept walking. "Berliners think they're something special—something very special. They even speak a kind of patois derived from Low and Middle German—"

"It comes from the original language of the *Mark Brandenburg,* the people who lived on the Prussian border," Anna added, knowing full well the history of *Berliner Deutsch.* "Yes, I know intellectually what it is to be a Berliner. But I think I would only really *feel* what it meant if I were away from Berlin. But you obviously don't think much of Berliners. Aren't you a Berliner?"

Kurt laughed—a laugh which sounded full of irony. "Not really. I'm certainly not the the kind of Berliner *you* are. I'm no member of the elite. I heard your friend say your father was a general . . . General von Bock, yes?"

They were walking toward the Social Democratic School, cutting through the park. Anna stopped by the pond and Kurt too paused. Two swans glided majestically across the tranquil water and Anna wondered if they were the same two swans she and Karla had watched several summers ago—swans, she recalled, mate for life. "I'm his younger daughter," she answered slowly, her eyes still fastened on the swans. "What has that to do with being a Berliner?"

"Everything. You were born here, reared in an aristocratic family. You're a person of privilege. Your family is a part of the despotism that has held the workers of this city—indeed all of Germany—prisoner."

Anna turned and looked into Kurt's face. His tone had grown suddenly hostile, his voice had a definite edge. She felt bewildered by his accusations, more so because it was he who had invited her to go to this Social Democratic School. "You're making assumptions about me because of my family," she answered defensively. "And they're as unjust as the accusations Ludwig made about your Social Democratic School.''

"Do you despise everything your father stands for?" He leaned closer to her face and his dark brown brows arched questioningly.

"Of course not! I'm not even certain I know what he stands for, as you put it. My father seldom sees fit to discuss his views with me. We certainly disagree on many things, but perhaps there are certain things we agree on.''

"He would say that he stands for law and order, for hard work and strict morals. But his law and order brings violence to the poor and the oppressed, his morals would ban all opposition political parties, jail Marxists, censor all creativity to suit his own taste and the taste of his 'class.' And he is also an anti-Semite. Your father is part of what a 'Berliner' is—he is arrogant and, worse, he is a despot.''

"I think there is more to being a Berliner than arrogance or even despotism. I think many Jews define themselves as 'Berliners' too. Most of all, I don't understand why you are making these accusations against my father—why did you want me to come with you if you feel as you say you feel?'' Anna spoke quickly, but she felt conflicting emotions surface even as she spoke. Much of what he said about her father was true, but because this condemnation came from someone who didn't even know him, she felt suspicious and even obligated to defend him.

A sudden smile flooded Kurt's face, and his eyes, which had been harsh only seconds earlier, softened. "Ah, you are quick to the defense of your father. It's true, blood *is* thicker than water. I just wanted to see how you would react,'' he said with a sweep of his hand. "I invited you because I've heard you are very intelligent, Anna von Bock. You see, I knew who you were before I interrupted your coffee. I'm a tutor at the university; I heard about you from one of the other tutors.'' He smiled and his smile was slightly crooked and very appealing. "You're also beautiful, and I won't lie to you. I like beautiful women. But most of all I want you to learn about us . . . I want you to visit our school and learn.''

"I would have thought you had concluded that I was hopeless—genetically predestined to serve the emperor as my father does."

"Very good. You have a sharp tongue."

"But I've not personally insulted you as you insulted me."

"I told you, I wanted to see your reaction. Besides, can you deny I have described your father accurately?"

"You're right about some things."

"Am I right that he is anti-Semitic?"

"He tolerates rich Jews and makes comments about the others, so I suppose you are right. Are you Jewish?"

"No . . . half Jewish. My mother was gentile, so I am not considered Jewish by Jews. But my father was Jewish, so I am considered Jewish by gentiles. A nice position, what?"

"I'm sure it can be difficult."

" 'Difficult' does not begin to describe it." He took her arm. "Come on, let's continue walking. I do want you to hear Rosa . . . not that I always agree with her. We disagree on many points. But that is what it is all about, Anna. It is about dialogue, argument, exposition. You'll see. And you'll see other things too. Anna, I'm going to show you a Berlin you didn't know existed." He felt satisfied with himself. Anna *was* impressed. She was vulnerable to arguments concerning social justice. Her conscience was the key—well, he knew all the right things to say.

Anna fell into step with him, though she wasn't entirely certain why. This man appeared moody and unpredictable. Yet he utterly fascinated her and she knew it was because she had never met anyone quite like him.

"It's crowded," Kurt lamented as they pushed their way into the overcrowded, smoke-filled hall. Anna looked about, her eyes scanning the mixed audience. Many appeared to be factory workers and were indeed dressed as if they had just left work. Others, a small group toward the front, were reasonably well-dressed. The group, she decided, were almost equally divided between men and women.

Rosa Luxemburg was a small, well-dressed woman. She wore her long dark hair in a roll that framed her face. Her eyes were lively, though, Anna noted, somehow sad. She limped when she walked and Anna wondered if she had been a victim of polio or whether she had been born with one leg slightly shorter than the other. Anna studied her and was surprised how well-dressed she was. Although not fashionable, her clothes were made in reasonably expensive fabrics. She looked like a middle-class hausfrau until she opened her mouth. Her voice was strong and deep for a woman. She was also direct and clear; from her very first word she held her listener's interest, and her intelligent and articulate presentation provided evidence of her own brilliance. Her every point incorporated the classics of world literature, and her talk, from start to finish, was an intellectual feast.

"Well, what did you think?" Kurt asked anxiously as the hall emptied out into the street.

"She was wonderful!" Anna said with undisguised admiration. "I thought she was better than my aunt said she was."

"Your aunt?" Kurt looked astonished. "I thought you had never heard of her—that all this was unknown to you."

Anna smiled. "You've made many assumptions about me, and more about my family." She did not mention that she and Karla were, as a matter of fact, close to being family outcasts. "In any case, I have never seen or heard Dr. Luxemburg for myself. My aunt mentioned her only once, and my aunt is gone now. She emigrated to America."

Kurt still looked puzzled. "But this aunt of yours, she liked Rosa?"

"My aunt admired her—though she might have disagreed with her on some points."

"I disagree on many points . . . I disagree with her criticism of Marx. She is always picking on his analysis of expanded reproduction."

"And what do you think about that?" Anna asked.

"You've read *Das Kapital?*"

"Yes."

Kurt half-smiled, "You are full of surprises, Anna von Bock."

Anna did not tell him that she had read Karla's copy or that she and Karla had discussed it often and for long hours. Put plainly, both she and Karla had concluded that Mr. Marx was too inflexible and that his system was also inflexible. But in the socialist system there were pluses, humanitarian concerns that should be adopted.

"Come walk with me," Kurt suggested, taking her arm. "Mental stimulation is like eating a heavy meal. One needs exercise afterward."

Anna went with him, her thoughts still on Rosa Luxemburg. The woman *was* a humanist who cared about other people. Her desire to help the poor and oppressed was obvious. Her politics, as Karla would have said, "has a human face."

Anna looked around furtively. This was the part of Berlin that needed reforms the most. Physically, Berlin's eastern and northern sections were not far from the Tiergarten and the grand Forum Fredericianum where the University of Berlin was located. But in terms of atmosphere they were as distanced as the sun and the moon. The *Tiergarten* was beautifully planted and the houses and apartments of its adjacent districts were well-appointed and well-kept. The Forum Fredericianum was wide, its architecture stately and its buildings magnificent. On one side was the Royal Library, in its center the University of Berlin—once a palace—and on the other side, the opera house. And Berlin had other wonderful streets and districts, not the least of which was the wide Unter den Linden in which every Berliner took pride.

The north and east were different. "No accident," Kurt informed her, "that the headquarters of the police is located in the Alexanderplatz, on the fringe of these sections. The better to enforce the law and keep the discontented from replaying the French revolution."

Anna had not commented, but she could not deny the poverty evident in the streets. Blocks of putrid basement flats, the smell of sewage and swill, and the sight of grubby ill-cared-for children and women who were old

and tired, though in years they were still reasonably
young. Der Alexanderplatz itself had a certain drabness.

"So, now what do you think?" Kurt asked. "What do
you think about the need for a revolution?"

"Insofar as revolution is defined as change—yes, I
think there is a need for change, dramatic change. I think
manning the barricades would bring only death and violence. We should work to force peaceful change."

"You're clinging to the past—the structures of power
will not change unless they're forced to change."

"Perhaps," she replied.

Kurt stopped walking and stepped in front of her.
"Will you meet me on the weekend?" he pressed.

Anna looked up into his eyes. "I am going home on
Saturday, but I could meet you Sunday."

"Home to the plush and the privileged," he said sarcastically; then, softening, "Meet me at the library at
two."

"Is our walk over?"

He nodded. "I have things I have to do," he replied,
not bothering to explain. Then he looked at her intently.
"Remember, Sunday at the library at two."

4

Frau Fischer sat in the center of her blue plush lounge. She wore a flowing robe made of dark blue velvet and her frizzy hair was tucked underneath a net snood. On the coffee table a half-empty bottle of schnapps stood next to a glass which was only partially full. To one side of the schnapps bottle, just under a porcelain figurine of Pan, there was a large box of bonbons.

Anna walked down the hall quietly, but Frau Fischer, even though she was into her schnapps, heard her and called out plaintively, "Is that you, Anna? Do come in for a moment."

Reluctantly Anna came into the living room, noting its odors seemed more obvious since she had come in from outside. Its musty smell combined with the odor of wood from the numerous clocks, the sweet aroma of chocolate, and stale smell of alcohol. And there was a smell she couldn't define, an aroma that seemed to fill the whole house. It was not an unpleasant smell, but it was distinctive.

"What's that odor?" Anna asked, crinkling her nose.

"Incense," Frau Fisher explained. "I discovered it in an Oriental shop. Pomegranates—it's bouquet of pomegranates." For a moment Frau Fischer looked dreamy, but she quickly recovered. "You missed dinner again," Frau Fischer admonished even as she lifted the schnapps and took a healthy and somewhat unladylike swig.

"I'm sorry. I was studying and time got away from me," Anna apologized. It wasn't mandatory to appear for meals and Anna did not feel that she need tell Frau Fischer the details of her life.

"Have a chocolate," Frau Fischer offered. Her eyes

went to the chocolate box. Anna looked down. All the chocolates were neatly cut in half, exposing the mysteries of their gooey sweet fillings.

"I cut them all in half so I'll know what's in them," Frau Fischer explained. "I like the ones filled with marzipan best."

Anna smirked, though she tried not to. "Then why don't you buy only the ones filled with marzipan?" she asked.

Frau Fischer frowned as if the idea had not occurred to her, but she did not answer, she only shrugged and said, "Well, aren't you going to have one?"

"No, thank you," Anna replied.

"You're a skinny little thing. You should eat more. If you don't come to meals you'll lose weight and your parents won't think I'm feeding you."

"I'll tell them that you are," Anna answered, though in truth, the meals Frau Fischer provided were less than nutritious and were, in fact, often mysterious concoctions of dumplings and sauces featuring little bits of unknown meats. Once Frau Fischer served a chocolate soufflé for dinner, and on occasion she served nothing more than rich cheese and heavy bread. Like the others who lived in the house, Anna ate a meal of sausage and sauerkraut at noon so that no matter what was served for dinner, she had eaten at least one good meal during the day.

"There isn't any leftover dinner," Frau Fischer revealed, "but if you're hungry there is chocolate *kuchen* in the icebox, and coffee . . . you can always have coffee."

"I'm not hungry," Anna answered.

"I just wanted you to know," Frau Fischer said, her eyes seemingly focused on something else. Then in the same distant tone she always seemed to use, "How do you like it here?"

"It is fine, I like it very much."

"Good. Good."

Anna watched as Frau Fischer took a long drink of schnapps.

"I like schnapps," Frau Fischer said unnecessarily.

"You didn't tell your parents about my schnapps, did you?"

Anna shook her head.

Frau Fischer smiled drunkenly. "Good," she murmured. "I don't think your mama and papa would approve."

She was certainly right about that, Anna thought.

"No, I should have known you wouldn't tell. You like it here, you don't like it at home."

"I need to live near the university."

"Of course, of course. You don't need to explain." She waved her hand in the air and almost knocked over the statue of Pan. "Your father's a strict old Prussian and your mama is going through the change—she's an erratic woman, I can tell. I understand people."

Anna didn't deny her observations.

"I know you're the youngest child. Probably your mother thought she was finished having babies. She's too possessive and critical, is that it?"

Anna nodded, surprised that Frau Fischer was so observant.

Frau Fischer smiled. "Well, you don't tell your parents about my schnapps and I won't tell your parents how often you are out late . . . even on nights when the library isn't open."

Anna felt a slight chill. She looked for a long moment into Frau Fischer's eyes and wondered if she could trust her. "I must go to my room now, it's late."

Frau Fischer only nodded; her eyes did not even follow as Anna left. Could she be trusted? Anna again wondered as she climbed the two flights of stairs to her little room. Unable to decide, she vowed to be more careful.

She opened the door of her room and went inside. This room had once been part of the attic, and the roof slanted downward on one side so that it met the floor. It was a long narrow room with a window at one end. Her bed lay along the straight wall, and in front of the window there were a desk and a straight-backed chair. Behind the door, also against the straight wall, there was a huge wardrobe. Along the slanted wall that met the floor, her books stretched out in a long line. The room was tiny and sparsely furnished compared to her room at home, but it was hers and already she had formed an attachment to it. She had allowed the one cuckoo clock in her room to run down so it at least was silent. At night she put a towel on the floor in front of her door to block out the sound of the hundreds of other clocks. In the weeks since she had come to this room she had grown used to the sound of the many clocks, and now with the towel providing a sound barrier, the din seemed far away, and, she thought with satisfaction, did not bother her at all.

Anna slipped off her shoes and slowly undressed. She put on her nightdress and brushed out her hair. Then she extinguished the light and lay down on the bed, pulling the duvet up over her.

As soon as she closed her eyes, Kurt's face appeared in her thoughts. He was truly different from any man she had ever known. His eyes fascinated her . . . his intensity fascinated her too. Yes, she wanted to see him again and again. But she thought Kurt was not a person her father would like, and certainly he would not approve of her seeing him. No, Anna thought, I shall be careful not to mention him to my parents. Papa would ask questions and object, and her mother's reaction was totally unpredictable. Yes, Papa would object to Kurt for many reasons, and only one of them was political.

"But it is I who should make such decisions about my life," Anna said aloud to herself with conviction. She sat up in bed, staring into the darkness, and, as if in defiance, folded her arms across her chest and began to mentally replay her recent conversation with Ludwig, a conversation that had distressed her because Ludwig was *not* a member of her family.

She had been walking alone across the wide lawn of the university when he'd run up to her. "Anna!" he called out, and she had turned and waited for him to catch up.

"Are you on your way to the coffeehouse?" he inquired hopefully.

"No. I'm going to meet Kurt."

Ludwig's hopeful tone and expression faded instantly

and he looked utterly crestfallen. "Are you going to go to the Social Democratic School again?"

Anna shook her head. "No. We're going to have dinner and then go to a play."

"Probably an avant-garde play. One of those plays full of political diatribes."

"I hope not. Actually, I think it's a comedy."

"Kurt Stein go to a comedy? I doubt it," Ludwig said, shaking his head in disgust.

'I know you don't like him and I admit he was very rude to you that day when we met—"

"He's rude to me every day," Ludwig fumed. "I see him all the time.'

Anna frowned. "Well, he shouldn't be rude."

"Anna, you're making a terrible mistake. Kurt Stein isn't a good person. You shouldn't be seeing him. He's . . . he's exploitive. And he has many women. He talks about them, brags about . . ."

Anna looked steadily at Ludwig. His Adam's apple quivered with emotion. He liked her himself and clearly he was jealous of Kurt. Still, she was touched that he cared and felt that although ill-advised, he was probably putting her best interests first. "I know you mean well," she said softly, stopping his flow of invective. "But I like Kurt and I intend seeing him often."

Ludwig had looked away. "He'll cause some sort of terrible trouble," Ludwig muttered darkly. "Please, Anna. Think of your family."

"No, Ludwig. The time has come for me to think of myself." She turned abruptly and walked away, sorry that she hadn't said more, yet unsure of what more there was to be said.

"I know you care," she said to the darkness of her room, thinking of Ludwig. Then Anna slipped back down in her bed and pulled the covers up once again. "Tomorrow," she whispered, thinking of Kurt. "Tomorrow we'll be together all day."

The past six weeks have changed my life, Anna thought as she stared into her coffee cup. It was mid-November and she and Kurt had met almost every day, and several

times a week they had gone to the Social Democratic
School to participate in discussions or listen to speakers.
Anna felt intellectually stimulated as never before, and
Kurt, though sometimes moody, had generally been both
warm and thoughtful. He had introduced her to everyone
and she felt accepted, which in turn contributed to a feeling of contentment.

Kurt Stein was, in Anna's eyes, handsome and intelligent. He genuinely appeared to care about her, and he
paid her compliments. No man had ever paid her compliments except Ludwig, and unhappily, she thought of
him more as a boy than a man.

Kurt was sitting across from her. He leaned toward
her, his dark eyes devouring her.

"Let's go to my place," he suggested in a low voice.
"It's more relaxing."

Anna studied his expression. She didn't want to sound
childish, she didn't want him to consider her immature.
Still, Kurt lived alone. "Would that be proper?" she
asked softly. And immediately she hated herself for so
stupid a question. She felt breathless, excited. She felt as
if she were absolutely drowning in his eyes.

"Proper? What's proper? Whose standards?" he
asked, scoffing.

She blushed slightly. "My family's, I suppose." She
forced herself to look away, to break eye contact with
him.

"Yes, that's what I thought. How can you be a revolutionary thinker unless you act on your beliefs, Anna?
You're afraid," he taunted.

"No," she replied quietly. "It's more a question of
propriety."

"Propriety?" he laughed. "Oh, God, I thought you
were different, I thought you were independent."

She lifted her eyes, almost afraid to look into his again
because she knew they affected her, weakened her re-
solve, made her question everything. "I want to be independent," she ventured.

"But you aren't. And you're being absurd. I asked you
to come to my place . . . it's where my books are. And
yes, Anna, I want to be alone with you. Does that make

me abnormal? Yes, I want to kiss you. Are you afraid I'll try to seduce you? Let me set your questions at rest. I *will* try to seduce you. I want to go to bed with you— there, shall I shout it out so everyone in here will know what my intentions are?''

Anna felt her face go hot. A part of her wanted to run away, a part of her responded so strongly that she couldn't move. She felt terribly attracted to this man, and she wasn't certain she wanted to spurn his advances. Yes, that was it. She wasn't afraid of being alone with him because of what *he* might do. She was afraid because of what she herself wanted. She dreamt about him at night . . . she had even imagined them in bed embracing and kissing. ''You're embarrassing me,'' she said softly.

He smiled knowingly and squeezed her arm. ''What you're thinking—no, what you desire, is embarrassing you, my darling.''

Anna looked down. Her face was crimson and her heart was beating rapidly.

''I'm not rich, Anna. I don't come from your circle of friends. I can't take you to expensive theaters or to dinner at fine restaurants. I admit it, I have nothing to offer you except a humble bowl of soup in my own rooms. And I can offer conversation and myself. Yes, Anna, I could make you enjoy it. I could teach you things you only think you know about now. But perhaps you don't want to be a woman. Perhaps you want to remain a girl.''

Anna looked around, and to her relief no one seemed to be within earshot of their secluded table. ''I do want to be a woman,'' she insisted.

''Well, then, have some courage. Be a revolutionary, stop acting as if your virginity was worth protecting. It means nothing. Those attitudes are all part of a system that has enslaved women for centuries. To be equal, you have to be willing to do what men do.''

No man she had ever known talked, thought, or acted as this man did.

Kurt stood up and pulled on his jacket. ''I'm going to my rooms. Are you coming, Anna?''

She followed him with her eyes, then slowly stood up and nodded silently.

He smiled and took her arm, propelling her forward out of the coffeehouse and into the night.

Kurt's rooms were in a working-class neighborhood, but they were not uncomfortable. In fact, Anna's first impression was that they appeared quite middle class. The main room was small, but furnished comfortably with a chair and sofa, a desk, and a small round table with several straight-backed chairs. To one side of this sitting room there was an alcove, inside of which were a sink, a small icebox, and a two-burner gas cooker. On the other side of the sitting room there was a bedroom with a large bed, a sink, and a chair. Books and papers littered every surface, and several unwashed coffee cups sat on the table.

"This is it," Kurt announced as he swung open the door and ushered her in. Anna set down her book bag and removed her coat. Kurt took it and hung it on the coat rack by the door; then he picked up the coffee cups and took them to the sink in the alcove which served as a kitchen. "I've been studying so I haven't cleaned in a while."

"Your rooms are nice," Anna commented as she looked about.

"Nicer than yours . . . I can't believe you live in the Cuckoo House." He grinned and raked his curly black hair with his hand.

"I'm not there very much."

"Perhaps in the future you will be there less, Anna."

He turned to face her and then drew her into his arms. "You're beautiful," he said, kissing her on the mouth and moving his hands over her back.

Anna felt her face flush with excitement. She did not pull away, but rather pressed herself against him. She felt warm and wonderful in his arms and she wondered if this was how Karla felt when Josef held her . . . and how, she wondered, did her mother feel when she was first held? Somehow she could not imagine her parents making love . . . although clearly they had.

Kurt drew back slightly and looked into her face. He

ran his hand through her hair. "So soft, so silky," he whispered as he kissed her neck and her ears.

Anna felt weak, unable to resist his advances. But she had known he was going to kiss her, indeed she had known he was going to make love to her. And she was willing, willing to discover the mysteries of love.

"Come," Kurt murmured as he lifted her into his strong arms and carried her into the still-dark bedroom.

Anna moved toward him as he stretched out beside her and began to undo the two dozen tiny buttons on her prim high-collared blouse.

"Don't tell me to stop," he said, kissing her cleavage as he brushed her blouse open. "A man can't stop when he has gone this far. You understand that, don't you?"

Anna nodded. Was that true? She wasn't certain, but she didn't care. The feel of his lips on her flesh sent chills of anticipation through her. Her whole body felt on fire. "Perhaps," she whispered, "a woman can't stop either."

He laughed lecherously and struggled with the little hooks on her corset. Removing it at last, he pulled her petticoats down with her skirt, leaving her only in her long dark stockings. "Let's leave your stockings on," he suggested as he kissed her neck, then moved his lips quickly down her neck to her breasts. "Later I'll want to look at you, so I'll turn the lights on. Your stockings make it more erotic—you have such lovely long white legs." He teasingly sucked on one nipple and toyed with the other and used his legs to rub over the lower half of her body.

Anna pressed herself to him. He was still dressed, but she could feel him against her. His movements and the way he touched her inflamed her and she wriggled as he moved his hands across her body, exploring and caressing her. Then he pulled himself atop her and whispered, "Open you legs." He unbuttoned his trousers and toyed with her for a second.

Anna's eyes were closed tightly and her arms were around his neck when he pushed into her. She cried out. It hurt and she hadn't expected it to hurt.

"It only hurts the first time," he told her quickly as he continued his movements, seemingly oblivious of her discomfort.

Anna moaned. In one way it felt good. In another it

still hurt, but she was certain he was right. He suddenly reared up and shook, then collapsed against her, damp with perspiration.

Anna lay there listening to his heavy breathing, holding him, wanting him to touch her further. Slowly the pain she had felt ceased.

He rolled off her then touched her intimately, moving his hand to and fro. "You should be happy too," he said. "I'll show you how and the next time it will happen when I'm in you."

He wriggled down in the bed and she felt his mouth caress her most sensitive region. He used his warm moist tongue and his movements were exquisite and Anna closed her eyes once again. He caressed her nipples with his fingers and continued to kiss her erotically till suddenly she felt a wild pulsation and she actually groaned with this new and intensely pleasurable sensation. He embraced her quickly and she shook in his arms, hugging him and aware that she felt more wonderful than she had ever felt before.

Outside, a harsh November wind blew sheets of rain down the street. Anna pulled Kurt's robe tightly around her as she lit the gas heater. The floor was cold through her stocking feet. In the bed Kurt turned restlessly, his foot sticking out from beneath the down-filled duvet.

Once the fire was lit. Anna blew on her hands and rubbed them together, then hastily retrieved her clothes and dressed. Once dressed, she went to the bed and sat down on the side, gently jostling Kurt. "Wake up," she whispered urgently. "Wake up."

Annoyed, he turned over, waving her away. But she persisted and after a moment he turned over and opened his eyes. "Why are you up and dressed?" he asked, frowning. "It's early, it's Saturday, and it's raining."

"I have to phone Frau Fischer, Kurt. I didn't go to my room last night. She might call my mother."

"Your mother will find out sooner or later about us. Why not sooner?" he asked, lifting a heavy brow.

"No, not yet."

He fell back against the pillows. "There's a phone in the café on the corner. Phone and then come back."

Anna nodded as Kurt, quite uninterested, rolled over and puffed his pillow up.

She left the door unlocked and hurried out of the building and down the street in the wind and rain.

Anna fairly blew into the café. It was almost empty and its windows were steamed over. Still, the smell of coffee and sausages made her hungry, and as Kurt was sleeping, she ordered some food before arranging to use the phone.

The phone rang its distinctive ring and finally Frau Fisher's voice answered crisply with the number.

"Frau Fischer? This is Anna. No, Anna von Bock."

"You didn't come home last night." Her voice was half-curious, half-accusative. Then, "I was about to call your mother."

"No," Anna said too quickly. Then, "I spent the night with a female friend. I should have called you."

"I worry," Frau Fischer returned. "You know I worry. You are all like my children. All of my students are important to me."

"I know. I'm sorry."

"Will you be home tonight?"

"Yes," Anna answered. "Yes, I'll be home tonight."

She returned the receiver to its cradle and walked to a nearby table. The proprietor had already poured her coffee, and she said down, drinking it quickly as her mind flooded with thoughts.

"You were gone long enough," Kurt said when she returned. To her surprise he was up and dressed and had prepared coffee. "I suppose you ate," he said, shaking his head.

"Yes. I thought you'd sleep longer."

"I would have if you'd been next to me."

His eyes lingered on her and she smiled at him knowingly. Somehow everything was different between them this morning. Before, she had been afraid to let him touch her; now she longed for him to touch her. And she wanted to do things for him . . . anything. "Shall I fix you something to eat?"

"No, I only drink coffee in the morning." He looked her up and down appraisingly. "You look pretty even when your hair is wet and clinging to your forehead."

"It's horrid out," she replied. "Very windy."

He sat down at the table and motioned for her to do the same. Silently he poured a coffee and handed it to her. "Come and live with me, Anna."

She stared at him in disbelief. It was an astonishing suggestion. She had not expected it at all and she was almost speechless. "How could I?" she blurted out.

He rolled his dark eyes and tossed his head back, laughing. "Oh, Anna, Anna! What do you mean, 'how could you?' You simply pack up your clothes, leave the Cuckoo House, and come here."

"I have no money of my own, Kurt. My parents wouldn't give me any money. How would I live? How could I continue my studies?"

"It's all quite simple. You can get a job. A real job. I can arrange that for you. You could profit from becoming a member of the working class, you'd learn what the problems really are. And you could stop attending the lectures at the university and go to the lectures at the Social Democratic School. It's free, after all. Then in three years you can be tutored for your examinations in law. You'd have to hire a crammer anyway, everyone does. With what I make as a tutor and what you earn, we would be quite comfortable here."

He was right about hiring a crammer to help prepare for examinations; it was the system. Students learned on their own and with tutors. He was, after all, a tutor, and if she worked well, she would pass her examinations anyway. But there were other considerations. "My parents would disown me."

"Eventually they would take you back."

She didn't verbally disagree, but she knew they would not. Still, living with Kurt would mean she would never have to live at home again. And I love him, she thought. "Would we marry?" she asked.

He leaned over and stroked her hair. "Eventually I suppose we might. Tell me, Anna, would having someone mumble over us change how we feel about each other? Many people in the new movement believe in free love. Rosa does. She had lovers, and one special love with whom she has an intellectual bond. We should be progressive thinkers, Anna. You should be willing to take risks. I do love you," he said, touching her throat and then lifting her hand to his lips and kissing her fingers.

"This is all so sudden for me," Anna replied softly. She could feel her own desire to be with him warring with her practicality, though even now she knew desire would win.

"Think about it," he said, draining his coffee cup. "And while you're thinking, come back to bed. It's Saturday. We have all day."

Dear Tante Karla,

How I long to hear from you, and how I wish you were here. I am so confused and there is no one I can talk with. No one, that is, who would understand.

A month ago I met a young man—a tutor at the university. He is a socialist and a free thinker. He is very intelligent, quite the most intelligent man I've ever met. I suppose I shouldn't even tell you this, Tante Karla, but I must take the chance that you will understand. Kurt and I—that's his name, Kurt Stein—have made love. In fact, I spent last night with him. I adore having him hold me, having him caress and kiss me. Oh, Tante Karla, Kurt makes me feel special and I know I will never love anyone else.

I hate being in my bed alone now. I long to have Kurt next to me and I know it's the same for him. He wants me to live with him. We would both work, and I suspect, if properly tutored, I could pass my examinations. I would also be able to attend lectures at the Social Democratic School. I think he is right when he says I need to learn more about the needs of the workers. I want to live with him, Tante Karla, but I know that living with him would mean breaking entirely with the family. If only you were here to talk with me . . . I feel so alone. Please write to me.

Love,
Anna

I'll wait to mail it, Anna thought as she folded the letter and put it in the top drawer of her dresser. Yes, I'll think about it and if I still want to tell her, I'll mail it then. But surely Karla would not condemn me, Anna decided. No, I *will* wait. I *will* think about it.

Anna closed the drawer and then put on her coat and hat. The walk to the university will clear my thoughts, she decided. And then, when I finish reading in the library, I'll meet Kurt.

Anna walked rapidly, feeling the cold damp wind on her cheeks. Her book bag was slung over her shoulder, and she pulled her green wool scarf tighter around her neck as she descended the steps of the library and headed for her rendezvous with Kurt outside Neues Schauspielhaus, an avant-garde theater on Moltz-Strasse near the Nollendorfplatz. It was the second time they'd come here, and she remembered how much she had enjoyed it the first time.

As she approached, she could see Kurt leaning against the wall, his hat pulled down and his collar up.

"You're early," she said, smiling.

He half-smiled back at her and raised his brow. "Are you sure you aren't late?"

Anna lifted her eyes to the big clock on the building across the square. She frowned slightly. "No, I don't think so."

"Oh, so serious. I was joking." He leaned over and kissed her cheek. Then, half whispering, "I have exciting news."

She squeezed his arm. "Tell me."

"I've found a job for you, Anna. A job as a seamstress in a sewing factory. It's not far from my apartment or from the school, darling. You can start next week."

Anna looked up into his eyes. Next week? She had not yet made a decision, but it seemed he had assumed she had already make up her mind.

"You don't seem too enthusiastic," he surmised; then, lowering his voice and assuming a thoroughly serious expression, "You do want to live with me, don't you, Anna? You are willing to make a commitment?"

"I've been thinking about it—"

"For more than a week! Anna, you either love me or you don't."

His eyes seemed to bore inside of her. She felt lost and almost overcome as he looked at her, his intensity enveloping her. Then his face softened and he touched her lips with his fingers lightly. "I want you, Anna. I know you want me . . . even now I know you're warm and moist and ready . . ."

His voice had become a near-whisper in her ear and his finger had moved from her lips to her neck, where he made small circles with it near her ear. He was right: she ached with desire—so much desire that she had lost all interest in the play they had planned to see. Her cheeks burned hot in spite of the cold and she broke his gaze, seeking some neutral spot with her eyes . . . but still she could feel the touch of his fingers on her throat. She shivered. "Of course I want you," she whispered.

"Then come home with me now. We'll go and get your belongings, Anna. Do it now."

Anna thought for a moment of her letter to Karla; then she nodded and they turned away from the theater.

"I'll help you pack your things—we'll call a cab."

"My family—" she started to object, to explain that she would have to tell them first.

"Your family!" he scoffed. "Oh, Anna, your father will be furious—he'll force you to stay home. If you try to tell them, there will be a terrible battle. Just leave, just do it. After a while they'll adjust."

"I don't have many things," Anna said softly. "I think I'd better go to Frau Fischer's alone. I can manage. I'll call a cab and meet you at your flat."

He smiled. "Good. Come along, I'll walk with you to the tram stop."

Anna felt the terrible tears of indecision fill her eyes. Was she doing the right thing? But she did not stop walking. She followed Kurt's lead, and slowly, silently, she knew she would continue to follow him.

Anna opened the front door of the Cuckoo House, almost hoping that Frau Fischer was taking her afternoon nap. I can pack and leave her a note, Anna thought.

Somehow the thought of even trying to explain anything to Frau Fischer made her uneasy. At the very least, Frau Fischer would pout. At worst, she would phone her mother, Anna decided.

Anna stepped into the hall and turned sharply at the sound of her name and her mother's almost shrill voice.

"Anna!"

Anna stepped into the living room with trepidation, her nostrils filling with the unseemly but now familiar aroma of pomegranates. "Mother?" she said almost uncomprehendingly. "What are you doing here?"

"I called her," Frau Fischer said as she lifted her eyebrows and scowled at Anna. "You are *not* the innocent child I took you for . . . you have embarrassed me, made a fool of me, and deceived me, Fräulein von Bock." She shook her frizzy curls and made a strange grunting sound.

Anna looked from one to the other. Her mother was strangely silent, allowing Frau Fischer to vent herself. "I don't understand," Anna said, already feeling defensive.

Her mother suddenly stood up from where she was sitting on the sofa. She waved a piece of paper in the air frantically. "This!" she screamed. "This letter written in your own hand! You're no better than a . . . a . . . a . . . slut!"

Anna inhaled slowly, deeply, as she held the side of the doorjamb. Her mother held the letter she had written to Karla. "Where did you get that?" she asked, forcing calm into her voice, though in fact a rage was beginning to well inside her.

"Frau Fischer found it in your room. She has been monitoring your activities at our request."

Anna felt cold anger completely seize her. "It was my private letter and it was sealed and in my drawer. You've done something I shall never forgive you for, Mother. You've spied on me."

"Apparently it was necessary," her mother fumed.

So great was Anna's anger that she was beyond shouting. She turned and walked up the stairs. "I'm packing," she said coldly. "I'm leaving here."

"I've already packed your things, Anna. You're coming home with me."

Anna looked beyond her mother and saw her suitcase. She marched across the room and picked it up. "Thank you for saving me the trouble of packing it," she said, looking at her mother. "I am not coming home with you. I'm going to live with my lover and I hope you go to hell."

"Anna! You can't talk to me that way in front of Frau Fischer!"

Anna turned and narrowed her eyes. "Frau Fischer is an old drunk and I'll do and speak as I please." She walked into the hall and opened the door. Without so much as looking back, she walked through it and slammed it behind her. Just as she did so, she heard the cuckoos begin to announce the time. Frau Fischer's face and her mother's face filled her mind, but she didn't turn back. She almost ran down the street and around the corner. On the busy Tiergarten she hailed a cab and got in. Now, she thought, there was absolutely no turning back.

It was a typically grim December day in Essen. Black clouds of smoke rose from the coal-fired furnaces of the city's many factories, and beneath the dull moisture-laden sky, the great Ruhr River ran gray through the bleak valley filled with steel and munitions plants. On the hillsides that rose from the riverbank, near the canal, thousands of identical attached houses meandered, row on row like stone soldiers with belching chimneys for rifles.

Not that Essen was entirely unrelenting in its pursuit of industrial supremacy, Markus thought as he alighted from the train. The south part of the town was largely parkland, and there was the sheer magnificence of Villa Hugel, the massive museumlike estate of the Krupp family. Still, he thought, Essen was not a place he would like to live. In fact, he did not even like Essen's suburbs—sheltered by the hills they might be, but if the wind blew the wrong way, there was an odor, and somehow it seemed to Markus as if the unkempt workers were too nearby. They were everywhere to be seen and smelled— yes, coal dust and cheap beer were the aromas that came to mind when he thought of Essen.

Markus walked quickly from the platform to the cabstand. It was the middle of the afternoon; the train he had taken was not a train that delivered hordes to Essen. Indeed, only a few others had gotten off the train with him. He was relieved to discover that there was no line at the cabstand, and more delighted that within minutes he was comfortably seated and on his way to Andreas' home.

Else opened the great wooden front door herself. Her lovely blond hair was loose and hung nearly to her waist. Her dress was too lavish for the hour, but he adored it, and he adored her in it. It was a pale blue empire gown that displayed Else in all of her swanlike glory. Almost her entire torso was visible save the very nipples of her soft, pliable, and most abundant breasts.

Markus stepped into the hall and looked around quickly as Else closed the door. He set down his little bag.

"We're alone," she announced. Then a wonderful smile filled her face. "All alone."

It was his signal, and Markus swept her into his arms hungrily, kissing her full lips, her neck, the tops of her breasts. "Oh, God!" he whispered into her ear. "Oh, Else!"

She returned his kisses, then pulled away, her face flushed. "We can go upstairs . . ."

Markus hesitated only momentarily. "Where is everyone?" he asked, as if he had to be certain they were indeed alone.

"Andreas is in Frankfurt and the children are with their governess—visiting friends for the entire day. They won't be home till after supper. I gave the rest of the servants the day off." She took his hand and fairly ran up the winding staircase.

Markus, breathless with his own eagerness, followed enthusiastically.

He smiled as Else, always thoughtful of his sensibilities, led him to the guest bedroom. It was true he would have had difficulty in Andreas' bed.

"I've missed you so," Else said as she closed the door behind them. "It's dreadful! Andreas is always gone and I'm always left here with the children. And when he is here, all he does is complain. He says your father is furious with Anna, that she's a scandal! I don't understand how she could do it, myself. I mean, goodness, your father is running for office. Does she know what a disgrace she is?''

Markus shrugged. "I suppose she must," he replied, though discussing his sister's transgressions was not, at this moment, on his mind. "Is Andreas really gone a lot?" he queried.

"Oh, all the time," Else pouted.

"My poor darling . . . were you mine, I'd lavish my attention on you." He sat down on the edge of the bed and pulled his boots off. Then he took her hand and pulled her toward him. She bent over and again he kissed her cleavage, his lips trembling. She was a magnificent creature, and as his tongue flicked over her flesh, he wondered why these great pink-tipped mounds so attracted him. He fell backward and pulled her down on top of him, then rolled over and positioned himself above her. Her cheeks were flushed and she wriggled seductively in his grasp. It was as if they were playing out roles in some ribald sixteenth-century drawing-room scandal. "God," he breathed in admiration as he pulled down her dress and exposed her breasts entirely.

She moaned loudly as his mouth fastened on her breast, and she moved about so that he could hardly stand it. With one hand he toyed with her other nipple while with his other he lifted her dress and tugged eagerly at her lacy undergarments.

She, in turn, fumbled with the buttons on his trousers till after a few minutes they were both undressed and panting like two wild young animals. Markus quickly entered her and she pressed against him, screaming out in delight as he took her. This game of plundering was one they both enjoyed, and they collapsed in one another's arms breathlessly laughing and giggling when they were finished.

For a short time they slept; then Markus awoke and found Else was wide-eyed and looking at the ceiling. "What's to become of us?" Else asked softly. "Oh, Markus. I can't give you up and I don't know how we can go on. Look what's happened to Anna . . . what if they found out about us?"

He ignored her question and stroked her gently. "You

don't know what my life is like, Else. I should have remained single, I shouldn't have married at all. She makes me miserable! I can't get her pregnant either . . . not that I care, but Father expects it.''

Else nodded and kissed the top of his head as he snuggled down to use her breast as a pillow for his cheek. "If you hadn't married, then everyone *would* have become suspicious.''

"I know, it's just that it's unbearable.''

"You mean you can't make love to her at all?''

There was, Markus noted, a tone of satisfaction in Else's voice. "I seldom succeed," he lied. The fact was that he had no trouble executing his husbandly duties with Dorcas. She could even be interesting at times, though he remained totally smitten with Else. Nevertheless, he deemed it better if Else felt in full command of him sexually. Women did not fully understand that men—most men, in any case—had no difficulty with multiple partners, even when those partners had nothing in common. Women demanded fidelity, if not absolute physical fidelity, then emotional fidelity. Vaguely Markus wondered about his brother, who seemed to spend more and more time in Frankfurt. Could it be that Andreas had wandered from Else? The thought made him feel somewhat less guilty.

"It you can't satisfy her, won't she suspect something?'' Else suddenly asked.

Markus kissed her once again. "Perhaps," he allowed, then, kissing her more intimately, added, "I shall just have to force myself so she won't suspect I love you.''

Else squirmed appreciatively. "Let's do it again,'' she whispered.

She needn't have asked. He turned on her eagerly, this time taking her more slowly.

5

February 1913

A bitter February wind swept up the street. Although it was only five-thirty, it was already dark owing to a combination of shortened winter days and the threatening storm clouds which blotted out the usual lingering light of early evening.

Anna finished washing the last dirty cup, and wiping her hands on her smudged apron, she walked across the center room of the flat she now shared with Kurt. Wearily she collapsed in the only comfortable chair. The lights were dim and, she thought, this room looked quite different than it had in November when she'd first come. Then the worn furniture and lack of amenities had seemed no more or less than normal student fare. Indeed, it had seemed a warm cozy flat with books and papers and glass ashtrays filled with Kurt's pipe tobacco. She had in those early days thought of the flat as being a romantic hideaway, a place where she and Kurt would read, study, talk, and make love together. But now the dim light and her familiarity with the rooms made them seem depressing. The furniture was soiled and shabby, the walls were in need of paint and were scraped and barren, dull and colorless. The clutter gathered dust, and the ashtrays, even though she emptied them daily, smelled of stale tobacco and cigarettes.

But what truly depressed her was the loneliness she felt. It was a more intense loneliness than she had ever known before, because before Kurt, she had not known real companionship. "You can't miss what you've never known," she told herself. But now she knew companionship, and when it was removed, when Kurt was away, she felt lost.

In the early weeks of their relationship they had lived intently for one another and were always together. But if those heady days of early love were not normal, the manner in which they now lived was the opposite extreme. They were both working, Kurt was home when she was at the factory, and she was home when he was tutoring. To make matters worse, he was absent long hours at night because he was tutoring a person he described as a particularly difficult student.

So many things to do, Anna contemplated as she looked about. How could two people make so much work? And it *was* work she had never thought about, since at home there had been maids and butlers, cooks and drivers. Now it was totally different; now her life had turned upside-down. She arose every morning except Sunday, and long before the sun burned brightly, she was at work in the factory. Abstractedly she held up her hands. Once soft and white, they were now red and somewhat puffy, and in places they even hurt, especially her forefinger, which she had pricked a number of times. She had never thought of sewing as being arduous before, but now she knew the long tedious hours that went into making clothes. When she returned from work, she made supper for herself and Kurt, tidied the flat, studied, and read before finally going to sleep. When Kurt came home he sometimes woke her to make love, but they made love less often now and she admitted to herself that she missed it on the one hand, and was almost grateful not to have her precious sleep interrupted on the other. Life, Anna thought, had become nothing more than a routine of eating, working, and sleeping. Each day she read less, each day they talked less, and days often passed without love-making.

Anna let her hands drop to her lap. Something of her own spirit had vanished, or been suppressed. I used to argue with Kurt, she thought. I used to be able to hold my own and speak my mind. Sadly, she realized, even that precious facet of her personality was weakening with her growing exhaustion. An exhaustion, she feared, that came as much from lack of mental stimulation as from sheer weariness.

"Kurt is right," she said aloud. "I am spoiled." She looked around. "What is the matter with me?" Anna asked aloud. Almost as if it were some kind of answer, there was knocking on the door and the noise startled Anna, who pulled herself up, and patting her hair into place, went to the door and opened it a crack.

"Anna?"

The voice that greeted her was questioning and filled with trepidation. Anna opened the door wider. The light in the hall was dim indeed, but there was no mistaking her mother, who stood before her, her gloved hands trembling.

"Mother . . ."

"Oh, God," her mother breathed, half in relief. "I've searched high and low for you. I finally got this address from a young man at the university—Ludwig. Oh, Anna, Anna . . . how could you?" Her eyes scanned the room even as she pulled off her gloves. "What have you done! My God, sleeping with him was one thing, but living like this . . . I don't understand. How can you?"

Her mother removed her hat and lifted her veil, revealing red-ringed eyes and a quivering lower lip. "Tell me!" she burst forth, and tears sprang from her eyes as she clenched her fists. "Tell me how you can do this! You've driven a stake through my heart, Anna!" She shook her head. "And your father is furious! He says you are a scandal! He may even cancel his plans to run for office for fear of having your . . . your living conditions made public."

"I didn't want to hurt you," Anna said, ignoring her mother's comments about her father's political future.

"Hurt me? Hurt me? What can I tell my friends? Anna, you've completely disgraced me—us—the entire family. And look at you! Look at you!" Her voice gained a certain strength as she repeated herself. "Living with some man to whom you aren't married! Living with a communist rabble-rouser . . . who knows what he is? Your father says he is a criminal! Your father says he has no daughter named Anna, that now he has only one daughter." More tears ran down her face. "I argue with him, I beg him to help you."

"I just wanted to be happy, to be on my own." Anna listened to her own voice and she knew she didn't sound convincing.

"Happy! And are you happy? Look at you, you look like a chimney sweep and you're as pale as a ghost and you've lost weight too. What is this beast doing to you?"

"Kurt is not a beast. He's a brilliant man."

"So brilliant that he's hoodwinked you into living in a pigsty!" She looked about quickly. "He isn't home, is he?"

Anna shook her head and tears also came to her eyes. She fought the desire to run to her mother . . . but what her mother said of Kurt wasn't true.

"Where is he?" her mother questioned.

"Tutoring a student."

"Yes, I was told he would be tutoring a student. I was told she's a pretty student and that he spends long hours with her. Anna, if this man loved you, he would be spending those hours with you." Gisela watched her daughter's face and knew that she had struck a chord. "He is gone a lot, isn't he?" she asked, pressing home her point.

Anna felt a sudden queasiness, and she had begun to shake. It had not occurred to her that Kurt's all-consuming student was another woman. But how did her mother know this? No, it was some kind of ploy, some trick her parents had conceived to get her back home. She summoned herself. "It is his job."

"*His* job is spending his nights with a beautiful young woman and yours is spending long hours in a factory! Well, I'd say he had the better part of the bargain!" Anna, Gisela noted, had lost some of her confidence.

"If what you say is true, how did you find out? Ludwig might have heard where we live, but he doesn't know about my job or about Kurt. I haven't seen him in almost two months."

"I have ways . . . what difference does it make how I found out, Anna? The fact is you are working long hours in a factory and living in a pigsty. You, you, who are almost a genius, are working in a factory! And did I bring you up to live in circumstances such as these? Oh, my God!'' She covered her face with her hands for emphasis. Then after a moment Gisela let her hands drop. She took a step toward Anna and seized her hands. "Look at your poor little hands! Oh, they look terrible.''

"It's from the sewing. And it's not as you think it is . . . Mother, I'm learning so much.''

"What are you learning? That it's miserable to be poor. I could have told you that . . . and do you really think you can pass your law exams without time to study?''

"I will. And I do go to lectures at the Social Democratic School and I do my reading. I am learning.''

"You hardly go to lectures at all. Don't lie to me. You're practically supporting this . . . this man. He has ruined your life, Anna.''

"How do you know about anything I'm doing, Mother?''

Her mother inhaled and pressed her lips together. "As soon as I found out where you lived, I hired someone . . . an investigator. You know your father has connections with the police. He was recommended. He's trustworthy and keeps everything confidential.''

"You hired someone to spy on me?'' Anna looked at her mother incredulously. "How could you?'' Anna stared at her mother, whom she had always known to be possessive. Still, this went beyond anything her mother had done before.

"I had to know for myself . . . I had to know,'' Gisela said, averting her eyes for dramatic effect. But I've lost, she thought, and just a moment ago I had the upper hand. Gisela cursed herself for telling Anna about the investigator.

Anna shook her head and backed slightly away from her mother. "Well, now you know. I love Kurt. I really do love him.''

"I doubt you know what love is. And even if you do love him, I sincerely doubt he loves you,'' Gisela persisted. "Look what you've done, Anna. You've given up everything. This man is using you, he's involved with other women. He doesn't love you . . . and what am I to do? Your father doesn't even know I'm here. Anna, he

won't take you back unless you beg . . . and even then
I'm not sure.''

"I don't want to come back!" Anna said firmly. "And
I don't believe you! Kurt loves me as much as I love him.
And I don't care that Papa won't forgive me. I don't
care!''

Hot angry tears tumbled down Anna's face. "Go away,
Mother. Please go away.''

"Why, so I won't make your life more miserable than
it already is? I can see through you . . . I know.''

"Please, Mother.''

"If you came with me now . . . perhaps we could make
your father understand. You could go to another university . . . Heidelberg, perhaps . . . please, Anna.''

Anna shook her head. "No, Mother. I don't want
Father's forgiveness.''

Her mother steadied herself by grasping the side of the
table. She wiped her cheeks with her hand, then picked
up her hat and put it back on, pulling the veil over her
face and then putting on her long gloves. "I will not
come again, Anna. This was your only chance. I want
you to understand that . . . do you understand that all
doors are now closed?''

Anna did not bother to wipe the tears from her own
cheeks. She only nodded silently and stared at the floor.
Her father had reacted as she expected, but her mother's
spying surprised her, though, she thought, it shouldn't
have, not after the incident with the letter at Frau Fischer's.

Her mother thrust out her tiny chin. "At least I still
have my darling Gerda," she said, "and my two wonderful sons and their wives.''

A kind of bitterness filled Anna. "And they're all perfect," she said sarcastically.

Her mother stared at her stonily. "They know the
rules," she answered, arching her brow. "And, Anna,
rules are everything, they are the very guidelines of our
lives.''

Anna shook her head, feeling totally alone in the face
of her mother's words. Rules, her mother firmly believed, were to be followed, but Kurt believed rules were

to be changed or even broken. Anna felt suddenly trapped between her parent's intransigence and her lover's dogmatism. She had been feeling unhappy when her mother came . . . but now she reluctantly reached inside herself, and what she briefly found was the glimmer of truth in her mother's accusations, the feeling that her life was less than what it should be and that she herself was to blame.

Except for two howling cats, the street in front of Anna and Kurt's flat was deserted as the immense clock in the old church tower struck three in the morning. Anna started at the sound, and sat up in her chair. The flat was cold and utterly dark, and as the door opened, emitting a triangle of dim light from the hall, she shivered and realized that she had dozed off, fully dressed.

"Kurt? Is that you?"

"Of course." He leaned over and lit the lamp. "Anna, what are you still doing up? You have to get up early." He looked about. "I see you didn't have time to straighten things."

"I fell asleep in the chair."

"Reading the material I left for you?" he questioned.

Anna shook her head. "I couldn't stay awake. I'm tired all the time. Sometimes I feel drugged."

He slung his coat over the chair by the door and walked over to her. Leaning down, he peered into her face. "Your eyes are red and watery. Perhaps you should see a doctor."

"I was crying." She hesitated, then added, "Kurt, my mother was here."

He stepped back and took a long look at her; then he turned toward the alcove which served as a kitchen. He filled the kettle from the sink and bent over and lit the burner, then set the kettle down. "A little tea will help me sleep." He avoided her puffy, yet somehow accusative eyes. She was every bit as intelligent as he had thought, but she was naive, a child, and they had been together for nearly two months. Since she'd begun working, she seemed to have stopped taking care of herself, he decided. Oh, she was still pretty, but somehow she seemed less sexy.

"You're not interested in what my mother had to say?"

He turned back to face her and shrugged. "I'm sure she ranted and raved. I'm sure your family has disowned you. I warned you they would. So why is her attitude a surprise? The day you walked out on your mother at Frau Fischer's was the day you began a new life. So, why the tears? The expected has happened. She's come, she's gone, it's over."

"It's true that I don't get on with my parents, but it's still not so easy to think that I'll never see them again, Kurt."

"You'll see them. I tell you, they'll get over it in a few years."

Anna frowned at him as he turned away again to see to the kettle, which, with little water, had quickly begun to boil on the open flame of the gas burner. "Why are you so late?" she queried, trying to sound utterly normal.

"A difficult student."

"What kind of student?" she asked. Anna watched him. There was no doubt he was being evasive.

He poured the water into the teapot and carried the pot to the table, where he pulled out a chair. "Tea?" he offered.

Anna nodded and sat down across from him at the table. "What kind of student?" she repeated evenly.

He scowled at her. "Why all these questions, Anna?"

"I'm curious . . . tell me, is your student a female?" She hated herself as soon as she asked. She was actually checking her mother's information.

Kurt set the teacup down with deliberate control. His eyes narrowed slightly. "Yes, Anna. My student is a female and a very desirable female. I enjoy being with her . . . Anna, I enjoy being with many women."

Anna stared back at him, unable for a moment to speak. He seemed calculated rather than angry . . . but why should *he* be angry?

"What do you mean by 'being with women'?" she questioned, her voice unsteady and quivering slightly. She knew she sounded like her mother, and again she censored herself.

"I mean exactly what I said. I enjoy laughing with other women, kissing them . . . yes, Anna, I enjoy exploring their bodies as I have explored yours. I enjoy having sex with them."

Her mouth opened in sheer distress, and tears immediately flooded her blue eyes. "But we . . . I thought you and I . . ."

"You and I live together. You and I are in the process of forming an intellectual relationship which shall last a lifetime. Naturally, our physical relationship will wane eventually. Anna, I believe you're jealous, and jealousy does not become you. You know what I believe in. I believe in free love. I believe that every person can enjoy experiencing many sexual encounters . . . no one relationship can satisfy me." He looked at her with a deliberately hard expression. His little speech sounded good, even to him. Intellectual relationship . . . high-sounding words for keeping her around as a convenience. She was, he acknowledged, earning enough to buy the essentials, and she wasn't bad in bed either.

"I'm satisfied with you," she said, trying to sound confident. "I want love and children. Kurt, I want a family."

He guffawed and slapped his knee. "You're a child. A lovely, naive, and brilliant child. It's my job to rear you, Anna, to mold you. I intend to turn you into another Rosa . . . and Rosa does not distract herself with such mundane matters as a husband and children. These are ideas which a woman must give up, ideas that are outdated."

"Have you slept with this student?" Anna demanded, cutting into his didactic exposition.

"Of course I have! And you're absolutely free to sleep with other men as well."

"I don't want to sleep with other men, Kurt. I love you." She felt as if he had stabbed her, but still she felt she loved him.

"Anna, I love you too. At least I love you insofar as I understand that word. But, Anna, I will not remain faithful to you physically, and I won't marry, nor will I allow you to have children. You must understand that these things are not for you. You are to be a brilliant woman and you have the potential to be a leader, a woman who will inspire all her sisters.''

Anna stared at him; his dark eyes bored through her and she felt lost, completely lost as she spoke. "I want to have your children," she blurted out, and she reached toward him, but he turned away and stood up. She fought to make sense of the contradictions he seemed to be expressing. He said he wanted one thing for her . . . but he treated her the way her father treated her, he was making decisions for her, decisions she wanted to make for herself. And how could she accomplish all the things he said he wanted her to accomplish when she was so tired she could hardly stay awake? Even as she asked herself questions, he droned on.

"No. You must grow up, Anna. You must realize your own potential in the movement." He waved his hand.

Anna felt her hands were shaking and she once again shivered. "I love you," she murmured, not knowing how else to plead for normalcy in the face of his cruel words and terrible admissions. "Kurt, I can forgive you this once, but you must be faithful to me, you must." And I'm contradictory too, she silently admitted. On the one hand she was rejecting him, on the other clinging to him.

He grimaced. "Anna, stop this at once!"

She struggled to her feet, and as she did so, the chair fell down and hit the floor. "I can't stop!" she screamed back at him, surprised by her own voice.

"Are you saying you cannot accept me as I am? That you can't rededicate yourself to our movement, give yourself over to it entirely?"

"I don't know . . . I'm so tired . . ." Anna lifted her hands to her temples. Her head throbbed and her eyes hurt from crying. Kurt's facial expression did not soften in the slightest.

"I'm going to bed, Anna. You can make your decision in the morning."

Anna watched as he turned on his heel and went off to the bedroom. She looked at the cold tea in their cups and then she checked the burner to make certain it was out. Lethargically she turned out the lamp and slumped back into the overstuffed chair. She could not bring herself to lie down next to Kurt, who might roll over and try to make love to her. No, she couldn't make love to him because he had probably already made love to another woman only a few hours ago, and the vision made her shiver and shake. She felt deceived and angry . . . she felt bewildered by his terrible betrayal and angry at his reasoned and unemotional response. As if deceiving her was his political right! And she admitted, she was angrier still because her mother had been right. The most disturbing element of all, however, was how she felt about her own reactions. For years she had fought her family, but suddenly she had given in to this man. She had allowed herself to become weak, yet somehow she didn't feel strong enough to fight—at least not now. She closed her eyes, knowing that when she awoke her eyes would be swollen shut because she had cried for so long. And all the time images of Kurt making love to other women filled her thoughts, torturing her as she forced herself to sleep, to forget, to feel utterly numb even if only for a few hours.

It had rained, but the winds had chased the clouds away for a time. The puddles in the gutter rippled softly in the predawn breeze. As the thin line of early-morning light in the east cast a strange purple on the streets of Berlin, Anna pulled herself out of the chair and walked across the room. She was vaguely aware of the ever-pervading dampness, and fully aware that her eyes were swollen and that her head throbbed. She went to the sink and splashed ice-cold water on her face; then, shivering, she squinted in the old mirror and studied the puffy-looking face that stared back at her. With her hand still trembling, she pulled the comb through her tangled hair and then washed and put on clean clothes. Perhaps, she thought, she had really made her decision immediately after talking to Kurt—perhaps she had thought of it during her deeply troubled sleep. No matter, it was made. As terrible as she felt both emotionally and physically, she knew she had to leave and she knew that the sooner she left, the better.

Kurt lay on the bed lost in a deep and apparently untroubled sleep. His mouth was slightly open and he snored, as he so often did when he had been up late.

Slowly, almost as if she herself were sleepwalking, Anna gathered up her clothes and poked them haphazardly into the old suitcase that had once belonged to her mother. Finished with the suitcase, Anna stuffed her family pictures, her beloved music box, and her personal papers into her smaller tapestry bag. Then she pulled on her boots and her coat, and, burdened with her suitcase and her bag, she hurried down the wooden staircase, through the dimly lit hall, and out into the cold February morning. For a long moment she stood by the side of the building and breathed deeply. Her eyes scanned the skies—it had stopped raining, but there were heavy clouds moving in and it had grown much colder. It seemed obvious that it was going to snow.

With determination she plodded on toward the post office. There, she reasoned, she could sit and write a letter to her mother. And it will be warm, she thought, contemplating where she might go after that.

Once inside the post office, Anna positioned herself at the writing desk and in a shaking hand wrote:

Dear Mama,
  It is urgent that I see you immediately. I'm sorry I've treated you so, and I hope you can find it in your heart to forgive me. I have left Kurt and I'm almost penniless. Mama, please help me. I'm not feeling at all well. Can you meet me in the café near the Kaiser Wilhelm Church? I will be there at two o'clock. I am sending this letter by messenger.

                                                    Anna

Anna folded the letter, carefully addressed it, and took it outside. There she paid a cabdriver to deliver her letter to her mother.

Then, returning to the warmth of the post office writing room, she wrote a letter to Karla.

When she had mailed her letter to Karla, Anna took the tram to the Potsdam Station. There she left her luggage in a locker, and, unburdened, took the tram to the café near the Kaiser Wilhelm Church.

It was two-thirty-five when Gisela, Anna's mother, slipped into the chair opposite. She looked around furtively before removing her coat and gloves. "You look dreadful," she whispered. "What's happened? Anna? What's happened since last night?"

Anna could see her mother was nervous . . . if not, she noticed, actually frightened. "I told you. I've left Kurt . . . we fought."

"He didn't hit you, did he?"

Anna shook her head and determined to tell her mother almost everything.

"I told you he was no good, that you had made a dreadful mistake, Anna."

Anna nodded silently. Her mother had been right for the wrong reasons, but discussion now was pointless, and in any case, she felt too ill to even want to talk.

"If your father knew I was here, he would be absolutely furious."

"I have nowhere to go," Anna said. "Please, Mother, help me. I'm not just upset, I really am ill."

Her mother's lips were characteristically pressed tightly and she wrung her handkerchief in her fingers, tying it, as she often did, into tiny tight knots. "I spoke to Gerda. Fortunately, Ernst is away for a week or two. Gerda says you can stay in the gardener's house, but you mustn't see the children, and if you come and go, you must do so after dark."

"Am I such a disgrace?" Anna asked.

"I told you, your father would be furious—Gerda doesn't want anyone to know you're there, and she doesn't want to upset your father."

Anna again nodded.

"You can take the train to Gerda's tonight. She'll leave the gardener's house open and put some tea and food in the kitchen. Here, I brought you some money . . . it's not much, it's all I have."

"Will you talk to Father?" Anna asked.

"I'll try . . . I will, but I have to be careful. And there

is one other thing, here is the address of a doctor. You had better go this afternoon, you do look terrible.''

"I can't go to Dr. Bauer?" Anna questioned. Dr. Bauer was their family doctor; he'd brought her into the world and he knew her well.

"No, he would mention it to your father. This Dr. Gunner has a clinic today, so you can see him this afternoon. Perhaps all you need is a good tonic.''

"Thank you, Mother.'' Anna looked at her mother and felt like crying anew. Why couldn't she get close . . . why did her mother seem to put the whole world between them?

Her mother sniffed and dabbed at her eyes with her knotted handkerchief. "I should be as angry as your father . . . but I am your mother and I do love you, no matter what you've done. Give me some time, Anna. I'll talk to him . . . we'll see, perhaps he'll relent.''

Gisela stood up and pulled on her fur coat; then she put on her long gloves. Anna stood too. She leaned across the table and kissed her mother gently on the cheek. "Thank you,'' she again whispered. Her mother sniffed again, then, dropping the veil over her face, turned and almost fled the restaurant.

Anna watched her as she disappeared into a cab. Then she put the money her mother had brought into her purse and dejectedly pulled on her own coat. She left the café, heading for the doctor's office.

Dr. Gunner's clinic was not off the Tiergarten, as was Dr. Bauer's clinic. Instead of that fashionable tree-lined avenue, which house the offices of fine doctors and specialists, Der Altmann Zahn Klinik where Dr. Gunner practiced was on the second floor of an undistinguished building on Der Alexanderplatz.

Having climbed the narrow, dirty staircase, Anna eased in the door and looked about. The people who sat stony-faced on the wooden benches which lined the wall were dressed poorly and their faces all bore that expression of defeat she had come to know so well in the past few months.

The woman behind the plain wooden desk in the cor-

ner looked up. "Name?" she asked loudly. All the faces
in the office turned toward her.

"Anna . . . Anna von Bock." The stares turned from
curiosity to mild antagonism. "Von" in a German name
indicated the elite class, and this was far from an upper-
class clinic. Not only that, but her father was a well-
known man, a man not universally admired or even liked.
Immediately she realized she shouldn't have used her real
name.

The woman behind the desk even sneered as she wrote
Anna's name in her enormous ledger. Then she looked
up and nodded toward a space on one of the benches.
"Sit down, princess, and wait your turn," she said
rudely. Some of the others snickered. Anna flushed
slightly, but she sat down in spite of the woman's nasti-
ness. She might have left had her stomach not been
churning, and quite apart from her emotional turmoil over
Kurt, she had realized for over a week that she felt physically weak and far more tired than she should have felt,
even considering her schedule.

Anna leaned back and closed her eyes against the drab
gray walls and the tight, weary faces of the other patients. But she could not forget where she was because
there was no way to close out the medicinal smells that
surrounded her. Most nauseating was the occasional whiff
of formaldehyde that escaped whenever someone opened
the laboratory door at the opposite end of the room.

It was over an hour before the receptionist called her
name and Anna was ushered into a small examining
room, outfitted in a white gown, and told to wait. Within
minutes a rotund balding man appeared, his stethoscope
dangling round his neck.

"Ah, Fräulein von Bock, and what brings you here?"
he queried.

"I'm ill," Anna said. "I'm tired all the time, and feel
dizzy and nauseated."

"Are you vomiting?"

Anna shook her head. "No, I'm just nauseated."

"Are you nauseated now?"

"I was earlier, I'm worse in the mornings."

He frowned and made a note on his pad. Then he

looked up at her. "And your monthly bleeding? How is it? Does it come on time?"

Anna flushed. "I've always been irregular . . . I'm late . . . it's been . . ." Her voice trailed off and she looked steadily at the doctor as strangely the truth came crashing in on her. How could she be so good in her studies and yet so stupid! "My God," she whispered, expelling her breath and leaning against the examination table. "You don't think I could be pregnant, do you?"

"I see my next question is unnecessary," he said coldly. "Up on the table, I'll have to examine you."

Anna lay down and heard the door open as the nurse came in. She was a huge woman in white and she pushed Anna down and lifted her legs, fastening her feet into metal stirrups. A sheet was then placed over her, and the doctor returned.

Anna closed her eyes tightly and clenched her fists. The doctor prodded and pushed. The instrument he inserted was ice cold, and she jumped. But he was quick, and in a few minutes he withdrew. "No question about it," he announced. "You are pregnant—three months, I would say."

The nurse grunted unpleasantly about immorality and released her feet. Anna sat up and looked at the doctor. She shivered once again. Pregnant? It hardly seemed possible. She thought of Kurt, whom only hours ago she had vowed never to see again. Now, she thought, I will have to see him. She bit her lip. It wasn't what she wanted, and she was certain it wasn't what he wanted. He had, after all, made it quite clear that he didn't want children. Still, it was possible the reality would make a difference in his attitude toward her. Surely at the very least he would assume his responsibility.

"You had better tell your family," the doctor's voice cut through her thoughts.

"Yes," Anna replied. "But I must think first."

"You'll feel better in a few days," the doctor said flatly. "You just have morning sickness. It's quite natural and it'll go away."

He opened the door of the examination room. "I suggest you get settled immediately," he advised. "Emotional upheaval is bad for you.'' With that, he followed the nurse, who had already left.

Anna quickly dressed, determining to go to Gerda's to rest and think. Tomorrow, she decided, would be soon enough to talk to Kurt. And I must talk to him, she thought unhappily, because Father will never forgive me now.

Gerda and Ernst's house was in the nearby suburb of Charlottenburg. Once the village of Lietzow, where Sophia Charlotte, the wife of Frederick I, had her palace, Charlottenburg was only a mile and a half from the Brandenburg Gate. But a large wooded district lay between Charlottenburg and Potsdam, and it was on the edge of this woods that Gerda and Ernst lived in a stately house with a garden that melted into the dense woodland. Their home was both in the city and in the country, and little Rudolf enjoyed, according to Gerda, the best of both worlds.

Anna crept round the side of the darkened house, and only because the moon was bright did she easily locate the small gardener's cottage. She hurried inside, grateful to find that Gerda had not only left open the door but also laid a fire in the fireplace. As a result, the small central room of the cottage was already warm and cozy. Anna put down her luggage, which she had retrieved from the station, and lit a small lamp. Then she collapsed into a comfortable chair to consider both her condition and her alternatives.

The room was decorated in blue and white and often served as a small guesthouse. It had never actually been used as a gardener's cottage—at least not since Gerda and Ernst had moved in. Anna inhaled, the smell of the burning wood permeated the room—pine, yes that was it. It was the clean, fresh smell of pine.

''Anna?''

At the sound of the urgent whisper, Anna started. ''Gerda?'' she questioned.

''Yes, Gerda . . . who else? Let me in.''

Anna got up from the chair and let her sister into the room.

Gerda peered at her, then pushed past her toward the kitchen. "I'll put on some water for coffee. What have you been doing?"

"Thinking," Anna replied.

"Praying would be better. You should pray that Father will take you back."

"He won't," Anna said firmly. "Not now."

Gerda turned from the coffeepot and stared harshly at her sister. "What do you mean, not now?"

"I mean my situation has changed since I talked with Mother. I have to talk to Kurt. He will have to take me back now, or at least help me. There's no choice."

"Kurt? Is that his name? Bad enough to have an affair before you are even married, Anna, but to have an affair with a poverty-stricken student . . . well, you couldn't have done worse. And what has changed? Tell me," she demanded.

Anna sank into a chair at the table. She didn't really want to discuss her condition with Gerda, but there was no point keeping it from her. Her mother had probably already found out from the doctor, and most certainly she would tell Gerda in any case. "I'm pregnant," she said softly, hardly able to push the words out of her mouth.

Gerda's face hardened. "God, no! Oh, Anna, you'll have to get rid of it. Right away!"

Anna stared at her sister uncomprehendingly. "Gerda, what are you saying?"

"That you must have an abortion, of course. Good Lord, Anna, what were you planning to do?"

Anna looked away. "I couldn't do that . . . I couldn't. I don't know what I'm going to do. But I must tell Kurt. Perhaps it will make a difference."

Gerda's expression grew harder and she shook Anna's shoulder. "What are you talking about? Make a difference? Did he leave you?"

"No, I left him."

"And if this man was so great that you gave up everything for him, Anna, why did you leave him?"

Anna looked back into Gerda's accusing face dumbly.

"Well, why?" Gerda insisted.

"He didn't want to make a commitment—there were other women."

Gerda stood up and slapped the sides of her hips. "God, Anna! You're such a goose I can't believe it! You have nothing to talk to this man about—nothing! Take my advice, get rid of the child. I know of a place."

Anna covered her face with her hands. "No! I won't! I couldn't." Again tears suddenly flooded her eyes.

Gerda went about the rest of the business of making coffee. She thrust a cup of the steaming brew at Anna. "Drink this," she said impatiently, "and stop that miserable crying. You need your wits about you, Anna. Honestly, how can someone as smart as you be so stupid!"

"I've asked myself that," Anna sobbed.

"And Mother doesn't know you're pregnant?"

"Not yet. At least not from me. She might have talked to the doctor. I really must talk to Kurt first . . . before I talk to Mother."

"You're stubborn and you'll lose everything, Anna." Gerda shook her head. "I don't know what will become of you."

Anna sipped her coffee. "I'm terribly tired," she admitted.

"I came to find out everything, but I see you are in no condition to talk. All right, Anna, go to bed and rest."

"You're going to tell Mother, aren't you?"

Gerda nodded. "She should know before she talks to Father."

Anna felt empty and tired as she rubbed her eyes and abstractedly ran her hand through her tangled golden hair. How in so short a time had everything fallen apart? she wondered. And how might some of it be put back together? She shivered with apprehension and touched her stomach thoughtfully. No, there was no question in her mind, she could not have an abortion.

Anna stood in the center of the middle room of Kurt's flat while he stood only a few feet from her, scowling angrily.

It hadn't been easy to find him at home. Anna had

spent three long days and nights at Gerda's, and on each of those days she had devoted long hours seeking out Kurt. Now, finally, she had found him alone at his flat. Uneasily she looked about the room. Even though she had been gone only three days, it didn't seem that she had ever been there, much less made it her home for over three months. There were books and papers everywhere and piles of dirty clothes sat in the corner. Dishes filled the sink, and the whole place smelled of cigarettes and garbage. It made her ill.

"You left and now you've come back." He sneered. "I knew you'd come back, Anna."

Anna looked at him steadily. "I've come to talk to you, Kurt. There's something important we must discuss."

"I expect you to apologize." He shook his head. "And you haven't been to work. I doubt I can get your job back for you."

His eyes looked strange to her; there was something in his eyes and even in his tone that made her feel uneasy, even a little frightened. "I didn't come here to apologize. I came to tell you I'm pregnant." She tried to keep her voice steady, she tried not to be unnerved by his cruel expression. But she was not prepared for the look that flooded over his face, nor the way he clenched his fist.

"You've done this on purpose!" Kurt roared. His face twisted hatefully.

Anna stared at him, and for the first time really saw him. He did not appear at all handsome, nor was he sensitive the way an intelligent man should be. She suddenly wondered what she had ever seen in him. At the same time, her fear increased. He looked capable of violence.

"I didn't get pregnant on purpose," she said steadily. "Don't you care? You are the father, Kurt, this child will be yours."

"Bitch!" He turned on her wildly, his dark eyes blazing and his fists still doubled in a fury. "Bitch! You did this to try to trap me. No, I don't care that I'm supposed to be the father!"

"What do you mean 'supposed to be the father'? You *are* the father, Kurt. I wasn't sleeping with other men as you were sleeping with other women. As you well know, you are the only man I've ever slept with.''

"How do I know that? Anyway, I wouldn't have cared if you had been sleeping with others, as long as you didn't get pregnant. No, Anna, I don't want a child. Get rid of it.'' His eyes were still narrowed and his voice still had a hateful tone.

Anna looked back at him unblinkingly. Her sister had said the same thing, albeit she had offered it as a suggestion, not given it as an order. "I don't understand you,'' she had replied as she struggled to keep her composure.

"If you had stayed with me, I wouldn't have tolerated your having a child. I would have taught you a few things . . .'' His fist doubled, and he moved forward menacingly.

Anna stepped backward. "You don't care about the working class as you profess to . . . all you care about is yourself. You use political slogans to exploit people—I think women in particular. I'm leaving, Kurt . . . and I will have the child.''

He moved to strike her, and she turned and fled the room. He despises my father, but he's just like him, she thought. No, he's worse, because he pretended to be something else. At least my father is honest about the things he believes in. Kurt was not honest. He lied to others, but worse, he lied to himself.

"Bitch!'' he cursed as he called after her.

But Anna didn't even turn around. She walked out the front door and she kept walking rapidly, grateful she was no longer alone with him.

It was the first of March, and though the sky was a brilliant blue, the strong wind blew cold and the sun was not yet warm enough to heat the soil and coax the crocuses from mother earth. Anna walked through the Tiergarten, her thoughts still very much on her encounter with Kurt.

She had turned her back on him, and now, she thought as she stood for a moment and looked across the park at the lake, she was on her way to face her father. She

watched as the brisk wind whipped up the usually tranquil water and sent ripples toward the pair of swans which
sat on the grass like porcelain figurines, their long necks
buried in their feathers.

She turned and trudged on. Her father frightened her
in many ways, but he could not hurt her the way Kurt
had hurt her. She closed her eyes. In a few months she
would come into a small sum of money her grandmother
had left her. If she worked till the child was due, it would
be enough to get her to America. There, she reasoned,
Karla would help her get started. It was half a plan, but
it gave her strength as she walked toward the tram to take
her to her parents' house.

Anna was ushered silently into her father's study. Emmerich, her father's manservant, looked at her as if she
were some stranger. His face was an unemotional mask.

Anna walked through the open door, half-expecting
her father to thunder at her, but instead he pointed to a
chair and his face revealed nothing save his strong Teutonic countenance.

Slowly he looked up and across at her. "You've behaved disgracefully," he said evenly, and almost without
any emotion at all. "But you are my daughter and I have
come to a decision."

"Father . . ." Anna attempted to interject.

"Just listen!" he commanded. "I'm sending you to
our retreat in Wildbad im Schwarzwald. I'm sending you
with a nurse I have engaged. As you know, it's a comfortable place and there are plenty of books, so you
should be happy. You'll have the child there, and after
it's born, you'll be sent to America. As you know, you
have a little money your grandmother left you. It should
be enough to get you started."

Anna felt as if her breath had been taken away. Her
father's solution was almost identical with what she had
planned for herself. But his was much better. She would
not have to work and she could build up her strength.
Moreover, the Schwartzwald, the Black Forest, would be
healthier than the city, far better for the little baby when

it was born. "Oh, Father, thank you." She lifted her eyes and sought her father's.

"It's what must be done to avoid scandal. I want you to pack your belongings and be ready to leave in three days with Helga, the woman I have engaged."

"Yes, Father."

"That's all that's required. When you have packed what you need, go back to Gerda's. Here are your tickets. You'll meet Helga on the train."

Anna took the tickets. "Thank you, Father," she said again.

Her father did not answer or even look at her. He returned his eyes to his papers and grunted. Anna turned and slowly headed upstairs to pack the clothing she had not initially taken with her to Frau Fischer's.

6

Helga Gassner was a huge woman with a thick, short neck that seemed to disappear into her collar. Her jowly face was set in an expression that appeared permanently stern and strict. Anna estimated Helga's height at nearly six feet and her weight was almost certainly well over one hundred kilos. She wore no makeup of any kind, and her hair was thin, blond, and pulled back into a little tiny tight bun that was held in place by two long skewers that looked like knitting needles. In spite of being so grim, and so utterly Teutonic in appearance, her hair and her build reminded Anna of a character out of an English comic operetta by Gilbert and Sullivan she had once seen at the theater of Komische Oper on the Friedrichstrasse. Yes, in some way Helga looked like a Germanic Katisha, the Mikado's "daughter-in-law elect."

And why had Helga worn her nurses uniform on the train? Anna asked herself. Why indeed did she need a uniform to live in an isolated lodge in the forest? But there she was, dressed from head to toe in white and wearing a full black cape which floated about her on the windy station platform outside the Wildbad station.

"Did the train ride make you ill?" Helga asked. She leaned over toward Anna.

"No, I'm not sick to my stomach anymore. But standing here in this cold wind isn't pleasant."

"A car and driver were ordered. In fact, the driver will live in the servants' quarters at the lodge. He should be here any moment. Naturally, he should be here now. I don't like to be kept waiting. But you can't expect much in this place."

Anna inhaled deeply. It was still chilly, but the smell

of the pine trees filled t...
would be acres of flowers...
"This place is quite lovely—
spas in all of Europe," Ann...
looked at Helga and thought to he...
to have a very negative personali...
missed her opinion. After all, she ha...
at all, and perhaps Helga's negativity d...
could be nothing more than a dislike for...

"This place is full of doddering old fools ...come
to take the mineral waters when what they re... need is
fresh air, exercise, and natural food. Beautiful it may be,
but this town is disorganized and its populace ineffi-
cient."

Anna ignored Helga's blanket condemnation. "The
lodge is only ten miles out of town. We can come into
town and go to the resort sometimes."

Helga scowled at her. "Such things are not for pregnant women. What you need is vigorous exercise to prepare yourself for childbirth. Three-hour walks, proper
breathing . . ." Helga sucked in her breath. "You're a
little thing, aren't you? Rather frail really."

Anna looked back at her, nonplussed. She did not think
of herself as frail—except perhaps by comparison with
Helga, whose stature was, to say the least, remarkable.
Still, Helga was right in one respect, she did need exercise to prepare for childbirth, and the truth was, she was
a little run-down physically. A car pulled up and Helga
all but attacked it, running alongside and banging on the
closed window with her fist.

"Ah, there! Herr Schroder?"

The car stopped and a tall thin mustached man climbed
out of the long sleek Daimler. He was dressed to perfection as a chauffeur, and he bowed dramatically from the
waist. "Frau Gassner? Fräulein von Bock? I'm sorry to
be late. Is this your luggage? Here, here, make yourself
comfortable in the car. I'll put the luggage in the trunk."

Anna climbed gratefully into the car. She leaned back
against the plush seats, relishing the smell of the fine
leather. Outside, Helga insisted on supervising the load-
ing of the luggage. "Put those smaller bags on the top!"

ly, then, seizing her black bag, "No,
one. I keep that one with me."

moment Helga bent over and surprisingly man-
ed to fold her bulk up to slide in next to Anna. The
seat sagged slightly under Helga's weight.

"A little over a half-hour's ride," Herr Schroder informed them. The car began to move and Anna turned
to look out the window as they proceeded down the street.

The houses they passed were made of wood, with
slanted roofs, and they featured intricately carved window boxes. It was a casual place, a place where people
came to relax. "You could have worn more comfortable
clothes," Anna said after the car had passed through the
town. "After all, I'm not sick, just pregnant."

"My uniform *is* comfortable. Besides, I don't have
other clothes. I do not indulge in frivolities," Helga announced self-righteously.

Anna digested the information and then leaned back
and closed her eyes. Helga seemed competent enough,
but she was also authoritarian and cold. But once they
were settled, Anna told herself, it would be all right. She
could escape Helga by reading, or perhaps by having Herr
Schroder bring her into town. And it wasn't as if her
confinement would last forever. After the baby was born
she would be immediately off to America and to Karla.
Unconsciously she patted her stomach and thought: We
will make a whole new world for ourselves in America—
everything will be different.

The late-May moon was nearly full, a slightly lopsided
plate of brightness as it rose over the Sommerberg Mountains. Its cold white blaze cast an eerie light in Anna's
room and she lay in the center of her huge bed and stared
at the log ceiling above.

This lodge was a place she had come to often. The last
time she'd been here was the summer of 1911—the summer after Karla had left. Generally, she had liked being
here.

Still, her recollections of Wildbad im Schwarzwald
were not all happy. Like her other recollections, her re-

membrances of summers past were tinged with loneliness.

Anna thought about a summer long ago . . . perhaps when I was five or six . . . yes, six, she remembered. Her father had come to Wildbad im Schwarzwald to hunt. She recalled being outside when her father returned. The servants he had taken with him bore a dead fawn. It was a beautiful young deer with soft huge soulful eyes that stared into space in death. She had seen it and she had cried hysterically because it was a creature that belonged to this place, and should have been as alive as she. In her revulsion for her father's act, she had doubled her small fists and cried and screamed, and in spite of her fear of her father, she had cried again and again, "I hate you! I hate you!" In cold anger he had hit her across the mouth hard and sent her to bed. She had been disciplined then, and, she thought miserably, I am being disciplined now.

"How could I have thought you were helping me?" she whispered aloud as she conjured up the image of her father's stern face. Tears filled her eyes, but she was too tired to cry for long. In a matter of hours the sun would replace the moon, and the moment it rose over the mountains, Helga would be there, jostling her into consciousness, not allowing her to rest longer than the seven hours decreed.

Anna shuddered as she thought of the day to come. It would be like all the other days that had preceded it—a nightmare regimen that surpassed that practiced in the strictest of nunneries.

As soon as it was light, Helga would make her take an ice-cold shower; then, before a meager breakfast of tea and porridge, she would be made to walk four full miles with Helga at her side.

After breakfast, Helga made her pray. "You have sinned," she would say sternly. "You must beg forgiveness." Prayers were followed by more exercises, and then she was given sauerkraut without sausages for lunch. Again Helga made her walk, and then she was allowed to read for a time before a dinner of vegetables and a small portion of bread and meat. Dinner was followed by more prayers, and prayers were followed by bed.

Helga had begun to give orders several weeks after their arrival, and in the beginning she had fought Helga's control, but it was no use. "You're supposed to look after me, do what I tell you," she had naively told Helga. But Helga had only laughed. "I work for your father and I am doing as he has told me."

Anna shuddered. All attempts to resist Helga were met either by force or by reduced food. She was watched constantly by Helga or Herr Schroder, and she was always kept away from others as well as from the town, which might as well have been a hundred miles away. And at night they locked her in her room, knowing full well that there was no way she could climb from the window and escape.

And it's worse now, she thought. I'm further along in my pregnancy and unable to run away. It was true, her belly was swollen with child, and she knew she waddled slightly when she walked.

Anna moved her arms to her sides and looked down on the mound that was her swollen uterus. The baby moved and she smiled through her tears at the sensation. It'll be over soon, she told herself. And when it's over, we'll be free, we'll go to America together. Again she fought off depression. There were no letters from Karla and none from her family either—not even a letter from Gerda. And she had written to them . . . all of them. Was Helga stealing her letters? It was a thought that had occurred to her before. Perhaps there had been letters; surely her mother would have written her.

Suddenly the room was plunged into darkness and Anna knew the bright, oddly shaped moon had slipped behind a dark cloud. She pressed her lips together and forced herself to close her eyes. Sleep . . . sleep. She imagined she was on one of her endless walks, but she imagined herself alone. She counted the trees silently, feeling her weary body going numb, and then she slipped into sleep, hearing only the sound of a single nightingale as it sang a lonely cry for its mate, or so she imagined.

* * *

In July, when Anna had walked with Helga along the main road, which was over two miles from the lodge, they had seen an occasional car or passed a wagon or a group of hikers. But as the cooler days of mid-August came to the mountains, strangers were seen less often.

Anna trudged along behind Helga, who set the pace with long purposeful strides. The forest, almost completely composed of coniferous trees, was seemingly unchanging from spring to late summer. Only when the winter snows covered the branches of the giant fir trees would the scenery radically change, but by then, Anna thought hopefully, I shall be on my way to America with my child. My family will be rid of me. Anna inhaled, slowed for a moment, and then began to walk on slowly.

"Hurry up!" Helga turned and shouted at her. "It's not good if you walk slowly! You must fill your lungs with air! Listen to marching music in your head and walk briskly!"

It was an order Helga gave often. Walking in the woods would be pleasant without her, Anna thought. She would be able to pause and enjoy the trees, she could have studied the plants on the forest floor or listened to the many songbirds. But as it was, these walks were not intended to be aesthetic experiences, rather they were militaristic. "Look neither to the left nor to the right, just walk rapidly," was Helga's motto.

Anna moved her arm to the small of her back, rubbed it, and frowned. Since early morning she had felt a slight pressure, a mild backache. But now it seemed worse, and she stopped walking to see if the pain would pass.

"Why are you stopping?" Helga called back.

"My back hurts," Anna replied as she began walking again.

Surprisingly, Helga did not forge on ahead; instead she waited until Anna reached her. She stood in the center of the path, hands on her giant hips, blocking the way.

"You needn't have waited," Anna said breathlessly, aware that once again she felt the pain in her back.

"Where is your pain?" Helga questioned. She stood behind Anna and roughly prodded her back with her giant hand.

"There . . . but it's not exactly a sharp pain, and it comes and goes."

"You're a goose!" Helga spat. "A simple goose! And your father told me you were smart! Well, how smart can you be to have gotten pregnant? Now you don't even know you are in the early stages of labor!"

"Labor . . . you mean the baby is coming, that I'll have it today?"

"Perhaps not today, but very soon."

"What will we do? It's two miles back to the lodge." Anna wondered if Helga could hear the panic in her voice. She hated this woman, and now she suddenly realized she would be at her mercy—completely at her mercy during the birth.

"We'll walk, naturally. You won't have the child right away. Walking will help you. Come along, don't waste any more time."

Anna pressed her lips together and followed as Helga marched off. God, had her father really known what a monster this woman was? Did he really intend for her to be held a prisoner? And why had her mother and her siblings deserted her? Tears began once again to roll from Anna's eyes—Kurt had been as cold and uncaring as her father, her mother had deserted her, and not even Gerda would help her. She felt alone and horribly depressed . . . and now, now she was in pain.

By the time the slanted log eaves of the lodge, which always reminded Anna of a gingerbread house, came into view, small beads of perspiration had broken out on her forehead and along her upper lip. The brisk walk back had caused her pains to come more rapidly, and more severely. Each time one came now, she had to stop walking and take a deep breath.

She staggered up the stairs that led to the door, grasping the rail. Helga held the door open, her face a mask of icy determination. "Go upstairs and put on that gown I showed you. Get into the bed. I shall be right along as soon as I have made certain preparations."

Anna gripped Helga's arm. "I want to go into town to the clinic. I don't want you to deliver my child." She forced the words out of her mouth in spite of her own fear. "Call Herr Schroder! Call him at once, I insist."

Helga's face hardened and she lifted her hand and slapped Anna hard. The sting of her hand left a red imprint on Anna's fair face, and she screamed and staggered, falling gently to the first step, sobbing.

"You are in no position to demand! Now, stop whining and get into bed! Either I shall deliver your child or you can deliver it yourself, you stupid child! Go!"

Another pain racked her body and she shook her head in fear. "No . . . don't leave me, Helga. Please."

Helga tugged on Anna's hair, and then, grasping her arm tightly, pulled her to her feet. Anna struggled for a moment, but another pain came suddenly and she sagged, gripping the banister tightly. She waited for a second, fearful that Helga might again hit her; then she turned and, sobbing, climbed the stairs slowly and fearfully.

Once upstairs, Anna threw herself on the bed and cried. Then, after yet another pain, she pulled herself up and took off her clothes, putting on the gown Helga had shown her. Then she once again climbed on the bed and lay shaking, torn between terror of Helga and terror of these pains she did not understand.

Helga came into the room shortly. She had a teakettle full of water, her bag, and she had changed into a clean new uniform. She did not speak to Anna, but rather roughly spread her legs and none too gently probed and prodded. Anna groaned and jerked as another labor pain surged through her body.

"You will do exactly as I tell you," Helga ordered. "If you do not, I shall tie your arms to the bed. Now, lift them up and grasp the bed here!" Helga pushed her arms into place. "And spread your legs and keep your knees up and bent . . . there, yes, that's it. Yes, you are well-dilated. When I tell you, you will inhale, when I tell you, you will exhale. When I tell you to push, push . . . but don't push till I tell you."

Anna nodded.

"Inhale deeply . . . hold it . . . now out . . . now in . . ."

The room was so utterly silent that Anna could hear

her own breathing as well as Helga's. And the rhythm of her breaths did help, though the pains grew closer and closer and more and more intense, till she screamed and writhed, gripping the bed.

"Pant, pant . . . like this . . . like a dog!"

Anna followed Helga's signals; then she screamed again.

"Now, push! Push!"

Anna pushed. She felt like a victim of the Inquisition being tortured on the rack. She screamed and she pushed and she was hardly aware that her whole body was bathed in sweat.

"Inhale . . . push one more time . . . hard!"

Anna closed her eyes and pushed, and then, cutting through her pain, she heard her child cry and she collapsed against the pillows, smiling through her perspiration and tears.

But another pain followed, and Helga yelled at her again and Anna again pushed on command.

"Just the afterbirth," Helga muttered. Then Helga put her child between her breasts, and after sterilizing her instruments, cut the umbilical cord.

"Nurse your daughter," she commanded.

Anna looked down on the tiny infant. Helga had wiped her off before placing her at the breast. She had huge blue eyes and her head was covered with soft blond down. "She's beautiful," Anna said, smiling. "So beautiful."

Anna snuggled her, then put her own nipple in the child's mouth. "Oh, she's strong!"

"Good . . . good," Helga said. "You don't have milk yet. But there's a liquid, and it's good for the child."

Anna nodded, but she couldn't take her eyes off her daughter. "Beloved daughter," she whispered. "I shall always take care of you and love you."

Anna watched in fascination as the baby's tiny little fingers caressed her bare breast. It was a wonderful feeling, having this child suckle, it was like nothing she had ever felt before, and the softness and helplessness of the little baby made her all the more determined to protect this child from the loneliness she herself had always felt until this wonderful moment. "I am whole now," she whispered. "You have made me whole."

"If you let her suck too long, your breast will get sore."

"I don't care," Anna said, snuggling the child closer.

"You really must sleep now . . . and you don't want to go to sleep with the child there," Helga said as she finished putting everything away. "You might roll over and smother her. Look, I'll put her in this basket right next to the bed. She'll sleep now."

Anna looked up at Helga. Was it possible she might roll over and hurt the baby? It was true that she was tired, terribly tired. Reluctantly she let Helga take the child and place it in the basket.

Helga withdrew a long needle from her bag. She filled it with fluid and took Anna's arm.

Anna pulled back. "What's that?" she questioned.

"Something to make certain you don't bleed. I *am* the nurse."

Anna winced as Helga pushed the needle into her arm and then pushed the plunger and withdrew the needle.

Anna rolled on her side so she could see the baby, whose eyes were closed and who curled up under the blanket in the basket.

"She looks like a little doll," Anna slurred as her eyes fluttered. She squinted to focus, but it was no use. Her body felt numb and soon her eyes closed, and try as she might, she couldn't again force them open.

Anna tossed on the bed, then forced her eyes open. The sun was pouring in the window and the low slanted roof made the room unbearably warm. Had she slept since the birth of her daughter yesterday afternoon? She quickly rolled over and then sat up, her heart pounding. The basket was gone. "Helga!" Anna's voice echoed through the house. "Helga!"

A frenzied panic gripped her and she pulled herself from the bed, hardly aware of the fact that she had been cleaned and her nightdress changed. "Helga!" she called again as she raced across the bedroom. Then a dizziness swept over her and she staggered, grasping the door as dreadful premonitions filled her thoughts.

Anna stood for a moment waiting for her eyes to focus and for the sensation to pass. The realization came slowly, but it increased her feeling of dread. Drugs! The shot Helga had given her! She'd been drugged! She wouldn't have bled. The birth had been entirely normal, and she was in fact in excellent physical condition. There was no need for a shot to keep her from bleeding. Oh, if only I hadn't been so tired, she thought, fighting even now for control. Her head pounded and Anna lifted her hands to her temples for a second. That was it. Morphine. Helga had given her morphine. She recalled once when she'd broken her arm she'd been given morphine and it had left her with a terrible hangover, a pounding headache that lasted for hours.

The feeling of weakness passed and she moved slowly into the hall. "Helga!" she called again, and this time she could hear anger as well as panic in her voice. She gripped the banister and went down the winding stairs. The house was utterly silent and completely empty. Even the furniture was covered with white sheets. Anna ran from room to room. "My baby," she whispered again and again, but she knew. Helga was gone and she had taken the baby. Anna slumped into a chair at the kitchen table. Herr Schroder's car was gone too . . . it was no longer parked between the cottage where he slept and the lodge.

Anna felt utterly rigid, too frightened even to cry. She shivered. Get dressed, she commanded herself. Get dressed and walk into town . . . get help and find Helga and the baby.

Stronger now, as her head gradually cleared, she hurried back upstairs. Quickly she got dressed and just as quickly she gathered what money she had and some essentials. She shoved them into a small rucksack and slung it over her shoulder and went back downstairs. It was early. If she walked rapidly, she could get to town within two hours . . . of course she would have to rest a little, and if she was fortunate, perhaps a wagon would come by, or even a car. She locked the door of the lodge after er and set off down the rough road that led to the main road into town.

Try as she would, Anna was unable to turn off her thoughts. Had her father arranged this? Or had Helga simply kidnapped the baby on her own? And what part did the wily Herr Schroder play?

For a few moments she concentrated on Herr Schroder. She had always assumed he was from the village, but now she wondered why she had made that assumption, especially as he and Helga did, in fact, appear to have met before. That was not her impression that first morning at the station, but as the weeks passed, she often saw Herr Schroder and Helga talking together conspiratorially. And it was not unusual for them to play cards long into the night. Yes, he most certainly was a part of this . . . he and Helga. The question was, had they committed this terrible crime on their own, or had her father put them up to it?

I must find my baby, she thought again and again. Why would her father do such a terrible thing? Why, when she had promised to leave Germany, would he have her child taken from her? No, Helga must have kidnapped the child on her own, Anna decided. Not even her father at his worst could be this cruel. The child was, after all, his flesh and blood too. No, it must all be Herr Schroder and Helga's doing. "You'll rot in jail!" Anna muttered as she reached the main road.

She walked as fast as she could, aware that she was not yet entirely over the hangover caused by Helga's drugs or the exertion caused by the ordeal of childbirth. Now and again she stopped to rest, and when she came to an outcropping in the rocks where a spring burst forth, she drank the cool, clean, fresh mountain water. Then, her thirst quenched, she went on, aware that the fresh air was gradually clearing her head.

She had been walking for nearly an hour when a wagon came clattering down the road. She waved and the driver slowed. "Help me," she called out. "I must get to town." The bearded old farmer who drove nodded and held out his arm to help her up onto the wagon. It hardly seemed faster than walking, though she knew it was. In half an hour they reached town and Anna hurried to the police station.

Like every other official building in Wildbad, the police station was built in a pseudo-Roman style. The style of the public buildings, the bank, and even the spa itself were all in sharp contrast to the private homes, all of which suddenly reminded Anna of Frau Fischer's cuckoo clocks. It struck Anna that while the scenery and the private homes were beautiful, the town and its great spa were ugly.

The police officer wore an ornate uniform with gold buttons and rows of gold braid. His head was half-buried beneath his absurd metal hat and he peered at her incredulously as she poured forth her story. "And the nurse has kidnapped my baby and run off . . . you must find her, you must find my baby at once."

The policeman's expression did not change. He withdrew a white form from a drawer, positioned his pencil, and looked up at her. "Name?"

Anna trembled. "Anna von Bock."

"Ah, Frau von Bock, you must be married to one of General von Bock's sons . . . were you at the lodge?"

His voice had taken on a syrupy indulgence. Since she had mentioned a baby, he thought she was married into the family rather than being the daughter. Well, none of those details were any of his business, she decided. "Yes, I was at the lodge with a nurse. The nurse has taken my child."

"And your husband, where is he?"

"In Berlin," she lied.

"Ah, so you were visiting the lodge with your child and the child's nurse. Not the usual thing, especially so late in the season." A strange girl, he thought, studying her. Still, he would have to look into the matter. The von Bocks were an important family.

Anna couldn't explain that she had just given birth. "And a driver too . . . a man from here, I believe, a Herr Schroder. He's gone too. I think he and the nurse kidnapped my child."

The police officer scowled at her. "Herr Schroder. I hardly think so. Herr Schroder is a good citizen."

"Well, he's gone and my baby is gone! And you're wasting time!" She could hear the edge in her voice. I can't hold myself together much longer, she thought. She was on the verge of hysteria and all she could picture was Helga—the cold, icy, mean Helga—with her poor little baby.

"I shall have to make some calls," the policeman explained. "In the meantime, why don't you wait at the hotel. Have a glass of schnapps to calm yourself."

"You don't understand. It's a tiny baby . . . my baby . . ." Tears started to run down her face and she began to shake. Why was this man such a dolt! What was happening? She'd been subjected . . . no, allowed herself to be subjected for months by Helga. Now she was shaking and crying and unable to think clearly. As never before, she felt weak and tired, totally shattered, and terrified that she would never again see her child. "Help me," she pleaded. "The nurse drugged me . . . I'm not well."

The policeman picked up his phone and dialed a number. "I'm sending for the doctor," he announced.

Anna sat in the chair staring into space, murmuring over and over, "My baby, my baby . . ."

The white-frocked doctor held her hand, took her pulse, felt her forehead, and finally peered into her face. "When did you have this child?"

"Yesterday," Anna murmured. "Please make them find my baby."

"Postpartum depression," the doctor declared, turning to the policeman. "Quite common, really. And sometimes it can be quite serious. I'll take her along to the clinic, and you contact her family and see to finding this nurse who may have the child.

"Come along . . ." The doctor helped her up. Anna looked into his eyes. It was as if her whole will had fled her body. She felt incapable of putting one leg in front of the other. Whatever source of strength she had tapped to get this far was used up. She let the doctor lead her away, and once in the confines of the clinic, she submitted to examination without objection. She did not even complain when he gave her some sleeping powders and spoke softly to her about "her ordeal."

When Anna opened her eyes she found herself in a small white room in a spotless white bed. The doctor looked down at her, but he no longer looked as concerned as he had previously. "Have you found my baby?" she asked anxiously.

"The police have called your father in Berlin," he said coldly. "Do you understand me? Are you fully aware of what I'm telling you?"

"Yes . . . have they found my baby?"

"Your father informed the police that as your legal guardian, he has given your child over for adoption. The nurse acted on his instructions. There has been no crime."

"Adoption . . ." Anna repeated the word. "No . . . she's my child."

"You're a young woman. Your father has every legal right to do what he has done."

"No! It's not just! No, she's my baby . . ." Anna cried out.

"It's been done. And you are quite well and free to go. There is, in fact, a train for Berlin within the hour. I suggest you take this matter up with your father. Neither I nor the local authorities can do anything further. Go back to Berlin. If you don't believe your father had the right, then consult a lawyer."

Anna shivered. Adoption? Her father had lied to her; he had been brutal, and not only would she never forgive him, but she vowed she would find her precious baby. It was that thought alone that enabled her to dress and gather herself up to leave for Berlin.

It was the first week in September and already there was a touch of fall in the air. Anna buttoned her jacket and closed the door of the room she had temporarily rented at a boardinghouse on the Unter den Linden. Located on the third floor at No. 29, it was run by the Stern family, who relished providing hearty German meals and all-too-cheerful conversation, at least too cheerful for Anna's mood. And the room was too expensive, though she reminded herself day after day that it was central. Nonetheless, the reality of her life was closing in on her. The money left to her by her grandmother was rapidly disappearing, and when it was gone, she would have to take work in a factory. Such a job would not give her the freedom to look for her baby, and she admitted to herself that she was growing discouraged.

Still, as the days and weeks had passed, Anna was aware that changes had come over her. The lawyers all told her the search was hopeless. The police would not help because, they insisted, no crime had been committed. Her father would not see her and he let it be known that his only daughter was Gerda and that Anna, as far as he was concerned, was dead. Nor would her mother consent to see her. In fact, her mother had been sent away to Vienna by her father. Gerda would not see or speak to her either, nor would Else or Andreas allow her to visit them in Essen. Only Markus would see her, and he would only meet her in cafés. It came as a surprise, but Anna admitted that only Markus had shown her affection, and he had even given her some money. Markus alone seemed to care.

Anna reached the ground floor and pushed through the double doors of the austere stone building that housed the boardinghouse. She walked out onto the busy Unter den Linden feeling alone as fashionably dressed women shoppers bustled by her, a sense of purpose, and indeed confidence evident in their step, as well as in their dress. It was already cold enough for fur stoles and flaring capes. The clouds hung threateningly over the city and Anna pulled her jacket tighter and walked hurriedly toward her rendezvous with Markus.

Helga, it appeared, had disappeared off the face of the earth, spirited away by her father. Herr Schroder was nowhere to be found either, and there wasn't a single clue to her child's whereabouts. Anna's sole comfort was Markus' contention that their father would have arranged for the child to go to a good home so that she need not worry for the baby's welfare. And Anna knew that Markus was right on that score. Her child had doubtless been given to some childless couple, and most certainly some lonely woman held the baby, lavishing affection on her.

Anna pushed into the busy Café Baur at No. 26 Unter den Linden. It was one of Berlin's many coffeehouses that specialized in cakes and other confections. The aroma of strong coffee and almond pastries filled her nose, and though she still felt badly, the wonderful smells reminded her of happier days.

"Over here!" Markus waved.

Anna pushed past a woman in a long black coat. She was a large woman, and for a single second Anna thought she was Helga. But it was not Helga. She shook her head to dispel the thought. It was true, she saw Helga everywhere.

"I'm glad to see you," Anna said, slipping into the seat across from Markus. He looked particularly handsome today, she thought.

"You look better," he said, studying her. "Yes, you look much better."

"I'm feeling a little stronger," she allowed. "I suppose I'm adjusting to being miserable. And when I visit the lawyer, I always hear about cases even worse than my own. Oh, Markus, it's so unjust." She shook her head.

"Life is unjust," Markus agreed.

"It's more unjust for women . . . you don't know." She clenched her fist unconsciously and looked steadily at him. "You know, Markus, if I ever have the opportunity to continue my studies in law, I shall specialize in trying to change things for women."

He half-smiled at her. "Ever since I can remember, you've had a passion for justice, Anna. You're a champion of lost causes."

"Is finding my baby a lost cause?" She frowned at him and watched as he nodded. A week ago she would have begun crying, but she was more in control now. She hadn't cried lately, and though she still had nightmares, they had grown less frequent. Anna knew her will was returning. For months now her will and her spirit had seemed to lie dormant. Kurt had found her emotionally vulnerable and used that vulnerability to subject her. He had tried to turn her into something she was not, bend her to fit the female role in his radical vision of a new society. Her father had taken advantage of her physical vulnerability and punished her for her immorality by taking away her child. But for days now she had felt her spirit being rekindled, and though her prospects remained grim, she knew now she could survive almost anything.

"Anna, you know I care about you, don't you?"

Markus' voice broke into her thoughts. "I think you are the only one who does, Markus." She reached across the table and covered his hand with hers. "How is Dorcas? Is she all right?"

"Yes . . . our baby isn't due just yet. She's with her parents in Munich. I haven't told her much about your situation."

"I'm pleased for you, Markus. She's a good person. Don't let Gerda eat her alive."

"I won't."

The waitress appeared. She looked at their entwined hands and smirked. Clearly she thought they were lovers rather than brother and sister sharing an affectionate moment.

"Two coffees and two almond pastries," Markus ordered. He smiled. "I know you like almond pastry."

"I do. Thank you. Have you talked to Father, Markus?"

"I tried. He's stubborn and he's distracted with affairs of state, Anna. No, he wouldn't tell me anything. He only said you must give up. He will never give in. I believe him, Anna."

Anna looked away, then slowly raised her eyes and looked into Markus' eyes. "He's done a terrible thing to me, Markus. He's been cruel beyond my wildest dreams . . . I didn't think he was capable of . . ."

"He believes he has done the right thing. He assured me the child has been given a good home and is well-loved. He says it would be better if you would join Karla in America—leave Germany and forget your child." Markus studied Anna's face, watching for her reaction. Yes, he thought. It would be much better if she left.

Anna trembled. "I can never forget my baby."

Markus nodded and squeezed her hand as the waitress set down the coffees and the pastries. "Then at least give up the search. Anna, your money is running out. Look, I have some money I'll give you. Karla wrote . . . I've told her you're coming."

"Karla wrote?" Anna felt a sudden burst of excitement.

Markus fished in his pocket and handed her a letter. "Here, it says she will meet you in New York. I wrote to her—I took the liberty of telling her you would sail from Hamburg next week."

"Next week?" Anna looked at him in surprise. "I haven't said I would go . . . how can I leave without my child?"

Markus leaned across the table. "You won't find her, Anna. Go, go to America and make a new beginning. I can't stand to see you suffer this way. I couldn't stand it if you ran out of money and had to work in some factory. Please go to America, Anna. Accept the fact that our father has defeated you."

"But to give up . . ."

"Look, Anna, you don't have to give up. I'll pay the lawyers, I'll continue the search for you."

"You would do that? Oh, Markus, you are my only real family apart from Karla."

"Take this opportunity. I'll keep you informed of progress. Anna, go and start a new life. If there are any developments, I'll send you passage money to return."

Anna listened to her brother's words, and even though she wanted terribly to reject his plea, she knew in her heart he was right. Perhaps in America she could finish law school and make enough money to return to Germany and find her daughter.

Slowly she nodded. "I'll go, Markus," she said softly. "I'll go to America."

Anna tied the woolen scarf around her neck and tucked it into her coat. Her hair was loose, but it was long enough and thick enough to keep her ears warm in the brisk breeze that made the waters of the Elbe ripple as the great passenger ship cut through the river on its voyage to the North Sea.

Although old and venerable, Hamburg had not entirely escaped being a port city. It had its share of bad neighborhoods and ribald nightclubs. But it was an attractive city, Anna thought as the Neo-Renaissance Rathus, built in the late 1800's, faded in the distance together with the spires of hundreds of churches. The harbor was busy and connected to all of Germany by hundreds of rail lines. The buildings she could see now were warehouses: they were drab and dull and the smoke from nearby factories climbed to meet an already gray sky.

She wondered what the sea would be like and she took comfort in the fact that it was only September. The Atlantic, she had read, did not grow truly treacherous till late October. Still, it would not be an easy voyage, and surely it would be crowded and stuffy belowdeck.

She glanced around and looked at the faces of her fellow travelers. On the whole they were young and, she hoped, adventurous. Unlike many, she was not so poverty-stricken she had to travel in steerage. Markus had arranged for her to travel third class in a cabin she would share with three other single women. For a moment she thought how strange it would be to live for so many days in a small room with women she didn't even know.

Anna thrust her hands into her pockets and inhaled deeply. What strange twists and turns her life had taken. It was as if the world had spun, and when it stopped, she found herself in circumstances completely in contrast to those in which she had begun. Once she had been seen as the intelligent university-bound daughter of an important German general, a woman destined to become a professor. And once she had been surrounded by the tangled web of her family relations. Then she had escaped the web and become entangled in a true trap. I was stupid and naive when I met Kurt, she admitted. And I am certainly no longer naive or protected. I am alone and I will have to work hard to make a new life. Anna pressed her lips together in determination and then she turned her back on the fading skyline of Hamburg and headed for her cabin. In it she would find three other young women who were also making a new beginning. Today, Anna thought, I am born anew . . . or as Karla might have said, I am about to reinvent myself.

The steel-gray North Atlantic churned and rolled as if, far beneath its surface, the earth pitched violently. But such was not the case. The tiny biting whitecaps and the sea's malevolent movements were caused only by the distant winds, the far-off sun, the stars, and the gravitational pull of the full white moon.

Anna walked carefully around the lower deck, feeling the salt spray on her face and the rocking of the ship beneath her feet. Not a few of her fellow passengers suffered seasickness, but she herself did not react badly to the rolls and pitches of the vessel, and in fact found she felt better for keeping a full stomach and staying out on deck where she could walk in the misty cold air.

After leaving Hamburg, the old *Deutschland,* a vessel built at the turn of the century, and the ship on which Anna traveled, had slipped into the turbulent North Sea to begin its 3,700-mile voyage to New York. It took on additional passengers in Portsmouth, England, and again in Brest on the coast of France. The additional passengers came from a dozen different lands, so that now half a dozen languages were heard on and belowdeck. But, Anna noted, the vast majority of English speakers were American rather than British. Europe was in turmoil and bad feelings existed between the English and Germans. Some, Anna thought unhappily, even spoke of a possible war.

Anna rounded the corner at the stern of the vessel and a gust of wind caught her skirt and it blew out and up. Awkwardly she held it down with her hands and looked up in annoyance at a jauntily dressed young man who was approaching her. He grinned at her and laughed. "Don't fly away, my beauty!"

Anna stared at him largely because his eyes lingered on her ankles. He was in his mid-twenties, she decided, and no doubt an American. He wore a tweed jacket with leather patches on the elbows, and he had a tweed hat too. The hat sported a small green feather in its ribboned band. He was a tall, well-built man with a face made more boyish by a line of freckles across his nose, and an unruly lock of red hair that protruded beneath his cap.

He stopped in front of her and tipped his hat, bowing from the waist. "You're in third class, aren't you?" he asked.

"Yes," Anna answered, avoiding his blatantly flirtatious stare.

"Ah and you're German, aren't you?"

Anna nodded, debating whether or not she should stand and talk to this young man, or whether she should step around him and continue her walk. He was bold, but if she avoided him, she would be rude. In any case, she was no longer an innocent, and to pretend she was would be sheer hypocrisy.

"Are you going to America alone? Not many girls go to American alone."

He spoke rapidly, and Anna tilted her head slightly. "My English is not very good," she said hesitantly. "Please speak a little slower."

He laughed, and after a moment he replied, "Yes, I'm American." Then he repeated his comment and question, and this time he spoke slowly.

"Yes, I travel alone," Anna confirmed. "But there are three other girls in my cabin. Three." She held up her fingers to indicate the number.

"And where are these three other lovely women?"

"Two are ill and the third is sleeping."

"I see. Tell me, are the others as beautiful as you are?"

Anna blushed slightly and wondered if all American men were so outspoken. "I don't think of myself as beautiful," she replied.

He chuckled again. "Well, modesty is becoming. Tell me, what's your name?"

"Anna Bock." She had decided the moment she left Germany to drop the "von" from her name. It would surely be thought pretentious in America.

"Jim Parnell," he said, doffing his hat and bowing absurdly.

"You're not traveling third class, are you?" she asked.

"Good heavens, no! I'm in first class. I have a fine cabin up there." He pointed to the deck above.

Anna followed his finger with her eyes. Then she looked at his clothing. He was well-dressed.

"I'm a student—a university student. I've been traveling in Europe and now I'm returning home to Chicago."

"Chicago," Anna repeated, digesting the pronunciation of the strange name she had only seen in print, but never heard spoken by a real American. "It's America's second-largest city, yes?"

"Yes. And where are you headed, New York?"

"Milwaukee. My aunt is meeting me in New York."

"Of course! All the Germans go to Milwaukee. I should have guessed. Well, it's not far from Chicago, you know. Not far at all." He paused as if thinking, then asked, "How is it in third class?"

"The cabins are small."

"You could come and visit me in first class. No need to spend the whole voyage down here."

Anna frowned at him and folded her arms. Just because she had stopped to talk to him and just because she had answered his questions, he seemed to think her willing to do other things. Well, he had taken her for a girl and didn't know what she had been through, or indeed how cautious her experiences had made her. "I like it down here," she replied somewhat coldly.

He looked a trifle taken aback. "I only wanted to be friends. Come on, Anna, let me get to know you."

"I'm not coming to your cabin," she said plainly.

He took her arm and turned so they could walk in the same direction. "Then just walk with me and meet me here tomorrow for a walk. That's all I want . . . really."

Anna did not pull her arm away, but she did steal a sideways glance at this Jim Parnell. He had an impish quality, an openness about him. His advances, she admitted, were not unflattering. Perhaps, she decided, I could learn more of America from him. And at the very least I can practice my English. "Very well. But we will meet only to talk."

"And what will we talk about today?"

"University," Anna said. "Tell me about American universities."

"Entirely different from those in Europe," he said with a sweeping gesture of his hand. "You must attend lectures and you are given examinations often . . . sometimes every week, but at least every semester."

"Semester?"

"The year is divided into two periods called semesters."

"Oh . . . and tutors?"

"No tutors, you're on your own. It's because there are no tutors that you must go to class. Anyway, after four years you graduate. But universities in America are more fun than in Europe. There's more social life . . . clubs and football games."

Anna took it all in and she asked more questions, which he answered patiently. Then after a time they stopped walking. "I have to go back to my cabin now," she told him.

"Tomorrow, then," he said cheerfully. "And what will we discuss then?"

Anna frowned and thought for a moment. "Shopping," she said, smiling. "Yes, I must know about shopping for food."

He turned and waved to her. "Same time," he said.

"Same time," she repeated as he disappeared up the stairs that led to the upper deck.

Uda Gersdorf was short and a bit stocky. Her hair was dark, thick, and straight and she wore it in long braids that were wrapped around her head, the result being that her round face seemed even fuller. She was a cheerful girl who made a joke of everything, and even as the ship rolled slowly and then pitched, she lamented, "See, I'm not seasick! If I were seasick I'd lose weight, but I never get illnesses that cause me to lose weight!"

Anna laughed with her new friend. "Did you want to lose weight?"

"Oh, yes. America's not like Germany. All the women in America are thin."

"You're not fat," Anna insisted.

"I am. I'm worried I don't look at all like the pictures of those willowy women in American magazines. Perhaps Oskar won't like me."

"He already likes you. That's why he wanted you to come to join him."

"Can you really like someone through her letters?" Uda asked seriously.

"Don't you like him because of his letters to you?"

Uda nodded, then said thoughtfully, "I just don't know exactly what to expect. I don't mean just what to expect where Oskar is concerned—I mean everything."

"That's what makes it an adventure," Anna returned. She sat on the edge of her bunk and ran the comb through her hair. In the bunk above, Hella slept soundly, too ill to care for either the conversation or her future adventure. Magda, their other roommate, had dragged herself up onto deck to sit in a chair wrapped in a blanket.

"I can't tell you how grateful I am that you're going to let me travel to Milwaukee with you," Uda said, looking at Anna. "I was so frightened, the thought of getting off this ship and arranging to take the train . . . to travel all that way in a strange country where I don't speak the language."

"And I'm glad Karla is meeting us," Anna said. "I wouldn't like to launch out on my own either."

Uda nodded. "Still, you speak some English. I speak practically none."

"I met an American today," Anna revealed. "I'm going to meet him tomorrow and talk with him so I can practice my English. Perhaps by the time we dock, I'll sound less like a textbook."

"I'll have to wait till I get settled. My cousin wrote that I can go to night school. He says English is easy for Germans."

Anna smiled. "Easier than German is for those who speak English, I imagine."

"Well, I must learn to speak well," Uda emphasized. "I'm going to get married and bring up lots of little

Americans, and a mother should be able to help her children with their schoolwork.''

Anna looked wistfully at Uda. She was so certain of herself, so sure of what her life would be like. ''I envy you,'' she said, smiling at her friend.

''You envy me? How could you? You've graduated from gymnasium. You . . . you're educated.''

''To do what I want to do, I must have even more education.''

Uda studied Anna's expression. ''You must really want to study law. You're very pretty, you know. You could easily find a husband and marry.''

Anna shook her head. ''This is something I must do, Uda. I've been thinking of it for a long while. There are so many injustices against women—even in America. They must be addressed.''

''You make hard choices for yourself, Anna.'' Uda decided her new friend was a special person. She was kind and friendly. But there was a sadness about her, and Uda wondered why anyone with so many advantages in life would be so sad.

Anna pulled her coat around her tightly and stared out across the choppy steel-gray water.

''See those gulls?'' Jim Parnell pointed skyward, his finger following the flight of a far-off twosome of seabirds. ''We're getting close to land—there'll be gulls with us the rest of the way now.''

''As we're scheduled to dock tomorrow morning, I don't think we need rely on birds to forecast our whereabouts,'' Anna replied, smiling.

''And aren't you sharp-tongued this morning,'' he returned.

''I didn't mean to be sharp-tongued, as you put it. I just meant that as we dock tomorrow, we *must* be getting close to land.''

''Perhaps I just like to state the obvious. You know, for days I've been trying to find a topic to discuss with you—something you don't know anything about.''

''Why?''

"I think I wanted to impress you. But you seem to be rather well-informed."

"I've asked you questions, and you've answered them. What makes you think I'm not impressed?" Anna asked, tilting her head slightly.

He shrugged. "You still keep me at arm's length."

Anna frowned and held out her arm. She turned it and looked at it. "I'm not sure I understand."

He laughed and shook his head. "It's just a phrase— an expression. It means you won't let me get close to you."

"At arm's length," Anna repeated the phrase. "An idiomatic expression," she said. Then she smiled. "I'll remember that."

"I imagine you will. You know, you have a pretty smile. You look small and vulnerable . . . but I don't think you are. I think you're a bit of shrew."

"A shrew? As in Shakespeare's play?"

"Yes."

Anna shook her head. "I'm not a shrew," she protested. "But I do have certain goals, certain ambitions."

"Is that why you won't let me get close to you?"

"Yes, that's part of the reason. I have . . . how would you say it? Yes, I have a commitment."

"To a man?"

"Oh, no. To something else . . . to my goal."

"I'm not used to being rejected by women, you know. I might feel better if you explained your commitment, or, as you say, your goal."

Anna didn't turn to look into his curious blue-green eyes. He was an appealing man, but there was no room for such a man in her life now, or in the near future. Any man who became a part of her life would have to understand her commitment, understand that he would have to play a minor role. Such men were not easy to find, and she was not looking. This man was certainly not a man who would play such a role. This was a man who wanted everything; she sensed it, just as she sensed anything but the most casual relationship with him would be dangerous.

"Will you explain?" he pressed.

Anna nodded slowly. "I'm what you might call wounded," she said slowly.

"Ah, an unhappy love affair," he surmised.

"There was an unhappy love affair, but that's not the source of my real wound. I've had a terrible injustice done . . . I feel it more deeply than I can tell you or anyone. I can only say that because of this injustice, I have made a commitment to the law. I will become a lawyer. I will fight not only the injustice done to me but also the injustices done to other women."

He raised both brows. "Good heavens!" he proclaimed, not looking at all serious. "I had no idea I was trying to seduce a reformer!"

Anna scowled at him, and gripping her coat, she turned abruptly. "You're making fun of me! You're not at all serious. I knew I shouldn't have begun talking with you!"

He reached out across the distance between them, and grasping her shoulders, pulled her forcibly toward him. He then leaned over and closed her partially open mouth with a hard kiss. A kiss that took her so by surprise she did not initially resist. Then she pulled away. "Why did you do that?" she said angrily.

He grinned at her and winked. "Because you're so damn pretty and I could never resist a pretty woman."

"You're a dreadful man!" She shook off his hands and turned sharply and tromped off, trying hard not to slide on the slippery deck. She reached the door that led to the stairs to the lower deck. "Damn him," she murmured as for some inexplicable reason tears flooded her eyes. "Damn him!" Anna all but ran to her cabin. He had made fun of her, and he certainly hadn't taken her at all seriously. Of course, she hadn't really explained about her child being stolen, but still he shouldn't have laughed. It was cruel . . . it was all cruel. Anna opened the door of the cabin and to her relief found it empty. She threw herself on the bunk and clenched her fists tightly and for a long while stared at the top bunk above her. Time will heal my wounds, she told herself. Time and doing what I must do.

7

Milwaukee curved around the shoreline of Lake Michigan, its factories belching out smoke, its breweries lending a pungent aroma to the air, while its many skilled workers toiled to craft the machines that would make the tools for America's rapidly expanding industry.

At times, when it was clear and sunny, Lake Michigan seemed to be a deep blue. At such times, Milwaukee appeared bold and brash, a sprawling potpourri of architecture that clearly marked it as a New World city. Some of its buildings were ornate and their design reminded newcomers of buildings found in European cities. But other buildings were as distinctly American as the city's sprawling patternless streets. Unlike so many European cities, which expanded in tight circles from the center, America's cities were undisciplined, stretching outward as if intoxicated with the endless space in which they could expand.

Milwaukee's second personality surfaced when the sky was dark and overcast, the wind biting, and the thunder clouds threatening. Then Milwaukee appeared gray and ugly; a depressing huddle of factories and expanding neighborhoods. At such times the populace seemed cheerlessly relentless in their pursuit of success, elevating self-discipline almost to the level of a new religion. The immigrants, perhaps more than those born in America, toiled long hours, performing hard, mind-numbing work. Sometimes, even recreation seemed routinized and planned.

The various communities were stereotyped by the native Americans. The Italians, who lived on one side of Canal Street, were seen as fun-loving, musical, and given to lavish weddings and boisterous street dances. The Irish, who lived on the other side of Canal Street, were seen as heavy drinkers, people who too quickly left their work behind them, and who always seemed to be having a party to literally "wake" the dead. The Poles, whose community was centered around Lincoln Avenue, were seen to be dour and somewhat plodding, while the Germans, who lived in the area of Walnut Street, were characterized as hardworking, sober, and above all frugal.

Sometimes it seemed that the various groups excelled in living up to their stereotypes; at other times they failed, and then, somehow, native Americans seemed puzzled, even angered. Wild Italian anarchists flew in the face of the party-loving musical Italian stereotype, as did a sober Irishman, a quick Pole, or a gregarious spendthrift German.

But on the whole, the communities seemed unconsciously to do what seemed expected of them, and the Germans, not terribly unhappy with their label of hardworking frugality, seemed to deviate the least.

There were Sunday-night church suppers, and Saturday-night beer-hall feasts that attempted to emulate life in the old country. But everyone worked, everyone "paid his dues," as Karla put it.

There was happiness and laughter in Germantown and there was still more joy on warm summer days. Blue skies and sunshine seemed to affect not only the appearance of the city but also the attitudes of its inhabitants. Or at least that was usually the case, Anna reflected. Today, even though the sun was strong and it was as warm and as beautiful a day in June as could be expected, a pall hung over Milwaukee. And the pall wouldn't pass quickly. In every newspaper—English, Polish, Italian, and German—headlines screamed out the unwelcome news: Germany was at war with England. Not that the signs of the impending conflagration had been hidden. But now reality brought a stunned depression to the German community. First there was apprehension over the fate of loved ones, second there existed an inescapable fear that everything gained in their new country might be lost. No matter how a conversation began, it soon turned to the war news.

It was the noon hour, and on the wide lawn behind the brewery, workers took advantage of the weather to eat their lunch outside. Anna sat on the grass, her legs folded up beneath her, her blue print dirndl skirt billowing around her. Her long thick blond hair was pinned up and enclosed in a net. Anna had been working in the brewery since she arrived in November, and she planned to work through the summer, after which she would leave for law school in Chicago, if all went well and she was accepted this year.

"You should be careful in the sun," Lili said, looking into Anna's eyes. "You're not used to it . . . and you're terribly pale."

"It's deceivingly strong—you don't think of it because we're so far north," Uda put in; then she looked away and ran her hand over the grass and shook her head. "What are we going to do? I'm so worried. I never thought it would come to this. My whole family is still in Germany."

Anna looked at her sympathetically. Her own brother Markus was already in the army. At twenty-nine he was certainly young enough to be sent to the front. Her other brother, Andreas, was safe enough . . . he still worked for Krupp, the manufacturers of the guns and bullets. Karla called them "the merchants of death." It was said Krupp had sold their weapons to both sides in the Balkans to encourage the war in the knowledge that however things turned out, they would benefit. Her father was too old to fight, but he would command and send others to fight, Anna thought bitterly. And there was her daughter, but Anna forced thoughts of her child away because they brought her great sadness.

"If America gets into the war, they might lock us all up," Lili suggested in a slightly high-pitched, nervous voice that brought Anna back to the present. "They call us the hyphenated Americans, German-Americans. Some of them say we're loyal to Germany." She bit her lip and looked down at her hands.

"America isn't in the war yet," Uda reminded them,

moving her hand from the grass to her skirt, which she smoothed out, nervously running her hand over and over it as if ironing out invisible wrinkles. She waited for Anna to say something, anything. Anna was the smartest among them, and she always saw things for what they were.

"I don't think they can lock us all up," Anna said, sounding more confident than she actually felt. "There are too many of us."

"But they might just lock up those of us who are not yet citizens . . . those of us who are really newcomers," Lili suggested.

"Perhaps America will stay out of the war," Uda ventured.

Anna looked from Uda to Lili. She did not know Lili Braun well. She had met her when she had begun working at the brewery eight months ago, and seldom saw her outside of work. But Uda Gersdorf was her closest friend. They had come to America together, they had traveled to Milwaukee together, and they studied English together at night school.

"I heard this morning that there was fighting between Italians and Germans on Canal Street," Lili told them in a near-whisper.

"If you're German, it's not safe to go down there," Uda agreed. Then, still seeking reassurance, "You don't think America will get into it, do you, Anna? I don't think I could stand it . . . I mean, the war is bad enough, but to be living in a country that's part of it . . . to know your neighbors here are going off to kill your relatives in Germany, or that your German relatives are killing your neighbors here . . . it's not a question of loyalty, it's not that simple."

Anna shook her head slowly and then shrugged to emphasize her own confusion. She couldn't ease Uda's concerns because she herself felt so apprehensive. If America becomes involved, she thought, then we shall all be in trouble. Anna glanced quickly at Uda and Lili. Uda had just summed up part of the dilemma—that part which defined the pull of the average German who had ties on both sides. But many German-Americans would support

Germany in the war . . . how could they not? If America entered, then what would they do? Not only would there be divisions between Americans and German-Americans, there would be suspicions among different sectors within the German community. She herself had no reason to be pro-German, and Karla and Josef were both pacifists, opposed to all war. But there were many who still counted themselves German patriots in spite of being American. How could they fight against their country of origin? And Lili had a point. What of people like herself, who did not yet have their citizenship? A cold chill passed through her. What if those without citizenship *were* deported back to Germany?

The brewery whistle blew three short blasts marking the end of the lunch period. "Back to work," Uda said, pulling herself up off the grass and brushing her skirt. Anna stood up, and so did Lili. The three of them walked back toward the stone building that housed the *Joe Schlitz Brewing Company*.

Anna stared down at the worn path that led across the grass to the doors of the brewery. Steps toward a new beginning, she thought . . . had it really only been eight months since that winter day she had arrived in New York? It seemed like yesterday, yet so much had happened, so much had already changed.

It had been a gray November day. Anna had grasped her bag tightly and expectantly allowed herself to be herded along with the other third-class passengers into the great warehouselike building on the famous—at least to immigrants—Ellis Island. It was cold and drafty even inside, and it was impossible for her to stay with Uda because they were divided alphabetically according to their last names almost as soon as they passed through the doors.

In all, it took Anna nearly three hours to pass through the various interviews and examinations. Finally she found herself thrust out another door and, after a short wait, onto a crowded ferry. It took only a short time to cross the water to the shore, and there the ferry unloaded its passengers. Onshore relatives mingled with organizations which carried identifying signs, and generally bedlam reigned supreme. Anna scanned the tired, anxious faces, and then she saw her aunt. Karla, a bit taller than average, wore a long tweed winter coat and a plain hat. She looked apprehensive and uncomfortable.

"Karla!" Anna fought her way through the mingling crowd even as Karla moved closer to her. Then Karla was hugging her and Anna was hugging back fiercely.

After a moment they stopped hugging and looked into one another's faces, concentrating on the changes time had wrought.

Under her aunt's broad-brimmed hat, Anna thought Karla looked wiser; she still seemed full of energy and enthusiasm. But Karla's eyes were filled with concern.

"What have they done to you?" Karla queried, soothing Anna's windblown hair. "You're so pale and so terribly thin."

"I'm so glad you're here," Anna managed. "Oh, Karla. I need you so much. But why didn't you write when I was in Wildbad?"

Karla frowned. "I did write! But I didn't know you were in Wildbad. Why were you there?"

Anna looked at her aunt and bit her own lip. "You didn't know?" she said incredulously.

"I didn't know anything till I heard from Markus. He said you wanted to come to America—he asked if I could meet you. Of course I said yes . . ." Karla looked at her darling Anna. She seemed older; she was certainly no longer a girl. But it was more than the passage of mere time. Anna has been subjected to some horrible ordeal; Karla felt it, and she reached out to her niece.

Anna frowned in disbelief and shook her head slowly, "No . . . no, I wrote to you . . . Oh, Karla, you don't know anything . . . you don't even know why I had to leave, why I'm here."

Karla now looked even more troubled. "No, we must talk right away. You must tell me everything."

Anna let out her breath slowly and looked around. "I promised to wait for Uda, a girl I met on the ship. They took us alphabetically. I don't know how long she'll be."

"Come along, come sit with me over here on one of these benches. When she comes, we'll see her."

Karla took one of Anna's bags and Anna followed her to the sheltered area where old rough benches lined a concrete wall. "It's a little warmer here," Karla commented. "What's your friend's last name?"

"Gersdorf," Anna replied, sitting down.

"Well, she shouldn't be too long. Now, Anna, tell me everything. The last letter I got from you, you were moving in with Kurt. When I heard from Markus, he seemed to suggest you'd had a breakdown over an unhappy affair—of course I didn't care what the reason was—I just told him you'd be welcome."

"I don't know why he didn't tell you everything," Anna said, taking Karla's hand. "I'm not sure I even know where to begin."

"You did have an unhappy affair, yes?"

"I got pregnant, Karla. I had a baby, a daughter."

"Oh, my poor Anna. What happened?"

"Father sent me to Wildbad with a woman he said was a nurse. She was a monster . . ." Anna felt the tears coming to her eyes, and she fought them back, even though she knew the moment she began to talk about it her voice began to quiver. "It's hard for me, Karla, even though it's been a few months."

Karla hugged her tightly. "I understand, go on."

"She kept me a prisoner . . . I suppose she kept your letters from me and didn't mail mine to you. I had the baby and she stole it, Karla. My father told her to . . . he gave my child to someone . . . I don't know who, I may never know where she is or who takes care of her . . ." Anna's voice drifted off and she stared out into the crowd, not seeing them or hearing them.

"Oh, Anna, how cruel your father has been. How could Gisela let this happen?"

"Mother has no strength to fight him. He sent her away in any case. He sent her to Vienna."

"Naturally, no one else would cross him."

"Markus was the only one who would even see me. He helped me to try to find the baby, but it was no use. Even the lawyers said it was no use. He thought I should come here. He promised to keep looking, to let me know if he found out anything.''

"Oh, Anna, I wish I'd been there. I wish I'd been able to help you.''

"Helga—the woman my father sent me away with—I couldn't fight her, Karla. She really kept me a prisoner.''

"And this man—the father of your child—he wouldn't help you either?''

"No. He's totally unlike Father, yet like him in some way.'' Anna looked into Karla's clear eyes. "I'm not a chattel, Karla. I never want to feel as if I belong to a man again . . . I mean belong in the sense of ownership. Karla, I want to finish law school and I want to fight for women . . . I have to fight. It's a promise I made to my little daughter. I will do it.''

Karla pressed her own lips together and willed herself not to cry, though she too was on the verge of tears. Impulsively she hugged Anna again; it was only partly a sympathetic hug. The other part was pride, pride that Anna had survived and was stronger. "You're not beaten, Anna. We'll get you a job and you'll live with us till you save some money and pass your examinations. I know you can do it. Listen, Crystal Eastman is a friend of mine. I've been staying with her here in New York. You'll meet her tonight. She went to Columbia Law School.''

"How can I talk with anyone? My English is still terrible.''

Karla smiled. "You're just shy. Crystal will understand your questions and you'll understand her answers. You've no need to worry. After a year of night school, you'll talk like a native American and you'll be able to sit the examinations for law school.''

Anna forced a smile. "You make it sound easy.''

"It won't be easy, but I know you'll succeed, Anna.''

"Anna! Anna!''

Anna looked up and saw Uda making her way through the crowd. "Over here!'' she called out.

"Thank goodness! I was so afraid you'd leave without me! God, I thought they'd never let me through. That place is like a prison, all those pens filled with people.''

Anna smiled and hugged Uda. "I told you we'd wait. Uda, this is my aunt, Karla Baer."

"Uda Gersdorf. I'm pleased to meet you and very glad you're going to Milwaukee."

"I'm afraid our train doesn't leave for two days, Uda. We'll be staying with friends here. There's plenty of room for you too."

"That's very kind," Uda said. "I could sleep on the floor if necessary—I don't mind."

"Oh, that won't be necessary. Come along, then, let's take the subway, since you two have so little luggage."

Uda picked up her bag and the three of them fell into step as they headed for the subway entrance. Uda walked next to Anna, and once they were standing on the platform waiting for the train, she nudged Anna's arm. "I thought you told me that man you met on the ship—the one you pointed out—was American," Uda said.

"You mean Mr. Parnell?"

"Yes, that one. He's not American. He was standing in the line with the rest of us. In fact, I learned he's Irish, never been in America before in his whole life."

Anna frowned. "I can't imagine why he lied to me."

"To get to know you, I expect. And he wasn't in first class either. He was in third class, just like us."

Anna shook her head and said nothing, although she felt strangely betrayed. He had seemed so genuine and so open . . . he had seemed to have a boyish honesty.

"Is something wrong?" Karla asked.

"I think I have very bad taste in men," Anna replied.

Karla squeezed her arm. "You're too young to feel such bitterness."

Anna didn't answer because with a cold whish of wind from the tunnel, the train shot forward and came to a halt by the platform. Karla led the way, and as if they'd climbed into a bullet, the train jolted and then suddenly sped forward, hurtling itself into the darkness.

They emerged from the netherworld of the subway into a delightful cityscape of tree-lined streets, parks, and gracious houses.

"It seems very European," Uda said softly. "Not at all what I expected."

Karla walked between them. "That's because this is New York, and New York is not typical of America—perhaps more so here because we're on Manhattan and Manhattan's an island." She smiled and turned toward Uda. "I promise you won't be disappointed in Milwaukee. It's a very American city in spite of the fact that over half its population is from somewhere else."

They crossed a busy triangular intersection and Karla steered them down a wide street. Anna looked at the street sign. "Greenwich Avenue," she said hesitantly.

"Pronounced *Gren*-itch." Karla smiled. "As in Greenwich time."

"It's a pretty neighborhood," Anna commented.

"There's a university nearby, and lots of writers and artists live here. It's rather like the area around the Nollendorfplatz in Berlin."

They stopped in front of a three-story brownstone. "This is it," Karla said, leading the way up the steps.

Before they reached the top of the stairs, a beautiful blond woman flung the door open. "I saw you coming," she said gaily. "Come in, come in . . . here, let me take those suitcases. We'll just put them here for now. We're all in the other room, come along in and meet everyone."

Karla leaned over and kissed the blond woman's cheek. "This is Crystal, she's irrepressible—the most enthusiastic woman in all of New York."

Crystal laughed. "And sometimes irresponsible," she said flippantly. "Well, you must be Anna, about whom I've heard so much, I feel I already know you."

Anna smiled. "This is Uda, I met her on the ship. She's traveling with us to Milwaukee."

"This is too much of an imposition," Uda said, looking embarrassed.

"Oh, what nonsense! We have lots of room, and one more young woman is no imposition at all. So, Anna, you will study the law, is that right?"

"I hope I will. First I have to improve my English."

"You sound fine to me," Crystal said. She took their coats and left their bags by the staircase. Then she took them by the hand and led them down the narrow hall of the town house and into a large room. Surprisingly, it was full of people of all ages and there was food sitting on every available surface, and everyone seemed to be drinking coffee, tea, wine, or whiskey. They were talking intently in small groups, some whispered, some shouted.

Anna glanced around the room. It was high-ceilinged and comfortably furnished. There were original sketches on the walls and books everywhere. "God, this will be a chore," Crystal said. "It's at times like this that I get mad when Max isn't here. He's so much better at names than I am . . . not that names always matter. You'll just have to join right in, you know. Force yourself into one of the conversations . . . and don't be shy. Nobody here is shy, and almost everyone has an accent. Let's see . . . that's Alex Webber—he's a famous lawyer from Chicago, rather well-known for his wonderfully liberal sentiments, and as a result, his spirited defense of first-amendment cases . . . you'll be particularly interested in him, Anna. And that's Gene . . . he drinks too much, swears too much, and is far too withdrawn for me. He's a serious . . . very serious playwright. And those two over there write for my brother's paper."

Karla leaned over. "Josef sometimes reprints articles from Max's paper, that's how we met."

Anna nodded, feeling somewhat assaulted by all the new faces and the barrage of information. She glanced at Uda and could clearly see that poor Uda was completely terrified of the possibility of even trying to speak English with such obviously formidable intellectuals.

"I think I'd like to go upstairs," Uda said almost pleadingly.

"Perhaps I should rinse my face and comb my hair," Anna remembered agreeing. Crystal had shown them where to go and Uda had remained upstairs, but Anna had returned to the gathering. It was, as she recalled, one of the most stimulating and exciting nights of her life. Karla had taken her right into her world and it was a wonderful world filled with men and women of ideas and convictions. But that first night had not been her last. Karla and Josef's home in Milwaukee was like the Eastmans' in New York. Intellectuals flocked there, and there was always conversation and music, talk of writing and of equality and justice.

"Anna?" Uda jostled Anna's arm. "You're lost in thought." Uda looked at Anna carefully; Anna did have a habit of drifting off—Uda called it mind travel.

"I was just remembering our first day in America," Anna replied.

"I wonder if our memories are exactly the same," Uda said. But somehow she knew they were not. She had been shy and frightened; Anna had been bold and excited and had talked half the night.

They walked to their places on the assembly line in the bottling section of the brewery. "Anna, Oskar has a friend he wants you to meet. There's a dance on Saturday, will you come?"

"I was going to study," Anna answered hesitantly.

"Please. I think you need to get out. You're either working or studying. And it's you who are always saying we Germans don't know how to enjoy ourselves . . . that we all work too hard. Well, you work too hard."

Anna smiled. "You make it impossible for me to refuse."

"Is that a yes, then?"

Anna nodded. "It's a yes," she confirmed.

In spite of its beer gardens, its breweries, and its waterways, Milwaukee was not at all like a German city. It was large, but somehow it seemed like a small town, a city of neighborhoods, a place were people readily greeted one another and friends were quickly made.

The neighborhoods were partly a result of the way in which the city had been settled. Long ago, the Indians had lived beside the tamarack swampland and called the area Mahn-a-wau-kee Seep, which meant "gathering place of the rivers." The city's rivers, the Menominee, the Kinnikinnic, and the Milwaukee, divided the city into three areas, and those areas sprang up as rival settlements. One came to be called Walker's Point, one Juneautown, and the third Kilbourntown for one Byron Kilbourn, a surveyor and canal builder. As the immigrants began to arrive, the various areas of the city were taken over by different groups. New Englanders settled on the high ground near Juneautown, and indeed, the highest hill in the area was called Yankee Hill. Most of the German immigrants settled in Kilbourntown and soon they renamed it Gartenstadt, or Garden City. The Poles lived on the South Side in row houses called "Polish flats," and the Irish lived near Grand Avenue, while the Italians lived below Canal Street down on the shores of Lake Michigan.

Anna lived with Karla and Josef. Their home was in the heart of Gartendstadt, on Washington Avenue. It was a comfortable two-story house with a veranda and a backyard garden. Downstairs there were a living room, a dining room, a kitchen, a small library, and the study that Karla had created from a pantry near the kitchen. Upstairs there were three bedrooms. Karla and Josef slept in one, Anna slept in one, and the third was for guests.

Anna brushed her hair and stared at her image in the mirror. There was no question about it, her experience with Kurt had caused her to avoid relationships with men. But her studied lack of interest, her fear of involvement, was hard for her friends to understand. And yet in the silence of her room, in the darkness, she admitted she missed a close relationship. Those three short months with Kurt had awakened her sexually and emotionally, and left her longing to be loved. Abstractedly she hugged herself and closed her eyes, remembering how it had felt to be held, kissed, and caressed . . . but as she remembered, she censored out Kurt's face in her thoughts and thought only of the sensations she remembered.

"Anna!" Karla's voice from downstairs caused Anna to jump. She glanced away from the mirror to look at the clock on the bedside table. She stood up and pulled on her dress. Karla's voice again called out from the hall, "Uda's here . . . Anna?"

"I'm coming," Anna called back. She slipped into her shoes and looked once again in the mirror before opening her door and heading downstairs. Perhaps, she thought, I should not have agreed to go out tonight. But no . . . she had been at home too much and everyone said she studied far too hard. Anna smiled as she reached the bottom of the stairs. "Good evening."

Uda was dressed in a flowered print skirt, plain blouse, and flat shoes for dancing. Her dark hair was pulled back and held by a red ribbon. Oskar stood proudly next to her. He looked a trifle stiff in his tight jacket, starched shirt, and high collar. He was smiling and had a personality as pleasant as Uda's, but he was also somewhat unusual-looking. He had dark brows and thinning light hair. The result of his conflicting coloring was that he often looked cross when he was not.

Next to Uda and Oskar stood a tall good-looking young man. He was younger than Oskar, Anna decided, and certainly he was much more attractive. He held a bouquet of daisies in his large hand, and he looked at her for a single long moment and then looked away a little shyly.

Oskar stepped forward. "Anna, I would like to present my friend Bernard Wittke."

Anna smiled. "I am pleased to meet you."

"Bernard, I would like to introduce you to Anna von Bock."

Bernard bowed. "I've looked forward to meeting you."

"I've dropped the 'von' since coming to America," Anna reminded Oskar, whose class-consciousness would not let him forget her origins. "It's too affected."

"And betrays her aristocratic heritage," Karla said as she stood in the doorway. "A 'von' is most inappropriate to someone as egalitarian and socially conscious as Anna."

Bernard glanced at Karla and then at Anna and then back at Karla. "Is she really an aristocrat?" he asked.

Anna laughed lightly. "Pay no attention to my aunt. She likes teasing me."

"I know the name von Bock . . . a general, yes, that's it. There was a general by that name."

"My father," Anna said. "But we're estranged. I'm afraid I've never lived up to the von Bock name . . . at least not by my father's standards."

Bernard frowned. "I can't imagine that," he said, looking at her and sounding truly genuine. So far, he thought, he'd managed to sound all right, but the truth was, he feared he'd become tongue-tied at any moment. Karla Baer was known throughout the German community. She was witty, intelligent, generous, and her husband owned a newspaper. And Anna, whom he'd just met, was delicate and beautiful and her voice was low and sensual, a deep throaty voice for a girl who looked so utterly doll-like.

"We should be going," Uda suggested.

"Have a good time," Karla called as she returned to her study.

Bernard took Anna's arm as they walked down the steps. "You're from Berlin," he said, trying to make small talk.

"Yes, I confess, I'm from Berlin."

"I'm afraid I'm from a farm . . . in fact, I'm a poor farmer's son. I've never been to Berlin. I think I'll bore you because I am what they call in America 'a country bumpkin.' "

"Don't let him fool you, Anna," Oskar said as he turned around and walked backward. "Bernard's smart. He's young and already he's a floor manager at the tool-and-dye factory. He goes to night school too. His English is good, better than mine, and I've lived here longer."

"Stop selling me, Oskar," Bernard called back. "I shall have to make her like me on my own."

It was still light, and Anna blushed slightly. To her surprise, she did like this Bernard, even if, compared with Karla's friends, he seemed unsophisticated.

"I doubt a Berliner can polka," he said teasingly. "It's a farmers' dance."

"I'm afraid you're right. I don't know how to polka. But then, I don't know how to dance at all."

"A deprived Berliner!" he said gleefully, suddenly feeling a spark of confidence. "Well, you shall have to learn to polka, Anna Bock. In fact, I think you shall have to learn to enjoy yourself."

Anna sat on the living-room sofa and looked out the window. It was five-thirty on Saturday afternoon and clouds had filled the sky over the city. A summer storm,

Anna thought. And she thought briefly that she was glad that the Fourth of July had been last weekend. She had gone to a picnic with Bernard, Uda, and Oskar and they'd had a marvelous time boating on the lake.

After a few minutes Anna picked up the newspaper and began reading it. Her eyes came to rest on a particular item. There was an arresting picture of a poorly clad young girl surrounded by three grubby children. The heading on the story read, "Twelve-Year-Old Sold." The story itself dealt with a poor white girl in Mississippi who had been sold into marriage by her father at the age of twelve. Now, only fourteen, she had two children of her own and two of her husband's children by a previous marriage. As if this situation were not shocking enough, the story went on to reveal the fact that many "poor" white girls in the South were sold into marriage by their parents, although, the reporter added, the practice was far more common "among coloreds." Anna clenched her hand in anger as she looked at the girl's picture. Even given the poor quality of reproduction on newsprint, she could see the girl looked much older than her chronological age, and terribly weary. Yes, anger and sadness were the two emotions evoked by the text and picture.

Anna closed the paper and let it drop to her lap, but she continued to think about the injustices done to women in certain states.

"It's going to rain," Karla said as she walked into the room. "We might even have an electrical storm."

Anna looked up. "I hope not."

"You're looking very pensive," Karla noted.

"I was just reading the paper."

"Are you going out with Bernard tonight?" Karla smiled and thought that she herself found Bernard a nice person and certainly Anna must also find him attractive. They had now been out four times, and each time they seemed to grow more at ease with one another.

"Yes." Anna looked down, then slowly lifted her eyes to meet her aunt's questioning look. "I like Bernard a lot," she said softly. "He's very intelligent and kind."

"He's a good man, Anna. And I think he's truly fond of you."

Anna leaned back and closed her eyes. "I have such mixed feelings, Karla. I'm fond of him too, but I want something more than marriage. I want to be successful in my own right. I want—no, I need—the independence of a career and . . ." Her voice trailed off and she looked down, moving her finger in small circles on the arm of the chair.

Karla watched Anna's expression and the way in which she moved her fingers. How difficult it was to be young! How terrible to be torn between sexual desire and intellectual fulfillment. And to the young it always seemed a choice. There was no way she could assure Anna that if she had patience she could have both.

"I want to be a lawyer—I want to work for legal reforms so other women don't suffer the loss of a child as I have," Anna continued. "Fathers, husbands, brothers—they shouldn't have the right to own women and children, Karla. It's unjust. I know it's not as bad here as it is in Germany, but I see laws that make women and children little more than chattels. Did you read this?" Anna handed her the paper and tapped the story with her finger.

"Yes, I read it. You're right, there are unlimited challenges. We won't soon run of out laws to change." Karla smiled and sat down next to Anna on the sofa. "Have you finished your applications to those five law schools?"

"Yes, I have one more and then I'll mail them."

Karla looked at Anna, and as she often did, she felt a surge of pride. "I couldn't love you more, Anna, if you were my own daughter. You're like my father, your grandfather. He was such a wonderful man. I'm sorry you never knew him."

"I am too," Anna said, looking into her aunt's face.

"You're intelligent enough to succeed. It's natural to be confused, to want marriage and a home and children . . . to want a good man like Bernard. You'll have to make up your own mind, Anna. But don't fight yourself so much. You're still young and now you're struggling with the temptations of youth." Karla took a deep breath. "One day, I hope you will find a man you can work with—a man who shares your desires to change things, to make a difference.''

The clock in the hall struck the hour of six.

''Bernard will be here soon. I have to get dressed now.''

Karla watched Anna as she climbed the staircase. Vaguely she wondered how close Anna and Bernard were really growing.

Anna sat in her room and thought about the evening before. Last night Josef and Karla had entertained a writer from California, two social workers from St. Louis, and the mayor of Milwaukee. It seemed as if there were always guests in the house on Washington Avenue. How fortunate I am to live here, Anna thought. It was a stimulating atmosphere. German-Americans of prominence came to visit Josef and Karla, journalists came to discuss articles that had appeared in Josef's paper, and because it was a socialist paper, socialists of note came to visit. Many were Germans, but others, like the Eastmans, whom Anna had met in New York, were from old New England families, families whose socialist leanings could be traced back to the Transcendentalists—the group of reformers who combined social thought with philosophy and whose ideas heralded the founding of Unitarianism. Anna had learned that the *Dial* was their publication and that Brook Farm had been their Utopian experiment in socialist communal living. Many great American writers had been a part of that movement, among them Emerson, Thoreau, Alcott, and Channing.

Anna tried to read those American writers as well as the essays in various publications. She found herself not just listening to discussions, but taking part in them. She knew the more she read and talked, the better her English got, but as important as her mastery of the language, she had formed her own views on many issues, and she felt secure in them.

But months of hard work had left her restless in a way she wasn't certain she understood, and she admitted she felt moody as well.

Anna put down her book of Emerson's essays and

looked around her room. It was not a large room, but it was homey and comfortable. The windows were covered with white sheer curtains, while flowered blue chintz draperies hung on either side and could be pulled over the window too. The twin bed was covered in the same blue chintz material. The walls were stark white, and she had a chest of drawers and a dressing table. Unlike bedrooms in Europe, bedrooms in America had closets built in so that valuable wall space need not be taken up with massive wardrobes. Anna looked at her dressing table. In its center was her precious music box. She lifted it up and wound it up. It played "The Blue Danube" and she closed her eyes and listened to it . . . yes, she loved America, and she loved this house, but in spite of everything there was a certain homesickness, a longing for the familiar, and now and again it overcame her, and she let her mind stray to Berlin and its lovely parks and stately buildings.

"May I come in?" Anna looked up at the sound of Karla's husky voice.

"Of course," Anna called back, and she looked up as Karla slipped into her room and sat down on the edge of the bed.

Karla listened as the music box wound down. "Homesick?" she asked, guessing Anna's mood.

"Perhaps a little . . . I love it here, you know that."

"It's natural. As much as I wanted to be here, as much as I loved Josef, I missed Berlin . . . I still do sometimes."

Anna shrugged and extended her arms as if in bewilderment. "I don't know why I feel this way. I haven't that many pleasant memories." She looked at Karla seriously, and then, out of the blue, "Was what I did so awful, Karla?"

Karla shook her head slowly and wondered if she should tell Anna about her mother . . . yes, it would help erase her guilt. It would help her to see things more clearly. "There's something I should have told you. I want to tell you now," Karla said carefully.

"Yes?"

"I was doubly angered by what your father did to you
. . . both your parents behaved like hypocrites."

"I don't understand."

"Oh, Anna. Your mother was pregnant with Andreas
before your father married her. If she hadn't been such
a beauty, he wouldn't have married her . . . he would
have left her and married a woman his family picked out.
We Gruns weren't aristocracy, you know . . . only the
von Bocks were aristocracy. Your father hated my father.
He hated intellectuals."

"Mother was pregnant before she married!" Anna ex-
claimed, an incredulous tone in her voice. For a moment
she couldn't say anything as she considered Karla's revelation. It seemed preposterous to her . . . no, mon-
strous, that her parents had treated her as they had. "They
told me *I* was immoral," Anna said, still shaking her
head with disbelief.

"Nonsense! Besides, it's their fault. They didn't prepare you for a person like Kurt . . . nor did I. I should
have, and I should have told you this sooner, but I wanted
you to heal a little first."

"I know you always cared about me, Karla. But you
couldn't have saved me from the experience I had with
Kurt. When you left, I was too young to have understood
about such men."

"Well, Anna, Kurt was not the first man to use politics
to seduce a woman. Nor was he the first man to be in-
sincere while hiding behind some ideology. He won't be
the last, either, so be warned."

"Bernard isn't like that."

Karla nodded. "No, Bernard is a real temptation simply because he *is* genuine."

"I'm very attracted to him," Anna admitted.

"And why not? Lovemaking is pleasurable . . . Anna,
what matters is not whether you and Bernard make love
. . . what matters is that you don't hurt one another."

"I don't want to hurt him."

"Anna, the person who cares the least is the one with
the power to hurt. Just be honest with Bernard."

Anna kissed Karla on the cheek. "You *are* my best
friend," she said. Then, smiling, "It's time I left."

"Meeting Bernard?"

"Yes. We're going to a film."

"Run along . . . be careful."

Anna got up and slipped on her sweater. She walked down the stairs. Yes, "careful" was the right word. And yet something in her cried out to be reckless, or at least a little reckless. There were too many memories, too much longing to be held, to be kissed, to be loved. She was filled with desire and she wasn't sure it shouldn't be satisfied.

A huge yellow moon hung in the sky like a shining giant unsculptured pumpkin. Anna and Bernard walked along the rim of the lake in the park.

"It's our anniversary, we first went out together on June 29, and tonight is the twenty-ninth of July," Bernard said slowly. "Anna, I think you know I really care for you, and I would like you to consider our relationship more seriously."

Anna stopped walking and turned to face him. "Oh, Bernard, I'm flattered, I really am. I care for you too, but it's too soon, much too soon."

"Does that mean there's hope?" He looked down at her and slipped his arm around her slender waist.

Anna opened her mouth to speak, then slowly closed it. It wasn't fair to lead him on. She had to be absolutely honest. "I'm not sure how to answer you," she said slowly. "For one thing, there are many things you don't know about me, Bernard."

"I know you're beautiful and intelligent. I know you're thoughtful and kind and honest and care about other people. What more do I need to know?"

"You need to know I'm not the person you think you see."

Anna paused, wondering if she could trust him enough to tell him the whole truth. Then, looking into his soft questioning eyes, she decided she could.

When she finished, Bernard looked at her for a long moment; then he reached out and touched her gently, running the back of his hand across her cheek. "Your honesty doesn't make me respect you less, Anna. I can see the pain in your eyes. I know you love your child . . . tell me about the father, Anna. Do you still love him?''

''He was a tutor at the university. He deceived me . . . though perhaps I wanted to be deceived. I was naive, very naive. And no, I don't still love him.''

''You can't punish yourself for such a relationship . . . it makes no difference to me, Anna. It changes nothing.''

Anna stared into Bernard's dark eyes. His huge hand caressed her cheek gently and then touched her neck lightly. He bent down and with an unusual gentleness kissed her tenderly first on the cheek, then on the neck, and finally he sought her lips, moving his against hers in small birdlike pecks of growing intensity. His arm around her waist was warm and exciting. Anna returned his kisses, closing her eyes and thinking that he was a good man, a kind man, and he was appealing.

''I think I love you,'' Bernard said, his breath coming in short gasps now. His big hands moved across her back and he seemed to rock her in his arms as he pressed her hard against him. Anna felt like a leaf clinging to a tree in the autumn wind. She could feel him against her, and she still remembered what it felt like to have a man touching you, arousing you, teasing you gently into a delirious fever of lovemaking.

His cheeks seemed hot to her touch, and Anna shivered with yearning, as once again Bernard kissed her neck, then her ears. He breathed deeply. ''I know you aren't a virgin, Anna. But I must stop, I respect you too much . . .'' He put his hands on her shoulders and stood still, looking at her now as he held her away from him.

Anna's eyes filled with tears. ''I'm sorry. I should have stopped you myself. I . . . I do like you, Bernard, I truly do.''

''I know you like me.''

''Oh, Bernard, it's not you, it's me.''

''But you responded to me.''

''I'm human. I have the needs all women have, the needs men have too.''

He inhaled deeply. ''Are you saying you would sleep with me, but you wouldn't marry me?''

"I don't know what I'm saying. If that were what I meant, would that shock you?"

His face knit into a deep frown. "I'm not sure . . . I don't know why it should be different for women than it is for men. No, I think I would still respect you. You're different. Anna, different from other women I've known." He looked at her steadily, and knew she wanted him physically. He wanted her too, but he wasn't certain he could let her go easily.

"Do you want to sleep with me?" she asked, surprised by her own question. The night was bright enough that she could see him actually blush. He looked down at the grass and nodded. "I would be a fool and a liar if I said no."

Anna sucked in her breath. Damn all the conventions in the world! Damn people like her parents! "I've applied to a law school in Chicago," she said slowly. "If I'm admitted, I'll move there."

"I want you," he said, kissing her again. "For however short a time, Anna. I want you."

"I'll go to bed with you if you want, but I won't change my plans. I can't."

He looked at her steadily and again touched her cheek. "If not for a lifetime, for as long as I can have you, even if it's only till you move to Chicago." He said it because he wanted her so terribly, but even as he spoke the words, he wasn't sure he was being honest with himself.

It was the first Saturday in August, and it was warm and the night air was filled with sounds of crickets.

Bernard lived in a small two-room flat above a bakery on Chestnut Street. It was a pleasant flat and rather nice, Anna thought, because it always smelled of freshly baked bread. It was furnished sparsely, but what furniture there was, was comfortable. Anna stood by the window in her snow-white camisole and looked out on the darkened houses, their rooftops illuminated by the stars and the silver sliver of the new moon.

She heard Bernard come across the room and she felt the warmth of his body as he stood close behind her and wrapped her in his arms, pulling her to him. He held her for a long while before he kissed the back of her neck and covered her small high breasts with his great hands. Then for a long time he simply held her tightly to him.

His lengthy embrace was special and it was as if they communicated silently while their bodies stood motionless against one another. Then Bernard ran his hands from her breasts down over her stomach; he touched her intimately and then spun her around to face him. He kissed her neck and her cleavage again and again and she could hear his growing excitement in his breathing and feel it in the heat of his body. Her own body grew heated with anticipation . . . with the memory of past sensations. He lifted her easily and carried her to the bed and stood looking down on her intently while he disrobed.

"You're small and perfect," he said, looking at her, "so beautiful, Anna. You are so beautiful." He lay down next to her and ever so gently caressed her breasts, her inner thighs, and her ears. He moved his hands over her slowly, arousing her to a fever pitch, a desire that while it did not surpass her past experiences, equaled them. He was a deliberate lover, a man sensitive to her needs, a man who enjoyed watching her pleasure.

He slipped down in the bed and kissed her thighs, touching her lightly again and again till she thought she would scream with pent-up passion. He touched her breasts and lightly pinched her nipples, kissing them and finally teasing them till she wriggled against him and pulled him across her. Anna closed her eyes and moved with him . . . it was wild and wonderful to feel this completeness again . . . it was breathtaking, and she shivered as she felt her body tensing for that most pleasurable of all releases. She shuddered against him and felt him shake against her. "I do love you, Anna . . . I do love you," he whispered, and pulled her still-trembling body tightly into his arms. Anna lay silently, her thoughts jumbled, her desires warring.

"It was just like that first night," he said after a while. "Each time I make love to you, I enjoy it more."

Anna didn't answer, but only lay against him, wondering if she should tell him about the letter she had received today—wondering if it would make him happy or sad.

"You're silent," he whispered. "Is something wrong?"

Anna shook her head. "No," she murmured. Then, "I got a letter today, Bernard."

"From your former lover?"

She almost smiled. "Oh, no. From the law school in Chicago."

"You've been accepted?" he asked.

"Not this year, but next year. A year from now I'll leave for Chicago."

"A year—a lot can happen in a year."

Anna nodded. "Yes," she replied, thinking of the last year. "Many things can change."

II

Temptations
1915–1922

8

The belching steam engine jerked the train forward, not once, but several times. Then the abrupt lurches were reversed as additional cars were coupled, making the train even longer. Then, the mating process complete, the train crept out of the Milwaukee station, then edged along a narrow track through a tunnel of factories before it passed rows of houses that were adjacent to the tracks. Gradually the houses grew further apart and the nearby road narrowed and then turned into a dirt lane. Soon the countryside was broken only by lone farmhouses which stood majestically on knolls overlooking green pastures neatly marked off by white fences. Overhead, a giant crow soared, then glided, its keen eyes no doubt seeking tiny rodents in the grass. From above, Anna thought, the land must have looked like a great game board composed of varying shades of green squares with white borders. The players, in their squares, were the farmhouses, the well-cared-for barns, and the tall straight silos that adjoined them.

Normally it would take the train two hours to travel the ninety-odd miles between Milwaukee and Chicago. But this train was not the express; this was what everyone called "the milk train," and it stopped at Franklin, Wind Point, Racine, Kenosha, Zion, Waukegan, Evanston, and finally crawled into Chicago some four hours after leaving Milwaukee.

The trip was, on the whole, a panorama of pastoral scenery, broke only by occasional glimpses of Lake Michigan. Isolated farms could be seen from the right side of the train and the low sloping hills that led to the shores of the lake could be seen on the left. Anna leaned back in her window seat and looked out. This country-side south of Milwaukee was hilly and green and was called the dairy capital of America. Its neat white farm-houses looked scrubbed clean and seemed to belong more to northern Europe than to America. But that was largely because the people who lived in them—Scandinavians, Swiss, Cornish, and German immigrants—clung to their heritage and lived as they might have lived, or, more accurately, have liked to live, in their country of origin. But in the countries they had come from, land ownership was a dream for most, while here in America it was a cherished reality.

In the north of Wisconsin the scenery was quite differ-ent. There it was densely forested, and there were clear, blue, rock-bottom lakes everywhere—"A lake for every person in the state," Bernard once joked, "and there are even more in Minnesota."

The train chugged into Racine, stopping by a long out-door platform, exhaled steam and sagged to rest as if it had exerted itself. Anna closed her eyes . . . saying good-bye to Bernard had been difficult, more difficult than she had imagined.

They had gone out together often, or, as Uda said, "they'd kept company."

Keeping company consisted of going to dances, at-tending picnics, and sometimes going to a concert or to the theater. Anna fought to keep their relationship from becoming serious, though she really admitted she liked Bernard and enjoyed talking with him.

"I did not lead him on," Anna whispered to herself. "As soon as I get into law school, I'll be leaving"—she had told him that again and again. "I was so sure you understood," Anna again murmured under her breath, but apparently he hadn't, she thought. And because he hadn't, their parting had been difficult.

"I can't believe you're really leaving Milwaukee," Bernard had said, looking into her eyes.

"I have to leave. I'm fortunate to have been accepted, and more fortunate that I've been accepted by a school in Chicago because I have a contact—a lawyer who may give me a part-time job that will help me to pay for my education.''

''Don't you care for me at all?'' he had asked. Unconsciously, Anna shook her head. Had he not listened to her? Had he thought she wasn't serious?

''Of course I care for you,'' she had answered. And before she had the chance to say ''You're my friend,'' he had said, ''Then change your mind and marry me. I love you, Anna . . . I could go to Chicago too, I could find work there, and you could still go to school. We don't have to be separated this way.''

His words were as clear now as they had been last night. Recalling them made her move uncomfortably in her seat. But I didn't lead him on, she reminded herself. But the reminder was small comfort. The fact was that he had grown to love her, and his love was honest and good. She, on the other hand, had taken great pleasure in their friendship, but known from the beginning that there was little else. And yet I let him love me, she thought unhappily as she recalled Karla's warning: ''the one who cares the least is the one with power to hurt.''

She remembered the pain in his eyes when she had shaken her head. ''No, I must go alone. I made myself clear from the beginning, Bernard. I have a goal, and I must fulfill it.''

''I'll never see you again,'' he whispered. ''Tomorrow you'll leave and I know I'll never see you.''

She had turned slightly away from him. ''It's not far to Chicago. I'll be coming back here to see Karla and Josef . . . you could visit.''

''I want you to marry me, to have my children,'' he had pleaded.

''I can't,'' she had answered, knowing now that she should have broken it off months ago, that she had let it go on too long.

''If you change your mind, Anna, I'll be here.''

''Don't wait for me, Bernard. You must find someone else, someone who can give you what you want.''

He had taken her suddenly into his arms and kissed her passionately, then whispered, ''I love you.''

She broke free of his embrace and fought not to cry,

though if she had cried, it would have only been because
she felt she'd hurt him. "I have to go now," she said,
allowing her hands to slip away from his.

"Will you write?" he had asked anxiously as she
picked up her white knit shawl from the bench.

"Yes, I'll write," she promised, but wondered if she
would, indeed, if she should. She had turned then and
tried hard to smile. She blew him a kiss and hurried
away.

Anna had not slept well. She wasn't certain if that was
because she had said good-bye to Bernard and now had
uneasy, somewhat guilty thoughts about him, or because
she was leaving to fulfill her dream and was filled with
excitement. The latter seemed the case, since in spite of
not having slept well, she was still very much awake and
filled with nervous energy.

She was going to live in Jane Addams' Hull House, a
settlement house primarily for immigrant women and
children. And she had a part-time job in the law firm of
Webber, Wyatt, and Prentice. Alex Webber, the famed
attorney, also taught at the law school. She had met him
her first day in America at the home of Crystal Eastman.

The train jerked forward and Anna opened her eyes.
In a short time she would be alighting on the crowded
platform of Deerborn station in Chicago. Chicago was a
much larger city than Milwaukee, a strange city which
she had passed through only once, on her way to Milwaukee from New York City. A chill of anticipation ran
through her. She'd been reading and studying lawbooks
almost since the day she came to America. Now, she
thought, she was really on the threshold of a career in
the law; it was the beginning of a whole new life.

The cluster of buildings that made up the Hull House
settlement was located at 800 Halstead Street, on the
corner where Halstead joined Polk. They were not lavish
buildings, but were instead sturdy and utilitarian; three
five-story brick buildings with gables and smoke-stained
chimneys. From the outside Hull House was almost indistinguishable from the flats and warehouses of the area,
an area populated by working-class immigrants. Once a

dreadfully poor neighborhood, the area remained lower class even now, though it was not as desperate a place as it had been when Hull House was established in 1889.

Anna had come to Hull House because Karla had been active in the establishment of the New Settlement House in Milwaukee. Through the settlement-house movement, Karla knew Jane Addams and she knew other women at Hull House as well.

Anna had been taken aback by the size and scope of the activities offered to both its residents and the community. Karla had told her a great deal about Jane Addams, the founder of Hull House, and what Hull House had become, but the reality was even more exciting than her description.

Facilities included a day nursery, a gymnasium, a community kitchen, and naturally, the boarding club for working women and students. Hull House offered college-level courses as well as training in typing, bookbinding, and bookkeeping. There was a theater group, and, if one wished, training in art and music. Here young working women found safety and respectability in communal living, while student social workers acquired training in the neighborhood around the settlement.

"As one of our legal students I hope you can find time to do some volunteer work," Hilda Hemmings suggested. "You'd be following in Jane's own footsteps," Hilda elaborated as she showed Anna around. "You'll meet Jane when she comes back from The Hague. You'll like her, she's full of energy and she always has ideas. You know, she began the reform group for the first juvenile court of law. She was active in obtaining regulations for tenement houses, for establishing an eight-hour working day for women, and she made Chicago pass laws to inspect factories. She fought for workman's compensation too," Hilda added proudly.

Hilda Hemmings was a short, stout, bustling woman with wavy gray-brown hair and intent green eyes. When she talked, she used her hands a great deal, and her facial expressions were animated. Anna wondered how anyone—even Jane Addams—could have more energy than Hilda.

"My aunt is devoted to Jane Addams' ideas, she never stops talking about her."

Hilda smiled. "I'm sorry, I have a tendency to rattle on. Perhaps because it's hard now . . . Jane's a pacifist and there's a lot of criticism concerning her position on the war. Naturally, when I find a sympathetic ear I tend to rattle on."

"But even President Wilson keeps restating our neutrality," Anna responded. She didn't mention the special problems of German-Americans, though she knew they grew more serious daily as Americans angered by the war in Europe vented their anger on those Germans with whom they had contact.

Hilda sighed. "I'm afraid the sinking of the *Lusitania* in May spoke louder than the President's neutrality speech." Hilda forced a smile. "Well, it all just makes it harder to raise funds. And when you have less funds, you have less power. We have to maintain constant vigilance to see that there's no slippage . . . you know, unless we keep at the city officials, they don't inspect the factories. A law on the books is no good, it has to be enforced.

"You'll like living here. We're like a family." Hilda ran her hand along the banister as they descended the stairs of the main residence for women. "A cross between a traditional home and a college dormitory. We've discovered a strength in each other. You're one of the single ones . . . most of the boarders are single," she sighed deeply, "but I'm married . . . it failed; he drank and when he drank he became violent. So I took my children and came here. Now I work and my children stay in the nursery. It's a way to survive, this cooperative living."

Karla and Bernard knew about her child, but Anna had never spoken of Kurt or the baby to whom she had given birth. Yet here she felt entirely comfortable and completely certain that she would be understood. "I had a child in Europe. My father arranged to have her taken away—"

Hilda turned and took Anna's hand. "Oh, my dear, how dreadful . . ."

"It's one of the reasons I want to study and practice law. Such things should not happen, and I know that in certain parts of this country they can happen too."

"We still have many battles to fight—even when we get the vote, it will only be the beginning of our fight."

"Our fight," Anna repeated. For a long while she had thought of it in personal terms, "her" fight. But through Karla and now here, at Hull House, she knew that other women were also joined in the battle for equal justice. Injustice had touched far too many women.

Hilda stopped before the window and with one hand moved the curtain aside so that the street could be seen. It was a grim street, and across from the settlement house, tenements stretched up the road. Their open, barren windows, their bleak sameness, all seemed to scream the word "poverty."

"The women who come here are often young university graduates . . . they say that bringing such unsullied young women to places like this is like casting lilies in the mud. But let me tell you, our muddied lilies leave here angry and armed to fight against child labor and lack of urban sanitation . . . we know how to organize," Hilda said with determination.

Anna felt a surge of solidarity, of pride, pride in being a woman. From now on, her life was going to be full and busy, and she felt truly strong and optimistic. "I like it here," she announced with enthusiasm, and she thought of what Karla often said about life being a grand adventure—this, Anna thought, is the real beginning of *my* grand adventure.

Hilda smiled knowingly. "And you'll like it more every day that you're here."

Alex Webber was stouter than Anna remembered, and his face was square and full and his hair was longish and absolutely straight. Parted on the left side, a thick swath of it was combed down so that it caressed his eyebrow. He was also a rumpled kind of man who, at this moment, wore a frown.

He sat behind a cluttered wooden desk and stared, moving his eyes appraisingly over her. He completed his silent survey with a grunt and then rubbed his chin thoughtfully. "Yes, you're as I remember you. You're small—that's good. It makes you seem vulnerable and that means people won't feel threatened by you."

"It might also mean I lack authority," Anna replied. "I don't think I see the advantage to being physically small."

His frown changed to a wide grin and he nodded his head up and down vigorously. "Good! Your voice is low. Lot of young women have high voices—too shrill for the law. But yours is low and, if I may say so, soothing. Mind you, you'll have to learn how to use it properly."

"I want to study law, not acting."

"And you say what you think. Well, you will study and learn both. Don't underestimate the need for theatrics. As for authority . . . well, that comes from intellect, and I'm told you have intellect to spare."

Anna forced herself to maintain eye contact, though she felt embarrassed by his praise. "I haven't had the chance to demonstrate any intellect yet. Perhaps you had better wait and see for yourself."

"False modesty is unbecoming, even in a woman. I wouldn't have hired you if you hadn't come with good recommendations." He chuckled. "Anyway, I got a peek at the results of your examinations. I am on the board, you know."

"I really don't know what to say."

"Well, then, don't say anything, just dig in. Look, if you really want to learn, you'll learn more here than in school—that's book learning, this is real life, little lady, and it's a far better teacher."

He poured some water from a pitcher on the corner of his desk into a foggy-looking glass and then gulped it down, quickly replacing the glass on the corner of the desk with a slight bang. "It's a hard profession for women, but we need more women in the law." He smiled again. "Used to be a woman lawyer in Kansas—named Mary Elizabeth Lease, an Irish lass she was, and she had a tongue as sharp as a razor and a mind to match. She told Kansas farmers, 'What you farmers need to do is raise less corn and more hell!' Pity, Mary Elizabeth was a member of the WCTU—and I don't hold with them at all. But apart from that little failing, she was quite the gal . . . yes, indeed, she was admitted to the Kansas bar in 1892.'' He looked up at Anna and cocked his dark brows. ''You're not against drink, are you?''

''No,'' she replied. ''Only against excess.''

''Seems reasonable. Well, I remember meeting you in New York, but we didn't talk. So tell me, what do you know about me?''

''I know you became well-known defending the anarchists charged with murder in the Haymarket riots some thirty years ago. I know you're a well-known criminal and labor lawyer . . . and, oh, yes, I know you defended Eugene Debs.''

He nodded as she spoke; then, when she paused, he interrupted. ''So, do you know why I hired you? I mean apart from Crystal Eastman's recommendation?''

''I'm afraid I didn't even know Crystal Eastman had recommended me.''

''Well, she did. But I hired you because you're German.''

Anna felt intrigued. ''We German immigrants aren't very popular these days. Do you mean you hired me as an act of defiance?''

He roared loudly and again scratched his stubbly chin. ''That too! But mostly I hired you because I suddenly seem to have a lot of clients who don't speak much English. I'm one of the lawyers working with the AUAM— the American Union Against Militarism. As you know, Crystal's the executive secretary. We're overwhelmed with attacks on dissent. There may be a war in Europe, but we've got our own war here . . . rights of assembly have and are being denied, rights of speech are being curtailed . . .'' His voice grew deeper and more moving as he spoke, his hand making a sweeping gesture. ''Hysteria! There are idiots who would bury democracy in the name of preserving it!'' He half-jumped out of his chair. ''I know you haven't yet begun your study of the law, but let's see what you do know, little lady. Have you ever heard of Mr. Justice Holmes?''

''Yes, I've heard about him.''

"And what might he have to say about all this banning?"

"He invented the 'clear and present danger' doctrine—that is, he wrote that 'all words not creating a clear and present danger to public order cannot be prohibited nor their authors punished.' Of course, Congress has the right to prevent substantive evils . . . it is, according to court decision, a matter of proximity and degree . . ."

"Very good, very good indeed," Alex Webber said, slapping his knee. "How old are you?"

"I'm twenty-one."

"You look even younger—I suppose you're one of those libertarian young women who go about flouting convention in the name of sexual equality and self-expression."

Anna half-smiled. "I try not to flout," she answered, "and I do live in Hull House."

He laughed. "Well, not much flouting there, I'll wager. Jane Addams is one of my oldest friends, but she can be a bit of a prude. Well, we can discuss liberty and license some other time. First I'm afraid you will have to discover the routine dullness that is, in reality, the stuff of law. I have here a deposition in German and I need an exact translation." He shuffled through the mess on his desk and pulled out a sheaf of papers. "Here," he said, handing them to her. Then, shaking his head, "I've never been very good at routine paperwork. It piles up."

Anna took the papers he gave her and followed Alex Webber into a long narrow room which held a library-style table and a few chairs. The walls on both sides were lined, floor to ceiling, with books . . . huge books. The room smelled of old leather bindings and dust, and while the lamps on the table were bright, the overhead bulbs were dim.

"You'll grow to feel at home in this room," Alex Webber predicted. "In time, you'll know it better than the feathers in your pillow." With that he waved casually and retreated back to his own office.

Kurt Stein huddled in the corner of his prison cell. It was dark and dank save for a square of moonlight that shone through a narrow slit near the top of the outside wall. Moonlight on barren stone. He shivered in spite of the fact that it was August; outside the temperature was warm, and a westerly breeze blew over the city. But it was never warm here in the cells of the military police, he concluded. It was never warm, clean, or dry, and his time here was never-ending.

Still, he was gratified for the bright night and the fact that he could see inside his cell. He looked at his skin. It was dark with dirt from the filthy stone floor of the cell, and it itched because lice multiplied in the thick dark hair on his head, in his pubic hair, and in the one blanket they had given him to cover his body. Yet in spite of his misery with being kept in such a wretched state, he dreaded Wednesdays, when all the male prisoners were herded together in the walled courtyard, stripped naked, and washed down with ice-cold water from gigantic fire hoses. It was painful and horrible and it left him shaking with cold for hours.

Again his eyes scanned the room. It was seven feet wide and nine feet long. There was a crude drain in the middle and a foul-smelling slop bucket in the corner. The door on the cell was steel, and there was a tiny slot in its center. In the morning and at night, the slot was opened and a tray of barely edible gruel was shoved through it to his eager waiting hands.

Forty days . . . yes, forty long days. He'd been arrested exactly forty days ago, and without explanation, he'd been thrown into this cell. Since then no one had come. He hadn't been questioned, he hadn't been charged, and no explanation had been given him. He shuddered, though in truth he was almost beyond panic.

He let his hands drop, then lethargically crawled over to his blanket and seized it, wrapping it about himself gratefully, even though he knew it crawled with the tiny gray bloodsucking parasites he had grown to hate.

Suddenly Kurt grew alert as he heard footsteps in the corridor. It wasn't mealtime; the footsteps were unexpected. He braced himself as he heard them stop outside his door. And then he heard the clinking of heavy keys and he watched wide-eyed and terrified as the door swung open. Were they going to torture him? He clutched the blanket tighter in apprehension.

Beyond his door, a light burned in the corridor. A man stood in the center of his open cell door, a large stout man. It was light in back of the man and dark in front of him. Kurt could not make out the man's features, but he saw the medals on the man's chest glimmer as they caught the moonlight, and he knew the man was an officer of high rank and distinguished service.

"Do you know where you are?" the silhouette in the doorway bellowed. "Answer!"

"In the military prison . . . I'm in the military prison." Kurt squinted at the silhouette. He wasn't the only person associated with the movement to be thrown in jail, but he'd been so careful! He'd never really been involved in anything. In fact, he felt no allegiance to any of them. If this officer wanted, he would name everyone he knew who was involved. Still, he was puzzled as well as frightened. Most of the others who had been arrested had at least been charged and sentenced. At least they knew of what they were accused and what they could expect as punishment. "I'm a patriot," he managed. "I'll give you names!"

"A patriot?" the silhouette thundered. "I haven't accused you of being a communist or even a socialist. As you've just proved, you're not even worthy of those traitorous labels."

Kurt felt his knees weaken. If he wasn't here for political reasons, why was he here?

"You're a prick," the silhouette spat. And the huge silhouette advanced on him and then swiftly kicked him viciously in the side with his heavy leather boot. "It took me a long while to find you. But now you're going to pay."

Kurt gurgled and tumbled onto the floor sideways, clutching himself in pain. Pay? He fought to understand his captor's words, to make sense out of them. This was clearly a personal vendetta. But why had this man been looking for *him* for a long while?

"Get up, you animal!"

Kurt felt salt tears in his eyes. He struggled to his feet

because he was too frightened to do otherwise. "What have I done?" he stuttered.

"You got my daughter pregnant. You almost ruined my political career!"

A fist struck him in the midsection and Kurt's head flopped down as he doubled up and gasped for breath. Still trying to organize the man's words in his addled brain, still trying to make sense of them, he staggered, then fell to his knees.

"Get him out of here! Take him for a long walk by the canal and don't bring him back alive!"

"No!" Kurt screamed, but his tiny cell seemed suddenly full of burly iron-helmeted soldiers. "You can't do this!" But he knew they could. Germany was at war, people disappeared everyday. Especially people who were suspected of political activity.

The soldiers prodded him with bayonets and he moved quickly past the silhouette. The man was a general! General von Bock . . . yes, that was it. Anna's father, he remembered now. Had Anna put her father up to this?

"Move!"

Kurt staggered on and the general remained inside. Kurt did not resist, and if he had, it would have been useless. He found himself securely in the center of some twelve men. The night air seemed cold, ice cold, even though in reality it was quite warm. Kurt realized it was fear, not cold that he felt.

They walked and walked. His feet were bare and he stumbled twice on the uneven stones, only to be roughly pushed on. He wanted to cry.

Then they stopped. They were by the shore of the canal. Its black waters lapped gently on the stone retaining wall; moonlight fell on the center of the canal.

The soldiers moved a little so that he was in their center. He wrapped his arms around his naked torso. Were they going to shoot him and then throw him in the canal?

"Was she good?" one of the soldiers sneered.

Kurt looked at him in near-disbelief. The interrogator appeared to be the one in command, and he smirked, a dirty expression on his fat face.

"Well, was she good?"

Kurt nodded.

"Tell us about it," he said, leering, and then lighting a cigarette.

"I . . . I can't." Then, "Are you going to kill me?"

The one in charge laughed, "Maybe yes, maybe no. Maybe none of us likes our general . . . maybe you can swim away before you're shot. Make it worth our while . . . tell us about our general's daughter."

Kurt looked from one of them to another. Were they serious? Was it a trap to make him say things for which he would be tortured? He was unsure of what to do.

The one in charge clicked his rifle and lifted it, pointing it at Kurt. "Go on, pig, entertain us!"

"She was blond . . . a beautiful virgin. She had little pink-tipped tits and golden fleece . . . she used to crawl on top of me . . . she loved it, she loved being screwed," he blurted out.

They laughed and clapped. "More!"

Kurt felt himself getting excited. It was an absurd scene, but as he talked, he became more excited, and the soldiers laughed. He finished one, then another lurid description of sex with Anna. He invented things and elaborated, he used words he knew they wanted to hear, dirty words.

Then suddenly the one in command fired a shot at the ground by Kurt's foot. "Swim!" he commanded. "Swim all the way out of Germany, you filthy little prick!"

A second fired and Kurt turned and ran for the canal, expecting at any moment to be hit with a bullet. He dived into the black waters and swam underwater till he thought his lungs would burst. When he surfaced, he heard gunfire, and he saw little circles in the water where the bullets hit. But he kept swimming with all his might . . . yes, they were letting him go! Either that or they were the worst shots in the entire German Army. He kept swimming . . . he had to get out of Germany. He had to get away before Anna's father discovered he *was* alive, before he really was tortured and killed.

The classrooms in the Union College of Law were entirely different from the ornate lecture halls of Berlin

University, but then, the Union College of Law had not originally been a palace. From the outside, the college could easily have been an office building, and it was, in fact, indistinguishable from any of the other buildings on Madison Avenue. The students usually met in classrooms so they could receive individualized instruction, but four times a week each class met in a larger hall for a lecture in each of the four areas studied.

Anna knew that in America students were expected to attend every class, partake in class discussions, and complete assignments. Here cases were argued in Moot Court—a mock court in which students argued hypothetical cases for practice. Essentially, the student of law studied four basic kinds of law, adding each year to his knowledge. The four broad areas were torts, criminal, contract, and property law.

An old Latin word, "torts" actually meant "twisted" in modern English. Generally, a tort was any violation of private rights not serious enough to be considered a crime. Libel and slander were torts; so was trespassing. It was a difficult area of the law, but one that was especially important to lawyers concerned with social issues, because cases involving harm done by landlords or employers fell under tort law, if there was no statute that might have prevented the damage.

The new class of students had just had their first lecture in property law, and their professor had left the hall as soon as he had completed his lecture and question period. At this moment, the male students—Anna was the only woman—were gathering up their books and papers and preparing to leave. Some had left already, but others had remained to talk with one another. Many of the male students, Anna noticed, seemed to know each other. She stood up and smoothed out her skirt. Her books were piled on her desk, and she paused to tie on her straw hat. It was September, but the sun was still strong and she had to walk nearly a mile to Alex Webber's law office.

"What's a woman want to study law for?" one of the male students asked. He was tall and thin, with thick glasses, and he scowled at her. There were two more young men behind him; they had all stopped to stare at her. "Hadn't you ought to be home in the kitchen?" another asked, laughing.

Anna felt unsure of exactly how to respond, so she decided to ignore them. She lifted her books and began to push by them. "Excuse me, I have to hurry," she said, ignoring their questions.

"Hey, what kind of accent is that?" the one who had first spoken asked. "You're a kraut aren't you?"

Anna frowned. "I'm from Germany," she replied, attempting to sound dignified.

"A kraut," he repeated with undisguised contempt.

Anna looked from one to another. They looked menacing and she felt uncomfortable.

"Leave her alone," a stronger, deeper voice said from behind her. Anna turned and peered into the familiar face—he looked more mature now, but there was no mistaking Jim Parnell. He grinned at her and held out his arm. "May I escort you?"

"When did you become a kraut lover?" one of the others asked meanly.

"When did you three take up persecuting young ladies?" he retorted. He glared at them and they stepped back.

Anna looked from him to the others, and though she felt able to take care of herself and quite able to rebuff their verbal assaults, she was glad to see him. She considered his offer for only a moment, then moved from behind her desk and took his arm. "I'm going to the law office of Alex Webber."

The others moved away, then without glancing back left the room. Jim Parnell continued to grin at her, and his eyes twinkled.

"I hadn't expected that kind of prejudice from law students," she said, looking after her band of tormentors as they closed the classroom door behind them.

"There's all kinds in law school. We've got the right, the left, and the center. We've also got the good, the bad, the ugly, and now the beautiful."

"I see you're still full of the blarney."

"And I see you've picked up quite a vocabulary."

"I've been living in Milwaukee. My aunt's house is in Germantown, but across the road there's an Irish neighborhood. I do know you're Irish . . . even though you told me you were American."

His facial expression didn't change at all. "So," he said, ignoring her comment, "you're going to Alex Webber's. Do you work there?"

"Yes." He took her arm and guided her away.

Jim Parnell shook his head knowingly. "Webber's is a den of reformers and pacifists. He's against America becoming involved in the war."

"Aren't you?" she asked pointedly.

"Hell, no. I think we should get right into it." He walked her rapidly down the hall and she allowed him to guide her till they were outside and down the steps before she stopped short. "I count myself a reformer. I'm a pacifist and I was born in Germany. I doubt you really want to be seen with me."

He laughed. "On the contrary, I want very much to be seen with you. Do I have to agree with you on absolutely every issue to want to be seen with you?"

She looked into his open face and shook her head slowly. He was a strange man—a puzzle. Still, he had stepped in and defended her a few moments earlier, though she wasn't sure why. And there was the past . . . the fact that he'd been untruthful when they'd first met, and though she'd just brought it up, he had said nothing. She suddenly decided to ask, to clear the air. "When I first met you, you lied to me," she said, looking him in the eyes. "Why did you do that? Why did you tell me you were an American traveling in first class?"

He arched his brow. "I said I was what I thought you wanted me to be. I'd read a lot about America so I knew I could answer your questions. Tell me, would you have been interested in meeting a poor Irishman traveling in steerage?"

"I think so. As it was, you made me feel like a fool. And why didn't you tell me you intended to study law?"

"I'm sorry I made you feel foolish. I only wanted to get to know you. As for studying law, well, I've never been one to confide my dreams to anyone."

It seemed a simple explanation. I'm making mountains out of molehills, she decided.

"Come on, I'll walk with you. You can tell me what you've been doing since you got off the boat. I'll even buy you a cup of coffee. You do drink coffee, don't you?"

Anna couldn't help smiling. "I do," she answered. Then, tilting her head, she looked at him and asked, "I haven't seen you before today. Are you in all my classes?"

"No, I was just sitting in today. I'm a second-year student."

"Is that absolutely the truth?" she asked.

"Absolutely." He grinned. "You can check on it in the registrar's office if you want."

She returned his smile. "I don't think that will be necessary." Then, "Where will you take me for coffee?"

"How about the Piggly Wiggly? It's on the way to Webber's office."

"Good," she answered, and this time she took his arm.

The warm days of September turned gradually cooler. October and the first two weeks of November brought a taste of Indian summer, but the last two weeks turned rainy, and by the first of December it was getting gray and cold. Anna did not see Jim Parnell often. Her classes and her job kept her too busy to socialize, and he was a year ahead of her in law school, so none of their classes were the same.

"You're a little late," Alex Webber said as Anna took off her felt hat, brown winter coat, and boots.

"I'm sorry. I had to wait to get a book from the library."

"It's quite all right. It's just that there's a telegram for you." He shuffled through the papers on his ever untidy desk and handed her the telegram.

Anna looked at it for a moment, then tore it open.

Please come home for the weekend, there's an urgent problem.

Love,
Karla

"Something wrong?" Alex Webber asked, his brow knit into a frown.

"It's from my aunt. She says it's urgent I come home for the weekend."

"Then you had better go."

"But we have work to do. I have research I haven't finished."

"Well, I won't pretend it will be easy without you, but an emergency is an emergency, and from what I know of your aunt, she isn't one to cry wolf."

Anna nodded.

"Well, don't just stand there. If you hurry you can catch the five-thirty train."

"Thank you," Anna said, turning to leave.

It was nearly eleven o'clock at night when Anna rang the bell on the door of the dark house on Washington Avenue. In a moment the porch light was snapped on, and it was Karla who flung open the door. "Anna! Oh, I thought you'd come in the morning. You should have phoned, we'd have met you."

"It's all right. I didn't have time to phone before I got on the train . . . and when I got here it was so late. Karla, what is it? Are you all right? Is Josef all right?"

Karla hugged her tightly. "Yes, come into the kitchen. I'll fix some tea and tell you everything."

Anna felt an immediate sense of relief, and slipping out of her boots, she followed her aunt down the darkened corridor. She had expected them to be asleep. Josef had to get up early to get the paper out. Saturday night was the night they had guests and stayed up late because there was no paper on Sunday.

"You didn't even bring any luggage," Karla said as she turned on the kitchen light and mechanically went about the business of preparing tea.

"I didn't have time to go back to Hull House before the train left. Karla, what's wrong? What's the emergency?"

"It's Uda. I wired you because of Uda," Karla said,

sitting down at the table while she waited for the kettle to boil.

Anna slipped her coat off and let it fall over the back of the chair. "Uda?" she asked. "I don't understand."

Karla looked at the red-and-white-checked tablecloth. "She had some sort of fight with Oskar . . . I don't know much about that. Anyway, she decided to go to Chicago and stay with you for a few days. She must have been terribly upset."

Behind them on the stove the kettle began to sing, and almost as if she were relieved to temporarily escape, Karla got up to turn off the gas and pour the water into the teapot.

Anna followed her aunt with her eyes, and she began to feel a terrible foreboding. "She never called me," Anna said. "Uda never called me."

"I know." Karla sank back into the chair. She sought Anna's eyes with hers. "She got off the train in Wauke-gan—I don't know why, perhaps just to walk on the platform for a few minutes. Some men came up to her—they'd been sitting near her on the train. According to her deposition, one of them said, 'Are you getting off here?' and Uda told them no, she was going on to Chicago. Then one of them said, 'No, you aren't.' He had a knife and they forced her to go with them. She was too frightened to scream . . . she didn't understand at all till they drove her out into the country. They kept calling her names—filthy names. They called her a kraut bitch and they . . . they beat her and raped her, Anna. They left her for dead in a ditch."

"Oh, my God," Anna breathed. "Is she . . . did she survive?"

Karla inhaled. "She's alive. She keeps asking for you."

Anna nodded and closed her eyes, thinking of Uda. She was from the German countryside and she was a real innocent. "I've written her only twice," she said after a few moments. It was a meaningless comment, but it embodied Anna's feeling that she should have kept in closer touch with Uda, that somehow this tragedy could have been prevented. And because she hadn't kept in touch, she felt unworthy of being the one for whom Uda kept asking.

"She knew you were busy. Don't feel guilty. I just thought if she could talk to you, it might help. Anna, you couldn't have done anything to prevent this." Karla looked at Anna intently and could almost read her thoughts. Anna was deeply sensitive.

"I'll try to help her. Oh, Karla, how could such a terrible crime happen?"

Karla's lips were pressed together. "I don't know, but I hope they burn in hell."

Anna poured herself a cup of tea with a trembling hand. Poor little Uda—she was certainly the least political of all her friends, and yet it seemed she would be the one to suffer the most. "She's asleep now," Karla said, "but you can talk to her first thing in the morning."

"She's here?" Anna said, looking at her aunt in surprise.

"Of course. I couldn't let her go home to her room alone. She's still very ill and terribly, terribly frightened."

Anna reached across the table and squeezed her aunt's hand. "Oh, Karla, you're such a good person."

Karla shook her head. "Not so good, Anna. You only see my good side."

"I don't know if I can sleep." Anna sipped her tea.

"Then let's talk for a while. Tell me about law school. Tell me about Hull House. Talk to me about anything except this damn war and what it's doing to us."

"All right. I'll tell you about property law—that's safe."

In the end, Anna fell into a troubled sleep on the sofa in the living room and awoke with the sun pouring through the window to find that Karla had covered her with a big Hudson's Bay wool blanket.

She rubbed her eyes and looked around. The room was as she remembered it. The old blue sofa and chair, the overflowing bookcases, and the newspapers and magazines that Karla tried to keep sorted and piled neatly, but which always seemed to willfully defy attempts at organization by tumbling over.

Anna stood up and looked out the window. It had snowed during the night, but now the sun was shining. Sun on snow. It made the day seem brighter.

Anna climbed the steps to the top floor and peeked inside the room that had been hers for almost two years. The blue chintz curtains still hung at the windows, and the matching bedspread was turned down. There, beneath a huge German down-filled comforter, Uda lay in the middle of the bed, her eyes open, staring at the ceiling.

"Uda?" Anna slipped into the room and went directly to the bed and sat down on its edge.

"Anna? Is that really you?" Uda's voice sounded small and almost childlike.

"Yes. I've come to see you."

Uda took her hand and squeezed it. "I tried to come to see you . . ." Her voice trailed off, and the expression in her eyes went from innocence to terror. Her lips quivered, and her hand shook. "There were five of them," she said in a near-whisper. Then, squeezing Anna's hand tightly, "Anna, they hurt me. They really hurt me. Why? Why did they do that . . . that terrible thing to me?" Tears began to flow down her face and Anna leaned over and put her arms around her friend and held her close and rocked her slowly in her arms. "I don't know, I don't know," she whispered. "Oh, Uda, you must get well. You must fight. This is not the end of the world."

But Uda remained silent and Anna could only go on holding her.

After a time, Anna kissed Uda on the forehead and left her to sleep once again. Karla was in the hall.

"Poor child," Karla said to Anna. "I don't know what more to do for her."

They walked back downstairs together. "Did they catch them?" Anna asked.

"Yes, but they let them go," Karla said with undisguised disgust.

"Let them go! How could they let them go?" Anna returned in a shocked, angry voice.

"They claimed she was a prostitute. They claimed she wanted them to have intercourse with her."

"But they beat her."

"They said they didn't. They claimed she had an accident. Oh, don't you see? They all came from 'good' American homes, and Uda . . . Uda was just a little German girl from Milwaukee. One of them said, 'What about all the French and Belgian women raped by German soldiers?' "

Anna leaned against the wall and clenched her fists. She felt absolutely outraged and she trembled with anger. Uda had been the victim of a vicious attack, and she suffered while her attackers went free. "It's a disgusting miscarriage of justice," Anna breathed.

Karla hugged her tightly. "We must all fight the attitudes that make it possible for criminals to get away with crimes like this. Fight, Anna. Didn't I just hear you tell Uda that?"

Anna nodded. "We will," she replied.

9

The January winds howled and the dark sky delivered a blizzard of snow and ice. Traffic on Chicago's slippery streets stalled to a standstill and only the occasional pedestrian was seen darting between the entrances of buildings. On the panes of the window, snow stuck round the edges till only a small foggy circle remained through which to see. Anna sat in Dr. Gluck's office, her thoughts on a problem she'd decided to broach with him.

Dr. Gluck was nearly sixty-five, but his mind was razor sharp and his voice robust and filled with enthusiasm and energy. He was a short man, barely five feet tall, and his head was nearly bald, though he did have a fringe of fuzzy gray hair that surrounded his skull. Still, when he was lecturing, no one noticed his diminutive size. His intelligence endowed him with intellectual stature, and many who didn't like him grudgingly respected him.

Anna sat opposite his desk. It was almost as disorganized as Alex Webber's desk, and Anna was beginning to feel that the more ordered the mind, the more cluttered the desk.

"You continue to make me proud," Dr. Gluck, her professor of criminal law, said without looking up from her examination paper. "It's good you are as bright in your other classes, or *someone* might think I was playing favorites."

"Someone?" Anna questioned.

"Are you so unaware?" He looked up at her and arched his brow.

"Professor Southam," she ventured. It was odd that Professor Gluck had mentioned him first. Professor Southam was the reason why she'd come. But then it occurred to her that Dr. Gluck had been born in Germany, although he had been brought to the United States when he was still in his teens. Nonetheless, he had a very slight German accent, nowhere near as pronounced as hers, but still quite recognizable.

"How you are getting on, Anna? Do your fellow students bother you much?" he asked. Then, "How about Professor Southam?"

"Some students needle me, others defend me. Professor Southam is . . . well, I came here to talk to you about him. He's very belligerent with me in class—he's asked to see me, and I'm a bit worried."

"He can't challenge your marks. They're judged independently and recorded. He *can* and might harass you in class. Anna, don't be intimidated. Southam's anti-German and he's against women studying law, so you have two strikes against you."

"I'll just have to prepare myself."

"And the students—they *just* needle you?"

"Yes, but as they've gotten to know me, well, even that's ceasing."

"In this instance being a woman is an advantage," he said, nodding his head slightly. "Women are not seen as being dangerous, but ah, Anna, there is fear sweeping this country, mass fear. I feel . . . I know America will not remain neutral. Then I fear German men may not be safe walking the streets."

"Women may not be seen as dangerous, but that doesn't mean that fear, anger, and prejudice aren't taken out on them. A German friend of mine was raped. The men who did it kept calling her a kraut bitch, and they told her they were raping her to avenge the women and children of Belgium and France."

Dr. Gluck looked aghast. "God. Anna, you must be careful. You must stay with friends at all times. I know men have been beaten, tarred and feathered, but I hadn't known about this rape."

"It's men like that George Creel and his American Protective League who are really responsible. He whips up a frenzy of hatred every time he speaks or there's a meeting," Anna said.

"He and others," Dr. Gluck agreed. "Limiting freedoms, destroying what this country stands for, what it is . . . it saddens me and people sadden me. Do they see us as all alike? Don't they know or understand that we Germans are being torn apart? They put all in the same basket—the unionists, the anarchists, the pacifists, the communists, the civil libertarians. I do not support this war, neither do I want my aunts, uncles, and cousins killed. And because I don't support it, it is assumed I am pro-German. What a dilemma!" He threw his arms up expressively. "Did you know there is a petition circulating—it asks for my resignation."

"Oh, no," Anna breathed, covering her mouth with her hand in dismay. Then she straightened up. "Such a dismissal would be wrong. You could sue."

"Torts is your best subject, yes?"

Anna blushed. "Yes."

"And should it come to that, do you think such a suit could be won?"

"Perhaps if Alex Webber argued it. I must confess that a lot would depend on the mood of the jury, though . . . and in the atmosphere of paranoia Creel has created, it might be difficult to find a sympathetic jury."

"Well, if I am dismissed, I'll consider a suit."

"In the meantime, let's start a counterpetition," Anna suggested.

Dr. Gluck shook his head. "No, Anna. I don't want *you* to start it. Perhaps someone else. I think that young man you argue with so frequently might be the right one."

"Jim Parnell? I'm not sure where he stands. He isn't a pacifist."

"Really?" Dr. Gluck rubbed his chin and looked somehow amused. "What makes you think that?"

"Well, he told me . . . more or less."

"I think Mr. Parnell, who by the way is also a very good student, is rather a typical male. I think he tries to make you angry so you will notice him."

"That's absurd," Anna answered.

"Perhaps I'm wrong. In any case, Jim Parnell is popular among the other students. And he is a second-year student.''

Anna listened, but didn't immediately comment. Then, after a time, ''Well, I can ask him to start a petition.''

''I suppose it might do some good.''

''I think I'd leave this school if they fired you,'' Anna murmured.

''You would absolutely do no such thing, Anna Bock. You would stay here and obtain the tools it takes to fight repression. Graduating number one in your class is the only real revenge you could exact. It is in any case the only revenge that would satisfy me.''

Anna smiled. ''I intend to do that anyway,'' she replied.

Anna stood outside Professor Southam's office. She drew in her breath and then knocked, trying to suppress her hesitancy and appear bold and confident.

''Come in!'' The professor's voice was stern, cool.

Anna opened the door and took in the room. It was larger than Professor Gluck's office, and it was more conservatively furnished. In fact, it looked less like a professor's office and more like an office in a high-class law firm, one of the firms on Wabash Avenue. The curtains were royal blue and so was the carpet. The desk was made of a light wood, white oak perhaps, and highly polished. To one side of it there was a large American flag. On the wall there was an autographed picture of the President of the United States, Woodrow Wilson.

Dr. Southam himself was a bulky man—not fat, but simply bulky. He was broad-shouldered and heavyset, but his expensive tailored suits hid his paunch. He had thinning light hair, a fair complexion, and wore rimless glasses. His voice was deep and he tended to speak in an absolute monotone. No matter what outrageous statement he made, he made it with an arrogant kind of authority. He was the sort of person who, if he said it were going to snow, would cause you to wear a sundress. Not that he was outrageous where the law was concerned, but he was given to making speeches on other subjects, the economy for one. All of his predictions were wrong, but

190 · Joyce Carlow

he was seemingly untouched by reality, and in a maddening way continued to insist that white was black, the moon was the sun, and ice was warm.

He looked up at her, unsmiling. "Sit down," he said, pointing to the chair.

Anna sat down and kept her silence. He had asked to see her.

He purposely ignored her for several minutes while he made a show of shuffling through papers; then he looked up. "I asked you to come here so I could warn you."

"About what?" she returned, forcing herself to sound cool and detached.

"To warn you that I tried to keep you out of this school and that I will do everything possible to keep you from graduating."

Anna looked at him unblinkingly. "Why, may I ask?"

"I don't believe there is a role for women in the law. Furthermore, it's no secret that I don't like Germans."

"Your first assumption shows ignorance and your second prejudice. Do you have something specific to say about my performance in the course you teach?"

"Not yet."

Anna stood up. "Well, I don't think you'll have cause for complaint in the future either."

He narrowed his eyes slightly. "I kept you out the first time you applied to this school. I do have some influence."

"I'm sure you do," Anna said as she turned. "And I have other matters to attend to."

Anna put on her hat, coat, scarf, and boots. Her hand was trembling with anger. It had been hard to control herself while talking to Southam, and, she feared, it might be harder in the future. Still, it was important not to give him cause to create more trouble.

Hurrying from the entrance of one building to another when the wind blew in unbearable gusts, and finally pulling her scarf up over her face, Anna trudged all the way to Alex Webber's law office. She was kept warm only by the fury she felt over her short meeting with Professor Southam. Clearly he had meant to intimidate her. She considered discussing it with Alex Webber, then decided against mentioning it just yet.

Anna arrived at two P.M. to find Alex Webber at his desk eating an egg sandwich and muttering, as he often did. He looked up as she walked in, and she could see the glint in his eyes . . . it was a glint that she had seen before. It meant long hours of searching and of trying to concentrate while he paced up and down, practicing his famed oratory. "Ah! You're here!" He jumped up and held out a sheaf of papers. "The proposed Espionage Act!" he said triumphantly. "I need your help . . . we have to find all the precedents. We'll go back to the Civil War . . . not that it was any more civil than any other war. You know, the bastards leave the Constitution alone in peacetime." He shook his head in disgust. "Then, just when we need protection most, they decide to try to turn this great country of ours into a two-bit fiefdom!"

Webber had what Americans called a "down-home folksy way" and he often used colorful language laden with slang. Sometimes she had to ask him to explain words, but this time she understood, and she frowned. "Will America go to war?" she asked earnestly.

Webber nodded. "The way they're acting, I imagine they will."

Anna drew in her breath. "It'll get worse for German-Americans."

Webber again nodded. "Gotta learn to keep your head down, missy. And when the bastards aren't looking, hurl a tomato or two back . . . that's a metaphor. I mean, we'll have to choose our times carefully or we'll all end up in the clinker while a bunch of yahoos parade up and down outside with our flag. See, the thing is, our rights and freedoms as individuals are exactly what Americans think they're fighting for . . . so we can't let the yahoos throw those rights and freedoms out and call it patriotism."

"Yahoos?" Anna asked.

"Swift—*Gulliver's Travels*. Read it, it's good seditious literature."

"You're a wicked man." Anna half-laughed as she

went to get the ladder that would enable her to reach the lawbooks on the top shelves.

"I'll be a good influence on you. You know, your English is getting better every day."

Anna pushed the ladder into place. "I'd better get to work."

"We'll send out for dinner."

Anna looked down in mild panic. "I have Moot Court tomorrow."

"I'll coach you sometime during the night. You can't lose."

"I could fall asleep."

"You'll have to learn to go without sleep—don't worry, you can have a nap."

"You're a slave driver."

"It's the only way to stay free."

Anna turned and watched him leave the library. She smiled to herself and began delving into the large dusty volumes. The impending entry of America into the war would cause her personal grief and it would cause all German-Americans turmoil and sadness, and unquestionably a great many would suffer. She sucked in her breath and leaned against the bookcase for a second. The implications were profound, but she admitted to herself that her whole being was filled with a kind of nervous wonder. She worked for a lawyer passionately involved in social issues, she lived in a wonderful place, surrounded by strong women with ideas—women who could put those ideas into action—and she was in law school and learning her profession in what seemed a living laboratory of First Amendment cases. It was an exciting time and she couldn't deny that while a part of her worried about Markus and her own lost child, another part of her was caught up in the frenetic pace set by her environment. There was so much to learn! There was so much to do! Anna trembled with excitement. She felt alive and vital—more alive than she had ever felt before.

Kurt Stein was thinner by twenty pounds than at the time of his arrest in Germany. And his appearance had changed in other ways as well. His curly hair was thinner, his complexion more sallow, and his once muscular body was now less toned. His personality was the same. He was still moody, but was able to be utterly and completely charming if necessary.

Allowed to escape, he had followed a difficult, complicated, and circuitous route to New York City. His survival he readily credited to three assets: his mastery of several languages, including English; his ability to bluff; and his cultivated charm. Over the last few months he had seen Turkey and the islands of the Aegean, Morocco and Spain, and then Cuba. It was via Cuba that he entered the United States. To keep alive he had stolen, been a rug trader, a tutor, a merchant seaman, and finally an exporter of fine Havana cigars. It was this latter role that enabled him to enter the United States legally. There were, he had discovered, many Germans in Cuba, and most had been there for several generations. It was easy for him to blend in, and because he spoke English well, he was able to convince the authorities he was genuine. "Born in Cuba of German parents" was his claim. It was always wise not to stray *too* far from the truth, and naturally he was most convincing when denouncing Germany, its military, and the war. But now, he thought with glee, it was over. He was in the United States, he was here legally, and he could do as he pleased.

Not that he found particular joy in New York City. It was big and impersonal, its immigrant neighborhoods were rigidly defined. His attempts at using American radical groups to help him financially failed. He discovered American radicals to be no more than sentimental idealists who enjoyed, yes, relished poverty. Nor was he at home among German immigrants, many of whom were either pacifists or quiet supporters of German expansion. Nothing made him happy, not even his prospects for work. He tried to find a position where his superior intellect would be appropriately rewarded with a good salary, but no one would hire him because, although he spoke English well, his accent was quite recognizable. For a short time he worked as a common laborer, then in disgust he took what meager funds he had accumulated and headed west. If one was going to be miserable, he concluded, one could at least be miserable in a warmer climate.

The train moved slowly even though the view from Kurt's window revealed the flattest, most barren land he had ever seen. Indeed, as he traveled west he began to question the wisdom of his decision. Though he knew it intellectually, he had not dreamed America was truly so unpopulated, and vaguely, as he journeyed across Kansas, he wondered if he would ever see another city again.

On either side of the train all that could be seen was an utterly flat expanse of white snow, punctuated only by solitary bleak grain elevators and the occasional ramshackle farmhouse and enormous barn.

The steel door at the far end of his railroad car opened as a woman walked from one car to another, and a whoosh of cold air blew down the aisle. Kurt looked up and watched as she navigated the distance from one end of the railway car to the other. She was rather extraordinary-looking, he thought, and he realized that he had not seen her previously, though daily, all the passengers made several treks through his car on the way to the dining car.

The woman, a willowy brunette, was ostentatiously dressed in a bright red suit, a swirling fur-trimmed cape, and a magnificent slouch hat. Not only was she ravishing-looking, but her jewelry indicated she was also wealthy.

As she passed his seat, Kurt got a whiff of her perfume. It was pungent, and clearly expensive. He followed her with his eyes; then, when she had disappeared through the door at the far end of his carriage, he checked his own pockets, counting his remaining money. He didn't usually eat in the dining car, but he thought tonight it might be worth his while and the expense.

Kurt went first to the men's room to wash and change into a clean shirt. He stared at his image. He wasn't poorly dressed, and he thought, looking at his now bearded face, he was still handsome. With that thought in mind, he headed for the dining car. Yes, it was time he met a new woman. And, he concluded, a rich woman was no doubt better than a poor one.

The winter months passed slowly and the summer months went by far too quickly. Autumn blended into fall, and fall once more turned to winter and then again to spring. As the new year 1917 was born, the United States edged slowly toward the abyss, drawn, Anna felt, by the irresistible forces of destruction. By spring the slow dance was over and the United States declared war on the sixth of April. Almost immediately a kind of fevered hysterical patriotism gripped the nation. It was said to be "The War to End All Wars," and posters boldly declared, "We are coming, brothers, coming, a hundred thousand strong."

Alex Webber leaned back in his chair and wiped his brow. Before he lifted his eyes to greet Anna, his eyes surveyed the piles of papers and books on his desk.

"It's your birthday today. You ought to be home with Clara."

His head wobbled slightly and he shrugged. "If it were a weekend I'd be home. But it's a Wednesday and it's a workday."

"Does that mean you only celebrate your birthday when it falls on a Saturday or Sunday?" she inquired.

He chuckled. "Well, that's how I stay young. Besides, we're up to here in work." He made a motion with his hand, lifting it to his chin. It wasn't an exaggeration; the law firm of Webber, Wyatt, and Prentice was drowning in a sea of cases brought on by the enactment of the Espionage Act. "War paranoia." Alex Webber sneered. "Damn Wyatt and Prentice . . . damn them for retiring and leaving me to fight this alone."

Wyatt and Prentice, whose names were still on the door, had been retired for years, and Prentice was on the verge of death. Alex Webber was alone and working long hours. Anna too was putting all her extra time to doing research. In addition, three other students helped out. Still, Webber pushed himself the hardest and to the limit.

In spite of little sleep and hard work, Webber didn't look his age. In fact, she had been surprised to learn that today he was celebrating his sixtieth birthday.

He ran his hand through his hair and frowned. "My father, grandfather, and great-grandfather were all undertakers. You might not be aware of this, but when graves are on flatland, you gotta be careful because if there's a lot of rain, the dead just float right up to the top again." He shook his head, then announced, "I've followed in their footsteps. I keep burying economic, social, and legal corpses and they insist on coming back up out of the ground every time there's a storm." He shook his head again, this time in utter disgust. "This is a big storm, Anna. All the bodies are resurfacing."

Freedom of speech, freedom of assembly—all the guarantees in the First Amendment were under fire. Editors, clergymen, educators, and women were being sent to jail for declaring that America did not belong in the war. The "bodies" Alex Webber spoke of were the rights of Americans to speak, to meet, and to write what they believed. "It's fear," Anna commented. "Fear has caused a suspension of judgment, and it's causing legal paralysis."

"It's causing dementia!" he declared, pounding the desk with his doubled fist. "People have been beaten for not buying Liberty Bonds. Today we're witnessing the most complete suspension of civil liberties since the Civil War. Can't say I blame you for looking distressed, but I'd be pleased to know specifically what you're thinking and how you feel at this moment." He leaned over and peered at her.

Anna thought for a long moment. She was, as Alex Webber well knew, in the position of having to sort out her emotional reactions from her legal study and knowledge. Long ago she had memorized the first ten amendments to the Constitution of the United States—they were fundamental amendments, they made America a unique country, even a unique democracy. The First Amendment, under which most of their cases fell, read:

> Congress shall make no law respecting an establishment of religion, or prohibiting the free exercise thereof; or abridging the freedom of the speech, or of the press; or the right of the people peaceably to assemble, and to petition the government for redress of grievances.

The Fourteenth Amendment, which also figured in the defense of rights, was more complicated. It defined citizens as all persons born or naturalized in the United States and being subject to the jurisdiction thereof, but more than these definitions, it forbade states to make laws that would abridge the rights of citizens or deprive any persons of life, liberty, or property without due process of law. But in spite of these protections, there were gray areas, areas left to the courts to decide. "I'm trying to understand exactly when personal prejudice infringes on individual rights," Anna confessed. "I mean, the line is perfectly clear when a law is broken—as in the case of the German lynched in downstate Illinois, or when the windows of the Settlement House were broken last week. One was murder and the other destruction of property. But when a company won't hire Germans or restaurants won't serve them . . . well, the issue isn't at all clear and there aren't many legal precedents. That is, there's a conflict—there's *my* right to be fairly considered for a job, and the employer's right to choose his employees—or the right of a restaurateur to serve whom he pleases."

Webber laughed, shoved his chair back, and stood up. He rubbed his chin. "A conflict of rights."

Anna looked at him. He was taller than average, a big man with heavy limbs and a bulging chest. He had a weathered complexion, and the skin on his face was loose, giving him a slightly jowly appearance. His face was deeply lined, and his lips were oddly colored. When he frowned, the lines in his forehead came together in a tangle of deep crisscross grooves. But when he smiled, his face turned infectiously jovial, and he could be irresistibly charming. He had a tendency to amble about most of the time, but when he had an idea or when he was about to deliver some profundity, his body imitated the quickness of his mind and he moved swiftly, like a cat pouncing on a mouse.

"It is up to you and others like you to set precedents," he said. "You've got to sort out the absurd from the truly harmful. Since we entered this damn war, all manner of foolishness abounds—persons being renamed, foods being called something they aren't . . ."

Anna couldn't keep from smiling. "Sauerkraut is now called victory cabbage."

"You see, those things are absurd. But tarring and feathering, vandalism, arrests for so-called unpatriotic utterances—that's dangerous, not simply personally dangerous for German-Americans, but dangerous for everything this country stands for."

"I know you're not a pacifist . . . you believe America should have entered the war."

"I started out as a pacifist, but I concluded that the German state was committing acts of barbarism and had to be stopped. But that doesn't mean I believe in the suspension of liberty, nor does it mean I won't defend those who, because of their religion, won't fight."

"You, Alex Webber, are a real humanist."

He frowned; then he grinned. "And you're too smart for what I hope are your lace breeches. Now, get thee off to our law library and start pulling cases for me. I have a pile of defenses here."

Anna smiled and left his office.

"Clara says to come over tonight!" he shouted after her.

"I wouldn't miss it," Anna called back. Webber's wife, Clara, encouraged the never-ending stream of law students who came to talk with Webber . . . not just law students, but admirers who ranged from the totally powerless and unknown to the famous, rich, and powerful. Jane Addams visited often, as did William Jennings Bryan, Harold Ickes, Hamlin Garland, Kenneth Harris, John M. Holmes, Clarence Darrow, and the journalist William Allen White.

In spite of the fact that it was Webber's birthday, she suspected tonight would not be different from other nights. Ten or twelve would gather in the comfortable living room of the Webber house. Some of those who came, like herself, would be young law students or newly graduated lawyers. A few others would have been in practice for a few years, and still others would be social workers, union organizers, or suffragettes. The constant factor would be the ever-stimulating conversation and the arguments. Like Karla and Josef's in Milwaukee, Webber's home was a gathering place, a place with which she never grew bored. Sometimes, Anna acknowledged, an evening with the Webbers was like an evening of heavy drinking. She would return home, her mind drunk with ideas, her spirit intoxicated with sheer energy, and her desire to get into a courtroom whetted with her desire to argue and to win. When I'm a lawyer, she thought, I will truly join this fascinating group of people who could change society by changing or moderating the rules under which society acts. And that, she thought, was what she really loved about America. It wasn't that America was perfect, it was that change could be effected through the ballot box and through law. In Europe, progress was all too often negated by a dictator or a monarch—dreams of equality and freedom were erased. But here, here in America, the ideal could be realized because Americans were builders rather than dreamers, and using their Constitution as a foundation, they built and were building a body of laws and interpretations that would gradually be expanded till every man, woman, and child would be protected and offered, not equality, but equality under the law and equality of opportunity.

Anna slipped into the library and started, surprised to see Jim Parnell poring over some musty volumes. As he was a year ahead of her in law school, she didn't see him often, and when she did, it was usually in Moot Court and more often than not he was her opponent. "What are you doing here?" she asked.

"Webber said I could come here and look a few things up—he has quite a collection, you know. Besides, it's quieter than the law library at the law school. You don't object, do you?"

Anna climbed the ladder which was attached to the wall and which slid around the perimeter of the room on tiny ball bearings. "Of course not, why should I care? I only work here." She didn't look at him. He was her friendly nemesis, always around, always arguing with her. She was quite certain that if it were raining and she said so, he would disagree with her simply for the joy of disagreeing. He was quite the most argumentative man she knew, and he could be grating and annoying as well.

"You're still mad at me," he concluded. "Just because of the fact that I outargued you in Moot Court last month and won my case."

Anna sucked in her breath and shook her shoulders in a slightly haughty motion. "I certainly am not. Besides, who said you outargued me?"

"The judges. Ah, the sting of a woman scorned, or in this case a woman beaten in argument."

"I assure you I do not feel one bit scorned and I certainly was not beaten, in spite of the decision." She gave her head a little toss and lifted her chin defiantly. He was so pompous!

Anna reached for a huge volume, and then, struggling slightly, climbed down from the ladder and headed for a small office down the hall. It wasn't her office, but it would allow her to get away from him.

But his voice called out to her, "I'll see you tonight."

"Damn," Anna murmured. Well, she wasn't going to stay home just because he was going to be at the Webbers'.

The comfortable Webber living room was filled with young male law students. Three were from the University of Illinois, and Anna didn't know them. Four others, including Jim Parnell, were from the Union College of Law. Three students sat on the green sofa, while two others sat on straight-backed chairs. The remaining two sat on the floor. Webber presided over the group from a large, shabby overstuffed chair, and Anna sat in the only other upholstered chair. Clara Webber had retired for the evening, pleading the need to get some extra sleep.

As Anna knew, this was the kind of evening about which Clara could relax. Clara Webber was a nervous woman, a woman given to fits of jealousy. Alex Webber was not good-looking, but he was charismatic and he attracted women by the score. It was not unusual to see him surrounded by women, and Anna was certain that her employer, friend, and mentor was not above adultery even though he had never approached her personally. Clara was not blind to her husband's shortcomings and she did not hide her jealousy. Still, she was relaxed when

Anna was around and Anna felt that Clara knew her sufficiently well to trust her. In fact, Webber had once told her, "You're the only pretty girl my wife trusts." He had pretended to be joking, and Anna had laughed lightly and replied, "And she's right to trust me." If Webber had taken that conversation amiss, he did not show it in any way.

Webber pulled himself up out of the chair, and leaning over the coffee table, poured a drop of coffee into his empty cup. "Oh, damn, all gone," he muttered.

Anna stood up. "I'll make some more," she offered.

"Let one of them make it," Webber proclaimed, waving his hand about. "Look at you all! Just because she's the only woman here doesn't mean she's your servant. This young lady is going to beat all of you in the courtroom . . . you know why? Because she knows her facts and she knows the law, but she leads with her heart." He looked at Anna and smiled warmly.

"I'll get the coffee," Jim Parnell said, standing.

Anna laughed. "I think I'd better help you. I know where things are kept."

He didn't argue, but instead gathered up the coffee set and followed her into the kitchen.

"Webber likes you," he said matter-of-factly. "Are you sleeping with him?"

Anna set the kettle on the stove with a thud and turned angrily toward Jim Parnell. "Of course not," she snapped. "Do you think he compliments me because we're lovers? You may be a year ahead of me, but you know I get good marks."

"Oh, I touched a raw nerve." He grinned. "Besides, how do I know you're not sleeping with Alex Webber?"

Anna clenched her fist. "You're despicable!"

He burst out laughing. "I'm only repeating what everyone else says."

"You mean everyone thinks I'm sleeping with Alex Webber?"

"Come on, Anna . . . I don't say nasty things about you. I'm not the one who calls you a kraut. Face it, a lot of the men don't like you. First off, you're smarter than most of them, second, you're German, and third . . .

well, you're a very attractive woman working for, and obviously very friendly with, the most brilliant lawyer in Chicago.''

Anna looked at the floor. He confounded her. She never knew when he was serious and when he wasn't. He looked playful just now, but the subject was to her very personal and quite serious. Did he not realize how important her reputation was to her? And what was he saying? First he was accusative; then he proclaimed he was only repeating what others said; now he had half-complimented her. "You flatter me," she replied without emotion. "But I would be interested in knowing the source of this vicious story—never mind how I personally feel about it, I'm a good friend of Clara's and it would be awful if someone told her such a thing.''

His expression turned completely serious. "I'm a clod," he said, shaking his head. "I guess I didn't realize how upset you'd be, and I admit I hadn't thought of Clara . . . I'm sorry.''

"Apology accepted," Anna said. Then she asked intently, "Do you know how this story got started?''

He took a deep breath. "I heard it from Bill Mathews, Southam's assistant.''

Anna pressed her lips together. "I really didn't think a professor would stoop that low.''

"You think it was Southam himself?''

"Yes. He makes his feelings about me quite clear.''

Jim Parnell nodded. "Watch him, Anna." Then he smiled, changing the mood. "You know, I really like you, Anna. Frankly, I'm glad you're not sleeping with Webber.''

She looked at him hard. She felt very competitive toward him, and he had such a capacity to anger her! But at the same time, when he was softer—when he said something nice—she didn't know how to deal with him. "I like you better as an adversary," she replied, sounding a trifle more cold than she intended, because she felt angry over the story she was certain Professor Southam had started.

"I'm afraid you're going to be deprived of me as an

adversary for quite a while,'' Jim answered. ''I'm going into the army.''

Anna turned and looked at him in surprise. ''The army?''

He laughed. ''Yes, the U.S. Army.''

''I thought you didn't want to be on the same side as the English.''

''I don't. But I'll be fighting for this country, not England. I'm certainly not pro-German . . . well, not usually. As I said, I like you.''

Anna felt her cheeks go hot. ''First you make me mad with a terrible insult, then you embarrass me. I don't know what to say to you.''

''Say good-bye.''

Anna frowned. ''You'd be fighting for America's freedoms if you stayed here and helped defend the Constitution.''

''You and Webber can defend the Constitution your way. I have to defend it my way.''

The boiling water on the stove distracted Anna and she turned to the kettle and picked it up, pouring its contents into the coffeemaker. It was a German coffeemaker and she had given it to Alex Webber for his birthday.

''What about law school?'' Anna asked while still pouring the water.

''I'll finish when I come back.''

She nodded, and having finished pouring the water, set the kettle down. ''I'll miss you in Moot Court.''

He cleared his throat and forced a smile. ''When I come back, I expect to see some changes.''

''Such as?''

He beamed, and as usual, she thought how much like a bad little boy he looked when he smiled . . . it was because he had a slightly crooked smile. ''How about your name? You know, 'Anna' is very old-fashioned. Especially for a woman who is going to be a lawyer.''

''But it's my name.''

''Well, you dropped the 'von' in front of 'Bock' . . . why not drop the 'a' at the end of 'Anna'? I think Ann Bock has a much more legal ring to it . . . yes, much more businesslike.''

"Ann Bock . . . it sounds a bit strange."

"You'll get used to it, Ann."

She arched her brow somewhat defiantly. "I'm not at all sure I'm going to let you change my name."

He raised his hands in surrender. "It's only a suggestion."

"We'd better go back, Webber is waiting for his coffee."

"I'll carry the tray."

Anna handed him the tray and for once returned his smile.

"May I see you home tonight?" he queried. "Remember, it's the last time you'll have to see me for awhile."

"Yes, thank you." She watched as he walked down the corridor with the coffee tray. Maybe, she thought, he really did like her.

It was past eleven o'clock when Anna and Jim Parnell left Webber's home.

"It's a beautiful spring night," Jim Parnell said as he took her arm. "Let's walk along Michigan Avenue and then up Polk."

"Oh, I see you know where I live."

"Yes, though I don't remember who told me. Maybe Webber."

"More likely you heard one of the other students muttering about me. Men seem very suspicious of the Settlement House."

"Seeing all those women surviving without us isn't a pretty sight," he said, once again smiling.

Anna smiled with him because this time she knew he was speaking tongue-in-cheek.

"Perhaps, if you really try, my girl, you might come to understand the Irish."

"You mean to understand you?"

He nodded. "May I suggest Swift."

"I believe you've suggested him before." Raising her right hand to her chin, Anna paused in thought, then continued, "No! It was Alex Webber who suggested him."

"Well, then you *must* read him. Read *Gulliver*, and perhaps more important, *A Modest Proposal*."

"Is it funny?"

"It's satire . . . I find it funny, you may find it quite sickening."

"I will read it," she promised. "We could take the trolley," Anna suggested.

"And miss the moon over Lake Michigan? Look at that, a perfect half-moon, and right over the stockyards too. It has the ring of a song, don't you think? 'Moon-light over the Stockyards . . . Moo! Moo! Moo!' "

Anna giggled.

"My God! She works from morning to night studying the law, she works at a law office, she advises immigrant women, and she can still laugh! Ah, Ann Bock, maybe there *is* hope for you yet."

"You really do misjudge me," she said.

"Well, when I first met you on the ship, you were deadly serious, and you've been so ever since."

"I have reasons."

"And secrets too, I imagine."

They turned the corner onto Polk and walked past the darkened tenements. From an upper balcony came the sound of washing flapping in the wind . . . someone had forgotten to bring it in.

"I think I'll worry about you," she said slowly. "I wish you weren't going to war."

They reached the outside of Hull House, and at the door they stopped and looked into one another's eyes.

"I kissed you once on the ship, Ann Bock, and you tried not to kiss me back . . . of course I admit it, I was young and frivolous then. Then you were just a pretty young girl, a girl I wanted to impress."

"By lying to me? By telling me you were an American just returning from Europe?"

"Well, half of it was true. I had been in Europe."

"You've impressed me more tonight," she said slowly. "Your mind impresses me."

"Your mind impresses me, but so, my pretty, does your derriere."

Anna felt her face flush. Why did he say such things? And why did he seem to want to embarrass her? It wasn't as if she were naive. She had had a child. Still, this man unnerved her.

"You have secrets, I can tell," he said, touching her hair. Then he leaned over and she felt his lips on hers, pecking as if he were tasting her lips. But the pecking stopped when he took her in his arms and pressed her to him and kissed her hard on the mouth. She let him hold her tightly, feeling the outline of his strong body against hers, and suddenly she felt very vulnerable and even more confused than she had been.

"Good-bye, Ann Bock." He released her and looked at her for a long, long moment. "That's a kiss to remember a woman by," he said just as he turned and suddenly, without explanation, burst into a full run down Polk Avenue.

Anna stood in the light of the Settlement House doorway and watched till Jim Parnell was a tiny running man darting underneath distant streetlights. Tears suddenly filled her eyes and she turned and hurried to her room.

10

Anna walked down the nearly deserted corridor of the Union College of Law toward Professor Southam's office. It was, she decided, time to confront his assistant, Bill Mathews, in person. Jim was the first to tell her of the vicious rumor concerning her relationship with Alex Webber, but now she had heard it from three others, all of whom swore they heard it from Mathews.

Anna sucked in her breath and paused for an instant to compose herself. Then she knocked.

"Come in," Professor Southam called out.

Anna stood for a moment and considered the situation. She had wanted to see Mathews alone, but instead she'd found the professor. Well, he was no doubt the source of the story, and perhaps it would be more direct to confront him in the first instance. Anna opened the door and walked in.

Professor Southam looked up, slightly surprised to see her. He was dressed casually in summer slacks, and his white shirt was open at the neck.

"May I sit down?" Anna asked crisply.

He looked at her for a long moment, moving his eyes from head to foot. She was wearing a light yellow dress that fell to just above her trim ankles. And, he noted, she had a good figure and a pretty face. Her short hair was a mass of naturally blond curls, and her eyes were deep blue. "Yes." He motioned her to a chair that sat to one side of the front of his desk. "It's not often that you come by," he commented as he returned his eyes to his papers.

"I came here to see Bill Mathews, but I see he's not here."

Professor Southam lifted his eyes to meet hers. "And what, may I ask, do you want from young Mr. Mathews?"

"I want him to stop spreading rumors about me."

Professor Southam scowled at her. "A lone woman in a school full of men is naturally going to be the subject of loose talk, Miss Bock. I foresaw this possibility some time ago. It is certainly one of the reasons why I don't approve of your being in this school."

"I believe, Professor Southam, that you are the original source of this so-called 'loose talk.' I want it stopped and I want it stopped now."

Southam jerked up as if he had suddenly been ordered to attention. His face grew exceptionally hard, and she noted that one hand remained doubled in a fist. The other was open, and he pointed his finger at her. "See here, young woman, I won't sit here and be talked to in such a way."

Anna narrowed her eyes. "And I do not intend to be talked *about* in such a way. I am most certainly not having an affair with Alex Webber. Several students have named Bill Mathews as the source of this story. I wonder, perhaps, if you did not put him up to telling such tales?"

His expression suddenly softened, and he reached across the distance between them and put his hand on her knee. "You're a pretty girl, Anna. I don't approve of women in the law . . . but I could make things easier for you."

His hand moved knowingly on her leg, and Anna clamped her hand over his wrist and forcibly removed it. "Get your hands off me!" she spat angrily as she jumped to her feet.

He too stood, and half-smiled. A lecherous kind of smile. "I see my little kitten can scratch. No matter. You are a mere student here, the only woman student, and if you expect to graduate, I think you had better learn to show respect for me . . . perhaps even friendship." He touched her neck and then let his hand slip down and over her breasts.

Anna stood absolutely frozen with shock and anger. She lifted her hand and struck him across the face. "I told you not to touch me,'' she reiterated. ''As for the rumor, well, I'm going to sue you. I think the students—perhaps even Mr. Mathews—will see fit to cite the source under oath, Professor.''

His face reddened and he stepped toward her menacingly. ''I will not be threatened,'' he muttered.

''And I will not be talked about in this way, nor will I trade favors for grades. You're a despicable man, and you won't get away with this.'' At that, Anna whirled around and almost ran out of his office.

Alex Webber sat at his desk making notes on a long lined piece of paper. He looked up when Anna came in, and he motioned her to a chair. ''What's up?'' he asked. ''You look a little nervous. Sort of like a long-tailed cat in a roomful of rocking chairs.''

Anna smiled in spite of her anger. ''You seem to read my moods rather well.''

''You see a person every day, you get to know her. What's wrong?'' He ran his hand over his rumpled tie and put the lined paper aside.

''I've just had a very unpleasant experience,'' she said slowly.

''Tell me about it.'' He leaned over toward her, an expression of concern on his face.

Anna told him the story, beginning with the rumor Jim Parnell had told her several weeks ago.

Alex Webber's face screwed up. ''He actually touched you?'' he questioned angrily.

''Yes.''

Alex Webber shook his head in disgust. ''Hell, I won't say you're not attractive. But trying to use his position that way . . . well, it's below the belt, it's despicable.''

''I don't know what to do about it. I threatened to sue.''

He laughed. ''Well, you could sue. You might win.'' Then his face became serious. ''But you probably wouldn't.''

''He can make things more difficult for me. I knew he didn't like me, I knew he didn't approve of women in the law . . . but he really surprised me when . . .''

"When he tried to seduce you?"

"I don't know if it was attempted seduction or just a display of what he thought he could get away with—a sort of supreme way to insult me. The question is, if I can't sue, what am I going to do about it."

Alex Webber steepled his hands and looked at them. Finally he said something. "Settle out of court. Look, I'll call him. I am, after all, a central character in this story."

"I think I should be able to handle this myself."

"I appreciate that, but this time you can't. Let him threaten me and let me be the one to threaten suit. I think it makes sense."

Anna nodded. "I suppose I should have talked to you before I went to see him."

Alex shrugged. "We can't always predict other people's actions. Look, you did the right thing. Just let me take it from here."

"Thank you," Anna said, smiling.

Alex actually blushed. "Hell, don't thank me. Get to work," he muttered in a tone of mock gruffness.

The Moot Court was assembled and the case before it had been carefully laid out with every detail of the imaginary situation stated. In essence, the trial involved fifteen anarchists who were being held responsible for a bomb blast that destroyed a police station and killed four people. The facts of the case were that the accused were being tried as a group, and there was no real evidence that any of them had been armed or actually been involved in the bombing. The main evidence against them was that they had been found with pamphlets that set forth the political virtues of anarchism.

Anna maintained a serious expression as she carefully listened to the prosecution. The precedent evoked was a precedent set some thirty years previously; it was called "The Haymarket Precedent." She might have smiled, but that would have tipped her hand, she thought. This precedent was a thorn in Alex Webber's side, since he had been one of the Haymarket lawyers and he spoke of it constantly. She not only thoroughly knew the original case, but she had been privy to Webber's meandering thoughts on all aspects of the case since the day she'd begun working for him.

The young prosecutor, nowhere near as good as Jim Parnell, who would have been in this exercise, summed up his argument. "He who inflames people's minds and induces them by violent means to accomplish an illegal object is himself a rioter, even if he doesn't take part in the riot."

"Lead with your heart," Webber had often told her. When Anna stood, she looked around, careful to establish eye contact with the jurors—her fellow students. Alex had taught her the importance of eye contact, and she always tried to follow his advice. Her voice was in any case low, but she kept it deliberately lower, and she moved instinctively, turning quickly when she wanted to make a point, or moving closer to the rail that separated her from the jury.

"These people are not being tried for throwing a bomb. I draw your attention to the fact that there is no evidence that actually links them with the bombing, or even indicates they knew the perpetrators of the bombing. They're being tried for carrying this literature." Anna held up a pamphlet that she took from the prosecutor's table. "Literature that seems to favor throwing bombs." She paused and moved slightly away from the jury box, then continued, "The atmosphere today is one of fear . . . fear of foreigners, fear of foreign forms of government, fear of unrest, of revolution. I suggest to you that this trial is not a criminal trial based on fact, but rather that it's a trial based on passion."

Anna moved forward again and leaned over. "Americans—all Americans, and all the people in America—have the right to believe in the idea that they can free themselves from real or imagined injustices by force . . . *believe*," she emphasized. "But only if it can be proved beyond a reasonable doubt that these defendants have actually used force to injure people can they be justly convicted. Only if they have violated the criminal code can they be convicted."

Anna paused, looked at the pamphlet, and frowned

slightly. "Perhaps we find their literature distasteful, even hateful. But literature is one thing and actions are another. Free speech—the maintenance of free speech—depends on keeping criticism open and alive. We must tolerate even politically distasteful literature . . ." She turned suddenly and then with considerable verbal force said firmly, "I put it to you that there is no such thing as a crime of thought, there is only a crime of action, and actions—criminal actions—must be proved." Anna looked at the faces of her student jury, and as she took her seat, she saw the smile on her professor's face.

In a few moments the Moot Court adjourned. Anna gathered up her books and began stuffing them into her bag.

"You were in superb form today," Professor Gluck said to her.

"Thank you."

"It's really I who should thank you. After all, without the counterpetition which was your idea, I might have been fired a year ago. You argued well today because you not only knew your material but also believe what you were saying."

"I'm glad you're here, but it's Jim who deserves the credit."

"Do you hear from him?" Professor Gluck asked as he took off his glasses to clean them.

"No. I wrote once, but he didn't answer."

Dr. Gluck nodded and held up his glasses to see if he'd fully removed the smudge. "Are you off to Webber's now?" he asked, peering through one half of his glasses.

"Yes . . . you know, we have a case that isn't unlike this one."

"In Milwaukee? The Italians?" he queried, replacing his glasses and crinkling his nose.

Anna nodded.

"I understand Webber is going to Milwaukee to fight the case."

"Yes . . . how did you know?"

"Alex called me. You have family in Milwaukee, yes?"

"My aunt and uncle."

"Alex said he would like you to come along . . . he hates being without his best law clerk."

Anna smiled. "Is that what he said?"

"I am pleased to report it is."

"Well, I'm flattered, but I can't go. I have exams next week."

"I'm quite confident you'll pass your exams. What if I let you write them later in the summer so you could go to Milwaukee and work on this case?"

"Oh, that would be wonderful."

Professor Gluck nodded. "Then that's what I'll do. My personal opinion is that you can benefit more from a real courtroom experience and from watching Webber fight a case than from staying here and writing your exams on time."

Anna smiled warmly at Dr. Gluck. She wanted to hug him, but she restrained herself. "And I really want to go," she admitted.

"You're going to make a fine lawyer, Anna. Tell me, if I'm not prying, what of your other problem . . . the one with my colleague?"

"Alex Webber told me not to worry. And I think the immediate problem's taken care of . . . I'm not sure, I'm still afraid I haven't heard the last of Professor Southam."

"He's a very strange man, very strange. Avoid him, Anna." Professor Gluck grinned. "And that's another good thing—you won't run into him in Milwaukee."

Cynthia Hudson tilted her rakish broad-brimmed red straw hat down on one side and adjusted her huge sunglasses. "It's a bore to be famous," she cooed as she slid across the leather seat of the open-top Packard next to Kurt. "Mind you, you're not famous, so you don't have to worry."

He ignored her comment, pressed the starter, and turned over the engine. The sun was hot and the sky was utterly cloudless. Cynthia, or Cynth, as he called her, was outfitted in an outlandish belted silk slack suit that clung to each of her comely curves. Like her hat, it was red, but the band on her hat, the belt, and her shoes were black. Moreover, the first four buttons on the blouse of her suit were open and one could see not only her cleavage but also the curve of her white breasts. Her hair beneath her hat was loose, and she sported immensely long silver earrings.

"I trust you're looking forward to this trip as much as I am," she said, leaning over and kissing him on the cheek. Then she breathed heavily. "God, you're handsome, so much more handsome than when I met you. But then, I always could tell a diamond in the rough."

She was right; his appearance had changed. He'd been exercising, he'd filled out, his muscles had tone, and he was deeply tanned. He was also expensively attired in tailored brown silk slacks and a handmade open-neck cream-colored shirt.

He turned slightly and returned her kiss; then he slipped his hand inside her blouse and squeezed her breast, causing her to give a slight squeal of delight. "I'm a lucky man," he said, and he meant it. If his short affair with beautiful Anna von Bock had caused him difficulty, his chance meeting with Cynthia Hudson was a stroke of genuine luck. But then, perhaps the trouble Anna's father had caused him was a good thing. Leaving Germany had turned out to be a good idea, as America had, indeed, turned out to be the land of opportunity.

He pulled the car out of the parking lot and headed out of Los Angeles.

"We'll just have a wonderful time masquerading as ordinary people. What an inspiration, leaving on a holiday weekend. No one will miss me till it's over. We'll stop at little hotels . . . won't it be wonderful, darling?"

"And you didn't tell anyone we were driving to Chicago?"

"Oh, heavens no! And of course no one knows about you. You're my little secret."

He smiled at her and patted her knee. They were headed for San Bernardino, the first stop on their trip east. Cynthia loved to travel and she loved most to travel incognito—understandable, since she *was* one of America's richest women and was recognized everywhere because of her wild life, which had included five marriages, and her party-girl reputation. She was also the darling of the scandal sheets. He hadn't known she was traveling secretly to Los Angeles when he'd designed to meet her over a year ago, but he had soon learned all about her, and he congratulated himself that it had taken no time at all to seduce her. She thought he was a member of the Russian aristocracy who'd fled to America, and he'd convinced her to keep his identity and their relationship a secret. As it turned out, she loved the subterfuge, and even thought it made their sexual relationship more fun.

Kurt turned to her and feigned a concerned expression. "I do hope you didn't bring all that jewelry with you."

"Of course I did! I never go anywhere without it. But never mind, no one will think it's real . . . not as we're traveling in this quite ordinary car. We look like anyone else, darling. And no one will bother us. I told my press agent I was going to a health resort in Mexico! We're free! Absolutely free!

"It's wonderful, darling. Yes, I didn't really feel I saw America on the train—"

"Of course you didn't!" she interrupted. "After we met, we spent the whole trip in my compartment!" She laughed and touched his thigh with her hand.

He gave her a knowing look, but returned his eyes quickly to the road. Yes, Cynthia was as close to a nymphomaniac as he'd ever known. He had marveled at her sexual appetite on the train, and he'd been amazed ever since. Fortunately, she was not given to loyalty, so he alone did not have to bear the burden of satisfying her. "You're a wicked woman," he said abstractedly.

"I know," she said breezily. "But it's not true that I was having sex under the table with that dreadful writer in El Mocambo. The columnists just love to write such terrible things about me."

"Probably because you're the heiress to a cereal empire," he said dryly. "Your living habits don't go with cereal. Anyway, Cynth, why don't you admit you were trying to have sex with him and would have had had you not been interrupted."

She giggled. "Well, just a quick trick. People make so much out of muscle spasms, darling, don't you think?"

He shook his head and grinned. She *did* have a way of putting things. And, he admitted, he might even miss her. "Do we have enough cash for the whole trip?"

"Oh, yes. It's all stashed in the lining of my purse, and there's more in the suitcase . . . yes, everything is just fine. We'll have a wonderful old time."

They passed the racetrack and the airfield and the blue-green outline of the mountains rose in the distance. Yes, Kurt thought. He was going to miss Cynth. He was going to miss her a lot.

The hot July sun shone brightly on the lake, creating shivering shimmers of light on the ripples as they washed against the grass-lined shore. Lazy fat ducks waddled about, quacking viciously at one another as they competed for bread crumbs offered by small, impeccably dressed little boys in blue-and-white sailor suits. The little girls in their ruffled dresses were made to sit on the sidelines watching.

On the hillside overlooking the park, picnic cloths were spread out, and all around Karla, Josef, and Anna other families sprawled on the grass or sat on blankets. The smell of spiced German sausages, hot potato salad, and spicy mustard filled the air. Around a large table, beneath an open-sided arbor, men drank beer from large tankards, and in the distance, from the bandstand, a brass band struck up patriotic tunes on this Fourth of July 1917.

In the June 30 edition of *The Saturday Evening Post*, Edward Lowry had written the lead article, "Germans and Germans." "Maybe it will help," Karla said, laying down the magazine on the grass. It featured a painting with George Washington on a white horse in the background, and young American soldiers with modern guns in the foreground. Underneath it said, "Fourth of July."

Josef grunted. "Calls us law-abiding, simple, industrious, frugal people, attending our own business and not disturbing our neighbors."

"I could do without the 'simple,' " Karla said. "Still, he is trying to differentiate between immigrants and the German government."

"And he readily admits most of us left to get away

from that government," Karla added, although she knew why Josef was less than satisfied.

"I doubt that article will make anyone less anti-German," Anna put in as she took a spoonful of potato salad. "Even if it is the most widely read magazine in America."

"And here we all are, in a display of patriotism on the Fourth of July." Karla smiled and took Anna's hand. "I'm glad you're not working."

"Alex Webber said, 'No work till Monday! A five day holiday!' "

"Personally, I'm not exactly here in a display of unqualified patriotism," Josef said, frowning. "I'm still a pacifist and I'm here because it's a lovely warm summer day, a perfect day to spend in the park with my two favorite women."

Anna smiled at her uncle. He was a burly man whose physical appearance made him look like a laborer rather than the intellectual he was. He had thin hair, a round face, and a ready smile. He had taken Karla's hand and was looking at her lovingly. "It's a delicious picnic lunch, Karla. You shouldn't have gone to so much trouble."

"No trouble," Karla said as she stretched out on her side, thinking how good it was to be alive and silently vowing to enjoy every moment and cherish every experience.

Anna looked at her for a long moment. Her eyes were closed, and she looked quite pale, even though she was dressed in a bright yellow outfit. And she was thinner too. Thinner than Anna had ever seen her. "Are you feeling all right, Karla?"

Karla opened her eyes and nodded. "Yes, yes, of course. Why do you ask?"

"You just look pale and tired. You've lost weight too."

Karla laughed, albeit a bit nervously. "Well, I'm always trying to lose weight, aren't I? I guess I've finally succeeded."

Josef opened a bottle of Phez loganberry juice and took a long gulp. "You know, you do look tired, Karla. I think you need a long vacation."

"I don't think this is the time for a vacation," she

replied. "Besides, I'm fine, and I wish you two would stop fussing just because I've finally succeeded in losing a few pounds."

Anna stood up and stretched. "I think I'll go down to the bandstand and see if I can find Uda and Lili."

"We old folks will stay here and plan the vacation we're going to take after the war."

Anna waved at her uncle and started down the hill toward the bandstand.

As she got closer, she saw Uda and Lili sitting on a bench. Uda had healed physically, but she still carried the mental scars of her ordeal. She went through the motions of a normal life without actually living a normal life. She had returned to work, but she never went out with men. In fact, she wouldn't go anywhere alone. Even when she had wanted to see the band, she had made Lili go with her down the hill.

"Anna! Over here," Lili called out.

Anna walked over and Lili stood up. "Henri wants me to go boating with him, but I couldn't leave Uda."

"We'll be fine," Anna replied. Lili immediately got up and hurried off toward a group of men standing by the lake. Anna, knowing what was expected, sat down next to Uda.

Uda ran her hand along the edge of the bench. "You all take turns being with me," she said without looking up. "Everyone accepts what I've become . . . I'll never be well again, Anna, never."

Anna covered her hand and held it tightly. "I hope that isn't so," she said sincerely.

"I think sometimes I'm getting better, and I try, Anna. I really try. But as soon as I'm alone, I become panic-stricken. I can't breathe and I shake all over. And I can't be alone with a man . . . Oh, Anna, I can never marry now, and I'll never have children." Uda looked at Anna imploringly and wondered how it felt to be unafraid. Anna always seemed unafraid.

"It hasn't been so long since it happened. You'll get better, I'm sure of it."

"Karla thinks I should go to a psychiatrist. There's one in Milwaukee. Do you think I should go, Anna?"

"Yes. I think you should try anything that might help, Uda. I know you had a terrible experience, but you could marry and you could have children. Physically you're well now."

"Perhaps I'm insane," Uda said, trembling. "You don't know what it's like to dread the night, to be afraid of being alone even in a crowd on a warm summer's day."

"I don't know, but I've tried to understand. I do know you can get over this and live normally, Uda."

"Then you think I should go to this doctor?"

"Yes."

"Then I will," Uda promised. The band began again to play and she leaned back against the bench and closed her eyes. "Tell me about your life, Anna. Take my thoughts away. You have such an exciting life."

Anna laughed. "Well, tiring," she admitted. "And sometimes exciting."

Berlin's Kaiser Wilhelm Hospital was overcrowded, so overcrowded that some patients lay on stretchers against the gray walls and cried out for overworked nurses. But Markus von Bock was an officer, the son of a member of the German General Staff, and an aristocrat. As a result, he was given a small narrow private room attended by his own personal nurse, a girl hired by his father at his mother's insistence.

Outside his window, a warm July rain fell in the stone courtyard below. Gisela clutched the heavy drapery and stared out the window, watching as the rain splattered into a round puddle beneath the stone statue of the kaiser, who had benevolently allowed this hospital to be built. She felt as if she were in a trance, unable to speak or move, mesmerized by the labored, heavy breathing of her younger son, whose life was ebbing slowly away as his lungs turned inside out, destroyed by the German gas he had inhaled accidentally when the wind shifted unexpectedly.

Dorcas, small and pale, sat by the side of the bed in a straight-backed chair. Over and over in a low monotone she murmured a prayer. It was a child's prayer, but she seemed to take comfort in it.

Gerda came once a day to be at her brother's side, and she brought Mathilde with her. Four-year-old Mathilde, Dorcas' and Markus' only daughter, had temporarily gone to live with her aunt Gerda and her older cousin Rudolf so that Dorcas could be free to spend all her time at the hospital sitting by her husband's side.

"He's not dead, and he's not alive," Gisela said flatly. "I don't understand why they can't make him better. I don't."

From his bed, Markus croaked, and Dorcas, unused to any noise from him, jumped and stopped in mid-prayer. She stood up and leaned over. "Do you want something?" she asked. "Tell me. What are you trying to say?"

"Mmmm . . . Mathilde . . ." he gasped, fighting for every breath.

Dorcas nodded, and checked the watch pinned on the lapel of her jacket. "Gerda should be here soon. She'll bring Mathilde with her. That's it, isn't it? You want to see Mathilde?"

He shook his head and tried to speak, but it was no use. The effort caused a sudden horrible convulsion and he began to gasp and flail about, struggling to suck air into his shrunken, burned-out lungs. It was a horrible sight and Gisela turned to stare, her mouth partially open in a silent scream as she watched her son struggle to breathe. Her hand still gripped the curtain and she pulled it hard and it suddenly gave way and fell to the floor. She screamed aloud as it fell about her, blotting out her vision of Markus' struggle.

Dorcas bent over, horrified, listening and watching as Markus' movements became more desperate and his gasps less full. Blood trickled from his mouth and she too screamed only seconds after her mother-in-law, who now fought the curtain as if it had attacked her.

The door to the room opened and the young nurse burst in, followed by the white-frocked doctor.

Markus reared up, and the doctor, recognizing the last gasps of life, restrained the nurse with his hand.

Markus collapsed back against the pillow and wheezed one last short breath; then his head rolled to one side and his wide eyes stared at Dorcas vacantly.

The doctor stepped forward, and reaching over, closed his eyes and summarily pulled up the sheet. "I'm sorry," he said crisply.

Gisela, freed from the drapery, tripped over it, trying to reach the bedside. The young nurse glared at her.

"Markus!" Gisela sobbed. "Markus!"

Dorcas turned slowly away, her face even more pale than before. She steadied herself, then allowed herself to fall back into the chair in which she had been sitting. "Dear God," she whispered, then covered her face with her hands.

"I'm afraid we need this room," the doctor said coolly. Then, turning toward Gisela, "Should I call your husband?"

Gisela nodded and grasped Dorcas' shoulder. "We must go," she said in an unnatural voice. "Come, there are things to do."

A scorching August sun beat down on the pavement, and even the humid breeze that blew off Lake Michigan did not relieve the heat. But Kurt Stein liked the warmth of a hot summer's day, and, he thought as he walked along Chicago's State Street, there was something he liked about Chicago.

It was more expansive than New York—more western. And while it was big and friendly, it had a sense of permanence, a sense of stability that California had lacked. True, it was cold in the winter—or so he'd been told—but it had its advantages, not the least of which were a large number of pawnshops where few questions were asked.

Kurt paused in front of the First National Bank and looked at his new image as it was reflected in the plate-glass window. He was clean-shaven and dressed in a dapper casual tan summer suit with a yellow ascot. The California sun had given his once sallow skin a healthy tanned glow, and his hair was impeccably groomed. In fact, everything about him appeared neat, clean, and reputable.

He continued on toward the clean but reasonable hotel where he had rented a room till he could find something more permanent. Yes, Chicago was where he intended to stay. It looked as if it were a town with a lot of opportunities for an enterprising young man.

His eye caught the image of a lady in red, and for an instant he was reminded of Cynthia, whose manner of dress had always been flamboyant. But Cynthia was gone, and, he reflected, it hadn't been difficult at all. They'd gone to a hotel in San Bernardino, and at Cynthia's insistence they'd registered under a false name, "Mr. and Mrs. James Carstairs." He smiled to himself as he relived the memory of their last night together.

"It's been a long day," Kurt had said, stretching. "All that driving—I need a cold shower and a stiff drink."

"You first," Cynthia had purred. "But I do hope you're not *too* tired."

He had smiled warmly at her and run his fingers through her raven tresses. "I'm never too tired for you."

She had flushed and wiggled up to him, pressing her body against his and kissing his neck.

"I'll be back," he'd told her. Then he had showered, and when he came back into the room, he found she had fixed him a drink. She then showered while he spread out on the bed and waited. She deserved the best tonight, he decided. Yes, he would give her the very best.

He remembered every detail of the room. The hotel was small, intimate, and off the main road. It was built in a fake adobe style and was obviously intended to look like a Spanish hacienda. Its rooms were furnished in a similar fashion. The furniture was large, heavy, and featured ornate Spanish carving on its trim. There was some sort of Mexican serape on the wall, a multicolored blanket in the brightest of reds, greens, golds, and blues. On another wall there were spurs and an intricately decorated leather harness. He remembered lying on the bed and taking it all in; he even remembered the smell of oleander blossoms on the bush outside the window. It was a heady aroma, almost like a drug.

Cynthia had come out of the bathroom adorned in a sheer white see-through negligee. It was trimmed in white feathers, and she wore little satin step-in shoes.

"Oh, look at you," she had beamed. "What's under that towel?"

He was naked except for the towel over his middle. "Come and find out," he said.

She came instantly, and he said, "Stop! Just stand there and let me look at you."

She stopped and he watched as her nipples hardened because of whatever thoughts were running through her head. "Take that thing off," he commanded.

"Oh, I love it when you're masterful," she said, slowly dropping her negligee as if she were a showgirl in a strip show.

He sat up and swung his legs over the side of the bed. He put his arms around her middle and drew her, still standing, to the bed. His hands were holding her tight little ass and he moved them around, watching as she closed her eyes and swayed back and forth like a snake moving to the music of a flute. He slowly moved his hands all over her naked body while she stood in front of him, flushed with excitement. He caressed her with his mouth and his fingers and toyed with her, enjoying her movements and listening to the strange sounds that emanated from her throat.

He pulled her down to him and then rolled her over on the bed. Cynthia had gasped in his arms and clawed at his back in a frenzy of fevered excitement. He held her squirming body with all his strength and he moved his hands over her roughly and she murmured and wiggled. In moments her whole body was glistening with perspiration and she was panting like a wild animal. He took her savagely and she responded in kind. Then, when he had had his pleasure, he toyed with her again and again, making her respond and feeling envious that women could experience pleasure so often while men had to pace themselves. Cynthia finally begged to be allowed to rest, and it was a wish he honored.

He remembered watching her sleep. The room was bathed in half-soft silver light from the full moon that poured through the window. Poor Cynth. It was too bad, he thought, but entirely necessary to kill her. She would tire of him and he would have nothing. This way he would have a nice nest egg and no responsibility. The situation was perfect; no one could ask for more.

After a time he had covered her pretty face with the pillow and held it down tightly. She woke for long enough to struggle, but it was no use. He was much stronger and he held her down with the weight of his body till she moved no more.

He took all the money she had brought—some two thousand dollars—and all of her jewelry. Then he had dressed, packed, put the "Do Not Disturb" sign on the door, and left by the back stairs. He'd taken the train back to Los Angeles, and there he had shaved, bought new clothes, and taken another train to San Francisco. After a few days there, he headed for Chicago alone.

It was fully forty-eight hours before the headlines in the papers screamed "Cereal Heiress Found Dead!" The initial headlines were followed by others: "Mysterious Companion Missing!" and "Who Murdered Cynthia?" He was scot-free and knew it. No one knew of his relationship with Cynthia Hudson and no one knew they'd gone away together. The police knew she'd checked into the hotel with a man, but in a few days the police had exhausted all their leads.

Kurt turned into a tobacco shop. He bought a pack of cigarettes and continued walking. Yes, he liked Chicago and he would probably stay. He didn't need to work for a long while; still, he didn't want to use up all his nest egg either. "Decisions, decisions," he muttered. He felt optimistic. Surely somewhere in this nice city there was a pretty woman who would be of use to him. Yes, that was what he really needed. He needed a woman of means, a woman who could give him security—at least until he tired of her.

11

It had been a rare Indian-summer day, but now that darkness had fallen, a cooler breeze swept off Lake Michigan and the dry brittle leaves that still clung to the maple trees shuddered and fell to the ground, skittering along the sidewalks and piling up in the gutters.

Anna sat on the blue sofa in the living room of the house on Washington Avenue and watched her Aunt Karla carefully. When she had been in Milwaukee over the summer, she had thought Karla looked tired, but now with a dreadful certainty she knew Karla was ill.

Although Karla wore her gray hair in a youthful short wavy style, her face looked drawn and tight. She was thinner too—almost gaunt. But it was Josef who confirmed Anna's suspicions. Normally good-humored and gregarious, he too seemed tired and worried. It appeared evident that he was under some strain, though he fought to hide it.

Josef was wearing his best blue serge suit, and he looked uncomfortable in his high stiff collar. Karla was dressed in a dark blue voile dress, her only party dress. But her dress did not hide her emaciated body, nor could makeup conceal her hollow cheeks, sunken eyes, and sallow complexion.

Anna felt the same apprehension she had felt earlier in the day when she'd arrived. But Karla insisted nothing was amiss and they'd gone directly from the train station to City Hall, where Anna, together with twenty-five other immigrants, was sworn in as an American citizen. Since then they'd been with friends, so Anna hadn't had the opportunity to talk with Karla and Josef alone. Now she found she felt frustrated by their studied avoidance of the subject of Karla's obvious physical condition.

"I'm so proud of you. What a grand moment, my darling! You're an American citizen now, how does it feel?"

Anna forced a smile. "It feels wonderful. I'm so glad I came here . . . came home, for the ceremony."

"And this *is* your home," Josef said, "even if you do intend to stay in Chicago to practice law when you graduate."

"It's certainly not far from Milwaukee to Chicago. I expect I can manage to get home once every few months," Anna said, still unable to take her eyes off Karla.

Karla smiled. "The last time you were here, when you came with Alex Webber to help with the case of the Italian anarchists, you were so busy we saw you for only two meals during the entire two weeks you were here." Then Karla patted Anna's arm. "Except for the Fourth of July holiday. You were with us then."

"But it was good of Anna to bring Alex Webber here for one of those meals. What a treat to meet and talk with him. I think if Abraham Lincoln were alive he and Alex Webber would have a lot in common," Josef said quickly.

It was as if he feared a pause in the conversation, Anna thought. Josef seemed to be watching her, gauging her reaction, waiting for her to broach the subject he so clearly seemed to want to avoid.

"I wouldn't have been working with him in the first place if it hadn't been for you two," Anna replied.

"Not us," Karla said. "Crystal Eastman."

"Well, she's your friend and she helped me a great deal."

Karla looked at Anna. "That's what friends are for . . . to help. I do wish you were coming back here to practice when you graduate, but I understand. Chicago is a more exciting city."

Anna sucked in her breath. "Karla, I don't want to talk about me. I want to talk about you," she announced bluntly.

Karla frowned. "Not now, Anna. Josef's reserved a

table at the dining room in the Statler. It's as posh as Milwaukee gets. It's going to be a real treat."

"You shouldn't have gone to so much trouble." Anna looked at her aunt steadily. "I really *do* want to talk with you seriously."

"All right, but not now, not tonight."

"Am I dressed well enough?" Anna asked helplessly, thinking that she didn't really want to go out. Whatever was wrong was overshadowing everything.

"Yes, that's a lovely outfit, you look stunning."

Anna ran her hand over her blue wool dress. It was a stylish dress, but it was also conservative.

Josef moved uneasily, also wishing they could talk, wishing that Karla weren't so stubborn. He checked his watch. "We can go now," he said. "By the time we get there it will be seven."

Karla turned away from Anna. "We're much too punctual a people," she said, sounding a little forced.

Josef laughed. And Anna knew it was not a sincere laugh. Something was wrong, very wrong.

"I am much too punctual. You are not punctual at all," Josef said, again attempting humor.

Small talk. It wasn't like either of them, but Anna couldn't make them confide in her. She followed them down the walk to Josef's black Ford, and in a few moments they were bouncing down the uneven streets toward the Statler. Karla and Josef in the front, Anna in the back.

"You seem very serious," Karla said, turning back toward Anna. "But then, the citizenship ceremony is serious . . . I don't know how to describe it, but it's profound. And no one could have been better prepared. The American Constitution is your forte, Anna."

"I wasn't prepared for the emotional feeling . . . not for what happened inside," Anna confessed. It was true; at the time she hadn't expected the tremendous surge of pride and responsibility that had flooded over her. Tears had filled her eyes as she recited the oath and then the preamble to the Constitution . . . it was such a strong constitution and yet it was fragile beyond ordinary comprehension. "We the people . . . we the people." What

wonderful words! Americans who had known no other
form of government didn't appreciate those words as
much as immigrants. In her mind she heard the preamble
and she remembered the feeling she'd had as she recited
its words, "We, the people of the United States, in order
to form a more perfect union, establish justice, insure
domestic tranquillity, provide for the common defense,
promote the general welfare, and secure the blessings of
liberty to ourselves and our posterity, do ordain and establish this Constitution for the United States of America." Only a few hours ago at the Federal Building she
had taken the oath and spoken those words. It was as if
she'd heard them for the very first time because she heard
those around her saying the words in unison, but with
different accents. She had been so moved that she'd actually cried. Everyone had a responsibility, but when she
was a practicing lawyer, her responsibility would be to
uphold that sacred document. Hers would be greater than
the responsibility of others. As a lawyer she would be
one of the guardians of justice, one of those pledged to
defend the Bill of Rights and all the articles and amendments of the Constitution so that all the people would be
protected equally under the law. In fact, her citizenship
ceremony had been so moving that she had temporarily
forgotten how worried she was about Karla.

"You're quiet," Josef said, glancing at Anna in his
rearview mirror.

"Just thinking about the ceremony," she admitted.

"You're right to be moved. It's a serious moment. It's
like being born, only this birth you will remember."

"I like that analogy," Anna replied.

Josef pulled up to the hotel and got out and helped
Karla and Anna out.

They stood by the hotel entrance, but milling people
prevented Anna from speaking her mind. Then Josef returned. He had parked the car and hurried to join them,
as if afraid to leave them alone.

The dining room was large, with high ceilings and
thick wall-to-wall carpeting in a subdued blue. From the
center of the ceiling a huge crystal chandelier hung from
gold chains. Its baubles sparkled in the light. The tables

were all set with white tablecloths, blue napkins, and fine crystal. The chairs were covered in blue velvet, and every table had a bouquet of flowers in its center. The waiters carried huge trays of tempting dishes.

They were waiting to be seated when Anna looked up to see Bernard walking toward them.

"Anna!" He held out his hands and took hers. He squeezed them and smiled. "I didn't know you were in Milwaukee."

"I only came for the citizenship ceremony. I'm going back to Chicago in three days."

Bernard nodded. "Good to see you, Josef, Karla . . ." Then he turned back to Anna. "I'd like to see you, talk with you," he said, his eyes riveted on hers.

How could she refuse? Anna nodded. "Tomorrow . . . lunch perhaps?"

"One o'clock . . . there's a little restaurant by Juneau Park. The Alps." He laughed nervously and whispered, "It used to be called the Heidelberg but they changed the name because of the war."

"One o'clock," Anna agreed.

Bernard nodded and walked back across the dining room. He sat down at a table with several other men, and he waved to her when the three of them were led to their table on the opposite side of the room.

"How nice to see Bernard again," Karla said abstractedly.

"I want to see Uda before I go back too," Anna put in. "I half-expected to see her today."

"We haven't seen her much since she moved into her own room at the Settlement House," Josef said.

"It was part of her treatment, living alone. You'll be surprised, Anna. She seems completely cured."

"I can tell from her letters that she's ever so much better. It makes me happy," Anna said thoughtfully. Then she turned to Karla. "Karla, I can't go on talking about the citizenship ceremony, or Bernard, or even Uda. Don't you understand? I can see something's wrong . . . I can feel it, and you won't talk to me." She looked into her aunt's eyes, and then said pleadingly, "Tell me,

Karla. Tell me what's wrong . . . I know you're ill. I can see it."

"Not now, Anna," Josef implored.

But Karla reached out and covered his hand and shook her head. "It's all right, Josef. She has to know."

"Know what?" Anna asked, her voice trembling.

"Know that I have cancer, that I'm dying."

Anna opened her mouth and stared at her aunt in utter distress. "Oh, Karla, no . . . no."

Karla nodded. "I've told you now, Anna. I can't tell you when, or how long I have. But I can tell you this: I planned tonight as a celebration and I intend to celebrate. I will not soon forgive you if you ruin this dinner for me by grieving over my death when I'm very much alive and even quite hungry."

Anna looked at Karla and couldn't say anything. She felt a miserable pain surging through her, a terrible sense of loss, a fear. And yet she well knew Karla's stubbornness, fierce pride, and strong will. "Oh, Karla, I love you so," she whispered.

Karla looked at her and smiled. "I know that. You're the daughter I never had. Anna, I've had a wonderful life and what I have left of it will be wonderful too. You are not going to change anything because of this. You are going to meet Bernard, see Uda, talk with me, and then go back to Chicago. I want things as they should be."

"I don't know if I can behave so normally," Anna murmured.

"You can," Karla said firmly. "And you will."

It was the second consecutive day of Indian summer, one of those clear crisp days when the smell of autumn is in the air, but the sun is warm during the day. Juneau Park was filled with people strolling during noon hour. It was as if the populace were storing up the warmth and sunshine to last them through the long cold winter that lay ahead.

Anna walked toward the restaurant slowly, reluctantly. When she'd been in town with Alex Webber to aid in his defense of the anarchists, she had avoided seeing Bernard, avoided giving him any hope that their relationship had any future beyond friendship. But there was no avoiding him this time, and the truth was, she was almost glad to escape the house for a short time. It was difficult now that she knew about Karla's illness, difficult because Karla insisted on absolute normalcy.

Anna stopped in front of the restaurant and checked her watch . . . it was a pretty little gold watch that pinned onto her lapel. Karla had given it to her last night to celebrate her citizenship, and she touched it fondly, and once again found she had to fight the tears that seemed so ready to come. She moved her fingers off the watch as if it were red hot, and forced herself to think about something else.

I'm early, she thought, looking around. She glanced down the street. Bernard was walking toward her purposefully, and although he was almost a block away, she recognized him.

He had increased his pace, and when he reached her he seemed out of breath. "Anna, Anna! I'm so glad you came. I was afraid you wouldn't."

"I said I would," she replied.

He took her arm and propelled her through the door into the restaurant. "They have wonderful schnitzel here," he said, talking rapidly, nervously. "Of course, if you don't like schnitzel they have bratwurst or sauerbraten . . . have whatever you want."

"Schnitzel is fine," she said. "Tell them not to put any dumplings on the plate."

Bernard ordered, then turned to her. "Don't you like dumplings?"

She shook her head. "They're too heavy."

"You're much too thin," he chided. "Much too thin."

The waiter poured them coffee and they sat at a table covered with a red-and-white-checked cloth by the window. Through the window you could see the park and the children playing on the swings.

"Is there someone else, Anna? Are you in love with someone else?" he suddenly asked.

Anna shook her head. "No. I have to spend most of my time studying, I really haven't had time to socialize much." She moved in her chair uneasily and wondered why they were having this discussion.

"You are getting older, Anna. You should be getting married." He looked into her blue eyes and thought that she was just as pretty as ever, but still he felt differently toward her. Nonetheless, it was important that he speak with her, that he make sure of his own feelings and of hers.

Anna stared at him. It was as if they spoke different languages. "Bernard, I have many things to do. I am not getting married now or in the near future."

He looked back at her steadily. "I thought you'd change your mind by now."

"No. I'm going to finish school and start a law practice."

"I was hoping you had found someone else. If you had, it would have made it easier for me to tell you . . ."

Anna looked at him and felt totally perplexed. "Tell me what?"

He looked at her sheepishly. "I thought I loved you, Anna, but I guess I didn't. I have found someone else— I've asked her to become my wife. But I felt, well, I felt I should talk to you first."

Anna looked at him and almost burst into relieved laughter. She had to force herself to remain serious. She could not begin to tell him how much they'd grown apart. How different their lives really were. Each of them had taken a different road. In his own way, Bernard was highly intelligent. He was a toolmaker, a precision machinist. Above all, he was kind and gentle, but they had nothing in common, and although she knew it, she had been afraid that he still wanted her to marry him—she had been afraid that was the reason he'd asked her last night to meet him today.

"Oh, Bernard, I'm very happy for you," Anna said sincerely. "Very happy."

"Then you think I should marry her?"

Anna smiled. "Oh, I think so, Bernard."

He nodded just as the schnitzel came to the table. Then, after a long moment, "She's a friend of yours. An old friend."

Anna looked at him in surprise. "Uda?" she asked, suddenly guessing.

He nodded. "She's well now. We've been seeing each other for a long while. You know that before she was attacked it was over between her and Oskar . . . in fact, he'd moved away."

"Yes, I knew all that. Why didn't Uda come with you today?" Anna asked.

"She asked me to tell you. She's coming later—in about half an hour."

Anna reached across the table and touched his arm gently. "Bernard, nothing could make me happier than to think of you and Uda together. I really am very pleased because you are both kind and gentle and I know you'll take care of each other. I know you'll be happy."

He grinned. "I told her you'd be glad. I told her you didn't love me."

"I love you, but not as a woman should love a man or a wife should love a husband. I love you like a brother and I love Uda as a sister." She looked down at the tablecloth. "This has been a strange visit for me," she said softly. "I've had terrible news and good news."

"Karla told you?"

Anna nodded. "I suppose Uda must have known."

"For two months—it's very hard for all of us."

Anna only nodded. She felt the tears running down her cheeks, and this time she didn't try to stop them.

The *eleventh hour* of the *eleventh day* of the *eleventh month* brought an end to the war. There were hysterical celebrations in New York, Paris, and London, but there were no celebrations in Essen in the Ruhr river valley.

Else von Bock stood by her bedroom window and stared outside. The sky was utterly, completely clear . . . not a single whiff of smoke escaped the huge smokestacks in Essen. The fires of Krupp had been extinguished, and the workers milled about apprehensively, angrily, as day after day their boredom, frustration, and fear of hunger grew. The men who had signed the armistice were sworn at, hanged in effigy, and were called "the November criminals."

Krupp was providing only bare sustenance for over one hundred thousand families in Essen alone, but sustenance was less than expected; indeed, it was far less than was needed. Talk of revolution filled the air, and while Else did not pretend to understand such talk, she well understood that all around her there was discontent, and possibly danger.

Else shuddered. Her own supplies of food were running low. What would she give the children? Andreas was never home to comfort her or even to help with the overwhelming problems of survival. In fact, she lamented, he had slept with her so seldom over the past two years, he probably suspected that he was not responsible for her last pregnancy. Yes, she knew it was true. Her youngest child was Markus' child. One day, Andreas would confront her . . . at the very least, he would suspect her. The very thought caused her more misery. "I hate it here," she muttered to no one.

It was all the fault of the war. And how could we have lost? Else asked herself for the millionth time. Not that I really understood it in the first place, she admitted. Still, in those days before the war, everyone had been working and happy. All the Kruppianer, the Krupp workers, had been employed night and day. The presses, wheels, belts, and hammers of the munitions factory had hummed with happiness, and on Saturdays there had been marching bands, and everyone had been attired in wonderful uniforms. The beloved kaiser—the All Highest—had the most wonderful uniforms of all. Oh, there had been so much gay pageantry and everyone had money . . . Else touched her dressing gown. Even if there were money now, there was nothing to spend it on.

"Mama! Mama!" Else turned quickly to face her eldest son. Eleven-year-old Klaus von Bock IV stood framed in the doorway of her bedroom. He was dressed from head to toe in one of his several little uniforms—uniforms patterned after those worn by the All Highest. It was a bright red uniform with big gold buttons, gold epaulets, and a drape of gold braid. He was holding his little helmet, the one with a foot-long plume on the tope.

Else frowned at her son. "Why are you dressed that way?" she demanded in a high, semihysterical voice.

"I like my uniform," Klaus protested as he stood at rigid attention. "After all, Mama, I begin military school this year."

Else stared at him and began to tremble. "There won't be any military school for you!" she shouted, and then, advancing on him, she tore the epaulets from his uniform and shrieked, "Take it off! Go to your room at once and take it off! The army has taken everything and lost it! I hated this war! We lost, do you understand *that*, you stupid child? We lost and now there's nothing!"

Klaus stared at his mother in sheer terror, and then, clutching his plumed helmet, he turned and ran down the empty corridor screaming, "I want Papa to come home! I want Papa to come home!"

Else leaned against the wall, and tears tumbled down her face; then she began to laugh. It was a high, hysterical laugh and she couldn't stop and no one came to help her. She laughed till her sides hurt, and then, weary, confused, and shaking, she slumped to the floor and sat in the semidarkness, slowly shredding her lovely gold dressing gown into long flimsy strips. Somewhere in the distance she heard gunfire, and she shuddered. There was lawlessness in the streets, and killing . . . they'd come for her . . . someone would come for her. They'd kill her because she lived in a big house. Else gathered up the shreds of her gown and crawled on her hands and knees back into her room. She bolted the door and crawled to the bed. She pushed herself under it in the darkness, and rolled herself into a fetal ball, clutching her knees. There in the darkness she lay fearfully shaking till finally she fell asleep.

Andreas walked rapidly along the street, thinking that he had never seen Frankfurt look so depressing. But perhaps, he reasoned, it was really the weather, the weather or perhaps his own mood. No, it was everything. Frankfurt, usually a humming industrial city, was quiet and still save for the almost audible sounds of discontent. Massive numbers of workers were unemployed, and they stood about on the streets and in doorways, bored and threatening. They swore at passersby or spit sullenly to indicate their disdain. Some shop windows had been broken, and many well-to-do residents had barricaded themselves in their homes. Not, he thought, that anyone was really well-to-do anymore. It was as if everything and everyone had slipped not one, but two or three notches down a steep economic ladder. Those who had been well-off looked a little down-at-the-heel; those who had been middle class looked seedy. The poor looked poorer, and some, he admitted, looked out-and-out dangerous. No, he wouldn't walk these streets after dark. The political and economic situation in Germany was critical and there had been a rash of robberies and violent murders—more than one hundred in the last month.

It seemed impossible that in the short five months since the armistice his life had crumbled so. Everything he'd worked for was gone . . . everything and more, he thought miserably as he approached the apartment of his mistress, Hedda Schnell.

He tapped lightly on the door. Hedda opened it a crack, and then, seeing it was him, opened it wider. He smiled, took her hands in his, and pulled her into his arms, kissing her passionately on the neck, then on the mouth.

"It's so good to see you," she breathed.

"Here." He pressed a package into her hands and she smiled. "Oh, darling, you've brought something." She eagerly tore away the wrapping and exposed a bottle of white Rhine wine. "Oh, it's wonderful," she said, smiling.

"Prewar," he told her. He hadn't bought it, he'd brought it from his own wine cellar in Essen. It was one of the few bottles he had left, but Else wouldn't miss it. He looked at Hedda and thought: I would have preferred perfume or perhaps some article of clothing, but neither were to be had . . . at least not with the amount of money I had left.

"We'll drink it with dinner," Hedda suggested. "A little celebration, yes?"

Vaguely he wondered what there was to celebrate. Certainly when he revealed the nature of his visit there wouldn't be anything. But he decided not to mention it just yet. He watched as she went to put the wine into the little icebox.

She was as beautiful as the day he'd first met her, he decided. She was still slim and curvacious, and her almond-shaped eyes still glistened, as did her thick red hair. Her hair was loose now, a wild, curly frame for her angular face.

He discarded his jacket and loosened his tie. Then he walked over to her and took her in his arms, holding her tightly, pressing himself against her, and inhaling her exquisite perfume. She always smelled delicious, her whole body a sensual feast.

"You're overanxious," she breathed, touching his cheek with her finger and tracing around his mouth while he nibbled on her. He reached up and took her hand and kissed her fingers; then he kissed her again.

She did not try to stop him or suggest they wait till later. She wore a long blue velvet robe underneath which she wore a flimsy blue diaphanous gown trimmed with ribbons. He pushed her robe back, off her shoulders, and then pulled her gown down, exposing her torso. For a long moment he looked at her beautiful naked body, and he remembered that when last he'd been here, she'd let him rub a warm perfumed oil all over her smooth, alluring skin. The memory made him instantly ready for sex, and he unbuttoned his pants. He seized her hand and placed it on his own organ. She folded her knowing fingers around him and let them dance on his pulsating flesh.

Eagerly now, he bent and kissed her nipples; then he tugged on her gown and it dropped to the floor on top of her robe. She moved her hand and ran it up his chest, undressing him quickly, efficiently. Then they stood naked, close together, their hands exploring one another. Unable to wait another second, he picked her up in his arms and carried her to the bed, kissing her ferociously as he went, then putting her down. He fell on her eagerly.

She wriggled as he caressed her urgently, and when she touched him, he responded instantly. There was something comforting in the sex act, something that momentarily relaxed him and made him forget the torment

238 · Joyce Carlow

his life had become. He roughly grasped her hips and pushed his hands under her buttocks, lifting them slightly. Then he straddled her, and breathing hard, took her while she moaned beneath him, scratching his back and moving with sinuous catlike undulations.

After an hour of rest, Hedda got up and pulled on her robe. He did not dress, but followed her into the kitchen. They often walked about nude. Hedda made coffee and they sat at the table.

"I don't know how you do it," he said, sipping the rich dark brew. "No one else has coffee. Ah, Hedda, your apartment is the last cheerful place in Frankfurt."

She smiled warmly. "How is Else?"

"Sinking into oblivion," he answered vaguely. There was no use trying to explain what had happened to Else. Else was stark raving mad. "She's in an institution," he revealed. "I don't even know if she'll get well."

Hedda looked mildly disturbed. "And your children?"

"I sent them to their grandparents in Berlin. They'll be better off there."

Hedda nodded. "I hope she's in a good institution. I've heard many bad stories . . ."

"It'll be all right," he said, and he wondered if his lack of conviction showed. The truth was that when he'd found her, he'd taken her right to the hospital. The doctors didn't hold out much hope for her, and he'd had no choice but to commit her. Not that he felt guilty about committing her. In her dementia she had confessed her affair with Markus, and had even revealed her suspicions about their youngest child. Even if Else recovered, he had decided on divorce.

"Poor Andreas," Hedda cooed. "You must miss the children."

He nodded and decided to take this opening. "I may have to move to Berlin," he announced.

Her face clouded over. "Berlin? It's so far."

"You could come—you could live and work in Berlin."

"There is no work in Berlin for me," she replied in a

slightly sarcastic tone. "If I left my job here, I wouldn't get another."

"I could—"

"Fully support me? I don't think so, darling." She smiled and reached across the table and touched his cheek. "At least not now."

Andreas automatically turned slightly in his chair when he heard footsteps in the hall, but when they heard the sound of a key being turned in the lock, Hedda too looked up. Suddenly her placid expression turned to alarm.

Andreas' mouth opened slightly as the door swung open. He tried vainly to cover himself with a napkin as Herr Henkle, the manager of the bank where Hedda worked, stood framed in the doorway. He was a large heavyset man with a nearly bald head. He had blue eyes and a ruddy complexion. He was, Andreas assumed, close to sixty, but he was in good physical condition.

In one hand Herr Henkle carried a large package wrapped in brown paper. When he saw Andreas, he slung it on a nearby chair and advanced into the room, slamming the door behind him.

Andreas was unsure of just what to do. He was naked, with only an absurd napkin covering him. Now, in spite of the coolness of the room, he could feel moisture on his skin as he broke out in a cold sweat. Hedda was wearing only her robe, and her long lovely bare legs were crossed, revealing her thighs. Clearly she had nothing on beneath the robe, and just as clearly their recent love-making seemed quite apparent.

"Alfred," Hedda breathed in a shocked tone. She pulled her robe tighter and stumbled as she struggled to her feet, knocking the chair over behind her.

"I suppose you thought I was still in Berlin," he surmised, taking a step toward them.

"Darling, I can explain . . ." Hedda walked toward Herr Henkle.

Andreas sucked in his breath and looked around, as if for the first time seeing the apartment in which he had spent so much time. It was expensively furnished . . . and then, Hedda always had fresh coffee—no one else had fresh coffee. And Hedda usually served him either chicken or meat, both of which cost a fortune on the black market. For the first time he asked himself how she could possibly afford such luxuries on her salary. Naturally, he gave her gifts and sometimes money, but not enough. No, till this moment he hadn't had the intelligence to even question how she survived. But now, in this instant, everything became obvious. He was not the only one! Hedda was not just *his* mistress! Andreas stared at her and then at the fat, wretched Herr Henkle. He felt betrayed . . . horribly betrayed. Was there no woman loyal to him? What was wrong with him?

"I doubt an explanation is necessary," Herr Henkle said coldly.

Andreas continued to stare at him. The old man's voice sounded hate-filled, almost dangerous.

"Darling . . ." Hedda had reached Herr Henkle, and Andreas saw only the old man's hand. His fist was doubled and he swung out furiously and caught Hedda across the face. She spun around and fell to the floor, emitting a short, gasping, pain-filled scream.

Andreas staggered to his feet, and absurdly the napkin fluttered to the floor, and stupidly he tried to catch it.

Herr Henkle looked at him as if he were an insect. And in a terrifying second, Andreas saw the old man held a small revolver. Its muzzle caught the light of the overhead lamp.

"The streets aren't safe anymore," the old man said evenly. He pointed the gun at Hedda's inert form. Her beautiful face twisted in fright, and he pulled the trigger.

Blood immediately gushed from the side of her temple. "I trusted her," Herr Henkle said as he lifted the gun and pointed it at Andreas, who still stood, his mouth open, clutching his napkin. Andreas closed his eyes, but he felt the bullet as he sank to the floor. Partially conscious, he heard a third shot, and as darkness closed in on him, he knew Herr Henkle had killed himself.

Andreas opened his eyes and looked about warily. He appeared to be in a long narrow white cubicle. The walls were absolutely white—in fact, a blinding white. Above him a light dangled from the ceiling. It was encased in a white fixture, and a glance downward revealed the fact that he was tucked tightly into a white bed with white covers. He tried to move his arms, and to his horror, he realized he was strapped down. He gurgled, and then, finding his voice, he yelled.

In a moment the door opened and a nursing sister sailed in. "Hush!" she said in irritation. "Hush! This a hospital, not a soccer field."

The nurse didn't look either kind or sympathetic. Her jaw was square and her lips narrow. Her dark eyes examined him unfeelingly as she brushed her straight dark hair away and off her brow. She was certainly not young, but he felt her manner made her seem older than she probably was. "Where am I?" he queried.

"As I just told you, you're in a hospital. Isn't it perfectly obvious? We have a lot of patients, a lot of casualties, you know."

"Why am I strapped down?"

"Because we have a lot of patients. I just explained that," she hissed angrily. "If you had half a brain, you'd realize you've got stitches. Normally someone would be with you, to see you don't do something stupid and break them open. But we're short-staffed and the wards are overflowing, so you're strapped."

"I won't do anything stupid. Please unstrap me."

"You already did something stupid. You got shot," she said meanly; then, arching her dark brow, "And under highly immoral circumstances," she muttered. "There was a prostitute, and the banker killed himself after shooting you and her. They're both dead, but you survived, and now you're in here taking up space." She glared at him and then continued her tirade. "Don't you realize how many wounded we have? You don't have to go about committing acts of immorality these days to get shot. You could have gotten shot more admirably . . . like our poor suffering war casualties. You make me ill."

Andreas looked at her in absolute amazement. "You're a nurse, you're supposed to be an angel of mercy," he said.

"Of course I am," she retorted coldly.

"You're supposed to love people and be generous and forgiving."

She shook her head. "No, *God* loves you and is generous and forgiving. I don't like you at all. You're taking up a bed that could be used by someone more deserving."

"I'm so sorry," Andreas replied sarcastically.

"You wouldn't be here if your father weren't a general. He had you brought here. I do not approve."

"I'm in Berlin?" Andreas asked.

"Yes. You were brought on a hospital train."

"Untie me!" he demanded again.

She pressed her lips together and leaned over him. "God has punished you." She sneered. "You'll never be able to copulate again. Personally, I hope you grow breasts, lose your facial hair, and develop a nice high shrill voice. Then your former friends will all call you a woman. No, I will not untie you. I will, however, notify your family that you are conscious."

She straightened up, glared at him for a second as she measured the effect of her words, then turned and left the room, closing the door hard behind her.

Never sleep with another woman? Grow breasts? Andreas broke out in a cold sweat and wiggled in his bonds. But it was no use. He couldn't move in any direction, and finally, exhausted, he lay still, his only motion an occasional involuntary spasm of fear.

How long he shook, he wasn't at all certain. Finally, after a long while, the door opened again. His father came in and loomed over him. He was a stern man and it crossed Andreas' mind that he would have been a good match for the nurse.

"I have no comment on your sexual liaisons," his father said without emotion, "but you were frivolous in the extreme, and I'm ashamed of you."

"I didn't know she had other lovers . . ."

"That's what I cannot forgive, your stupidity. Well, it's over. The banker is dead and so is the woman. There are enough scandals and unrest that soon everyone will forget. Besides, what happens in Frankfurt isn't necessarily known in Berlin."

"Else . . ." Andreas said, his face knit into a frown.

"She killed herself," his father said emotionlessly. "Just as well, the state can't afford to care for lunatics in these difficult times."

"My children, how are they?"

"Splendid. Little Klaus is at boarding school. A good strict school. Hermann will follow in his footsteps next year. Emma and little Markus have a nurse. Everything is fine."

Andreas looked at his father. It was such an irony. His parents had asked that his youngest be named after his dead brother, but they didn't know that little Markus was in fact Markus' son. Andreas inhaled and pondered how to ask his next question. "My injury," he finally said. "Is it . . . is it serious?"

"You'll live," his father said without explanation.

"As good as I was? I mean, no aftereffects?"

His father looked at him with disdain. "When you get your balls shot off, there are bound to be aftereffects, Andreas."

"Oh, God! Oh, God! What will become of me? I'm going to turn into a woman!" Andreas wailed, and he tossed, trying once again to break his bonds.

"You're babbling," his father proclaimed harshly. "Have you no self-discipline?"

"I'm afraid," he muttered.

His father scowled. "You didn't get hurt honorably, as your brother did. He was a hero, a man of honor." His father shook his head. "We should have won the war," he said slowly, "The German Army was betrayed . . . the treaty is an abomination. But we will rise from the ashes, Andreas."

Andreas stared at his father. Didn't he understand what he felt like? That frankly, he didn't give a shit about the war?

"You didn't answer," his father observed.

"Yes, rise from the ashes," Andreas repeated, feeling as if he'd been thrust into an alien land where no person understood what the other was saying or feeling.

"I have decided you will go into the army, Andreas.

Markus is dead, I must have a son in the army. You will join as soon as you are better.''

Andreas looked into his father's cold eyes. There was no argument, and he knew it. He also knew he would make a very bad soldier, especially given his condition.

He forced his thoughts away from his father's ravings and glanced downward. Surely there were medications he could take, something to prevent him looking and sounding like a woman.

"Are you all right?" his father queried.

"I'd like to be unstrapped."

His father shrugged. "I'll speak to the surgeon," he promised. "In the meantime, think about your sins. Think about how you can restore honor to the family name."

12

It was June, and all along Chicago's lakeshore the willows, poplars, and maples blossomed anew with lacy greenery. The white sand of Oak Beach, in front of hotels, beckoned tourists, although residents knew it was still far too cold to swim. But in Garfied Park, brave boaters set off across the lake. Oarsmen sporting straw hats guided wooden vessels filled with bonneted young ladies, their parasols open to protect them from the sun. The boats and their passengers floated lazily in front of the old boathouse. It was a masterpiece of Carpenter's Gothic with its alcoved balconies and red roof. Anna walked briskly around the edge of the lake, inhaling the spring air and aware that she didn't even need her blue crocheted shawl in the warm sunshine.

"You look more beautiful than I remembered," Jim Parnell said as they paused under a freshly leaved weeping willow. Its far branches bent down toward the still water, and its reflection created another tree—an almost perfect mirror image.

Anna looked up at him. His reddish-gold hair was still unruly and refused to be tamed by any oils. His blue-green eyes twinkled, and he still had a faint line of freckles across his nose. But he was thinner than he had been, and because he was tall, he looked lanky. There was, she noted, a new seriousness about him, a seriousness that hadn't been an obvious part of his personality before he'd left to fight. He was wearing tan slacks and a white shirt with his sleeves rolled up. He had a straw hat, but it was tilted slightly back, giving him a rakish look. There was, she thought, still something of the bad little boy in his appearance, but there was also something else, something she struggled to understand.

She ignored his flattering comment. "Are you coming back to finish law school in September?" He had missed a year, so they would now be graduating in the same class. But they wouldn't see much of each other because in actual fact, their last year was spent working full-time in a law office and they only returned at the end of the year to sit final examinations.

"Of course. Now we can graduate together."

"You mean now I'll have you for competition in exams."

He put his hands in his pockets and they started walking again, slowly. "You still want to be number one," he surmised.

"I'm a woman. I have to do well."

He nodded, for once adopting her statement without argument. "I thought about you a lot while I was gone," he admitted. "But I suppose you didn't give me a second thought."

"Of course I did. But you didn't write."

"I'm not much of a writer . . . letters are inadequate for me, not my form of communication."

"I wouldn't have made much of a correspondent myself. I've been terribly busy." Anna shook her head. "You know, I thought the hysteria during the war was bad enough, but it's worse now."

"There's less anti-German feeling."

"That's true. But we have more First Amendment cases than ever before. The unions are under fire, the anarchists and socialists are persecuted . . . the slightest deviation is intolerable, it seems. Did you know a socialist was attacked for making a speech? A speech he'd actually plagiarized from Abraham Lincoln!"

"I admit that paranoia's running wild. It's bad, but it'll pass."

"It will pass into law if it isn't fought," Anna said with conviction. She stopped walking. "I don't think you realize how serious this is."

She looked terribly concerned and, yes, determined. He frowned at her. "Of course I do. This war has torn up the world, Ann—think about what's happened. There's been a revolution in Russia, an uprising in Dublin, which our allies put down with a terrible force—they all but destroyed the city! And the European economy is a shambles—the graves are all full, Ann, and there are more being dug as the victims of the gas die slowly.''

His expression had become twisted and he had placed his hand on her arm, which he now held tightly.

''I saw the victims of gas . . . I've watched men die of it. A light puffy cloud, and it burns you from the inside, it shrivels your lungs until you're gasping for breath and praying, just praying to have one more real breath.''

Anna's face clouded over as she listened to him. The war *had* changed him. What he had experienced had made him concerned. He seemed to have a new empathy, an increased sensitivity.

''There weren't enough masks to go around. We were dug into trenches like groundhogs, covered with mud and filth and bugs and waiting for the cloud, praying we'd have a mask.''

Anna reached up and touched his cheek. ''It must have been terrible,'' she said softly.

''Don't you see, Ann? Americans are afraid. They're afraid *that* kind of war, *that* kind of chaos, will come here.''

''Fear is no excuse for intolerance. We can only stay free if we protect our Constitution and the freedoms it gives us.''

''Fear is *the* reason for prejudice and loathing. *Fear*, Ann. Prejudiced, intolerant men are fearful men.''

''Who shouldn't be allowed to undermine our rights,'' she countered, knowing they were in disagreement. ''I know you've seen war and I know you want me to understand. But I can't understand the destruction of our justice system. We can yield nothing, not a single freedom.''

He let out his breath, shrugged, and dropped his hand from her arm. ''You may be right. I may be wrong. Maybe both of us are half-wrong. I don't know, I didn't bring you here to argue.''

"And I didn't come here to argue. Anyway, perhaps we're not really arguing."

"Nonsense, we always argue," he said, changing his tone.

She smiled and changed the subject. "Do you think you can get back into the swing and studying without any trouble?"

"Sure. I read a lot when I was over there . . . look, I've already been approached by the district attorney's office. That's where I'm going to work next year, during our 'year' of practical experience. Then, as soon as I graduate, I'm going to take a job with them."

"That's exciting."

"I've always wanted to be a prosecutor. Working there will be great." He paused. "I guess I don't have to ask where you'll be taking your practical year?"

Anna smiled. "No, you don't. Yes, I'm certainly going to stay with Alex Webber."

"He's a great guy—a little abstract and not too good with the paperwork, but a fine lawyer."

"He's very abstract just now. Mr. Prentice just died. He was nearly eighty—much older than Alex, but I guess it's made Alex feel his own mortality. Not that it was a shock, it was expected. He's been retired for years."

"Webber's lucky to have you," Jim Parnell said: then, "Ann Bock for the Defense," he said officiously. "Hey, maybe we'll face each other in court."

"Maybe," she allowed.

"We don't live in a peaceful city," Alex Webber said with an ironic smirk. The hot July sun streamed through the window at one end of his law library. Anna sat at the long table with piles of papers and books in front of her. She was wearing a light white summer dress with short sleeves and a V neck.

"Do you think you can sort all that out?" Alex asked. "I know there's a lot."

Anna smiled. "I miss the law office when I'm gone, and when I'm here, I don't know how I'll get all the work done. Right now I'm burdened with case law."

"Not all as romantic a profession as it's made out, is it?"

"No, most of it's quite dry . . . but I love it anyway."

He chuckled, then his mobile face returned to its more serious expression. "Pretty bad," he said, shaking his head. "Those Negroes will have to be defended—the ones that were arrested yesterday."

Anna looked up at him, fully aware of what he was talking about. It was an ugly summer, not that the events of the past week had come as a total surprise to anyone with eyes to see. Still, it was surprising how many people didn't want to see.

When she had first moved to Chicago, there had been a long narrow Negro ghetto that stretched along Twelfth Street on the South Side. The war had brought increased Negro migration from the South, as there were jobs and employment opportunities offered by new industries. As she well knew, housing was always difficult. The social workers at Hull House complained constantly. On any single day during 1918, more than two hundred housing applications had been received by the Urban League. Seldom was the League able to find more than twenty-five dwellings a day. The result was that the migrants crowded into what tenements were available, till they were overflowing. The ghetto could not be contained and it spilled over block by block all along South Park and down Grand Boulevard. The aristocratic old homes of Prairie Avenue were taken over, and as far south as Sixty-seventh Avenue, Negro neighborhoods appeared. All along the edge of the ghetto, fighting broke out, and for over a year now there had been bombings and crimes. Seven days ago, a hot July day like this one, race tensions had turned truly violent. When the rioting finally ended, six Negroes were dead and one white person had been killed. Many more Negroes were in hospitals lying injured. Negroes had been pulled off streetcars and beaten, bands of white mobs had roamed neighborhoods ransacking and burning. Finally the governor had sent in troops, and while a few whites were arrested, hundreds of Negroes were in jail, and it was said that property damage was in the millions.

"Six days of pillaging, fighting, stabbings, and shootings," Alex Webber lamented, shaking his head. "And it all started with a stone-throwing incident at the beach."

"No, it all started with inadequate housing and lack of social services," Anna corrected. "It started with prejudice."

"Yes, but there were laws broken."

"Most of the accused white people got off—only one was arrested."

"But some of the Negroes arrested *did* commit crimes," Alex reminded her.

"It still isn't just that so few white lawbreakers were arrested when they committed most of the crimes."

"Sometimes raw justice has little to do with the law. Do you agree that the Negroes who were arrested have to be prosecuted?"

"If real evidence exists to show the law was broken."

"And could you prosecute such a case?"

"I wouldn't necessarily want to, but I could," Anna replied.

Alex smiled. "Parnell has been taken on by the district attorney's office for the year. Usually they take only one student, but they're interested in two this year. Anna, they're interested in you."

Anna looked at Alex. "I'm honored," she said softly.

"It's a compliment."

"You're absolutely the first woman they've ever considered."

"I'm doubly flattered."

"They've asked for an interview with you. Shall I tell them you're interested?"

Anna sought Alex's eyes, then slowly shook her head. "I *am* honored, but I can't. I want to stay here. I don't want to be a prosecutor. When I graduate, I'll be setting up my own practice. I want to concentrate on women's cases and, where they interact, First Amendment cases."

"You won't make a fortune in that kind of law . . . you won't have the opportunity to build the kind of reputation you could build as a prosecutor."

"I know. I hope I haven't disappointed you . . . you've done so much for me."

"You're certain?"

It was, Anna thought, a major temptation. If she worked for the prosecutor, she'd have financial security and the chance to handle highly visible cases. But she would be working with Jim Parnell too, and, she concluded, that just might lead to complications, because she realized she liked him in spite of everything. Yes, this job offer was a temptation, and so was he, but she was determined not to give in to either. "I'm certain," she finally said.

Alex smiled broadly. "Good, good. You know, I think I would have been disappointed if you'd been interested in that job. Besides, my girl, I need you."

"Are we going to have a busy summer?" She smiled, guessing his intentions.

"Oh, yes. You are going to be very busy. I want you to file *habeas corpus* papers for all the Negroes arrested during the riots." He paused and rubbed his chin with his hand. "What might *you* have in mind for a defense strategy?"

Anna thought for a moment. "You know, since there was only one white person arrested, and all the injured in the hospitals are Negroes, I think there may be a possibility of building a case for unequal justice."

"And what of the murdered white man?"

"It still has to be proved that a Negro committed the murder."

Alex took off his glasses and cleaned them with his handkerchief. He chuckled. "The district attorney's loss is a gain for judicial fairness. Go see if you can get blind justice to open just one eye and take a peek into the ghetto. You certainly have my blessing."

He watched as Anna left. Then he stood up, and taking the wrinkled jacket to his summer seersucker suit off the back of his chair, he put it on and went out. It was time to visit Mavis Prentice—he'd been putting it off ever since the funeral.

Mavis Prentice was younger than her husband by ten years, but women age differently than men, whose faces sometimes appear younger than their years. At seventy

Mavis was magnificently wrinkled, the lines in her face like a map of her life. Her white hair was thin, but coiffed into a short, waved fashionable hairstyle. She was a small woman, just under five feet in height, and she still had a small wiry body. Her hands were expressive, and each of her fingers—long thin fingers—was adorned with a ring. She mixed white gold with yellow gold, diamonds with emeralds, and both with a strange agate of no particular value.

"You put off coming," Mavis said sharply as she ushered Alex into her library. "You were my husband's first protégé—he was so proud of you."

"He was my mentor."

"I believe you, but no one else will. My daughter, Christiana—you remember her—keeps asking me if you've come. And I keep telling her, no, he hasn't come. He's an old fuddy-duddy. He doesn't like people dying because it reminds him he's not immortal."

"I don't like people dying because my father was an undertaker and I've seen enough of it."

Mavis nodded and self-consciously touched her finger to her lips. He realized she hated her dentures and probably hadn't put them in. "Pearly said you were the best lawyer in Chicago."

"Pearly . . ." Alex Webber said the name. It had been Prentice's nickname, but it was known to only a few intimate friends. Pearly Prentice was so called because of his dazzling smile. "I'll miss him," Alex said. "I'll never take his name off the door."

"How are things at the firm?" Mavis asked.

"As usual, short of cash. Too many *pro bono* cases, not so many rich clients. I'm not a rich man's lawyer."

"Pearly left me a sizable trust fund, Alex. You're the keeper of that fund. You know if you ever need it you can take what you want. I'll never live long enough to need it."

"That's your money."

"I have more money than I need. Use it, Alex. Pay the bills and take care of things. I know how many cases you have."

He pressed his lips together and nodded. "You're a

wonderful woman, Mavis. Pearly was a lucky man. I'll send some papers over for you to sign—a formality, giving me access to the fund if necessary.''

"How many nonpaying clients do you have now?"

He shrugged. "Ten—all important cases."

Mavis smiled and touched his hand. "You wouldn't take an unimportant case," she said. "Pearly would approve."

Alex stood up. "Can I take a lovely lady out to dinner?"

"Your wife won't mind?"

He grinned and shook his head. "How about the Addison?"

"The Addison will be fine."

The Cook County Jail was a depressing place, and the so-called "interview area" where lawyers were allowed to meet with their clients was no exception. It was a barren room with dirty mustard-colored walls and the only furniture consisted of a pockmarked table and several straight-backed chairs. At the far end of the room there was a long narrow window with heavy iron bars over it. But it was open, and given the hot, sticky, humid atmosphere in the room, Anna was grateful that a slight breeze could be felt every now and again. August in Chicago could be deadly, and this was as deadly an August as she remembered.

Anna wiped her brow, aware that her hair was damp with perspiration and strands of it clung to her forehead. She had now interviewed thirty-five of the blacks who had been arrested. It was a long and tedious process, not relieved in any way by the fact that she had a difficult time understanding some of them because her ear was not attuned to their heavy Southern accents mixed with slang, and she had to keep asking people to repeat themselves. Her thirty-sixth and last interview of the day was the most serious case. He was accused of murder, while the previous thirty-five had been charged with everything from disorderly conduct to assault and battery.

The door opened and the stony-faced guard pushed a young black man roughly into the room. The guard was wearing blue trousers and a lighter blue shirt. He had, because of the heat, discarded his uniform jacket, and the sleeves of his shirt were rolled up. He was a burly man with bulging muscles and short, neatly combed hair. The black man was young and was by contrast much smaller, perhaps, Anna gauged, only five-feet-three or so. And he was thin, pitifully thin, and frightened-looking.

"Sit down, please," Anna said, indicating the chair on the other side of the table.

"I thought I was comin' to see the lawyer," the young black said.

"I'm studying to be a lawyer. I'm in my last year. I'll do this interview, but someone from our firm will actually represent you in court." Anna paused. The guard was still there, standing by the door, his feet wide apart, clearly listening. "I'd like to be alone with my client," she said, looking up in annoyance.

"Can't leave no little girl with a murderer," he snapped back.

Anna scowled at him. "*Alleged* murderer, and I have a right to be alone with my client. I want you to leave," she stated authoritatively.

"Nope. Can't do that, honey."

Anna felt a wave of absolute anger wash over her. "I am not your honey," she said icily. "There are laws governing client-lawyer relations. I insist you leave."

"I don't want no woman lawyer," the young black man mumbled.

Anna looked from the guard to the young black man. She stood up, and her chair scraped across the floor. She tugged on her cotton skirt; it was so warm it was stuck to her because she'd been sitting so long. She walked over to the prisoner's side of the table. "You," she said, "will stay right where you are. You will answer all the questions I ask you, and you will not complain anymore." Then she walked up to the guard, and thrusting her hand behind him, turned the knob and opened the door. She edged past him. "I'll be back with your superior."

Anna stomped down the hall, feeling the blood rush

to her face. How dare the guard refuse her request! How dare he call her "honey"! As for the prisoner, well, he was lucky to have Alex Webber's firm representing him. It was hardly the moment to complain because she was a woman.

"Hey, you could run right into a person," Jim Parnell said cheerfully.

Anna looked up, surprised to see him. "Sorry," she said. "I was just on my way to the superintendent's office."

Jim grinned at her. "Trouble?"

"Yes, the guard won't leave me alone with my client."

"Ah, and who might your client be?"

"Jimmy Washington, the young man accused of murdering that Tom Andrews during the rioting . . . you probably know the case."

"Sure, I know the case. Look, the guy only wants to protect you . . . what's the problem? You look like you've really got a bee in your bonnet."

Anna looked up at him and then stamped her foot. "Damm it!" she swore. "I don't expect that from you! I want to be alone with my client! I want the rules enforced! And don't you dare call me 'honey' too!"

Jim took a step backward and held up his hands in surrender. "I wouldn't dream of calling you 'honey.' Okay, okay . . . come on, I'll talk to the guard. I am from the D.A.'s office, remember."

Anna looked at him, but her expression did not soften, nor did her mood change. "You do that," she said, following him as he turned to head for the interview room. Anna forged ahead of him, and she wiped the perspiration off her brow. She would have to face this sort of thing over and over, she told herself. And learn to deal with it . . . still, she felt truly angry, and she admitted to herself that her inability to be patient had something to do with the heat. She inhaled and pressed her lips together; no wonder there were race riots in the summer. At the moment she herself felt like rioting.

Jim watched her as she flung open the door and tramped across the room to sit down. He looked at the guard, then at the prisoner. "Jim Parnell, D.A.'s office," he introduced himself to the guard.

The guard immediately smiled and nodded, showing Jim the respect he hadn't showed her, Anna noticed.

"You can leave her alone with the prisoner. It's required by law."

The guard looked dubious. "Is that wise, sir?"

Jim nodded and then grinned. "Take it from me, she can take care of herself."

Anna looked at both of them coldly. But the guard acquiesced and stepped outside.

Anna was still seething, but she fought to control herself. "Thank you very much," she said, looking at him skeptically.

"Don't make more of it than it is," he advised. He turned to leave, and as he did so, he closed the door. Poor Anna, he thought, she had a fierce pride and a healthy temper. She was going to have to learn to control her anger and decide on which issues she would make her stand. It was not going to be easy for her to do her job; she had her work cut out for her. But, he thought, she was smart as well as beautiful, and she would make it because she really wanted to make it.

It was autumn, and the magnificent hardwoods that were interspersed with the conifers turned gold, red, and orange. Anna sat by Karla's bedside and looked out the back window into the small yard. A maple tree shed golden leaves on the browning grass and Anna watched as a neighborhood boy clad in an Oshkosh plaid jacket and work pants raked them lethargically.

Karla opened her eyes, "Are you still here?" she asked in an unnaturally small, weakened voice.

Anna looked away from the window immediately. "Of course I'm still here."

Karla sighed. "I'm going to die soon," she said slowly. "I know because if you're not here, Josef is here."

"We want to be here."

"Thank you for wanting to be with me, and thank you for not bothering to say, 'You'll get better, Karla . . .

you'll be just fine.' I won't be fine, and I don't want to be lied to, I want the truth.''

Anna bit her lip. "The trouble is, you're braver than we are.''

"I'm not brave at all. I love life, I've hugged it and I've kissed it every day I've been on this earth. I'm frightened of nothingness—of the void.''

"I don't know how to comfort you.''

"You comfort me just by being here, by seeing me off. I told you, life is a grand adventure. I've been blessed.''

"You're going to make me cry again,'' Anna said. "Don't, because when I cry, you get mad.''

"Well, I don't want to leave with everyone moaning and groaning. I want you to hold my hand and kiss my cheek. I want you to smile and say good-bye.''

Her voice seemed to be getting smaller and smaller as she spoke. It came harder and she kept closing her eyes and opening them, as if drifting off into sleep for just an instant.

Anna leaned over and kissed her aunt on the cheek. "You get weaker when you talk too much.''

Karla half-laughed. "That's because I'm dying . . . a moment or two of rest will not prolong my life, my darling.''

"It makes me angry,'' Anna said suddenly. "This makes me angry. Karla, you're only forty-two! You're young and this shouldn't be happening.''

"It happens . . . I had a huge growth on my left ovary when I was younger . . . they took it out, but they told me then I'd not have children. It's where the cancer started . . . they say it moves faster when you're young.''

"Oh, Karla . . .'' Anna laid her head down on the side of the bed and pressed Karla's hand to her face. "You've always been a mother to me . . . I'd have been miserable without you.''

"And you've always been like our father, Anna. You were never like the von Bocks. I knew it from the beginning. I knew you were intelligent and gentle, a special child.''

"Please . . . don't flatter me when all I want is to let you know how much I care for you.''

"I'm so proud of you. You must promise me, Anna. Promise to practice law. To defend the principles of justice."

Anna embraced her and Karla began coughing. When she stopped, she leaned back and groaned a little. "Is it time for my medication?"

Anna nodded. "You're in pain, aren't you?"

Karla nodded.

Anna got the pills and the water. She helped Karla take her medicine and she watched as Karla grew drowsier and drowsier. Soon her eyes were glazed over and she finally closed them, slipping off into a merciful drug-induced sleep.

Anna sat in the room while the sun set, and then Josef came.

"Is she asleep?"

"Yes, she's just had the morphine."

"You go rest for a while. I'll stay."

"All right." Anna pulled herself up, surprised how stiff she was from sitting for so long. She went down the corridor and then down the stairs to the kitchen to fix some tea.

When she had finished her tea, she lay down on the sofa and for a time slept herself.

"Anna! Anna!" Josef's agonized cry filled the house and Anna opened her eyes and sat up suddenly. She clenched her fingers and waited for a second as she tried to gather strength. She could tell from the tone of his cry that it was over, that Karla had died in her sleep.

Anna stood up and then forced herself to climb the stairs. Josef was standing outside Karla's door, his mouth still open, his face knit in pain, silent tears running down his face. Anna ran to him and held him. They stood for a long while, trembling in each other's arms, crying quietly for Karla, whom they had both loved so much.

It was a gray day, and threatening December winds blew across Lake Michigan. The windowpane in Jim Parnell's fifth-floor office shuddered with a particularly ferocious gust, and for a moment both Anna and Jim looked up, half-expecting the wind to shatter the glass.

"They don't call it the windy city for nothing," he quipped. "Take off your coat, Ann, stay awhile.

He looked relaxed in spite of what she knew his job demanded. He closed an open file folder and tossed it into a tray on the corner of his desk. Anna undid her warm scarf and unbuttoned her coat. She slipped it off and hung it on the rack by the door. "Don't tell me you have all the time in the world. I know better. This place is overburdened with cases."

"You can't let it get to you. Have a seat"—he motioned to a chair opposite his desk. "I don't suppose this is a social call . . . I couldn't be that lucky."

"You're right, it's not a social call."

"Too bad. This has been a hell of a year. We've hardly seen each other at all."

"It's been busy," she agreed. Jim was wearing casual slacks and an Irish fisherman's sweater with a shirt underneath. Clearly he liked it here, Anna thought.

"So, to what do I owe the pleasure of this visit?"

Anna reached down for her briefcase. She snapped it open and took out some papers. "I've been told you're the junior counsel on the Jimmy Washington case."

He grinned. "And let me guess . . . you're the junior defense counsel?"

"You know perfectly well I am. You met me at the jail the day I was doing the initial interview."

He held up his hands in surrender. "I confess. As a matter of fact, I requested this case just so I could see you."

Anna blushed and then quickly recovered. "Could we stick to business?" He was teasing her again, but somehow she wished she could believe it was more than teasing. He was an attractive man, and as she well knew by now, a good man.

"Your wish is my command."

He deliberately sat up straight and looked across the desk at her, an expression of mock seriousness covering his face.

"Jimmy Washington has been in jail without bail since July," she began.

"Not unusual for someone charged with murder."

260 · Joyce Carlow

"He didn't commit murder, he acted in self-defense. He hit Anderson with a plank—we don't deny that, but I've evidence that Anderson was armed."

Jim screwed up his face. "With what?"

"A Saturday Night Special. He's a Ku Klux Klan member, did you know that?"

Jim sucked in his breath. "Can you prove that?"

"I can prove he participated in Klan activities . . . I can prove he has a criminal record."

Jim's face had taken on an expression of interest, and now, she noted with satisfaction, he seemed sincerely concerned.

"Exactly what have you got?" he asked.

"He has a record with the St. Louis police and the Bureau of Investigation."

"Even if the victim did have a record, and even if he was armed, I will argue that your client used unreasonable force to defend himself if you argue your client acted in self-defense."

Anna looked at Jim hard. "You can certainly do that, but wouldn't it be better to save time, taxpayers' money, and your esteemed efforts by reducing the charge to manslaughter?"

"Is that what you want?"

"That, and time off for time served as well as recognition of the fact that my client has no previous record."

For a long moment Jim Parnell tapped his fingers on the corner of his desk. Anna watched him carefully and could see he was running through all the alternatives in his head. Finally he looked up and nodded. "I'll recommend the reduced charge," he relented.

He then smiled broadly. "Don't be so suspicious," he said, reading her thoughts. "I'm not doing it for personal reasons . . . believe me, Ann, I'm reducing it because I think you've got a good case. Besides, racial tensions are high. Why heighten them by going to trial in such a questionable case? This way justice can be served and people won't get their backs up."

Anna looked at him and then cautiously returned his smile. "Thank you," she said.

"You can thank me by letting me take you out. How about it?"

"I'm not free till the weekend."

He nodded. "Saturday night?"

She smiled. "I'll look forward to it."

William Pridmore was tall, smooth, and slick. He wasn't Chicago's most notorious criminal, but he was one of the most successful. He owned and operated an elegant restaurant on the near North Side.

The restaurant served him well. It provided a legitimate front for his illegal activities, it enabled him to meet and entertain the political and financial elite of Illinois, and it satisfied his passion for explorations into gourmet cooking. Pridmore's wife, Agnes, knew nothing of his activities as "brothel keeper," nor did any of Pridmore's wealthy and influential friends guess his true interests, or suspect that he had become active in the new and lucrative area of bootlegging. In spite of his success, Pridmore was well aware of the fact that in order to remain successful he had to protect his territory as well as his access to the rich and influential. At this moment he was in what a financier would call "a period of consolidation." Toward that end, he had ferreted out all his local competitors and either bought them out, or hired them, or killed them. If at all possible, and if they were talented and had certain resources, he preferred hiring them.

The office at the rear of Pridmore's North Side Bistro was spacious and decorated in the best of taste. The wallpaper was red and gold, a textured swirling pattern that harked back to the Victorian era. The lamps, while electric, were made to look like gaslights and they gave off a muted golden glow. The furniture was made of highly polished oak, and the sofa and all the chairs were richly upholstered in forest-green velvet.

Pridmore leaned back in his own plush chair and steepled his fingers. He stared at his impeccably manicured fingernails and slowly lifted his eyes to assess the well-dressed man who sat opposite. Pridmore decided the man was in his late thirties . . . and, he admitted, he was well-groomed and good-looking. Not really the type to be running a small prostitution ring . . . yet it wasn't the average small operation. This one had a certain reputation.

"So, they call you the professor," Pridmore said.

Kurt Stein looked Pridmore in the eye. "So I hear," he replied.

"And why might they call you that?"

Kurt shrugged. "I suppose because I was once a tutor at a European university—perhaps it's because I speak several languages and I'm a hell of a lot smarter than most of my competition."

"I'm glad you said 'most,' " Pridmore said dryly.

Kurt glanced around. "You've got a class operation," he admitted.

"I was initially going to buy you out, Professor, but I think you might be an asset to my business. As America's second-largest city, we sometimes have diplomatic customers. I could use an educated type. What do you think?"

Kurt half-smiled. "I wouldn't want to lower my standard of living."

"I don't think you'd have to lower it . . . in fact, I think you could raise it. How about it? I'll run the cathouses and you can have full control over the call girls. I'll cut you in on the booze too."

Kurt raised his brow. "What are we talking here? A month, that is. What's my share?"

"Ten grand minimum."

Kurt smiled. "And a new Duesenberg . . . black."

Pridmore smiled and walked around his massive desk. He reached out, and he and Kurt Stein shook hands. "Deal," he agreed, and as he looked into Kurt's eyes, he felt good about it. This man, he decided, was a better partner than an enemy.

The long table in the von Bock dining room was set with silver and fine china. General Klaus von Bock sat, as always, at the head of the table. He still stood ramrod straight when he stood, but his walk was slower now, and his gray hair had fallen out, leaving him entirely bald. At sixty-two he was beginning to feel his age, and this New Year's Eve he drank less and ate less, aware of the tightness of his belt.

He looked down the long table. The chairs were further apart now, but if he tried very hard he could fill in the missing faces, could conjure up New Year's Eves past.

The past was a dream; his reality was more depressing. Those seated round his table were primarily women and children. The pride of his life, young Markus, was dead. In his place sat his simpering widow, Dorcas, and her six-year-old daughter, Mathilde. Gerda too was a widow with two children, though one, Rudolf, was a son. Little Markus was too young to be present. And of course there were Andreas' four children—three boys and little Emma.

He looked down to the foot of the table. His wife, Gisela, sat placidly staring into her soup. Yes, there he was, the only real man among three women and seven children, the eldest of whom was twelve-year-old Rudolf, a pale asthmatic child who would never be fit enough for military service. He glanced at Mathilde. She was the only one of the grandchildren that showed a real spark of intelligence. But then, he reasoned, it was too soon to tell. She was only seven and was, after all, a girl.

Klaus forced himself to look at Andreas. Andreas was dressed in his uniform and he looked like a stuffed pig. He had put on a great deal of weight, and he was nervous too, incredibly high-strung and nervous. It was the shooting. Andreas would never be the same, but they didn't speak of it, and truth be known, he himself felt little or no sympathy for his son.

His eyes settled on little Klaus von Bock IV. There was real hope for the lad. In spite of having a mother who had gone stark, raving mad and a father who had managed to get his balls shot off while enjoying a flight of fancy, little Klaus would probably make the perfect German soldier. He was in fact completely intrigued with everything military and he moved his toy soldiers with sureness and true commanding skill. Yes, in spite of his mad mother and undisciplined father, little Klaus already knew what was important. But the boy was still young and what he needed was self-denial and training.

"It's almost midnight," Mathilde announced.

Drawn out of his thoughts by Mathilde's voice, Klaus von Bock stood up and Andreas and the three male children also stood up. "To the new year," Klaus toasted. "To 1920!"

"To 1920!" they all repeated in unison.

Klaus began the countdown as he watched the second hand on his pocket watch move around the clock face— 59 . . . 58 . . . 57 . . . Their combined voices grew fainter as the hour approached, and then only Klaus was counting—3 . . . 2 . . . 1 . . . He lifted his glass. "Happy New Year."

There were several moments of uncomfortable silence; then Gisela unexpectedly struggled to her feet. "What's happy about it!" she screamed down the length of the table. With those words she threw her Rosenthal china plate to the floor, smashing it into a hundred pieces. "My son is dead! My daughter is a widow! My grandchildren are fatherless! I hate this place! I hate you!" She hurled her crystal goblet the length of the dining room and the children automatically ducked and yelled.

Then Gisela ran from the room. "Damn the German Army!" she shrieked. "Damn the kaiser and all the stupid fools who followed him!" Her voice grew fainter as the front door opened and then slammed shut.

All eyes were turned to where Gisela had been seated. Klaus stared openmouthed and then he gurgled and clasped his chest. A sharp, horrible pain spread up his left arm and across his chest. He gasped, but the eyes of everyone in the room were still on the door through which Gisela had fled. They did not turn till the tablecloth beneath the plates moved and Klaus von Bock crumpled to the floor with a great thud, his fingers grasping the white damask cloth tightly.

Gerda screamed and ran to her father. Dorcas stood over him looking down. "He's dead," she said flatly. "He's had a heart attack."

13

Anna's golden hair was cut short and combed so it curved under gently. Her haircut and the style of her clothes were a studied attempt to appear completely business-like, and she felt satisfied that she had succeeded. She wore a beige linen skirt that fell to her stockinged ankles, and a matching jacket that had small gold buttons on it. Underneath, she wore a plain tailored white blouse. Her shoes were leather with a small heel, but they were good sturdy walking shoes, sensible shoes.

She sat behind her secondhand maple desk and looked at the block letters on the door across the room. As the top half of the door was made of opaque glass, and the lettering was on the outside, the letters appeared to her upside down and backward, and rather resembled Cyrillic script. But Anna knew what they said: *Ann Bock, Attorney-at-Law.*

"This is a cubbyhole," she said aloud to herself. "But mine, all mine." Anna smiled and got up from behind her desk and walked around, stopping at the only window, a long narrow one that overlooked Randolph Street. "My law office," she said, because saying it aloud made it seem more real. It is real, she thought. Yet a year in limbo and four years of study, her own tiny office and the practice it represented, all still seemed like a dream.

The room was only nine by twelve feet, and there wasn't any reception area, or even room for a secretary. Still, she felt proud. And, she told herself, the size of the office didn't matter because there was no money for a secretary or a law clerk in any case. She had room for her desk, four chairs, a filing cabinet, and a small corner table. The most positive feature of her office was its location in the Shilling Building. The Shilling Building was a brisk walk down Randolph Street from City Hall and the County Building located on a block bounded by Randolph, Clark, Washington, and LaSalle. It was also near the Wabash Street elevated station, as well as the law office and library of Alex Webber. "Come and use my books anytime," he had told her, and since it would be years before she built up her own collection, she was grateful for his generosity.

Originally Anna had planned to set up her office in the Settlement House, but in the end she had been persuaded by Alex that she needed to be closer to the courts, and that, located elsewhere, she would be able to attract paying clients in addition to those *pro bono publico*—or welfare cases—which she intended to pursue. "Doing good is one matter," Alex advised, "but, my dear, goodness doesn't pay the rent, and in order to do good, the rent *does* have to be paid."

He was right, she had thought when he'd finished his little lecture. Still, she could not help chiding him, "You're a fine one to give advice."

He'd looked at her and winked. "I'm not just starting out. I've been in practice a long time."

"Next you'll tell me you're independently wealthy," she had teased.

He had laughed and waved her away. Nonetheless, she took his advice and was, in fact, now waiting for her very first paying customer.

Anna checked her lapel watch and then looked about her little office nervously. The desk was in order, and what books she had were neatly arranged on the shelves. There were gold curtains at the window, and several chairs in which her clients could sit. She was still taking inventory when a shadow appeared outside the opaque glass door and there was a knock. Anna smiled. Her very first client was early.

"Come in," Anna said as she opened the door, then, smiling, "I warned you on the phone that my office was small."

The woman who came in appeared to be neither rich nor poor. In fact she appeared to be almost relentlessly middle class. She wore a high-collared suit with a full jacket, three-quarter-length sleeves, and deep pockets. She wore gloves and her hat matched her suit and was trimmed with little flowers. Her skirt fell just above her ankles and her shoes were pointy, with big buckles. Definitely not designer clothes, but rather an off-the-rack ensemble from Marshall Field. "I'm Ann Bock," Anna said, holding out her hand.

"Mary Ellen Olsen," the woman responded as she eased into the office. "Mr. Webber's office recommended you . . . he's too involved to take my sister's case . . ." Her voice trailed off and she slumped into one of the chairs and folded her hands resolutely.

Mary Ellen Olsen looked tired and discouraged. "Tell me why you're here," Anna urged kindly. "And please, don't hold anything back."

Miss Olsen nodded and began to talk, though she didn't look up at all, but continued to stare at her hands.

"It's my sister. She was brutally raped and she's been accused of killing the man who did it. She's in jail . . . how could they put her in jail? It was self-defense."

Anna frowned. "Obviously the police don't think so."

Miss Olsen glanced up, then returned her eyes to her hands. "There's a problem," she said hesitantly. "A terrible problem."

"You must tell me everything if I'm to help her," Anna coaxed.

Miss Olsen paused, then slowly began, "My sister isn't like me . . . she's . . . she's loose . . ." Miss Olsen's voice got softer and softer, till Anna could hardly hear her.

"A prostitute," Miss Olsen finished, and her gloved hands covered her face and she began to cry. "I love my sister in spite of everything, Miss Bock. She's not a murderer, it *was* self-defense. But the man was one of her . . . her clients. The police say it's murder . . . that rape couldn't take place under such circumstances."

"Criminal law isn't my specialty," Anna said honestly.

"I can't pay you a big fee, but I can afford to pay. Mr.

Webber told me a woman should fight this case . . . please, you must help me.''

"I'll be glad to take your sister's case. I just wanted you to know that there are experienced criminal lawyers available.''

"I understand. But Mr. Webber recommended you and I trust his judgment.''

"All right, I'll be glad to take your sister's case, if, after I've spoken to her, she too is agreeable. Is she being held in the Cook County Jail.''

"Yes, they won't grant bail because of her . . . her profession.''

Anna opened the top drawer of her desk and took out a printed form. "This is an agreement stating that you've hired me to represent your sister. Please read it and then sign it. I can't get in to see her or talk with her until I'm officially representing her. Naturally, I will have her sign it too if she agrees.''

The woman took the proffered form and read it slowly.

Anna watched, and when the woman had finished, Anna asked, "Are there any questions?''

The woman shook her head, and Anna handed her the pen. When the woman passed the document back to her, Anna took out a large pad. "What is your sister's full name?''

"Margaret Jane Olsen.''

Anna wrote it down together with Mary Ellen's address and phone number. "I'll request the particulars of the charges from the district attorney's office, and I'll try to see your sister today.''

Miss Olsen nodded, then held out her trembling gloved hand. "Thank you . . . please, try to help her. She's terribly frightened.''

After Mary Ellen Olsen left, Anna carefully put away the file. She then prepared to leave the office in order to go to the Cook County Jail. Absorbed in thought, she opened the door to leave the office and was surprised to see a man standing in front of it, his hand raised as if he were about to knock.

"Miss Bock?'' he said hesitantly.

"Yes, but I'm afraid I'm on my way out." Even as she spoke the words, his expression turned to one of distress. He was, she saw, about forty and well-dressed in a conservative tan summer suit. Perhaps, she guessed, he was a business executive, or even a banker.

"I must speak with you. It's really urgent, quite urgent."

His voice was soft, yet insistent. His rimless glasses gave him a severity that his voice belied. "I'm afraid I have to get down to the Cook County Jail," Anna responded. "But I could see you tomorrow morning."

"That would be too late. I must speak with you now, this minute."

"I wish you had phoned—I'm terribly sorry, but I have a previous commitment."

"Then let me drive you to the Cook County Jail. I'll explain myself on the way."

It certainly wasn't her policy to accept rides from total strangers, but this man seemed troubled and genuine. "All right," she agreed. "Talk as we walk. I'll try to take it all in."

"My name is Robert Stackhouse. I work at the Illinois Central Bank on Wabash."

As they hurried down the stairs, Anna mentally smiled. It might be a stereotype, but there was something about bankers . . . she could always tell a banker.

They walked through the door, and he indicated a car parked at the curb. It was an undistinguished black Ford. "What is the nature of your legal problem?"

"It's my daughter . . . Louise. She's ten . . . well, she will be ten in three days' time."

He opened the door and Anna slid into the front seat. In a moment he was sitting beside her and the car was was pulling out into traffic.

"Her mother and I are divorced. Lilian—my ex-wife— Lilian got custody of Louise."

Anna frowned slightly. In her heart she supposed she was prejudiced; she believed mothers should have custody. Quickly she reminded herself that there were exceptions. "Is this really urgent?" Anna asked. "You know, it takes a long while to reopen a custody case."

"No. I mean, yes. Yes, I know that part takes time, but there is something urgent. Lilian is taking Louise away—she's leaving tomorrow. I'm never going to see my little girl again . . . and . . . and I'm afraid for her."

Anna glanced at him. His face was red, and tears had formed in the corners of his eyes. His hand shook slightly. Clearly he believed what he was saying, and believed it passionately. "I imagine you want a court injunction to prevent your wife from taking the child."

"Yes. It's imperative. Lilian is leaving with a man who is . . . well, dangerous. I don't trust him with my daughter. You must help me, you must."

Anna stared out the windshield of the car. She had always championed women . . . always assumed . . . Could this man be right? Could this young girl be at risk with her mother? At that moment she realized she had always made other assumptions too. She had always thought that fathers cared less for their children than mothers. Perhaps, she thought, she had made that assumption because of her own personal experience—because Kurt hadn't cared.

"Do you have any proof of the allegations you're making against this man?"

Mr. Stackhouse nodded. "Please, you must help me."

"You came to me because I'm a woman, didn't you? You think a judge would be more sympathetic if a woman tried for this injunction."

"Yes, I admit it. Is that so wrong? I'm desperate."

Anna turned to him as the car came to a stop in front of the Cook County Jail. "Wait for me here. Then we'll go back to my office and fill out some papers. Then we'll try to see a judge."

"And then?"

"If we're lucky, we'll get a court order—then the police won't let her leave Chicago."

He still gripped the steering wheel, but now he leaned back and closed his eyes. "Thank you," he whispered. "Thank you."

During her apprentice year with Alex Webber, Anna had spent a considerable amount of time attending and conducting interviews with prisoners, as well as in the courts assisting at trials. As a result, the the Cook Country Jail was not new to her. Still, familiarity did not make the place seem less depressing, and the section in which women were held was even more unnerving than the rest of the place.

Anna walked along the corridor between the cells slowly, her eyes drawn to the women behind bars, her sense of rage growing with each passing cell. There were more than a few prisoners who ought to have been in mental hospitals rather than jails. These were women who had committed crimes ranging from shoplifting to murder, but whose states of either wretched suicidal depression or maniacal hysteria branded them as ill rather than criminal. Still, they were here—some lost, withdrawn, weeping souls, others frantic and tearing at their clothing, hair, and bodies.

Anna stopped in front of a cell holding a single woman. Her hands were tied to the sides of her bunk, and she sobbed, choking now and again as she tugged on her bonds in violent frustration. So intent was the woman that she didn't even look up, but even without seeing her face, Anna could see that her arms and legs were covered with vicious scratches, some of which were still bloody.

"Matron!" Anna called out, knowing the anger in her voice was all too evident.

Big Betty, as she was known in the jail, padded down the corridor. Anna looked up at her—in the distance her silhouette against the light in the dimly lit corridor appeared frighteningly familiar. Big Betty, in stature at least, reminded Anna of Helga, the militant and cruel nurse who had stolen her child. But Anna knew Big Betty, and even as her own memories flooded over her, she pushed them from her mind.

"Yes, counselor?" Big Betty sneered. She didn't treat Anna as she treated the male lawyers. Indeed, in the beginning she hadn't even believed she *was* a lawyer.

Anna ignored her insolent tone. "Why is that woman tied?" she asked sharply.

"She your client?" Big Betty asked, looking confused.

"No. But I want to know why she's tied."

Big Betty shrugged as if the answer were all too evident. "She hurts herself. See all them scratches?"

"Who is her lawyer?" Anna asked.

"Court ain't appointed one yet."

Anna looked into the cell. "May I represent you?" she called out.

The woman looked up. Her expression was fearful, like that of a trapped animal. But she seemed to understand and she murmured, "Yes."

Anna turned back to Big Betty. "What's she here for?"

"Attempted murder. Tried to kill her husband."

"I want her sent to the hospital. I want a doctor to examine her immediately."

Big Betty scowled down at Anna.

Anna stood fast. "I can get a court order if necessary, but I know she can be sent to a hospital on *your* recommendation. Let's not waste time. Send her for assessment."

"You going to stop by my office and fill out the papers?"

"On my way out," Anna promised.

"Okay, what do I care? One more loony gone out of here is one less to take care of." Big Betty turned slightly. "Who you come to see?"

"Margaret Olsen."

"Oh, the hooker. She's three cells down, around that corner. How many stray cats do ya intend to pick up 'tween here and there?"

Anna didn't reply; she just turned and walked away. As she did so, she heard Big Betty mutter something distasteful about lady lawyers.

The cells between the tethered woman and her client were filled with prostitutes. There were a great many in Chicago, and if they did not pay off the police, they landed in jail for a few nights. Naturally, there were also thieves and murderers, women who planned their crimes and knew exactly what they were doing. Unfortunately, they were not segregated from the mentally ill or the clearly nonviolent.

So many crimes resulted from poverty—more than

Anna could have possibly counted. Worse yet, punishment was what society wanted, not rehabilitation.

Anna stopped in front of cell fifty-three. She opened it with the key Big Betty had given her, and let herself into the cubicle.

Margaret Olsen was in her twenties . . . younger by ten years than her sister. She was blond and brown-eyed, and even in plain prison garb Anna could tell she had good figure, the kind of figure men like. Her breasts were heavy, her waist small, and her hips rounded. Her mouth was full and a little pouty. She was an appealing woman in a sensuous way, a woman who would have had little difficulty attracting men. The minute Margaret opened her mouth, it was evident that, unlike her sister, she had dropped out of school and spent a number of years on the street.

"I'm your lawyer," Anna said. Then, correcting herself, "I'm the lawyer your sister hired, and I'll represent you if you consent."

Margaret looked up. "Sure, you're okay, I guess."

Anna gestured toward the bunk. "May I sit down?"

"Be my guest," Margaret replied.

Anna sat down and opened her briefcase, withdrawing her pad and pencil.

"You really a lawyer?" Margaret asked, scrutinizing her more closely.

"I certainly am. My name is Ann Bock, Margaret. Your sister has asked me to help you."

"Wouldn't I be better off with a man?"

Anna raised her brow and looked at her new client. Women, as much as men, doubted the ability of the female sex. "Not unless you want to sleep with him," Anna replied flippantly. "Frankly, because of your profession, there's a certain psychological advantage to having a woman defend you. In fact, I think if we can get a predominantly female jury, we'll do better."

Margaret half-smiled. "I see you're not as naive or as la-di-da as my sister . . . maybe you'll be okay."

"I will," Anna said confidently. "Now, start at the very beginning and tell me everything. Don't leave out a single detail, do you understand?"

"Some of it's not very pretty . . . I mean, you don't seem the type to be used to hearing certain things—maybe even knowing about certain kinds of men or what they want to do."

"I'm not a flower," Anna said. "I must have *all* the details, please."

"Well, I've been a working girl for . . . let's see . . . three years now. I don't work the streets much, I've got a deal with this speakeasy off State Street. They let me hang out there, that's where I find my customers. I haven't got a pimp—that's a man who acts as your, uh, sort of . . . manager."

"I know what a pimp is," Anna said. "Go on."

"Anyway, I met this man . . . I'm not really certain of the date. It was about two weeks before it happened . . . maybe August 1. This man, he didn't tell me his real name. He told me his name was Jason and that's all . . . he took me to a hotel, Marshall's over on South State . . . in the six-hundred block. It's upstairs."

"I know the hotel," Anna said, making a note to speak to the manager.

"We got room 406—I remember that, isn't that funny? Anyway, we got to the room and he lay down on the bed and he told me to undress . . ." She paused and moved uncomfortably. "You sure you want to hear *all* of this?" she asked Anna.

"All of it," Anna reiterated.

"Well, I took off all my clothes . . . he wanted me to do it slowly, like a stripper in a club. So I did, and he watched. Then he told me to come over to the bed, and I thought he was going to lay me, but that wasn't it. He grabbed me and twisted my arm. He made me kneel in front of him and he pulled out his . . . his pecker . . . ah, I mean penis, and he told me to . . ." Margaret stopped. "I'm going to shock you," she said.

"I doubt it, go on," Anna replied as she continued to take notes.

Margaret sucked in her breath. "He told me to put it in my mouth and . . . and do him."

"And?" Anna said. "Did you?"

"No. I broke away from him and I told him I didn't

do that. Well, he was mad as hell, and he got up and hit me, but I grabbed my dress and opened the door and screamed. The house dick came running. You know, they know me there, they sort of look after me, and I pass them a few bucks in return.''

Anna nodded. ''And when did you next see this man?''

''Four nights ago . . . on Thursday the nineteenth. I'd just left the bar . . .''

''Alone?'' Anna queried, looking up.

''Yes, alone. Smitty will tell you that, he's the barkeep. Thursday's always a lousy night, not many guys around.''

Anna nodded. ''Go on.''

''I was walking down State Street when this car pulled up at the curb. It was a long sleek car, I'd never seen it before. I'm not much on cars, but I remember this one. It was a Duesenberg and it was new, brand-new . . . it had the new smell. 'Course, I didn't notice the smell till I was inside it.''

''And then what happened?''

''The guy in the back rolled down the window and he called, 'Hey, girlie!' and I stopped and then I went over to the car. I don't usually pay attention to cars, but this one was kind of nice, so I figured the guy had money and was okay.''

''You said he was in the back . . . someone else was driving?''

''Yes, I think he was his chauffeur.''

Anna nodded again and motioned for Margaret to continue.

''He opened the door and he pulled me in. The car took off and it was only when we passed under a streetlight that I saw his face and recognized him. I told him I wanted to get out, but he just laughed. They took me to an isolated section of the park. It was real dark. The car stopped and this guy dragged me out of the car and started hitting me. He slapped me a couple of times and then he started tearing my clothes off. He got me down . . . and he . . .'' Tears flooded her eyes, and she shuddered. ''He hurt me real bad . . . I mean, I'm not a virgin, but he hurt me real bad. See, he didn't do it normally . . . he . . ."

"Sodomized you," Anna concluded.

Margaret shook her head and started to cry. Anna reached across the distance between them and pressed Margaret's hand. "Go on, I understand." Anna did not drop Margaret's hand, and for a moment her thoughts filled with Uda, who had nearly lost her sanity because of such a crime. Uda had not received justice; her attackers had gone free.

"He finally finished and then he rolled off me. I guess he thought I'd fainted. I reached around as soon as he turned his back. I felt this rock . . . it was a good-size rock. I was hurt . . . I was afraid he'd come back or send that other fella in the car back . . . I lunged at him from behind. I hit him with the rock real hard and he fell down . . . it's rocky around there, I guess he hit his head when he fell too, 'cause I don't think I hit him hard enough to kill him."

"And the chauffeur?"

"I don't know if he really was a chauffeur or what. But he got out of the car and ran away. I was scared. I put my clothes on and started walking. After fifteen minutes or so, I walked into a police patrol. I guess there was blood on my dress . . . it was my blood, but they asked me what had happened. I tried to tell them and they took me back and found the body . . ."

Anna put down her pencil and looked at Margaret. "The man you killed was a well-known Chicago businessman. A restaurateur. His name was William Pridmore. I'm not sure what the prosecution will attempt, but they'll certainly try to show this man was your customer—"

"But it was self-defense, not murder."

Anna nodded. "If he'd been a less important man, you probably wouldn't be here—we seem to have one law for the rich and another for everyone else," she said bitterly. No, Uda had not received justice, but this woman would, Anna silently vowed.

"The chauffeur, the man driving the car—he knows the

man wasn't my customer. He knows I was grabbed,'' Margaret emphasized.

"And as far as I know, he hasn't come forward to testify. I'll have to find out what the D.A. has," Anna said, tapping her pencil. "Did you get a look at this chauffeur?"

Margaret shrugged. "He had real tight curly hair . . . but it was dark. I couldn't see much."

"He could have gone back and killed Pridmore," Anna suggested as she thought aloud. "We'll have to look into that, into possible motive . . . especially if you don't think you hit him hard enough to kill him."

"Can you get me out of here?" Margaret suddenly asked.

Anna looked at her steadily. "I can try," she replied. Then she stood up and smoothed out her skirt. Turning back to Margaret, she tried to smile. "I'll do the best I can," she promised.

It was after seven when Anna and Robert Stackhouse were shown into the library of Judge Gluck's house. Once her law professor, Judge Gluck had been appointed to the bench last year. In just a short time on the bench he had built a solid reputation for fairness and he was a real exception to those political appointees who were the beneficiaries of Illinois' corrupt government. As far as the case itself was concerned, he would do her no favors, but he would see her immediately, and right now, time was of the essence.

Judge Gluck examined the contents of Mr. Stackhouse's file folder with care. His studious manner betrayed nothing of what he was thinking.

"I don't have the actual police records, of course. They're confidential," Robert Stackhouse explained nervously. "See, I went to the newspaper library and checked this guy out . . . as the story explains, he's served time for armed robbery and assault."

"I can obtain the police records," Judge Gluck said with a wave of his hand. "Now, what ties this man to your wife?"

"That other envelope. It's got pictures of my wife and

278 • Joyce Carlow

daughter with this man. And there are pictures of my
wife in bed with this man . . . this is urgent, they're
leaving town. She's packed up everything—I know that.
She's leaving.''

Judge Gluck opened the other envelope and quickly
looked at the photos of Lilian Stackhouse in assorted
compromising situations. He blushed slightly and shoved
the photos back into their envelope. ''I assume you hired
a detective?''

''Yes.''

''Miss Bock, do you intend to reopen the question of
custody?''

Anna was glad he spoke to her formally, almost as if
they hadn't known each other well. ''Yes, your honor, I
intend to explore that possibility.''

''Is that a yes or a no?''

Anna frowned. ''It's a probably. I'll want to interview
both the mother and the child first.''

Judge Gluck turned to Stackhouse. ''Perhaps you
should consider a lawyer slightly more committed to your
cause.''

Anna stiffened in surprise at Judge Gluck's comment.
Then she realized he'd made it precisely because he knew
her and he knew her views. ''It's true that I've always
believed children should be with their mothers if a choice
must be made, but I know there are exceptions. I've only
just met Mr. Stackhouse and I'm only just beginning to
look into this case.''

''I trust her,'' Mr. Stackhouse said firmly.

Judge Gluck lifted a heavy brow and shrugged. ''I'll
grant a sixty-day injunction. Reopen the custody case
before then, Miss Bock, or Mrs. Stackhouse is free to
leave the state of Illinois.''

It was businesslike and just. Judge Gluck wouldn't do
her any favors, but he wasn't prejudiced either. ''Thank
you,'' Anna replied in a cool tone. She turned to her
client. ''You'll have to go to police headquarters and see
to it that the injunction is enforced. I'll see that your wife
is notified.''

Mr. Stackhouse nodded and Anna tried hard to read

his expression. Vaguely, she wondered what she was getting into.

Jim Parnell's office was on the eighth floor of City Hall, a massive building that also held the county offices as well as the courts. It was a gray-white stone building with great Doric columns that stretched from the fourth to the tenth floor on all four sides. The windows peeked out between the Doric columns and the offices were large, spacious, and well-furnished. The big ceiling fans helped keep the offices cool during the long days of the hot, humid Chicago summers.

For a moment Anna stood in front of Jim's office wondering if, under the circumstances, they should discuss this case. They had been going out now for months, at least as often as their mutual schedules permitted, and, she acknowledged, their friendship had grown till now they teetered on the edge of the precipice, wanting each other but still hesitating.

"C'mon in," he called out.

Anna opened the door and stepped in. "I've come to meet the lion in his den," she said cheerfully.

"Have a seat, Ann," Jim Parnell said with a sweeping gesture of his hand. "It's nice to have you in my domain. Better than the hole-in-the-wall they gave me here when I was serving my practical. Do you remember it?"

"Of course I do. Are you trying to make me feel bad? You know you could fit my office into your waiting room and have space left over."

He laughed. "Look, you could have had the office next door."

Anna shook her head. "I like my cubbyhole. Besides, too much togetherness isn't a good thing."

"I'm not so sure of that," he replied. He rubbed his chin. "This place is a treadmill . . . I suppose if we both worked here, we wouldn't have any spare time."

Anna sat down on a blue leather chair. "I've taken on the Margaret Olsen case," she revealed.

"I'm prosecuting," he replied quickly.

"I was afraid of that when they sent me up here,"

Anna said under her breath. Then, looking him in the eye, "How can you? It was self-defense, she was raped."

"That's her story. Look, no witnesses . . . he was hit from behind, when the police found him his wallet had been taken—"

"What?"

"His wallet was lifted. According to his wife, he had a bundle on him too . . . at least a grand. Your Miss Olsen says self-defense, my investigators say he was rolled by a prostitute and maybe there was some involvement from her pimp."

"She doesn't have a pimp. Did you find the wallet on my client?"

"Nope. But she could have stashed it. She could be planning to go back after it when she gets out."

"She says there was a chauffeur . . . have you found him?"

"The victim's wife says there was no chauffeur. Look, the little lady killed him. She had motive, we've got the weapon with her fingerprints all over it . . . open and shut."

"Was she examined by a doctor?"

"Yeah, sure. He said she'd had a rough time, but that doesn't prove rape."

Anna scowled at him, because now, just for this second, he was her adversary.

He held up his hands as if in surrender. "Hey, look, I'm not the bad guy. I'm just a young D.A. doing my job. I'll give you everything I've got. No surprises—that's more than you'd get from a lot of D.A.'s."

"It's what the law says I'm supposed to have," she returned. "Full disclosure."

Jim laughed. "This is Chicago," he reminded her.

Anna looked at him. Regrettably, he was right and she considered herself lucky because he would be honest about his case. "I think you should consider reducing the charge to manslaughter," Anna said evenly.

Jim laughed. "Hey, you talked me into that before—I recommended it in the Jimmy Washington case, and his charge was reduced. Washington got only six months and

took criticism for a year on that one. Nope, the charge
ays the same.''

"I think you're being unnecessarily harsh, perhaps
en foolish.''

He grinned. "Want to discuss it at dinner?''

"No. You know that would be, or could be, considered
conflict . . .'' She bit her lip and looked hard at him.
We ought not see each other till this case is over.''

"You're going to go by the book, aren't you?''

Anna looked at him steadily. "Yes. No dinner dates
ll after the trial.''

"I know you're right, but I don't like it.''

She let down her guard for a minute. "Neither do I,''
e confessed; then, "There are unexplored areas of this
se,'' Anna said thoughtfully.

"And it's no secret that you're not at all happy with
e current legal interpretations of rape, specifically,
Velch v. the State of Georgia.''

"You're absolutely right, I'm not one single bit happy
ith that decision.''

He slapped his desk with the open palm of his hand.
Maybe you'll triumph on self-righteousness alone.''

"Maybe you'll be defeated by overconfidence,'' she
uipped as she stood up to leave.

"See you in court,'' he said cheerfully.

"Send me over a copy of the charge.''

He nodded, and Anna left. As she walked down Ran-
olph Street toward her own office, she thought that Jim
ould be a tough opponent for her first case. Tough and
onest. Now all she had to pray for was a fair judge.

There was, she reminded herself, a lot to be done.
irst she would have to study the evidence turned over
 her by the district attorney's office. But she would also
ave to talk to the victim's wife, his business associates,
nd his friends. Smitty at the bar might be able to help
o, and so might the house detective at the hotel. There
ere two important matters—the first was to establish the
xistence of the elusive chauffeur, and the second was to
stablish the fact that Margaret had been kidnapped off
e street and then forcibly raped.

282 • Joyce Carlow

Anna reached the Shilling Building and pushed throug
the door. She trudged up the three flights of stairs to he
office and, once inside, collapsed in her chair. It wa
nearly one hundred degrees outside, a real scorcher wit
humidity to match. She caught her breath, then took ou
her notepad. One by one, over the next hour, she mad
the vital appointments. "Open and shut," Jim had tol
her. But if she was lucky, she would find out the Chicag
police hadn't really checked out Margaret's story. The
had a bad habit of not doing their job, and Jim wouldn
be the first novice D.A. to discover his "open-and-shu
case" was built on the sand of bad investigative work.

Anna worked long into the evening, then gathered u
her papers, and catching a streetcar out front, headed fo
the Settlement House.

"There's a letter for you," Hilda said as Anna cam
in. "It's from Germany."

Anna frowned and reached for the letter. It had bee
forwarded from Milwaukee by Josef.

Anna took the letter into the quiet sitting room and sa
down in a comfortable old rocking chair under a readin
lamp. Carefully she tore open the letter, which looke
old and fragile, as if it had been lost for months in th
mail . . . which, as soon as she read the date, she real
ized was the case.

March 1920

Dear Anna,

I don't know how to begin this letter to you. Surely I
should begin by begging your forgiveness for the terrible
wrong I did you. I should have helped you, my darling
daughter, but I was afraid of your father. I hope you can
find it in your heart to forgive me, Anna.

You can't imagine how terrible it is here in Germany.
There is no real money, the government is unstable, and
there is violence and murder everywhere. I have sold all
my jewelry—I would sell the house, but there is no one
with enough money to buy it . . . everything is worth-
less.

The war cost us everything, Anna. Everything. Your
brother Markus died as a result of gas poisoning. He has

left his widow, Dorcas, and a daughter, Mathilde. They live with me and together we can hardly survive.

Your brother Andreas was in the army, but he was dismissed. Now he has grown fat and lethargic. He barely has enough to support his own children, since he must hire a housekeeper. Else died in a mental institution. She went quite mad after the war.

Gerda survives better than the rest of us. She refuses to see me or help the three of us (Dorcas, myself, and Mathilde). She is only friendly with her husband's family. She too is a widow, but the von Raeders help her.

Your father died of a heart attack on New Year's Eve. He left us very little, which I can't understand at all, because I always thought we had money.

Anna, I know you have every reason to hate me, but I beg you to help us. Please, if not for me, then for Mathilde and Dorcas. Please send us some money, and if possible—or when it becomes possible—help them to emigrate to America. It is too late for me, but not for Dorcas and Mathilde. Please be charitable and kind.

Lovingly,
Your mother

Anna let the letter drop into her lap. Her father was dead, so the secret of her child's disappearance and the whereabouts of the nurse had probably died with him. Clearly her mother didn't know to whom her daughter had been given. And Markus was dead too. She could hardly believe the multiple misfortunes which had befallen all of them.

Anna thought for a long while. Markus had helped her a great deal. He was, in fact, the only person who had helped her. I'll help Dorcas and Mathilde, she vowed, I owe it to Markus' memory.

Anna stood up, shoving the letter into its worn envelope. Tomorrow I'll go to the bank and see about sending some money, she decided.

Lilian Stackhouse was not what Anna had expected. In the still, somewhat badly focused photographs taken by the detective, she had appeared to be a dark-haired

temptress. In person her hair was light brown, her eye,
soft and doelike, and her figure trim. She was dressed in
a plain housedress when she answered the door, and ove
it she wore an apron.

"I'm Ann Bock . . . your ex-husband's attorney."

Lilian Stackhouse's expression turned from curiosity
to dismay. She pressed her lips together. "You're the one
who got that paper for him . . . the one that won't let me
leave."

"Yes. I'd like to speak with you, if I might."

The dismay in her expression was turning to another
emotion. Fear? Anger? Lilian's lips were pressed to
gether tightly, and her lower lip quivered. "You don'
know what you've done. I have to get away from him
He's a monster now . . . now I don't know what I'm
going to do."

Anna frowned as she edged past the distraught woman.
She had rather hoped this woman would be brazen and
hard. But she wasn't, and Anna realized this would be
more difficult than she had thought . . . or hoped.
"Please, I want to hear both sides."

"Why? You're *his* lawyer."

"There are allegations . . . he claims you're mixed up
with a man who is dangerous, that you're leaving town
with this man and that your child is in danger."

"If she's in danger, it's from him. Look around this
place, can't you see I haven't any money? He wants to
take my daughter away . . . not because he wants her,
because he wants to hurt me. Sure, I'll admit it. Willie
has a criminal record, but he's good to us, and he's
changed. He wants to make a new start and I have to get
away. Bob will kill me, you know. He wants to kill me."

Anna sank into the chair. Charge and countercharge.
And though she kept it to herself, she admitted she found
both Mr. and Mrs. Stackhouse incredibly convincing.
"Has he ever beaten you?" she asked.

"Yes, and it's only a question of time before he does
the same to Louise. I tell you, he's not what he appears
to be, he's a monster."

Anna studied her hands. They were tightly folded and

she wondered if her tense emotions betrayed her own doubts. "I'd really like to talk to your daughter."

"It upsets her . . . this all upsets her. Naturally she loves her father . . . he always buys her presents. She doesn't understand that he doesn't give us money for food. All she understands is that he buys her presents."

"Please," Anna said softly. "Please let me talk to your daughter."

"She's not here now."

"Then bring her to my office," Anna said, taking out her card. "Please, I need to get the facts straight."

"I suppose I have to," Lilian Stackhouse said.

Anna shook her head. "No, you don't have to let me talk to her. I want to talk to her because I think it would help."

Slowly Lilian Stackhouse nodded. "I'll bring her," she agreed. "Day after tomorrow."

Kurt Stein tilted his comfortable mahogany desk chair back, and smiling, lifted his feet to the desk. Agnes Pridmore might own the restaurant on paper, but for all intents and purposes it was now his. And, he reflected, he would soon buy it from her, using her own money—the skimmed-off profits and the money he'd taken that she didn't even know her husband had . . . cash and negotiable securities that were kept in the safe. Yes, there was no doubt that Pridmore's sexual perversities had played right into his own hands. If he had planned it, he could not have come upon a better scheme. He'd driven Pridmore, and had, for a time, even considered having the girl himself. But the truth was, he didn't enjoy rape the way Pridmore did. Now he was glad he hadn't had her, because she didn't know him, and while there had been some talk of a chauffeur, he was not a chauffeur. He had been, he thought, smiling, a business partner, one with enough sense to seize the opportunity presented when the girl hit Pridmore and knocked him unconscious. The girl had fled and he had returned and finished the job. Now he had the business, the securities, and a position. He felt altogether satisfied with himself—altogether in charge.

He looked up from his folded hands when someone knocked on his office door. "Who is it?"

"Tiny," the deep voice of the bouncer replied.

Vaguely Kurt wondered why every three-hundred-pound bouncer in Chicago was named "Tiny." "Come in," he called out.

Tiny, who acted as bouncer for the speakeasy and casino in the basement, ambled in. He was half-chewing, half-smoking a big black Havana. "Got the *Tribune* here, Professor."

Kurt nodded and took the paper. He'd already forgotten he'd sent Tiny out for it half an hour ago.

"Anything else, boss?"

"Nope," Kurt answered as he unfolded the *Chicago Tribune*.

He slowly read through the front page; then he opened the paper and saw a picture of the late William Pridmore staring out at him. Kurt smiled. No one would guess that someone who looked like such a stuffed-shirt bastard could have such weird sexual perversions. His eyes lingered on Pridmore for only a second; then he moved on, staring at a much smaller picture under the heading "Lady Lawyer to Defend Hooker." Kurt squinted. It was a picture of a woman in a graduation gown, and underneath it said, "Ann Bock, Attorney."

Her hair was short, but her face was as beautiful as he remembered it . . . and there was no doubt. It couldn't be anyone else. All that had changed was that she'd dropped the "von" from her name and she'd matured. He grinned. Small world, he thought. Real small.

Louise Stackhouse looked surprisingly like her mother. Her voice was soft and very small. She wore long white stockings and black patent-leather shoes. Her dress was a faded blue cotton sundress with a ruffled skirt. She sat straight in the chair, her eyes glued on the corner of Anna's desk.

"Please don't be frightened, Louise."

"Mama told me you're Daddy's lawyer."

Anna inhaled and for a moment studied the child. She wasn't exactly a child, Anna thought. She was on the threshold of biological womanhood, a tall lanky girl who looked older than the average ten-year-old. Anna leaned over. "Anything you tell me is absolutely confidential, Louise. I won't even tell your father."

"How about my mother? Or the judge? Don't you have to tell the judge?"

For a single second Louise looked up; then quickly her blue eyes returned to the corner of the desk.

"I don't have to tell anyone," Anna reiterated. "Unless you agree to let me . . . please, help me, Louise. I know this can't be easy for you."

Louise didn't respond.

"Did your father ever hurt you . . . I mean physically?"

Louise shook her head.

"Did he hurt your mother? Did you ever see him hurt her?"

Again Louise shook her head.

"You know your mother says your father beat her."

"I never saw it," Louise said emphatically. Then, in a lower voice, "I used to hear her scream and cry . . . but I never saw it." Her eyes filled with tears and she looked up at Anna. She had that terrible look of a trapped animal. "I want my daddy," she said as the tears ran down her cheeks, "and my mama."

Anna waited a moment. She felt defeated inside; there was no black and white here, just yards of gray. "What about the man who sometimes stays with your mother, Willie?"

Louise shrugged. "He's okay."

"Louise, it's terribly important that you've told me the truth, you know that, don't you?"

Louise nodded.

Anna returned her own eyes to her desk. "I'll talk to the judge," she said quietly. "Tell me, if you can only live with one parent, whom would you want to be with?"

Louise looked up. "Daddy," she replied evenly. "He needs me more. There's nobody to cook dinner for him anymore. Daddy works hard."

Poor Louise, Anna thought miserably. She was caught in the pincers between her parents' hatred of one another. But she wanted to stay with her father to protect him. Need? Anna wondered what Louise needed, and she wondered how a young girl could feel such adult responsibility. "I'll talk to the judge," Anna promised. "And to your father as well."

14

Anna walked briskly toward her appointment with Robert Stackhouse. A cool wind blew off Lake Michigan, a reminder that it was the first of September and fall had arrived, bringing with it the unpredictability of weather that characterized Chicago. Here, swirling dry winds from the great flat farmlands to the south merged with the churning winds of the Great Lakes. The change of seasons was often heralded by spectacular electrical storms as hot air met cold in a violent clash of noise and light. Today it was clear and the cool breeze and the cloud bank on the horizon were only a warning. Anna thought back on her recent conversation with Judge Gluck.

"It's not the parents who need a lawyer appointed by the court," Anna had told the judge. "It's the child. Who represents her?"

Judge Gluck had looked at her curiously and half-smiled. "A court-appointed lawyer to represent the interests of the child? That is a novel idea."

"Well, what's to be done? The girl loves her parents and they hate each other. They'll fight over her till she's old enough to be on her own. They'll ruin her life. If she's given to her mother, she may never see her father again. If she's given to her father, she'll spend her childhood keeping house for him and playing wife. I wish I hadn't gotten involved in this case."

The judge lifted his brow. In spite of his imposing robes, he was suddenly her professor again. "You can't just take cases you can win, Anna. And by 'win' I mean win in more than the adversarial sense. You can't go out looking for easy cut-and-dried cases where the woman is wronged and where your defense makes matters right and somehow changes the course of history. Our legal system is about choices—just choices. You're an idealist, and in order to really make your mark, you'll have to learn to compromise." He smiled. "Though I rather like your idea of a child having counsel, but I think it's far in the future."

"I thought you thought it was a crazy idea."

"I said novel, not crazy. In any case, that's not what's going to happen."

"What is going to happen?"

Judge Gluck rubbed his chin thoughtfully. "I'm leaving the child with her mother—no ands, ifs, buts, or maybes. I'm also ordering that the child is not to leave the state of Illinois without the written permission of the father."

"Her mother will test that decision in a higher court."

"Let her. It's the best we can do, Ann."

Anna looked into Judge Gluck's eyes and could not help thinking that in spite of the fact that she was a practicing lawyer and he was a judge, she was still very much the student. He was still teaching her, and his lessons were valuable.

Anna hurried into the Shilling Building and up the stairs. There, in the corridor outside her door, Robert Stackhouse waited for her.

Automatically she glanced at her watch.

"I'm early," he said before she had time to say anything. "I was just so anxious—you can't imagine what its like waiting to find out what's going to happen."

His voice had grown lower and now his eyes were glued on the floor. "You've got bad news for me, haven't you? I can tell."

"Not entirely," Anna answered as she poked the key in the lock and opened the door. "Come in, sit down."

He slumped dejectedly into the chair opposite her desk. She pulled up the blinds on the window and then sat down herself.

"Tell me straight out," Robert Stackhouse said, looking at her hard.

"The judge will leave Louise in you ex-wife's custody,

but he's also made a provision that makes it illegal to take Louise out of Illinois without your written permission.'' Anna paused, then added, ''It's a kind of compromise.''

But Robert Stackhouse had already sprung to his feet, and the reasonable man she'd seen before disappeared in a frenzy of anger. ''I didn't want a compromise! I wanted my daughter!''

''I'm sorry—it's the best we can do.''

''I don't believe that! That judge was right, dammit! I should have gone to a lawyer who was *really* on my side!''

Anna stared at him. Whatever she had expected in the way of a reaction, she had not expected this. ''I really did do my best,'' she managed, knowing she sounded defensive and realizing that she needed more experience in handling irate clients.

''Well, your best isn't good enough!'' Robert Stackhouse stormed. ''I'll appeal this!'' He turned and strode out of her office, slamming the door hard enough to rattle the glass.

Anna leaned back and closed her eyes. Internally she questioned herself, but she kept coming back to the fact that both she and Judge Gluck had done what seemed best for the child. Finally she turned to her preparations for the trial of Margaret Olsen. It was, she reminded herself, only a few days away.

The September sun streamed through the four windows that lined one side of the courtroom. But in spite of the sun, the courtroom smelled musty. It was the same smell that often permeated libraries and schools. At one table Jim Parnell sat with his several law clerks, documents and books in front of him. At the other, Anna sat with her client, Margaret Olsen. She had more documents and fewer books, but she felt confident, and that, she knew, was important.

Anna glanced at her client. At her request, Margaret Olsen was devoid of all makeup and she was outfitted in the simplest and most conservative of dresses. It was navy blue and had a large white collar and white cuffs. Margaret Olsen looked nothing less than demure.

Thus far Jim had offered up the murder weapon—a duly marked rock—and the evidence of the fingerprint expert. Further, the two police officers who had made the arrest had testified, as had the hotel clerk from the Marshall. The former explained Margaret had been apprehended running away from the scene of the crime; the latter had told the jury that Margaret Olsen often brought men to his hotel and that she was, indeed, a prostitute.

Jim was finishing up his case now and she listened as he cited Welch v. Georgia.

"And so, ladies and gentlemen of the jury, you may accept the claim of the accused that she resisted a sexual liaison with the victim, but I remind you that although consent may be reluctantly given, and although there may be some force used to obtain consent, a coupling under such circumstances cannot be called rape. Opposition to the sexual act by mere words is not sufficient."

He stopped, looked at Anna, and then strode back to his seat.

Anna stood up and walked closer to the jury. "The defense would like to call Agnes Ann Pridmore to the stand."

There was an audible murmur of surprise in the courtroom, and one quick glance told Anna that Jim Parnell looked as surprised as the spectators when a prim, well-dressed, middle-aged woman came forward, her face partially obscured by a dark veil. She was sworn in.

Jim expected her to fight Welch v. Georgia. But, she thought happily, it won't be necessary. In fact, she'd built quite a strong case.

Anna waited till the whispers ceased; then she approached the witness. "I know this is difficult for you, Mrs. Pridmore, but I'm going to ask you a few questions—just to clarify matters. Were you aware that your husband was in the habit of visiting prostitutes?"

Jim Parnell wriggled in his chair and frowned. "Objection!" he shouted out. "This is irrelevant."

Anna looked at the judge. "The prosecution has gone to great lengths to present my client's character, background, and reputation. He opened this line of testimony and I ask only to establish the character, background, and reputation of the victim. It's pertinent to my defense, your honor.''

The judge screwed up his face a bit, then muttered, "I'll allow it, but don't let it get out of hand.''

"Thank you, your honor," Anna replied, thinking that there were plenty of judges who would not have allowed her to continue. Anna repeated her question to Mrs. Pridmore.

Mrs. Pridmore looked around, then in the smallest of voices replied, "Yes." She ran her finger around the collar of her black suit, then repeated "Yes" in a louder voice.

"And how long had you known that your husband availed himself of prostitutes?" Anna asked.

"For several years . . .''

Anna moved slightly so the jury could better see Mrs. Pridmore. "Mrs. Pridmore, did your husband ever hit you?"

"I object," Jim Parnell said loudly.

Anna turned to the judge. "I must show the nature of the victim's character, your honor. His character is directly related to my client's plea of self-defense.''

"Objection denied. You may answer the question, madam.''

"No.''

Anna looked up at the judge, then at the jury. "I would like it recorded that this is a hostile witness.''

"So recorded," the judge muttered.

Anna looked at Mrs. Pridmore steadily, trying to establish eye contact through her veil. "Isn't it true, Mrs. Pridmore, that only two weeks before your husband was killed, you went to the emergency room of Cook County Hospital—that you were treated there for severe lacerations of the face and arms? I warn you, Mrs. Pridmore, perjury is a crime.''

"Yes . . . yes, I went to the hospital, to the emergency room.''

"I'm going to ask you again. Did your husband beat you?"

Mrs. Pridmore glanced around helplessly, then murmured, "Yes . . . yes, he beat me."

"Regularly?" Anna queried.

"Yes. He had a vile temper . . ."

Anna nodded, and noted the whispers in the courtroom. "You may step down, Mrs. Pridmore. The defense calls Andrew J. Smit," Anna announced.

Smitty, the bartender, hobbled to the stand and was duly sworn in. He was outfitted in a tight-fitting brown suit and wore a checkered shirt.

"Mr. Smit, what is your occupation?"

"Before that there Prohibition Act was passed, I was a bartender at O'Leary's. After that I got work in a speakeasy. I worked there until a week ago."

"You know that selling liquor is an illegal act."

"Yes, but I don't work there no more."

"Was Mr. Pridmore, the victim, a regular customer at the speakeasy where you worked?"

"Sure was."

"Can you tell us what you know about him?"

"I suppose you mean besides the fact he's dead." Mr. Smit grinned foolishly. "Well, he used to come in once a week. He had a big car, a Duesenberg, and sometimes a fella drove it for him. I never got a look at the driver, though."

A ripple of comment again went through the courtroom, and Anna turned slightly so she could better judge the reaction of those listening. "Did you see Mr. Pridmore—"

Anna stopped in mid-sentence. Her eye had caught sight of a man sitting in the rear of the courtroom, a man with a familiar face.

"Please continue, Miss Bock," the judge said.

Anna turned back to face him. Her mouth felt dry. It couldn't be Kurt. It couldn't . . .

"Miss Bock!"

Anna looked up. "I'm sorry, your honor." Anna looked at the witness. "Did you see Mr. Pridmore the night of the murder?"

"Yes, ma'am. He was in half an hour before Maggie over there."

It was like an irresistible force. Anna turned again to glance nervously at the spectators. But the seat where the man had been sitting was empty! She ran her hand across her forehead. I've got to concentrate, she thought. God, I'm having hallucinations. She forced herself back to the witness. "And did he have his driver with him?"

"Yes."

"But he must not have been driving. The police fingerprint expert has testified that only Mr. Pridmore's prints were on the wheel of the car."

"Hell, ma'am, that's easy to explain. The fella—the driver—he always wore these leather driving gloves. Had them on that night, I remember."

There was a collective muttering.

"Were you questioned by the police on this matter?" Anna asked.

"Nope."

Anna looked hard at Jim Parnell. "I'm finished with this witness," she said, sitting down.

"Cross-examination?" the judge droned.

Jim was on his feet in an instant. Clearly he was going to try to discredit Smit. True, Smit was a bartender, and such activity meant he'd been illegally employed. But there were twelve thousand speakeasies in Chicago, and if the state stopped taking evidence from bartenders, they'd have to let half the criminals in the state prison out. Anna sat down and looked at Margaret.

"You all right?" Margaret whispered, a look of concern on her face.

"Yes . . . I just thought I saw someone I knew. But it couldn't have been that person."

"You've been working too hard," Margaret whispered back.

Carefully, block by block, Anna built her case. But Jim did not back off easily, as she had hoped he might. Two days after she began her defense, Anna found herself in front of the jury making her all-important summation. And, she thought as she rose to deliver it, the face she had thought was Kurt Stein had not reappeared. Someone who looked similar, she decided. Yes, that was the only possible explanation. That and the fact that she was over-tired.

Anna cleared her throat. "The prosecution has implied that a woman who sells her favors cannot be raped. Even if I agreed with that absurd premise, I would have to point out to you, the jury, that Margaret Olsen did not receive money from the victim, and there is no evidence to suggest that an agreement existed between them. Margaret Olsen was taken off the street—kidnapped by a man whose own wife has characterized him as brutal. Margaret Olsen was taken to a remote section of Jackson Park and there brutally raped by the victim. Thinking she would be assaulted by the driver of the car as well, and perhaps further beaten by both men, she seized the opportunity to defend herself. She hit the victim with a rock, and it appears he fell and hit his head on another rock. There is no absolute medical evidence to indicate which blow killed him. I put it to you that Margaret Olsen acted entirely in self-defense. She carried no weapon, but used what was at hand. The prosecutor well knows that *intent* is part of the legal definition of murder. Margaret Olsen did not plan the victim's death . . . she acted out of fear and in self-defense of her own life. Yes, the defendant hit Mr. Pridmore on the head with a rock, a rock which a desperate hand found by chance to stop a violent attack on her person. That Mr. Pridmore's head hit a rock when he fell was also by chance, and both of these chance occurrences prove there was no criminal intent on the part of Miss Olsen. Further, the manner in which she earned her living should have no bearing on your deliberations." Anna paused for dramatic effect. "Jack the Ripper murdered prostitutes, but not one of you would suggest that he wasn't a murderer. William Pridmore raped a prostitute, but he was still a rapist. Perhaps if one of your daughters or wives had spurned his advances, as did the accused, he might have raped her. We have no way of knowing if William Pridmore raped other women. We *do* know he beat his wife so brutally that she was forced to seek emergency medical services.

"The prosecution has further suggested that Margaret

Olsen robbed William Pridmore. But there was no money found on Miss Olsen, and I suggest to you that Mr. Pridmore's driver may have taken that money. You cannot convict Miss Olsen if, in your minds, there is reasonable doubt concerning her guilt. I put it to you that the police did not properly investigate this crime. That they did not interview Mrs. Pridmore, or look into the victim's life at all. They assumed that because he was a wealthy man, he was an honorable, law-abiding man. Nor did the police examine Miss Olsen's claims. Why? Because Miss Olsen is not wealthy, Miss Olsen is poor. Miss Olsen is a woman forced into degradation by economic circumstances.'' Anna paused again, then leaned forward. ''I urge you to look into your hearts. Try to understand that Margaret Olsen was deserted by society. Her sister cares, but she too has responsibilities, and little money to spare. I urge you to recognize the fact that Miss Olsen's actions—her means of making money—do not justify her brutalization by a monster. Margaret Olsen had the right to defend herself and, indeed, had the right to expect the police to protect and not persecute her. I put it to you that the police must seek and find the missing driver, that the case as it currently exists against Margaret Olsen is no case at all, and that reasonable doubt most certainly exists.'' Anna continued to look at the jury for a long moment, then turned and sat down, not daring to look at her opponent, Jim Parnell.

Just outside the courtroom door, which was partially ajar, Kurt Stein swore under his breath. It was stupid enough of him to have gone in and been seated, thus allowing Anna to see him. Had she recognized him? He felt certain she had. But now her summation had raised real questions, and soon someone would investigate his role as Pridmore's associate. Shit! There was no choice. He would have to take what he could of his ill-gotten gains and move on. He absolutely could not risk trying to run the restaurant. ''Damn you, Anna,'' he cursed. ''This is the second time you've caused me problems.'' He walked rapidly down the hall. One day, he thought, he'd have the opportunity to get even, but, he admitted, right now he had other things to think about.

* * *

Anna sat next to Margaret as the jury after six long hours of deliberation marched in, their faces a mask she could not read.

The judge brought his gavel down. "Has the jury reached a verdict?" he asked.

"We have," the foreman replied, holding a piece of paper.

"How find thee?" the judge bellowed.

"We find the defendant, Margaret Olsen, not guilty."

There was clapping from a contingent of women who had been sitting in the back row, and Margaret turned to Anna and hugged her, even as her sister reached from behind to touch Anna's shoulder gratefully.

Anna looked at Margaret seriously, aware that the woman who pretended to be so hard was crying. "Come to the Settlement House," Anna suggested. "There are other ways . . . you don't have to sell yourself, Margaret."

Margaret nodded. "I was thinking of asking you what I could do. I mean, I've got no education. Unlike my sister, I never learned to read. I always hated school."

Hilda from the Settlement House had been among the women in the back. Almost seeming to sense the conversation in the front of the courtroom, she had come forward and was standing now just behind Margaret's sister.

"There are women at the Settlement House who can help you learn to read. We can get you a job, Margaret. Here, I'd like you to meet Hilda. Why don't you go with her now and have a look around?"

"You'll be pleasantly surprised," Hilda said, taking Margaret's hand.

"Okay," Margaret said slowly. "Okay, I'll have a look-see. C'mon, sis . . . you come too."

Anna smiled and watched as they made their way through the crowd. She slowly turned and began putting her documents in her bag. Winning a case was satisfying—especially if you believed in your client. But setting a person on a new path was even more satisfying.

"I knew I was going to regret going up against you in

this case," Jim said as he unprofessionally perched on the end of the table.

Anna looked up; he was grinning mischievously.

"You fought it hard, and you deserved to win. The police did a sloppy job and I should have forced them to do more investigating."

"They were sloppy," Anna agreed. "But the trouble with your job is, you have to presume guilt. I'm more fortunate. I can presume innocence."

"Well, if it's any comfort, I think your client was innocent."

"Even if she weren't—even if I didn't believe she was innocent—I'd have defended her. Everyone must have a defense."

"That's the law," he said with a slight wink. "Well, Ann, this trial is over. It's no longer a conflict of interest for us to share a meal. How would you like to go to the Leland Hotel for dinner? It'll be a sort of celebration. After all, criminal law isn't your specialty."

Anna returned his smile. "The Leland is rather expensive."

"I can afford it . . . mind you, if I never get a conviction, I could lose my job," he joked.

"Cheer up! You won't always be up against me," she laughed.

He looked at her for a long moment. "Good thing too," he said, moving around the table and taking her arm. "Can I pick you up around seven?"

"Seven is just fine," Anna replied.

Anna wore her best dress. It was black, fell slightly off the shoulder, had a V neck and lovely white embroidered flowers on the clinging folds of its skirt. It also had a long sash which tied loosely and fell scarflike from her waist. She wore white stockings and black shoes trimmed with little white fan-shaped buckles.

Jim stared at her across the candlelit table in the small intimate dining room of The Leland Hotel. "You look absolutely beautiful. You know, I like your hair short."

"It's easier to care for."

"And a busy working girl like yourself is short of time, right?"

"Right."

"How's Webber these days?"

"He and Clara are enjoying his partial retirement. Actually he's turned two of his cases over to me—both appeals. One is going to be routine, the other is the appeal of the anarchists. It's very complicated."

"Jesus. Is that still going on? When you were a student you went up to Milwaukee with him one summer to do the research on that one."

Anna laughed. "That's why the appeal's been turned over to me. I know the case inside out."

"I hear you're doing pretty well, all in all. I know you've taken over more than one of Webber's cases."

"Yes, I'm even making money."

"Do you plan to go on living in the Settlement House?"

"Yes. It's cheaper than having an apartment, and I like the company and the mental stimulation."

"But you could afford a place of your own."

"No. I'm sending money to my sister-in-law and niece. My family was devastated by the war . . . the situation is very bad in Germany."

"There's a lot of bitterness over the peace treaty. Well, cheer up, you're not the only one sending money home. Ireland is always devastated. I send money home too."

The waiter came and gave them the menu. Anna looked at it for a long while.

"Have the catfish," Jim advised. "It's always fresh and always sensational."

"I've never had catfish," she admitted.

"All the more reason to try it then," he urged.

"Fine, I'll try it."

He ordered the main course and a bottle of dry white wine, a cold Chablis. He studied her expression and felt good about the fact that they had so easily slipped back into their relationship after this separation. I'll tell her my news later, he decided. He looked up. "After dinner, why not come by my place for coffee?"

Anna tilted her head slightly and returned his smile.

For a second she tried to imagine his apartment; then she nodded her agreement.

Jim's apartment was not quite what Anna had expected. It was, for one thing, neat and tidy. The furniture was new except for the massive desk in the corner of the living room, and the balcony overlooked Lake Michigan.

She sat on the sofa with her coffee on the table in front of her. Jim sat next to her. He turned and looked at her seriously. "I've put this off all evening," he said slowly. "Anna, I asked you out tonight to say good-bye for a while."

"Good-bye? Are you leaving Chicago?" Anna felt shocked by his admission; her heart began to pound and she looked at him hard.

"I'm going to Springfield to the state attorney's office. A sort of training program. I think I'll move up the ladder faster in the state government. More scope . . ." He stopped and looked at her. "Hey, you look really upset. Ann, I'll be back, you can count on that."

Anna continued to stare into his eyes, wondering if she had been wrong to begin trusting him with her emotions.

His expression remained serious; then silently he pulled her into his arms. "It's not just for me, it's for us. Ann, I want you. I want to marry you."

Anna felt her skin grow warm. She continued to look into his eyes . . . they were wonderful eyes, eyes like the sea, and she knew if she let herself she could become lost in their depths. This man who often made her angry was also the most appealing man she'd ever met. She touched his cheek with her hand and he returned her intent gaze. Then after a moment he leaned over and kissed her hard, his lips moving against hers, his hands roaming her back sensuously. "Tell me you love me as much as I love you," he whispered as he kissed her neck, then her ear.

Anna pressed herself against him, allowing her emotions full rein . . . there had been too much suppression. In the warmth of his arms she felt suddenly overwhelmed. All their conversations, their moments of tenderness, converged as their friendship suddenly seemed to turn to fire. They had long denied each other, but there was no denying this moment. "I do love you," she breathed, "I do."

"And when I finish in Springfield and come back, will you marry me?"

"Yes . . . I will. Oh, I love you so much—" Her words were silenced as once again he kissed her lips. His hands touched her lovingly, yet they seemed like red-hot irons on her flesh, exciting her, arousing feelings and desires long dead.

He touched the curve of her breast through the soft material of her dress, then kissed her shoulder as her dress slipped down. "If you want me to stop, tell me now," he whispered urgently. She could hear the desire in his voice, and her only answer was to embrace him tightly.

He undid her dress and slipped it off; then, kissing her again, he carried her to the bed. She lay on the dark spread in her white camisole and lacy undergarments. She watched him as he shed his own clothes, revealing his strong broad shoulders and muscular arms.

"You're beautiful," he said, stretching out next to her. He gently pulled her camisole away and kissed her bare breasts, her neck, and then her nipples slowly, lovingly, then passionately.

Anna felt as if she were on fire, and she responded with twists and turns, with embraces of her own, and finally by touching him.

He kissed her again and again as he aroused her, toyed with her, and brought her to the very edge of fulfillment with teasing touches and intimate caresses. Then he entered her and she moaned beneath him, pressing to him as he moved within her. Then they were tumbling together, holding each other tightly as they both felt the surge of satisfaction.

Hours later they lay in each other's arms. "Will you come with me to Springfield or wait here?" he asked.

Anna looked at him, then whispered, "I'm not sure how to answer that. I have things I must do."

"Mysterious lady," he said, touching her hand. "Well, see that you have done them by the time I return."

"I will."

"It's not so far. I'll come down on weekends when I can. You can come up too. We'll write . . . promise you'll write."

"Yes, I will, I promise," Anna said, kissing his fingers. Then, sadly, "It's going to be the longest year of my life."

A cold, unrelenting March wind blew off Lake Michigan and down Chicago's wide avenues, whipping round the corners and sending a chill through the populace who braved the streets in the early-morning hours.

Morning in Chicago was a cacophony of sounds and a kaleidoscope of sights. It seemed as if the sounds increased with each minute, as the city, like a giant awakening from a deep sleep, first tossed and turned, then stretched and stood. Beyond the rooftops of the inner Loop, smoke curled from the factories of the South Side, and traveling on the wind, mingled with the steam expelled from the office buildings which rose like sentinels around Lake Michigan. To the left, the lake stretched out to meet the horizon, though the place of their meeting was blurred, and lake and sky seemed one in the peculiar smoky light of the giant's heavy first breaths of morning. To the north and to the south, for thirty miles, the sprawling city stretched till it dissolved into prairie grasses where only the cold steel arteries of the rail lines that fed the city provided visible promise of a distant metropolis.

The sounds of early morning began with the far-off whistle of a steamer on the lake; then came the clicking of heels on the pavement, the tooting of horns, and the clamor of industry coming to life. And beneath the bridges that spanned the narrow rivers that segmented the inner city, thick brown waters flowed into the lake.

The year 1921 brought a new surge of construction to Chicago, and every day it seemed there was a new factory, another windowless warehouse, or a tall stark grain elevator. The great steamers that moved on the lake carried coal and grain and a thousand manufactured items. Deerborn, Randolph, and State streets were a mass of traffic as cars, trucks, streetcars, and pedestrians surged to life.

Anna fought her way through the early-morning crowds as she hurried down Randolph Avenue toward her office. New York, with its great financial center, was said to be the head of the nation—the brain that directed it—but Chicago was always called the heart. As she joined a million pairs of feet, it seemed to Anna that calling Chicago the heart of the nation was an apt description of this prairie anomaly.

Anna caught sight of her image as she passed the windows of the Ashland Block. She was wearing low-heeled laced shoes that matched her three-piece suit. It was a wonderfully stylish suit with a straight skirt, the hem of which caressed her lower calves, a belted jacket, and a heavy cape that matched skirt and jacket. All three pieces were trimmed in identical plaid. Beneath her belted jacket she wore a tailored white shirt with a brown bow necktie, and she had long gloves and a slouch hat that matched the bow. Her blond hair had been cut into a softly curved bob, but it was nearly obscured by her hat.

Passersby noticed Anna and observed that she walked with an enthusiastic spring—everything about her spoke of her liberation of mind, spirit, and body. And, she acknowledged, she felt happy. Jim wrote often, and they'd spent three weekends together. She missed him terribly, but still she was happy. Happy and, yes, even contented.

She was a long way from Anna von Bock, the shy intellectual girl who had been ruled by her father and who in desperation had sought freedom with an unworthy man. Nor was she any longer in need of a man to justify her existence. This time she knew she had fallen in love with a man who respected her equality.

I'm no longer a dependent student either, she thought. I am a free and independent woman. I make a good living, I dress as I wish, I go where I wish and with whom I wish. Most important, I and every other woman in this country who chooses to do so can now vote. She smiled at her own image and thought that even though the law giving women the vote had been enacted in 1920, it was still new and important to her because it opened up whole new interpretations in the law . . . whole new arguments for issues such as child custody and the responsibility of the father.

She turned away and walked on, letting yesterday's events flood over her. Strange, she thought, she felt wonderfully optimistic today, even though yesterday she'd lost the appeal case for the convicted anarchists.

When she'd come home to the Settlement House, Hilda had taken one look at her and said simply, "You lost, didn't you?"

"I was sure I was going to win," Anna had confided. "I feel defeated."

"Don't be so hard on yourself, Anna. After all, you wouldn't have been appealing if Alex Webber hadn't lost the case in the first place. If he couldn't win it, well, it's a tough case."

"Tough indeed," Anna agreed, but she couldn't help wondering if she'd really done her best.

"There's nothing to do but pick yourself up and file another appeal," Hilda had said matter-of-factly.

Anna had looked at her in surprise. "Another appeal? That would have to be an appeal to the Supreme Court! They've never heard an appeal filed by a woman."

Hilda had winked slyly. "Exactly. Take this opportunity, risk it . . . for God's sake, try it!"

"The Supreme Court . . . ." Anna smiled too, then said softly, "I'll do it!" and hugged Hilda.

Somehow, making that decision had restored her optimism.

Anna reached her office building and climbed the three flights of stairs. Outside her office door, her morning's mail awaited.

Anna hung up her cloak and jacket and took off her hat. She opened the curtains and surveyed the sky. Perhaps the wind would carry the clouds away and by noon the sun would shine.

She took her little pile of mail and sat down at her desk. She opened the letter from Germany first.

Dear Anna,
     Mathilde and I want to thank you sincerely for the

money you have sent and keep sending. You can't imagine what U.S. dollars mean to us in these trying times. Without your help, we would starve to death.

Anna, I have terribly sad news for you. As you know, your mother has had many physical problems since she had influenza. A few nights ago, she developed pneumonia and was taken to the hospital. She died early this morning. I know you were not close, but I also know this will sadden you greatly. I suppose I should have wired you, but it seemed such a cold way to tell you, I decided to write instead. Everything that could be done for her was done, and in the end, she died peacefully in her sleep.

Dear Anna, we do thank you for all you have done, but our need is great. I worry mostly for Mathilde. Would it be possible for us to come to America? I would do anything—anything. I would work and pay you back every cent, I promise you. Could you help us? There is no hope for Mathilde in this country, and she is a very bright girl.

Yours sincerely,
Dorcas

Anna looked at the letter for a long while. Her mother had outlived Karla, but her life had certainly not been as happy. Karla had gone after what she wanted, had taken something from life, and had given too. "Poor Mother," Anna said, thinking aloud. "She always lived in Father's shadow, she never really lived for herself."

After a moment Anna laid Dorcas' letter down and tried to picture Mathilde. The same age as my own daughter—wherever she is, Anna thought. Well, Markus had helped her, she ought to help his widow and daughter. She checked her calendar and decided she could go to the Federal Building after lunch. Yes, she decided, she would go and see about sponsoring them. It would take ages, but it would, she decided, be good to have family here with her.

Outside the window of the visitor's room at Joliet, a mist-fine March rain fell on cold concrete walkways.

Anna looked out for a moment, then returned her attention to her notes.

The priority of civil libertarians was now a fight against the repression of the war years. She was flooded with cases, and so were other law offices across the country. During the war and for some time after, censorship of the mail had been carried out with a vengeance, and it clearly demonstrated the paranoia that gripped the country. What, exactly, could be legally mailed was left up to the postmaster general. The postal censorship laws were used to fight the growing union movement. Notices of union meetings, pamphlets, indeed any material that called for workers to organize could be legally seized. In addition to postal censorship, lawyers were fighting to have political prisoners released and state sedition laws repealed.

The legal profession was having the best luck with the postal authorities. The *Milwaukee Leader,* which had been banned by the mails for so long, had already had its mailing privileges restored, and only four books remained on the old banned mailing list.

The political cases were absolutely the toughest, Anna thought. She herself had launched one major appeal to the Supreme Court over the Milwaukee anarchists, and she was considering a second appeal to the Federal Court of Appeals. In the latter case she planned on appealing a thirty-year sentence given to a conscientious objector. The harsh judgment he had received was rendered doubly unjust because those who had been charged under the Espionage Act had, for the most part, received only ten-year sentences.

Anna looked up as her client, William Kerns, was escorted into the room by a guard. Anna smiled warmly. "Please sit down," she said.

William Kerns was a pale, sincere-looking young man of twenty. He had kind green eyes and an open, honest face. His hair was dark, and he had a slight build. He came from Quaker stock, and had refused to join the army when America had joined the war in 1918. The difficulty was that although his background was Quaker, he did not practice the religion, although he claimed that serving in an army—any army—was contradictory to his beliefs.

"How are you?" Anna asked.

"As well as can be expected," he returned.

"I've come to tell you I want to launch another appeal."

"Will it do any good?" he asked, sitting down across from her.

"I certainly hope so. But our strategy is important and I want to make certain you understand the options."

He half-smiled and ran his hand through his hair. "I have options?" he asked.

"Well, you could apply for a pardon."

He looked thoughtful. "Doesn't a pardon imply forgiveness for wrongdoing?"

"Yes, and for that reason I advise against it," Anna said slowly.

"I agree. I've come this far and I'd like to help establish a precedent."

"There's also the possibility of a commutation," Anna put forward.

"What would that imply?"

"Again, the element of forgiveness—and it wouldn't erase your record. At best, you would receive a shorter term, and since your present term is extremely harsh, I imagine the authorities would look favorably on a commutation."

"And an appeal?"

"An appeal can result in amnesty. Amnesty implies you've done nothing whatsoever wrong."

"And if I received an amnesty, would it set a precedent?"

"Yes. It would be a precedent that would legitimate political dissent."

He smiled. "That's what I want to do."

"There are dangers," Anna warned. "If we lose the appeal . . . well, then we'll have to find new grounds, or we'll have to appeal to a higher court. At worst, we'll have to pursue one of the other two options. And appeals take time, so you will remain in prison."

He nodded. "I'm working in the prison hospital. I feel

I'm doing some good here. Please, go ahead and file the appeal.''

Anna reached across the table and touched his hand. "Right away," she promised. Then she looked him in the eye. "I admire what you're doing," she said honestly. "It takes courage."

He shyly acknowledged her compliment and replied softly, "Most people don't call a man who won't fight courageous."

"Most people don't know you," Anna said.

Anna returned directly from Joliet to Chicago on the train. By three she was ready for her next client, Helen James. While she waited, she reviewed the file of Mary Hanson. Mary Hanson was a librarian who was taking a customs official to court for seizing some books. The books had been taken from her on her return from Europe. Were it not such a dangerous example of authority run amok, it might have been funny, Anna thought. The books she had attempted to import were Boccaccio's *Decameron* and *The Complete Works of Rabelais*. Anna shook her head. The books were classics, taught to every European schoolchild, and it was unbelievable that they had been banned by U.S. customs. To make matters worse, even though only four books remained on the banned lists of the postal authorities, there were over seven hundred books on the banned list of the customs authorities. It wasn't a case Anna expected to win; in fact, it probably wouldn't get to court because the government wouldn't recognize Miss Hanson's right to sue. But Miss Hanson, an eccentric and wealthy woman dedicated to civil rights, insisted it was worth trying. "I know lots of people who write for newspapers," she had told Anna emphatically. "At the very least this outrage will get some much-needed publicity." It was a strategy with which Anna could not disagree.

Anna put aside Mary Hanson's file and picked up the file of Helen James. This case, she admitted, was close to her heart.

Anna had not yet met and interviewed James, but she already had a thick file of press clippings and notes on the issue, a file which she intended going over with Helen in the next hour.

It was ten after the hour when Anna answered her office door and greeted a tall, thin, stylishly dressed matron with bobbed white hair.

"Ann Bock," Anna said, holding open the door.

"Helen James."

Anna ushered her into the office and showed her to a chair. "I'm pleased to meet you," she said enthusiastically, then, smiling, "I'm afraid you don't look like a 'purveyor of immorality.' "

Helen laughed. "I see you read the *Herald*. Isn't it wonderful being called a purveyor of immorality! Can I sue?"

"Under the circumstances, I think not," Anna said, still smiling. "I'm a fan of yours, I have a file of clippings."

"Do you? How flattering," Helen James said.

Anna studied Helen James. She was extremely well-dressed, in a belted beige coat dress. It had a high flaring collar and she wore a trimmed beige hat that all but covered her white hair. Her pumps had wide tongues that came up over the front of the shoes and she was carrying a thin walking stick tipped in gold. In all, she was highly stylish in appearance and distinctly well-off-looking.

She tilted her head toward Anna as if guessing Anna's thoughts and said, "I think that sex education has too long been the province of radicals like Emma Goldman and Mary Ware Dennette. Control of reproduction is *the* key to changing the role of women in our society, and I intend to fight for the education that will give our young women that control."

"I admire your stand," Anna said forthrightly. "And I can assure you, I will give your case my all if you decide to hire me."

Helen nodded. "Oh, I already decided. You've got the right sort of reputation, and Good Lord, a woman should be fighting this case, don't you think?"

"I certainly do. But I also think a male co-counsel wouldn't hurt. Someone with stature, an older person perhaps."

"Do you have someone in mind?"

"Alex Webber. I would suggest Clarence Darrow, but he's tied up with the Scopes trial as well as a number of other cases."

"I intend to place this squarely in your hands, Miss Bock. Of course, I'll take your advice. A male co-counsel is just fine."

"As I told you, I do have a file, and I have read your pamphlet—"

"You were able to obtain a copy? Well, that *is* hopeful!"

"I borrowed Jane Addams' copy."

"Ah, of course, of course . . . well, I knew you hadn't bought it in a bookstore."

"But I *should* have been able to buy it in a bookstore. In any case, I'd like you to go over this entire matter with me. Please start at the beginning and include your motivation for becoming involved in such a controversial area."

Helen James moved slightly to be more comfortable in the chair. "It all started when my children—three daughters—reached what I might call the critical years."

"After puberty," Anna surmised.

"Yes. After puberty. I began to look for something I could use to teach them about their own bodies and about male bodies. I wanted something that would help them to understand the reproductive system."

"And you couldn't find anything?"

"Not a word outside medical texts, which are far too complicated. But I did get a medical text . . . I studied science at Smith so I didn't have much trouble with it. In any case, I translated it into simple, straightforward information. It was never my purpose to encourage loose morality. I included a long chapter on married love."

"I understand the purpose was strictly educational."

"And aimed at young married women. You know, in terms of financial security. I'm among the fortunate. I married a wealthy man, and when he died, he left me his money. I've never wanted for anything, but I'm a rare case. There are too many women who begin having babies immediately . . . who can't afford them, and who find themselves unable to care for their children properly.''

"I think you'll be very good in your own defense," Anna noted.

"I hope so . . . you understand that I know if I'm convicted I'll be fined . . . and I don't mind that. It's outrageous that I've even been charged!''

"The postal authorities have considerable power," Anna said. "Power they shouldn't have under our Constitution. But we've made a lot of progress with them. Yours is the first new case in quite a while.''

"I have some powerful allies," Helen James said, leaning over. "Many Republican women support me, and Mrs. Marshall Field will help my defense committee.''

"We'll need all that help and more," Anna said thoughtfully. It *was* true, ideas in America were changing, but alas, the government, as usual, was being dragged along after public opinion.

"I'll begin preparing your case immediately," Anna promised.

"And what can I do?" Helen James asked.

"Encourage your friends to start a letter-writing campaign. At the very least, that might result in the assignment of a sympathetic federal judge to the case.''

"I'll do just that," Helen promised.

15

Courtroom 23 was filled with milling people. Willard Harrington, the federal attorney, walked restlessly around the prosecution's table. He was a heavyset man, a man whose expression appeared tight and tense, as if his teeth were permanently clenched. Unlike many heavyset men, Willard Harrington's clothes were not rumpled and stretched over his swelling stomach, rather they were superbly tailored and cut from the most expensive British fabric. His shirt was crisp and spotless, his tie a conservative blue, and in his lapel he wore a fresh pink carnation.

Anna discreetly watched Willard for a few minutes. He had a staunchly conservative reputation—or more accurately a reputation for publicly upholding conservative positions. He was a man who had decided the parameters of ideal public morality for himself, and with his foe carefully targeted, he plunged into the fray, claiming to serve all men by protecting what he referred to as "the frailer sex" from all knowledge that would, in reality, free them.

Regardless of Willard Harrington's personal views, he was, Anna reminded herself, simply a conduit of the federal government, for it was the postal authorities that were prosecuting Helen James. But there was no doubt in Anna's mind that Harrington would make it more difficult simply because he believed in the case.

Anna watched her opponent as he moved about, conferring with his staff of underlings. Certainly in the matter of assistants she was outnumbered six to none, and vaguely she wondered if she shouldn't have hired four or five people to sit around with her simply to even the psychological odds. And the worst of it was Alex Webber. He was her co-counsel, but he'd taken ill and couldn't be with her on this all-important day. They had discussed a postponement, but Helen had made the decision to go with Anna alone. "Let's brave the lions in their den," she had proclaimed.

To calm her nerves, Anna reminded herself that this *was* a jury trial, and juries always reacted better to the underdog.

The court clerk, a dark-haired woman in a slim lined red dress, with thick glasses, also walked around restlessly. She flexed her fingers as though exercising them for the task ahead. And outside the courtroom, in the anteroom, observers shuffled back and forth talking in low voices. This wasn't a sensational murder trial—indeed, even if convicted, Helen James would probably only be fined and restrained from printing and distributing her pamphlet. But because the nature of the pamphlet was sex education, it drew a large crowd. Supporters ranged from out-and-out libertarians to those who felt a purely intellectual battle had been joined. Detractors included members of the Ku Klux Klan, albeit without their outlandish costumes. Today they only wore little identifying lapel pins. There were outraged women with signs pro and con, and political types who felt it their duty to legislate and uphold their particular vision of public morality. Naturally the press was present, because above all, Chicago was a newspaper town. Some would write reasoned, researched, and thoughtful pieces; others would fasten on to any purloined headlines they could conjure up, ignoring the central legal issues of the Constitution. Certainly the many placards—some quite mystifying—would provide grist for the mill as well as good pictures. One strange sign read, "Keep Sex in Church!" and another oddly read, "Sex Is a Family Matter." Anna wondered if its holder meant sexual instruction was a family matter or whether he was an advocate of incest.

Helen James, looking every inch the decent and even conservative matron from Evanston, walked slowly into the courtroom.

Magnificent, Anna thought. Helen was dressed in a well-tailored and clearly expensive gold silk summer suit. She smiled radiantly, and stopped to chat briefly with a huddle of reporters. Then she turned when she saw Anna, and moved quickly to her side, taking a seat at the long table. She leaned over. "Someone called me a hussy as I came down the hall," she whispered. "Imagine being called a hussy at my age! Let me tell you, I *am* flattered."

Anna smiled back. "I'm glad your sense of humor is intact. I'm afraid you'll need it before this is over."

The court clerk rang a bell and those members of the public not already seated hurried into the courtroom and jostled for seats.

In a moment Judge Samuel Martindale swept into the room. He was, to Anna's knowledge, neither wildly conservative nor given to radical flights of jurisprudence. He was dead center, and the best she could have hoped for. He stood and in a loud clear voice called the court to order in the case of the Federal Government *v.* Helen James. Then he sat down and called the prosecutor and counsel for defense.

Willard Harrington stood and allowed his presence to be felt. Then, surprisingly, he called Helen to the stand as his first witness.

He immediately introduced the pamphlet and established that she had authored and distributed it. He wasted not a moment branding it "pure and simple smut."

Anna watched Harrington strut about like an overfed peacock. His argument, which was the argument of the postal authorities, was absurd. She thought of Chicago's speakeasies, of the literally thousands of prostitutes available, and of the mobsters—these things were not labeled obscene, but this rather prim-and-proper guide for married women was labeled smut. Ah, she thought gleefully, if only one could argue on the basis of reality and emotions . . . but the law was a hard taskmaster. One could be involved and one could really care. But one could not argue merely on the basis of common sense and reality—speakeasies, mobsters, and prostitutes were not, alas, "pertinent." But the thought gave Anna an idea, and the idea began to germinate.

"Suppose," Willard said, pacing in front of the jury, "suppose some sexual deviant were to obtain this so-called innocent pamphlet. Certainly the descriptions might urge him to an uncontrollable passion resulting in some terrible crime. Or suppose an innocent young woman read it and was persuaded to take up a life of sin!"

Willard Harrington continued to hammer on his point that women would be made immoral by exposure to the pamphlet and men would be driven to lust by it. When he finished with Helen, Anna rejected cross-examination, stating that she intended to call Helen James to the stand herself and would postpone questions till that time. After Helen James, Willard Harrington called five witnesses in all. Two were mothers who railed against the pamphlet, and three were men—two Catholic priests and a Baptist minister. By the time Willard Harrington had finished, it was noon and the judge adjourned for lunch, ordering everyone back to the court by two P.M.

Helen disappeared almost instantly with an entourage of female supporters. Anna carefully picked up and sorted out her notes, putting them in her briefcase.

"Your power of concentration is immense," a strong, familiar male voice said.

Anna turned. "Jim! I didn't see you in court."

"As I said, your power of concentration is immense." He edged closer and quickly pecked her on the cheek.

"When did you get into town?"

"This morning. C'mon, I can't even give you a proper greeting in here."

Anna tilted her head and smiled.

He grinned boyishly and brushed a lock of his red hair off his forehead. "I've got a big surprise. May I introduce you to the new state's attorney?"

"You? Oh, that's wonderful!"

He took her hand and squeezed it. "I rather fancy it myself," he said, and she continued to smile at the sound of his voice and his faint Irish brogue.

"I fought my way in here and I'm looking forward to

this afternoon when you make mincemeat out of Harrington—what a pompous bastard.''

"You're very irreverent for a state's attorney.''

"I wouldn't touch a case like this—leave it to the feds to be ridiculous.''

"It *is* ridiculous, but serious. It's a clear First Amendment case.''

He reached out impulsively and touched her hair. "I like your hair this way,'' he said, caressing her with his eyes. "You know, when you say the words 'First Amendment,' your face lights up. I'm starting to think of you as my little German-American Don Quixote—tilting at the windmills of injustice.''

"Are you making fun of me?'' Anna asked, frowning.

"Certainly not. I admire you. Liberty is, after all, a lady, so she should be defended by one.''

"And you, as the saying goes, are full of blarney.''

"I've reserved a table at the Drake. May I take you to lunch?''

"You reserved a table? How did you know I'd be free?''

"Well, if you hadn't been, I'd have had to invite someone else.''

Anna took his arm. "Well, I am free and I'm not turning down lunch at the Drake. They have the best catfish in town.''

"You've become not just a real American, but a real Midwesterner.''

"I could say the same for you,'' Anna quipped.

Arm in arm they left the courtroom. Outside Jim hailed a cab and soon they were in the quiet, elegant world of the Drake dining room, overlooking the white sands of Oak Beach. An odd sight, Anna reflected, because it was fall, and while the beach looked inviting, the water was already cold and the trees beyond the sand had turned color and already lost many leaves.

"And what, may I ask, are you thinking?'' Jim asked.

Anna turned from the window to face him. "Nothing, really. I was only imagining how the beach will look in the winter when the temperature drops and it freezes. I'm always fascinated by the huge slabs of ice along the shore.''

"Personally, I like the warm sand more.'' He leaned over the table. "It's good to be back in Chicago, and even better to be looking across a table at you.''

"It's wonderful to have you back. You're good luck. Now I know I'll win.''

"So you've filed an appeal to the Supreme Court. I read that letter to all my friends. I said, 'Listen to this—the woman I'm going to marry is taking a case to the Supreme Court!' God, I am proud of you.''

"Did you really tell everyone? Oh, Jim, it'll be a while before I know if they'll hear it.''

"They'll hear it! After all, you won an Appeal Court case for William Kerns, that conscientious objector.''

"I have pluses and minuses. The court ruled that Mary Hanson, one of my other clients, couldn't sue the government.''

He grinned at her. "Busy lady. Tell me, when I come back, will you have time to marry me?''

Anna looked at him seriously and nodded. "I'll make time.'' She felt a wonderful calm with him now, yet she still felt a thrill when he touched her, and she felt warm when his eyes rested on her. He was a wonderful lover too, and over the months he'd told her about his family, his childhood, and about his youth in Dublin. Anna looked down. There were things she had yet to tell him . . . important things.

He touched her hand, and for now she pushed her thoughts away. "I've rented an apartment. I was going to write to you this week. My widowed sister-in-law and niece are coming to live in Chicago, so I've taken an apartment on the near North Side. I'll live there till we get married.''

He squeezed her hand. "That won't be long. I should be back in a matter of months now.''

Anna smiled. "Well, lunch is taking too long. We'd better hurry. I've got an obscenity charge to defend.''

At two-fifteen, following the judge's call to order, Anna rose to present her defense. She recalled Helen James to

the stand and had Helen tell the jury in her own words
why she had written the pamphlet.

When she had finished, Anna took the pamphlet and
walked slowly toward the jury. "You have heard the
prosecution suggest—no, claim—that a person or persons
might be influenced in some way by this pamphlet . . .
a woman might take up immorality, a man might be
driven to dreadful deeds by these rather clinical descriptions
of the female anatomy." She kept a true deadpan.
"I must agree. Heaven knows how a man might be
aroused by the very word 'ovaries.' "

There was a snicker through the courtroom and Harrington
shouted his objection.

"What is your intention?" the judge asked her.

"To illustrate, your honor, that this material is written
not in obscene or pornographic language. Further, I will
prove that it is not even written in even mildly erotic
language. I shall show it to be written in medical language,
and if such language is so provoking, it would
seem we can hardly trust male doctors, who are, on a
daily basis, subjected to such language."

The judge smirked slightly. "Objection overruled,
continue, Miss Bock."

"There are hundreds of prostitutes on the streets of
Chicago who have never heard of this pamphlet, nor are
they familiar with its contents. If we assume they were
driven to immorality by something they saw or read, then
apparently they were inflamed by some other, more
widely available reading material . . . perhaps indeed by
something read by one of the good men of the cloth who
appeared for the prosecution."

"This is absurd! I object!" Mr. Harrington shouted.

Anna looked at the judge. "I intend to show, your
honor, that there are more arousing passages in the Bible
than in this pamphlet." She bent over and picked up a
Bible from beneath her reference papers.

"Continue," he muttered, leaning over slightly.

" 'My beloved is to me a bag of myrrh that lies between
my breasts . . .' " Anna read slowly. " 'Upon my
bed by night I sought him whom my soul loves; . . . your
breasts are like two fawns, twins of a gazelle. . . . Make

haste, my beloved, and be like a gazelle or a young stag upon the mountains of spices.' " Anna stopped reading. "Now let us examine the meaning of some of these illusions—if indeed they are not obvious."

"These passages from the Bible are not readily understood!" Willard Harrington exploded as he jumped to his feet.

Anna turned sharply. "Neither are they banned by the postal services," she replied coldly; then, turning to judge and jury, "The issue is not whether the passages are understandable, it is whether they are obscene. Further, the prosecution has spoken of the pamphlet arousing men and women to wantonness. He has suggested that those with a predilection to loose behavior will be encouraged to immorality. But a judgment cannot be made with consideration for a few exceptions—if indeed they exist and could be so influenced. A judgment must be made on how this pamphlet would affect the reasonable man." The law was peppered with the "reasonable-man" argument, and she turned to her desk to begin citing precedents. "I cite the case of the Federal Government v. Henderson, the case of the Federal Government v. Tierney, the case of Massachusetts v. Walker . . ."

The judge nodded as Anna laid out her precedent cases. When she had finished, she called a doctor to the witness stand. Then she questioned him on the medical validity of the pamphlet's contents.

It was four o'clock when she finally gave her summation. "First," she argued, "you must consider intent. I put it to you that the intent of this pamphlet is to educate, not to titillate. Second, you must consider availability. True, it was sent through the mail, but only when it was requested. It is available only on request and therefore is not placed in the hands of the general public. Third, no reasonable person could be inflamed by the contents of this pamphlet, and fourth, it is doubtful that this pamphlet is, in any legal or literary definition of the word, obscene. It is not erotic—indeed, as I have illustrated, there are passages of the Bible that are quite erotic. No, ladies and gentlemen, this pamphlet has not been seized by the postal authorities because it is obscene, it has been seized precisely because it is educational. Women have been given the vote, but many men still consider us children from whom certain knowledge—knowledge of our own bodies—must be withheld. But we are citizens, voters, and persons. We are entitled to knowledge and we are guaranteed the same rights, freedoms, and protections as men under the First and Fourteenth amendments.'' Anna spoke firmly, in a low voice, and as always, she kept eye contact with the jurors. "I ask you to find my client not guilty," she finished.

It took the jury only an hour to find Helen James not guilty. Helen hugged her and was then absorbed by a crowd of reporters, all of whom wanted pictures to augment their stories.

Jim grinned at her. "Great defense." Then he leaned over and whispered in her ear, "Take me home with you, read me more from the Songs of Solomon. I love your voice."

"Miss Bock?"

Anna turned sharply to see a messenger bearing a gold embossed envelope. "Yes, I'm Ann Bock."

"I'm to deliver this letter," he said officially.

Anna took the letter and fished in her purse for a tip. The letter was from the Illinois Bar Association. She looked at it curiously, then opened it carefully and read it slowly:

Dear Miss Bock,

You have been highly recommended for membership in the Illinois Bar Association and it is my pleasure to extend this membership invitation to you on behalf of the governing committee.

If you accept our invitation, you will become the first woman in the history of Illinois to become a member. We would like to welcome you at our annual dinner to be held on Saturday, November 5, at seven P.M. at the Sherman House in Chicago. Please let me know your decision as soon as possible.

> Yours sincerely,
> Carlton J. Anderson,
> General Secretary, Illinois Bar
> Association

"My goodness," she breathed as she handed the letter to Jim.

"Double cause for celebration," he said after he read it. "We'll pick up some champagne on the way home."

It was Friday, the twenty-eighth of October. A damp, windy, cloudy day. It was the kind of day that was the harbinger of a cold winter to follow. But Anna felt excited, and her excitement blotted out the clouds and filled her with happiness.

She hurried across the street to Chicago's Deerborn Station and glanced up at the clock set into the ornate cupola that loomed far above the street. It was ten to four and the train from New York was due at four sharp.

She hurried through the arched doors of the station and into its large interior. Travelers stood in lines behind the brass rails leading to the ticket windows, a crowd gathered in front of the information booth, and several women stood by the Traveler's Aid desk looking bewildered by the throngs of people who seemed to surge through the station. As she well knew, Friday afternoon was always a madhouse. People flooded to the station to head out of town for the weekend, many would, as she so often had, leave for a weekend in Milwaukee. Others would head down to St. Louis, and still others would seek the quiet solitude of one of the many little communities that hugged the lake, far from the crowds, the slaughterhouses, and the steel mills of the Calumet.

Anna consulted the board, found that the train from New York was arriving on Track 16, and then headed out of the warm station and onto the cold, though covered platform. Trains stood at rest on many of the adjacent tracks, but they did not block the wind, which swirled up underneath them, causing a chill draft that caught Anna's skirt and caused it to billow.

Train tracks, Anna thought, were the arteries that fed the city. The "hump" thirteen miles west of the city was the largest railyard in the world. It was proudly stated that it could break up, sort, and dispatch a hundred-car train in less than two hours.

An engine on a nearby track gave a sudden loud hiss of white steam, and Anna jumped, slightly startled by the sound. The steam quickly dissipated in the afternoon breeze. Out here on the platform, odd smells assaulted her nose. The smell of food from the dining cars of the resting trains on nearby tracks, the smell of the oil used to keep the trains running smoothly, and the odor of milling humanity as it moved around, restlessly waiting.

Anna shivered in anticipation. Perhaps she would have the cab drive them down Michigan Avenue. The new Drake Hotel where Jim had so recently taken her for lunch was impressive, and the broad white sand of Oak Beach offered promises for lazy summer days to come. The parks were lovely too, and certainly the wide avenue of what was called "the Gold Coast" would make Dorcas and Mathilde think of Berlin with its wide streets and parks.

Perhaps, she thought, the similarity between Berlin and Chicago would help them to feel more at ease in this new country. She closed her eyes and for a long moment tried to remember how she had felt when she had first come to America. Everything had seemed strange, different. Then, in Milwaukee she had encountered a culture that was something in between the new world and the old. The similarities had helped ease her into all things American. Milwaukee had prepared her for Chicago. Chicago too had a large German population, but Chicago was truly the melting pot, truly the place where immigrants became really Americanized, where they became part of the energy and the bustle, part of a kind of new-world spirit. Immigrants sought to free themselves from Europe's burdens and be born again, and they embraced their newfound equality—the right to an equal opportunity to succeed. Here names and bloodlines ceased to mean much, and what mattered most was ambition, hard work, and accomplishment. Yes, she embraced her own excitement and thought how grand it was going to be to introduce Dorcas and Mathilde to this new challenging world.

The loudspeaker announced the train from New York and Anna watched as the engine pulled the long train

slowly up the platform. She trembled again, thinking that
although Dorcas was only her sister-in-law, Mathilde was
Markus' daughter, her real niece, and that Mathilde
would be her only blood relation in America—indeed,
the only family she had been in contact with since she
left Germany. And she felt good, good that she was able
to offer Dorcas and Mathilde a helping hand and a new
beginning.

The train jolted to a stop, and slowly, all along one
side, its doors opened and white-clad porters pulled down
the iron stairs and set step stools in place. Then passengers began to pour from the train. Anna positioned herself where she could scrutinize their faces, and she held
up a sign with her name on it in case, after all these
years, Dorcas didn't recognize her.

Then Anna saw them and dropped her sign, as there
was no need for it. Dorcas looked older and thinner than
she remembered her, and eight-year-old Mathilde was
taller than Anna had thought she would be. But there was
no mistaking them. They carried tapestry bags and looked
tired and hesitant, taken aback by the bustle and bewildered by the language. And there was no mistaking them
for another reason. Looking at Mathilde was like gazing
into a mirror nineteen years ago when she herself was
eight. Mathilde had her exact build, hair, and eyes. She
was dressed in an embroidered emerald-green skirt and
vest over which she wore a plain cream-colored coat.
Anna blinked back tears, and couldn't help thinking: She
could be my own daughter. But quickly she forced the
thought out of her mind, reminding herself that children
often looked like their aunts and uncles. She walked
forward. "Dorcas," she said, ". . . Mathilde?"

The two of them stopped and stared at her; then Mathilde smiled and embraced her. "Tante Anna!"

Anna returned her hug and closed her own eyes, feeling a strong, fierce emotion surge through her. Tante
Anna. How often she herself had said "Tante Karla" in
that same voice. I want to be to you what Karla was to
me, Anna thought. Then, unable to hold back her own
tears, she held Mathilde back and looked into her face.
Her eyes were blue and Anna fastened on them, spell-

bound. She couldn't shake the memory of that moment when she had held her own sweet little blue-eyed baby to her breast. She shivered, feeling quite shaken by this moment and by her unexpected emotional reaction.

"Tante Anna, are you all right?"

Anna nodded. The smooth, suave lawyer Ann Bock had fled her body, and for just this instant she was Anna von Bock and she had returned to another time, another place . . . in fact, almost a different lifetime. "I'm fine," she whispered. "I'm just glad to see you, Mathilde."

The young girl beamed and said in halting English, "I want a new name for my new country," she said. "I want to be called Mattie."

Anna nodded. "Mattie it is," she agreed.

Then Anna turned and hugged Dorcas, who whispered, "You have saved our lives, Anna. I shall always be grateful."

"I wanted to help," Anna said; then, "I've rented a small apartment, but there's plenty of room for the three of us."

"I'll have to find work," Dorcas said.

"I too," Mattie put in.

Anna shook her head. "You're going to school," she said firmly. "You're much too young to work."

Dorcas inhaled. "She had to work in Germany."

"Not here," Anna said.

"I don't know if I can find a job that will pay enough for me to send her to school."

"I have enough," Anna told her, "and I insist, Dorcas."

"You've already done so much, I don't want us to be a financial burden any longer."

Anna smiled and took one of Dorcas' bags from her. "I promise you won't be," she said. "Come, let's get a cab and I'll give you your first look at Chicago."

"I'm so excited," Mattie said. "I've dreamed of this day."

Anna smiled. "Today your dream will come true."

Anna's pale mauve Callot evening dress fell in pleated tiers from its bloused waist. It was trimmed with a filmy wisp of material that hung from its neckline. Her shoes were dyed to match her gown, and she wore a thin head-band across her forehead. Although stylish, her gown was extremely conservative compared to the gowns sported by the many lawyers' wives present at the annual meeting of the Illinois Bar Association.

Anna had arrived a trifle early and gone to the ladies' lounge to comb her hair. Even though she had come by cab, she'd been windblown on leaving the cab and run-ning from the cab to the front door of the Sherman House.

The woman standing next to her at the mirror was wearing a gown in what was called "the Egyptian mode." It was white and featured a draped beaded sash around the hips and folds that were reminiscent of an-cient Rome or Greece, if not of Egypt. She wore a glit-tering beaded bracelet and matching headband over dark wavy bobbed hair. Her gown fell daringly over one shoulder and her earrings hung almost to her shoulders. She turned toward Anna and smiled warmly. "I don't think we've ever met. I'm Carol Thompson."

Anna knew a Robert Thompson, although she didn't know him well. He was a partner in one of the city's more prestigious firms.

"Mrs. Robert Thompson," the woman confirmed without being asked. "My husband's with Freeman, Freeman, Bach, and Thompson."

"I'm familiar with the firm," Anna replied in as friendly a fashion as she could muster.

"Who's your husband?" Mrs. Thompson asked, turn-ing toward Anna once again, and still holding her lipstick in one hand.

"I'm not married," Anna replied. "I'm Ann Bock. I'm an attorney."

Carol Thompson whipped her head around and almost dropped her lipstick. She looked at her as if she had fallen to earth from a distant planet. "An attorney?" she questioned, tilting her head slightly.

"Yes, I have my own practice."

"I didn't know there *were* any women attorneys," Carol said, still looking slightly doubtful.

"There aren't many," Anna allowed cheerfully.

"Are you a member of the bar . . . of the association?"

"I'm to become the first woman member tonight," Anna replied. "And I'm very excited about it."

Carol Thompson looked her over very carefully. "Are you engaged?" she queried.

"Unofficially," Anna answered, beginning to feel a little uncomfortable.

"Goodness," Carol said, "if women who look like you are going to be attending meetings with . . . with . . . well, I mean most of the men are married already."

Anna raised her brow slightly; the emphasis of Carol's sentence had been on "already." Well, Carol Thompson didn't have to come right out and say it, even though she was honest enough to have come close: the wives of lawyers weren't going to be too excited about the thought of females belonging to the association. They didn't mind their husbands being out with the boys, but it was obvious from Carol's reaction that many of them would not like having their husbands out in mixed company without them. It was an aspect of membership in the association she hadn't considered, but she considered it now, and wondered if there would, in fact, be much hostility from wives.

"I didn't mean you were a vamp," Carol suddenly said.

Anna almost laughed. "Not with married men," she answered. "Please, let me assure you, when I'm with my colleagues we only discuss our cases."

"Well, there *are* single lawyers . . . I could introduce you to some. Think of how perfect it would be if you married a lawyer and you could work with your husband." She smiled and turned back to look in the mirror, the smile faded from her pretty face and replaced by a more serious expression. "I wish I could spend more time with Robert. Sometimes I wish I could work with him. I even envy the girl in the office who knows how to use the typewriting machine." Carol shook her head. "The truth is, I hardly understand what he's talking about most of the time."

Anna touched Carol gently on the arm. In spite of this

woman's honestly expressed envy, her heart went out to Carol Thompson, whom she didn't even know. This woman had, almost inadvertently, made a heartfelt confession of inadequacy. It was painful to hear, more painful to really understand. Carol Thompson felt she was only an appendage of her very successful husband. "There will come a time," Anna said, "when things change."

"Not for me," Carol answered as she stared into the mirror.

"Do you have daughters?" Anna asked.

"Yes. We have two sons and two daughters."

"Then make a vow that your daughters will never feel as you do. See that they study and get a good education. We women need that. And don't you believe for one minute that you're not important. Mothering is a profession too, and perhaps it's the most important one."

"Do you really believe that?"

"I wouldn't say it if I didn't. I had a wonderful aunt who mothered me properly—she gave me everything."

Carol smiled. "You're interesting," she said, looking at Anna. "I don't believe they've assigned tables. Will you sit with us?" Carol brightened. "Actually, if he makes it down from Springfield, Jim Parnell will probably join us too. He's not married, and he's devastatingly good-looking."

Anna laughed. "Jim Parnell is my unofficial fiancé!"

Carol raised her brow. "Oh, you must be his mystery woman! He's a devil, that one!"

Robert Thompson and Jim Parnell both stood up as Carol and Anna approached the table.

"Carol, you're a genuine psychic," Jim said, holding out his hands. "I should have called you, Ann, but I wasn't at all certain I was going to make it."

"You came all this way for this dinner? I thought you'd be here. You know, I am catching on to your surprises," Anna said playfully.

"No, I came all this way to welcome the first woman member of the association. I'm afraid I have to go back tonight. You know, the next two months are going to be the longest in my life, but when they're over . . . well, no more separations."

"Going back on the milk train?" Robert Thompson asked, then turned to Anna. "He must really like you. That's four hours down and six back."

Anna blushed.

Jim moved behind her and pulled out her chair, while Robert did the same for Carol. "Bob's making this into much, too much of a gallant effort. Actually, I can work on the train. Besides, I really came to see your old nemesis, Southam. He'll walk out on this dinner."

Anna looked at him in distress. "Professor Southam? Is he here?"

"You bet. And when you're introduced, he's going to publicly walk out. He fought your membership every inch of the way."

"Was he the only one?" Anna asked.

Jim smiled. "No, but he's the only one who will resign his own membership in protest."

"I'd hate to think I'd caused a major rift," Anna commented.

"Is Alex Webber coming?" Jim asked.

"Yes. He'll be introducing me. I don't have to make a long speech or anything, but I have to say a few words. You know, I am nervous. More so now that you've told me about Southam."

Robert Thompson laughed. "Isn't that the way? Hell, I can get up and hold a jury in verbal captivity for hours—"

"It's true," Carol said proudly. "He's very charismatic."

Robert patted her hand. "What I was going to say was that no matter how much speaking I do, in the courtroom and out, the audience that always makes me the most nervous is this one." He gave a short laugh. "But don't worry about Southam. He's not beloved in any case."

"One's peers are always the toughest. Anyway, we're all seasoned public speakers," Jim agreed.

"I wish we could get it over with before dinner. I'll be too nervous to enjoy my meal," Anna confessed.

"We're having you for dessert," Jim said, winking.

Then he shook his head in disgust. "God, this is irritating. I hate Prohibition. Imagine not being able to have wine at a dinner like this."

"If you miss your Irish whiskey, I know where you can get some. Good stuff, comes from Canada."

Jim raised his brow. "I'm working in the state attorney's office, for God's sake. I don't want to know where you get your hooch, or even how it's getting into the country."

"You mean you never tipple?" Carol asked.

"My secret," Jim replied, smiling slyly.

Discreetly, waiters began to bring the food, and after dinner, dessert and coffee were served. Then, while the guests sipped their coffee, the master of ceremonies introduced the head table. Following that, and before the speaker of the evening, Alex Webber stood to make his announcement.

"Tonight," he said solemnly, "is a historic night. Tonight we are welcoming to our midst the first woman to become a member of the Illinois Bar Association, Miss Ann Bock.

"Miss Bock distinguished herself as a student, graduating first in her class at the Illinois Union College of Law. In her own practice she has further distinguished herself defending the basic rights of individual citizens, rights guaranteed under the Constitution. Perhaps because she herself emigrated from a country where individual freedoms were granted only at the behest of the monarchy, rather than being guaranteed by a democratic constitution, Ann Bock has a special understanding of—even affection for—the importance of defending the First and Fourteenth amendments of our precious Constitution. She has worked tirelessly for those without a voice—women and children. She has been an advocate for the oppressed and she has demonstrated a rare passion for justice. It is with pleasure that we welcome her to our ranks and wish for her a long and distinguished career."

All the men in the room stood and clapped loudly as Alex Webber gestured for Anna to come forward to speak.

Anna stood up and looked around. In the far corner of

the room, Professor Southam, her old nemesis, stood alone. He marched down the long aisle between tables and out the door. A few eyes followed him, but most of the group applauded her and the crowd parted as she moved toward the podium and stood before the assembled lawyers and their wives.

Anna trembled slightly. "Earlier," she confessed in an even, low voice, "I told one of my colleagues that I was nervous at the thought of speaking before you, my peers." She smiled. "I was and am. But I am also moved deeply by Alex Webber's words and by the honor you do me tonight. A short eighteen months ago, women obtained the vote in this country, and with that vote I expect new avenues will open up to them, new careers will become an option. I may be the first woman to be honored by this association, but I know I will not be the last. I thank you, and I promise to continue down the legal path I have chosen."

There was clapping and Anna slowly worked her way through the crowd and back to her table. Jim kissed her on the cheek and squeezed her hand tightly. Then he whispered in her ear, "I wish I weren't going back to Springfield tonight."

Anna squeezed his hand back. "I wish you weren't either," she murmured.

"We'll be together soon," he told her, and for a moment it was as if they were the only two people in the room. Then he asked almost anxiously, "You are going to be down in Springfield for the Law Society's annual seminar, aren't you?"

Anna smiled. "Yes . . . yes, I made reservations yesterday."

"We'll be together then," he said softly, and she returned his smile. It sounded far more like an assignation than a seminar.

16

Although it was three weeks till Christmas, a large full spruce tree decorated with red and silver balls stood in the lobby of the venerable Athena Hotel in Springfield. Built at the turn of the century, it had the same old-world charm as the governor's mansion, where the reception for the Law Society Annual Seminar had just been held.

Inside, Anna and Jim sat at a small table in an alcove of the dining room. Anna felt a certain tranquillity, and concluded it was caused by the room's comfortable, intimate atmosphere. Decorated in the Victorian mode, it featured long heavily draped windows, high ceilings, and a huge fireplace. Copies of famous paintings, meticulously done in oils by local artists, hung on the walls. They looked almost genuine in the muted light of the flickering candles that sat in the center of each table.

Anna wore a black crepe satin dress with three separate tunics, each lined with satin. Her shoe buckles, evening bag, and slouch hat were trimmed in pearls to match the rope of pearls she wore around her neck.

Jim leaned toward her. "You've been thoughtful all evening, Ann. Is something troubling you?"

Anna studied Jim's ruggedly handsome face. The light from the candle played on his ruddy complexion. "I've been thinking," she said slowly.

"Ah, secrets again . . ."

"I'm afraid I have serious things to confess, Jim."

"Anna, you don't have to tell me everything, or even anything. There have been women in my life, lots of them. But over the years I kept thinking of you—it was as if I'd always known you were the right one.

"I wasn't talking about 'just' a boyfriend," Anna said

carefully. Jim, years ago, before I ever met you, when I was a student in Berlin . . . there was someone.''

His face clouded over and he leaned toward her because he could see the pain in her face. "You don't have to tell me this," he reiterated.

"I do." She shook her head as if to deny her own past. "I was so young and so naive. I met a man. He professed to be a sort of political radical. He was a kind of mad genius and, as it turned out violent. I didn't see through him at the time. I lived with him for a short time and I got pregnant and I had a daughter."

Jim looked at her seriously, but nothing in his eyes seemed to condemn her. His expression of concern gave her the courage to continue. "My father sent me away to have the child. The nurse who cared for me was a tyrant and she was in my father's employ. Right after my daughter was born, she drugged me and stole my child. I understand she was given up for adoption, but I don't know to whom. I never saw her again."

Jim let out his breath slowly and shook his head. He reached across the table and took her hand. "God, Anna, I know you well enough to know you must have been devastated."

"I almost went out of my mind. Only my brother Markus tried to help me. That's why I had to help Dorcas and Mattie . . . though I admit that just in the short time since they've been here, they've come to mean a lot to me. Dorcas, as it turns out, is very loving, and Mattie . . . well, Mattie is the same age as my daughter. She means a lot to me. But more, she's made me realize that I have to go back to Germany and try one more time to locate my own daughter—I have to exhaust all possibilities before I can truly close the door on that part of my life."

"So you did try once to find your child?"

"Yes. But there were only two people who knew where she was placed. One was my father and the other was the nurse, Helga. My father's dead, but perhaps I can trace the nurse. I've decided I have to go to Germany after Christmas. To try one more time."

"I understand. How about your family, have you remained estranged from them?"

"Yes, but I was especially estranged from my father. I hated him—hated what he did to me. I suppose that's why I became so attached to Alex Webber. He was my surrogate father. He always treated me like his daughter."

He half-smiled at her, then took her hand. "Now that I'm finally coming back to Chicago, you're leaving."

"I didn't mean for it to work out that way. Can you spend Christmas with us? You won't be alone in a den of women. My Uncle Josef is coming down from Milwaukee. He's a journalist and I think you'd find him a very interesting person."

"What about your aunt?"

"She died. Josef is a widower." Anna leaned closer. "One thing, Jim . . . Dorcas and Mattie don't know about my child. When I go to Germany I'll just tell them it's to visit the other members of my family. I do still have a brother and sister in Berlin, and a host of nieces and nephews."

"I won't say anything. Not that it's likely to come up. How about the father of your child? Will you see him in Germany?"

Anna shook her head. "He's one person I never want to see again. He frightens me."

Jim studied her face and thought to himself that she was haunted by old ghosts. Later he would make love to her and hold her. "Of course we'll spend Christmas together. This Christmas and all the Christmases to come."

"Jim . . . you're a wonderfully sensitive man," she said in a near-whisper.

He caressed her with his eyes. "Let's get out of here. I want to be alone with you."

Anna felt a thrill of anticipation as the memory of their last assignation flooded over her. She nodded.

Once in the privacy of his room, Jim poured the champagne he'd arranged for; it bubbled and fizzed in the glasses. Then he walked over to her, held out the glass, and they silently toasted, each lifting the glass to the other's lips.

Anna crinkled her nose as the bubbles tickled her.

"I love you," he told her, looking deeply into her marvelous blue eyes. "And this is for you." He handed her a small black velvet box.

"Oh, Jim," she breathed as she opened it and the diamond engagement ring sparkled in the soft light.

"I don't want to be your unofficial fiancé anymore."

"At this moment I feel as I've never felt before in my entire life." Tears filled her eyes. "I feel lighter than air . . ."

He set his half-filled glass down on the table and she did the same, though neither took their eyes off the other.

He reached out and ran his hand over her gently waved silky blond hair, then he gently kissed her neck, her ears, her cheeks and eyelids, and finally her lips, which he seemed to taste before pressing them hard against his own. She responded with all the passion he knew her to possess, moving her lips against his, embracing him, caressing him.

The apartment on the near North Side where Anna, Dorcas, and Mattie lived was in one of Chicago's many new buildings. It was a six-story yellow-brick building with modern rounded corners. The apartment itself had three small bedrooms, a living room, kitchen, sun room, and bath.

Mattie attended the North Side School, and Dorcas, who had completed a course on the typewriter in Germany, found a job in an insurance office. The three women shared the housework and the task of preparing meals, though Anna was not always there for dinner. The apartment, which was normally large enough, was somewhat crowded owing to Josef's visit. Still, he was only to be there for a few days, and the inconvenience was far outweighed by the joy of feeling a "real" family.

Anna looked at the Christmas tree. Mattie had just placed the final decoration on the top. She looked down from the chair on which she stood and smiled at her aunt. "What do you think?"

"It takes up almost the whole sun room," Anna replied good-naturedly, "but of course Christmas must be celebrated."

"Even in our new country," Dorcas said as she stood in the doorway that led to the kitchen.

"It's a huge holiday in Milwaukee," Josef put in. He was sitting in the overstuffed chair in the living room, midway between the sun room and the kitchen. "Just as it is in Germany. Ask Anna if you don't believe me. You can smell the sausages all over Germantown on Christmas—sausages and roasted goose. People in America don't know how to cook goose, and what's worse, they throw the drippings out!"

"Well, we won't throw ours out. We'll save them for you to eat at breakfast with your bread," Dorcas promised.

He grinned. "You're a good cook. I can smell your handiwork from here."

"I read that it was German immigrants who first introduced the Christmas tree to America," Mattie said as both she and Anna came into the living room from the alcove that was the sun room.

There was a knock on the door and Mattie hurried across the room to open it. "I imagine it's your fiancé, Mr. Jim Parnell," she said gaily. Expectantly she flung open the door. "Merry Christmas!"

Jim stood outside holding an armful of gifts.

"You shouldn't have brought anything," Dorcas admonished.

"Of course I should have! I rarely spend Christmas with a real family. Here, here, do put this illicit champagne on ice," he said, holding out a paper sack that clearly held a bottle.

Anna laughed, "Oh, dear! A state's attorney breaking Prohibition."

Jim grinned mischievously. "If I don't know where to get good hooch, who does?" He kissed her on the cheek and whispered in her ear, "And it's not the first champagne we've ever had, is it?"

Anna blushed and smiled knowingly at him.

Dorcas looked at them for a moment, pleased that

Anna looked contented and happy. "We have German white wine too," Dorcas confided, "and the right German cheeses to go with it."

"Smells good to me." Jim sniffed and then slapped his leg. "Goose! I smell a goose! Thank goodness, I thought we were going to have a turkey. I couldn't stand it, you know. Christmas is not Christmas without a fat goose. Mind you, I think we Irish cook them differently."

Josef stood up. "You probably stuff them with potatoes."

"I'm so rude. Josef, this is Jim Parnell. Jim, this is my uncle, Josef Baer."

The two men warmly shook hands and then pointed to one another and laughed because they were wearing identical Christmas ties. Both were red with small green wreaths.

"And we have almond kuchen," Mattie said.

Jim smiled and fished again into the large shopping bag he carried. "And these go under the tree." He handed Anna three boxes.

Anna took the gifts. She thought that the love she and Jim felt for one another was visible and that Mattie, Dorcas, and Josef were probably aware of the intensity of their relationship. Not that they had tried to hide it. They were just simply in love, and it showed.

"Let's have a drink," Jim suggested.

"Dear, dear, all this lawlessness," Anna said mockingly.

Jim laughed. "At least I'm not a revenue agent. Why do I suspect they're all drinking on Christmas Eve too?"

"Because in all likelihood they are," Anna concluded. She turned and walked toward the archway that led to the sun room. "Our tree is in here."

Jim followed. "A fine tree," he said, watching her as she bent over and put his packages beneath it.

"I must go see to the goose," Dorcas said, and she returned to the kitchen.

Josef pulled himself from the chair. "I think I'd like a look at that bird myself."

Mattie looked at Anna conspiratorially and whispered, "I think Josef likes my mother."

Anna tilted her head slightly and looked through the living room toward the kitchen. Josef had been there three days, and it was true . . . he did seem interested in Dorcas. She smiled, feeling rather pleased. Josef and Karla had been wonderfully happy, but now Josef was terribly lonely. Dorcas wasn't at all like Karla, but then, no one was, and perhaps it was better that he was interested in someone totally different. Yes, she decided. Dorcas and Josef—though he was older—were a good idea. "Does your mother like him?" Anna quietly questioned.

"Oh, I think so. I think she might like him more when she gets to know him better. I think she might even have a crush on him."

"And I have one on your aunt," Jim said, leaning over and kissing Anna on the cheek. He looked at Anna. "You know, she looks like you," he observed.

"Well, she is my niece," Anna replied proudly.

Mattie looked at Jim and then at Anna. "I'll be back," she said, excusing herself from the room and leaving them momentarily alone.

"Ah, we're alone!" He pulled Anna into his arms and kissed her passionately, moving his lips against hers.

She returned his kiss. "They know we're in love," she whispered.

He kissed her throat. "I should hope so. I certainly can't hide it."

Anna leaned against him. "I'm going to miss you, even if it is for only a month."

"Have you told them you're going to Germany?" Jim asked.

Anna shook her head. "No. I'll tell them after the holiday. I have reservations on a ship that sails on the fifteenth of January."

"Rough winter crossing," he commented.

Anna nodded. "I know, but it's best now. I'm between cases and the appeal won't be heard by the Supreme Court till at least March or April—if it's heard at all."

He looked at her for a long moment, as if he'd been thinking about what he wanted to say. "You know, Anna,

if you found your daughter now, it would be difficult.
She only knows the people who have her, the people who
have reared her. What exactly would you do?''

"The answer depends on her situation. The most important thing for me now is to know that she's safe and
happy. I don't have to have her back. I just have to
know . . .''

Jim took Anna in his arms. "I understand," he said
softly.

It was the day after New Year's and winter attacked
Chicago with a vengeance. Snow propelled by high winds
drifted against the sides of buildings and the gray cold
waters of the lake blended with gray snow-laden clouds,
blurring the line of the distant horizon.

"Good thing Josef caught the train for Milwaukee last
night," Anna said, looking out the kitchen window. "He
wouldn't have made it today. I'll bet all the trains have
been canceled."

"Or at least delayed," Dorcas said. Then she looked
up at Anna, her blue eyes wide. "I liked Josef . . . I
liked him a lot." She blushed a soft pink at her own
confession and distractedly finished drying the last
breakfast dish.

Anna put the dish away and sat down at the kitchen
table. "I think I'll have another cup of coffee before I
begin drafting my appeal case. If they decide to hear it,
I want to be ready," she explained to her sister-in-law.

Dorcas nodded. "I'll put the coffee on," she said,
placing the pot on the gas burner. "I suppose Josef thinks
I'm a dolt. I hardly said a word all the time he was here."

"I'm sure he thinks no such thing. Don't be so hard
on yourself. Besides, a dolt couldn't have a daughter as
wonderful as Mattie."

Dorcas shifted uneasily and looked away. "She is an
intelligent girl," Dorcas said, "and pretty too. She's very
fond of you, Anna."

"I adore her," Anna confessed. Then, looking at Dorcas more seriously, "I think you and Josef should see
each other again—soon."

Again Dorcas blushed. "Oh, I don't think he'd be interested in me. Besides, he lives in Milwaukee and I live here. And there's Karla—I mean Karla's memory. You've spoken of her a lot. I couldn't live up to her . . . I'm too plain and not at all bright.''

"You are not plain and you are bright! In any case, you don't have to live up to Karla, or even be like her. No, I think you're wrong. I think Josef was as interested in you as you were in him. Write to him, Dorcas, and go and visit Milwaukee—soon.''

"I thought you would want me to be loyal to the memory of Markus—I've probably shocked you.''

"Oh, Dorcas, not at all. Markus has been dead for some time, and so has Karla. You have a right to a life of your own, and so does Josef.''

Dorcas' eyes sought the floor, and a frown filled her face. "I know you loved Markus,'' she said slowly.

"He was the only person besides Karla in the family who cared about me,'' Anna said, without revealing any details.

"But were you close?'' Dorcas asked.

Anna shook her head. "I was the family baby. We grew up separately. No, I don't think you could say we were close.''

"There are things about Markus you don't know,'' Dorcas confided in a voice that seemed to be growing ever smaller.

"Should I know them?'' Anna asked.

"I don't know. If I tell you, please don't think ill of me.''

"I won't,'' Anna promised.

"Anna, Markus never loved me.''

Anna frowned and studied her sister-in-law's face. Vaguely, a memory returned . . . a buried memory. She was in the library reading and Markus had come in with Else . . . and she had forgotten Gerda's contention that Markus and Else were having an affair, but she remembered now. "Did he love someone else?'' Anna asked.

"Else . . . he loved Else.''

"Did Andreas know?'' Anna queried.

"The whole story was complicated. I wasn't told all of it. But as far as I know, Andreas had a mistress. It was one of her other lovers who shot Andreas, then killed her and shot himself. It was a terrible scandal. No, Markus only married me to have an heir and to cover up his feelings for Else. That way he could go on seeing her and no one would suspect because he was 'happily married with a wife and child.' I felt used, Anna.''

"How terrible for you. I'm sorry, Dorcas.''

Dorcas again moved uneasily. Then the coffee finished perking and she jumped up to retrieve it from the stove.

"I have something to tell you,'' Anna said as she watched Dorcas pour the rich dark coffee into the porcelain cups. "I suppose I should have told you before, but I wanted to wait till after Christmas.''

"I hope it's nothing bad.''

"No, nothing bad. I'm going to Germany for a visit, that's all. I won't be gone long.''

Dorcas set down the pot with surprise. "Germany? All that way? In the winter?''

"It's the only time I can get away. I have to see Gerda and I have to settle a few things.''

"I won't know what to do without you.''

Anna lifted the coffee to her lips. "Go visit Milwaukee,'' she suggested.

Dorcas smiled coyly. "I suppose I ought to get used to being without you. I rather think you and Jim will get married soon—when you get back, perhaps?''

Anna smiled at Dorcas. "We're so obvious, I suppose the whole law society knows we're lovers by now. Is it the way we look at each other?''

"Oh, no! It's the distance. You sit close now, lean closer together—there's no space at all between you. That's how I always tell when people have a relationship.''

"That's very perceptive.'' Anna winked. "I'll be keeping my eye on you and Josef.''

"Perhaps,'' Dorcas allowed, "I will go to Milwaukee while you're gone.''

The winter ocean had been angry and turbulent, but the inland river was merely choppy, as if by comparison the waters were nagging rather than having a full-blown tantrum.

Anna watched with fascination as the ship slowly navigated the biting waters, making its way to dock in Hamburg. Outwardly the city appeared as she had left it; there were no signs of the Great War, nor was there evidence of the terrible economic tribulations that gripped the land.

For years she had thought of returning to Germany to look for her daughter; now the enormity—perhaps impossibility—of her task loomed before her. Clearly she would have to go to Gerda first. Gerda was, after all, her sister, and if Gerda knew anything, she might tell. Especially now that their father was dead.

Concentrating, Anna tried to conjure up Gerda's image in her mind. No, she couldn't imagine what Gerda looked like now, and she wondered if Gerda was still a politician, and still struggling within her husband's family for a foothold. She sighed. Going back, even for this short visit, would not be pleasant.

Anna shivered in the cold as the ship finally docked and the deckhands hastily put the gangplanks in place so that the passengers might leave.

It had been a positively horrible voyage. She had fought to spend most of the time buried in blankets in a deck chair because only in the fresh air was she able to ignore the rolling of the vessel on the choppy waters on the North Atlantic. And precisely because it had been so horrible, it had seemed twice as long as it actually had been.

Anna disembarked and quickly cleared customs because she'd brought little luggage. Within two hours she was aboard the boat train and headed for Berlin.

Almost immediately she felt a strange hostility directed toward her by her countrymen. Perhaps it's my clothes, she thought. None of the Germans she encountered looked at all prosperous, though, she reminded herself, she had hardly expected them to look prosperous. Still, it was not the poor way in which they dressed that made her uncomfortable, it was instead the sullen bitterness that seemed to pervade the atmosphere and poison even the most innocent of exchanges.

The Germans, it seemed, placed everyone in one of three categories: you were one of the villainous conquerors who imposed the vile and unfair Versailles Treaty; you were one of the Germans who had somehow escaped the widely felt effects of the treaty; or you were one of that great mass of Germans who felt they were being punished. The former were met with true hatred, though a civility existed long enough to overcharge the unsuspecting; the latter were simply ignored, for in this atmosphere it was everyone for himself. The middle group were looked on with wonderment, with a combination of jealousy and admiration, and were greeted with unspoken questions: How did you manage? Why am I not among you?

By the time the train pulled into Berlin, Anna felt prepared for the worst. But the familiarity of the streets and the rhythm of the capital set her temporarily at ease. She went to the small Linden Hotel at 70 Unter den Linden, and there, from her balcony, she looked down on Berlin's most famous street and in her mind relived her childhood years.

The next morning Anna awoke prepared to brave the city and what was left of her family. Gerda still lived in the district of Charlottenburg, but not in the same house with its spacious grounds. Now she lived in a small house not far from the Royal Porcelain Factory. It was not a bad neighborhood, but certainly not as good as the one in which she had formerly lived.

Anna walked down the Berliner Strasse slowly, in spite of the brisk wind and the overcast sky, which, had she been going elsewhere, might have urged her to hasten her steps. Everything, Anna noted, had a somewhat shabby appearance. Otherwise elegant homes needed paint and repair, the walkways were rutted, and as she had noticed before, the other pedestrians were dressed plainly in clothes that were several years out of fashion. But again it was attitude that struck Anna. Not only did Germans put everyone into categories, but they appeared to take an annoying kind of pride in their misery. Their punishment became an excuse for everything from inflation to laziness. The atmosphere which Anna seemed to absorb slowly, hour by hour, was at odds with everything she remembered about Germany and Berlin in particular. It was certainly at odds with German culture in America too. And, Anna admitted, she found the atmosphere irritating. Germans were simply not prepared to take any responsibility for their situation. Their poverty, indeed all the misery caused by the war, was the fault of the French and the English. It was the fault of Germany's small Jewish population, of the Social Democrats, of the men who had signed the surrender . . . it was everyone's fault, and yet it was most decidedly someone else's rather than theirs.

Anna reached the house, a modest two-story house on a small plot of land. When she had called, Gerda had not even sounded surprised. Certainly she had not sounded welcoming either. Instead her reply had been snappish and the mood conveyed was decidedly one of: I suppose you've come to gloat—to see how far I've fallen.

Anna sucked in her breath and climbed up the stairs that led to the porch. She knocked.

Shockingly, Gerda's hair was snow white and she wore it in long thick braids twisted around her head. Her features had sharpened with age, and she was rail thin and seemed to Anna, even during the first few seconds of their encounter, brittle in body, mind, and spirit.

Nor was her house furnished pleasantly. Like almost everything else, it had seen better days. The furniture was old and massive. It was dark too, and seemed to blend into the walls, which were peeling and much in need of paint.

Gerda herself opened the door, and instead of hugging her sister, she stared at her as if they were total strangers. "Anna?" she asked.

Anna tried desperately to mask her own shock at Gerda's appearance. "Yes, of course, Gerda—of course it's Anna."

There followed an awkward moment of silence. Then quickly, perfunctorily, Gerda leaned over and hugged her sister. She jumped back almost instantly, and there was little or no warmth in the greeting.

"Come in. Excuse the house," Gerda muttered as they walked into the sitting room. Gerda cleared chairs as she moved around the room, and Anna noted the tables were dusty, the room cluttered, and there was a musty smell, as if all the doors and windows had been closed for a year or more.

"I have no servants," Gerda complained. Then, bitterly, "I can't afford them." She nervously rubbed her hands over her faded gray cotton dress, as if she were trying to make it disappear.

Anna sat down on the edge of the sofa. On one worn arm the stuffing was peeking through the faded fabric as if it were trying to escape. Anna forced a smile. "I suppose you were surprised to get my call."

"Yes. I'm surprised you came home."

"This isn't my home," Anna said somewhat coldly.

"I suppose not. Naturally you wouldn't come back to Germany. You're a rich American now . . . I can tell by your clothes. Do you have your rich American husband with you?"

"I have no rich American husband," Anna answered, trying not to sound as exasperated and as irritated as she felt.

Gerda looked at her crossly. "Well, then, how do you afford to dress so well? To travel?"

"I finished law school, Gerda. I have my own practice and I earn my own salary." She stopped short of telling Gerda how much she earned, not that she had an immense income, but it would sound huge in German terms, and so she did not reveal it.

Gerda looked at her disbelievingly and shook her head. "So," she finally said, "you've come to lord it over me, to rub in your success. Well I haven't failed, Germany has failed. Our leaders sold us out, we're all suffering."

Anna tensed, anger welling inside her. She had not expected to be happy on this visit, she had not even expected to be welcomed by her sister. But she had not expected such selfish bitterness and such a miserable outlook either. She felt overwhelmed with Gerda's self-pity;

it was the statement of all she had felt since she had arrived.

"I have not come to lord anything over you," Anna stressed. "I've suffered myself, and worked hard for everything I now have. I'm not ashamed of that. You, on the other hand, are drowning in your own misery. Germany wasn't and isn't an innocent victim, Gerda."

Gerda looked taken aback, but she chose not to respond. "Why have you come here?" she asked without emotion.

"I've come back to try to find my child. I came to ask you if Father ever told you what he did with my child. I have not forgotten, Gerda. I have not forgotten her, and if you know anything, you must tell me. Father cannot do anything to you now, so there is no reason why you can't tell me anything you know."

Gerda looked at the pattern in her faded Persian rug. Her hands were folded in her lap tightly. "He never told me anything," she said. "It's the truth. I have no reason to lie to you now, none at all. But you could have written me. You didn't need to be so frivolous and spend so much coming here. But then, I suppose you can afford it."

Anna ignored the barb. "You are not the only one I have to see," Anna replied. "Besides, I wanted to see Germany." Anna paused because Gerda, who had never left, could not imagine some of the warring emotions felt by those who emigrated. Anna realized that even though she'd always been the family outcast, she had still loved her country and missed it in ways unknown to those who had not experienced the uprooting experience of the immigrant. And perhaps, she admitted, she felt even more uprooted because she had left a child here, a child whose whereabouts were unknown to her. "Do you think Father told Andreas?" she pressed, leaning toward her sister.

"No. Markus knew and I knew. It's no use. If that's why you came, your visit will be a failure. Our father did not share his thoughts unless he had reason."

Anna frowned. "Markus knew I had a child before I told him?"

Gerda shrugged. "Yes, but I don't know why he was old."

Anna leaned back against the sofa. "Dorcas and Mathilde have come to America. We live together."

Gerda looked up, mildly interested. "I didn't see them much after Markus died." Then, bitterly, "Are they also rich and successful?"

"I'm not rich, Gerda. And neither are they. We're just comfortable. Dorcas has a job and Mathilde—Mattie is going to school."

"Pity Markus is dead. If he knew about your child, perhaps Father told him more."

Anna felt a chill pass through her. She looked at her sister and shook her head in denial. "No, that's impossible. No, Markus was the only one to help me."

"Our father never did anything without reason. He sent Mother away and he only told Andreas and Else not to see you or answer inquiries. And Dorcas was away with her family having her own child . . . so if Markus knew, he knew because Father had a reason for telling him. Likely, Father wanted Markus to do something . . . perhaps he hired the nurse, or something like that."

"You must be wrong," Anna said, hearing the distress in her own voice.

"I think Markus only pretended to help you so you would leave Germany. Father knew Markus was seeing you, helping you."

"What makes you say that?" Anna asked.

"I heard him talking to Father one night. They knew you'd keep looking for your child if you stayed here. Father said you were too stubborn to give up, and Markus helped you to leave, isn't that so?"

Anna nodded, aware only of a creeping sense of betrayal. She had always thought her brother was helping her. Then she thought of poor Dorcas and of the fact that Markus had had an affair with Else. It was possible, she conceded, that Markus had lied to her. But what difference did it make now? Anna closed her eyes and bit her lower lip. Where should she begin, where?

"You should try to find the nurse," Gerda said as she

lit a cigarette and expelled the smoke quickly and somehow dramatically into the stale air.

Anna watched as Gerda's hand trembled. "I don'
know where to start looking for the nurse. When I lef
Germany, Markus kept paying the lawyers . . . he wa:
supposed to have continued the search."

"Well, he didn't. He just told you that so you woulc
leave. Aren't nurses registered?" Gerda asked. "Aren'
we Germans famous for keeping records of everything
Private nurses are registered too. Perhaps you can fin
out where she lives from the registry office."

Gerda had after all given her an idea. "I'll try that,'
Anna said thoughtfully. "Do you think I should talk tc
Andreas?"

"I doubt it would do any good. Though you may wan
to see him. I should warn you, Andreas has changed mos
of all. He's . . . he's not the person he used to be."

"I don't understand."

Gerda shrugged. "He's grown terribly strange . . . I
suppose it's physical, but who knows? I never see him
and I certainly wouldn't let him near the children."

Anna frowned. "I still don't understand," she said,
perplexed.

"He was castrated as a result of his wound. I mean,
he is more like a woman than a man . . . is that clea
enough?"

Anna looked at her sister and felt both shock and bewilderment as she remembered her once-handsome
brother. Andreas had been a real ladies' man, but it appeared that those days were gone forever. And how cold
and cruel Gerda was!

Gerda stood up and the ash from her cigarette fell on
the floor. "I'll fix us some tea," she suggested. "If we
have any."

It was a clear hint. "Come out with me, Gerda. I'll
take you to a coffeehouse for a coffee and some pastry."

Gerda half-smiled. "I haven't been out in a long
while," she admitted. "You'll have to pay. I have no
money for such luxuries."

Anna felt totally exasperated. "Of course I'll pay,"
she muttered. Well, Gerda was Gerda. She was getting

the terms all straight before she accepted. Perhaps, Anna thought hopefully, her sister would be less bitter in a different place where she wasn't constantly reminded of her fallen status. "Then come along," Anna said, "We'll discuss the children."

"Rudolf is an honor student," Gerda said proudly.

"That's wonderful," Anna said, trying to imagine the young man that Rudolf, a child who had once always been dressed like Little Lord Fauntleroy, had become.

Gerda put on her coat and together they left. "Let's go right into Berlin," Anna suggested. "To one of the fine cafés on the Unter den Linden."

"Perhaps I can remember what it was like," Gerda said wistfully. "What it was like when I had my own money."

Jim Parnell looked around his new office. He was a full-fledged state's attorney and the fine leather chair, the good view, and the expansive desk all forecast a bright future, a future that would enable him to marry Ann, to have children, to travel, and to buy a home. This position and the opportunity for advancement that it offered was all he had worked for, and he ought to feel optimistic. But he didn't feel at all optimistic. In fact, he felt almost ill. His first case, a case he could not refuse because those senior to him in the department had already refused to handle it, was a case he wasn't certain he could prosecute. Because he was new, because he had no say in the matter, he had been ordered to take this case. He wiped his brow and shook his head. No, he *could* prosecute. It was more that he had no heart for it. His objections were strong and they were personal—his feelings were feelings a man in his position simply shouldn't have.

He pressed his lips together and stared down at the file in front of him. It was marked "Alex Webber" in large black letters. Cautiously, as if the contents were volatile, he opened the file. A long official document—a deposition—stared back at him. It stated that over twenty-five thousand dollars was missing from the trust fund of the late Mavis Prentice. Mavis' husband, long dead, had been Alex Webber's law partner. Webber was the administrator of the trust fund and he alone had access to it. The deposition was signed by Christiana Prentice, Mavis' middle-aged daughter.

"Shit," Jim said under his breath. Alex Webber was his friend, he was Anna's mentor. He'd worked hard over the years to help other young lawyers as well.

Jim shuffled through the papers. Certainly this was not a clever theft. Webber had made no attempt to cover it. Jim shook his head and for the one hundredth time asked himself, "Why?" But the answer was obvious. Webber always had financial troubles. He took too many *pro bono* cases. "Probably rationalized it all," he muttered aloud.

Again he shook his head in rejection of the facts and in disgust over what he would now have to do. He closed the file and stood up, shoving his chair back against the wall. It was a little unorthodox, but he decided to go to see Webber. Again he wished that Christiana Prentice had waited . . . but she was not the waiting kind. She had already gone to the press. The world would soon know that Alex Webber, renowned civil libertarian, was accused of theft. It was, Jim reflected as he pulled on his coat, a tragedy of Shakespearean dimensions. Webber would be a man destroyed by his most admirable quality, his overwhelming desire to defend liberty.

Anna walked down the Unter den Linden to the grandiose magnificence of the Brandenburg Gate. There, for a long moment, she paused before trudging on to face again the unbearable bureaucracy of the nurses' registry.

The registry was located on the fourth floor of an undistinguished building off the Unter den Linden. Anna pushed through the glass door, and finding the elevator still out of order, walked wearily up the four flights of worn stairs. She went directly to the main desk where yesterday she had waited for over an hour, only to be told to return today.

"Helga Gassner," Anna repeated for what seemed the hundredth time. "I suppose she'd be around fifty-five now," Anna explained as patiently as possible. The woman looked up over her glasses and fingered her cheap beads.

"We have thousands of nurses registered here. Any one of them is qualified. Why must you have this one?" she complained from behind her old desk.

"I don't want to hire her," Anna said as she felt herself beginning to lose patience. "I explained all this yesterday. I'm a lawyer and I need information from this woman. There was another woman here yesterday—she wrote it all down."

"Yes, I have her note, but it doesn't say why you wanted to find this woman."

"Well, now I've told you. Do you or do you not have such a person registered here?"

The woman frowned. "It was so long ago. I had to go all the way to the basement. I finally did find her record."

"Where is she? Do you have an address?"

"I have an address. But she probably isn't there anymore. She was in the inactive file, so the address hasn't been updated."

"Give me the address you have," Anna persisted. "I'll check it out myself."

"It's not in the best of neighborhoods."

"Please, just give it to me," Anna insisted.

The woman didn't look up at her again. She scribbled down an address which she copied from a yellowed file and handed it to Anna.

Anna took it. "Thank you," she said. But the woman only grunted. Yet another pleasant German, Anna thought with annoyance.

Oddly, Helga Gassner's last-known address was on a street off Der Alexanderplatz, not far from where Anna had lived with Kurt. Anna trudged along in the cold, preferring to walk from the station than take a cab. When she took a cab, people stared at her, and it was a chore having the right payment. Inflation was absurd, one had to carry thousands of marks, and if you didn't have the right change, the driver always tried to cheat you by refusing to give change.

Anna stared at the nondescript building and then went inside. There was no directory, so there was no choice but to knock on doors.

Anna knocked on one and an elderly man opened it. He was bald and had a thick gray mustache. His old brown work pants were held up by red suspenders. He squinted at her over the top of thick reading glasses. "Do you know a Helga Gassner?" Anna inquired.

"Ja," he answered, pointing a finger upward.

Anna felt her heart leap. Helga still lived here! "Which apartment?" Anna pressed; then, realizing he was deaf, she asked again in a louder voice.

"Number ten," he answered, still pointing upward.

"Thank you," Anna said. "Oh, thank you." She hurried up the stairs and down the dark, dank, smelly corridor. She stopped short in front of the door; her heart was pounding and she steadied herself, waiting for a moment before knocking.

The woman who came to the door was still heavyset, but her face was deeply lined and her neck was thick. Her once-blond hair was thin and white and she stood framed in the doorway staring at Anna.

Anna didn't need to ask; she immediately recognized her nemesis, even though years had passed. "Do you remember me?" Anna demanded.

Helga Gassner continued to look at her, and her lips began to move, though no words actually came out. She lifted her finger like a teacher and waved it limply, as if the action would help her remember. "So many years," she finally muttered; then, "I remember the Black Forest . . . yes, you had a child, a daughter."

Anna looked at her hard. "You took her," she snapped. "Tell me where you took her! I demand it!"

The woman blinked at her. She scratched the side of her head slowly. "No need to yell. What difference does it make now?"

Anna had to force herself not reach out and shake the woman. "Tell me," she said, forcing control into her voice.

"I took her to your brother," Helga said. "Yes . . . I remember now. Those were the instructions your father gave me. I took her to your brother . . . a nice young man. He was in the army, I remember."

"Markus?" Anna wasn't really asking Helga; she just

said the name in utter amazement. It was all true . . .
Gerda was right. Markus had deceived her at their father's request.

"I don't remember his name," Helga said. "But he said he had to have the child because his wife's child had died. He said not to worry . . . I wasn't . . ."

"What!" Anna's voice resounded down the hall and she seized the old woman's shoulders and shook her hard. "Repeat that! What did you just tell me?"

"He said his wife's child died. He said he would raise the baby as his own and you'd be sent to America."

Anna let her hands slide down the sides of Helga's arms. She felt almost as if she might faint. Mattie was *her* daughter! But Dorcas didn't know . . . how could she? I never told her I had a daughter. Anna's mind raced, though gradually her heart stopped pounding wildly and she began to feel a release, a sense of happiness, even a sense of pride. Mattie was *her* daughter. She kept saying it over and over to herself.

"Is that all you want," Helga said impatiently.

Anna heard her voice through the fog of her own thoughts. "Yes," she managed; then she turned and literally ran down the corridor and then the stairs. Once out on the street, she walked rapidly along, everything taking shape in her mind, everything finally making sense.

At nine in the morning, a short two days later, Anna boarded the train for Hamburg. As it pulled slowly out of the station she leaned back and closed her eyes, thinking of her visit with Andreas, whom she had seen in spite of Gerda's warning.

She had met him in the wine bar of the Hotel Monopol on the Friedrichstrasse, and in all truth they would have failed to connect had he not recognized her. Always a tall man, Andreas had grown extremely heavy as well. That he was gross was one thing, but his voice was high-pitched and his face round, feminine, and hairless.

Shortly after they had been seated in a secluded corner, he had implored her, "I'm not a freak, I'm not. Don't look at me that way!"

"Andreas, I didn't mean my look to convey any judgment. But you have changed."

"The doctors say it's because of the hormones . . . that's what they call it, a hormonal abnormality." He bit his lips and his blue eyes filled with watery tears. "Underneath—you can't tell because of my clothes—underneath, I have breasts like a woman! Oh, Anna, my life is horrible. I am much abused."

Anna looked at him sympathetically, not knowing exactly how to respond.

"I am not a homosexual, but I am treated as one. Actually I have no sexual desires at all."

"I'm sorry your life is so miserable," Anna said sincerely. Of all those she had met, Andreas seemed the most pitiful, and he did not seem to blame others either, he seemed to bear his own burden of guilt.

"I deserve to suffer," he blurted out, leaning toward her and running his hand nervously through his thin hair. "It's my fault Else's dead, you know. She went mad, and I let them put her in a terrible place. At the time I didn't care. I think they killed her—I don't believe she killed herself."

Anna felt shock mingle with nausea. "Oh, Andreas, how could you?" she asked in bewilderment. "How could you not care about her?"

"She was having an affair with Markus."

"But you had a mistress yourself."

"I know . . . but Else had Markus' child. I know it wasn't mine. I'm not proud of what I did, and I'm paying, Anna, paying just as if I'd gone to prison. You don't know what a hell my life is . . . my children have been taken away from me. I have to do terrible things simply to get enough money to eat."

Anna had not asked what things, because his constant references to being physically abused were enough. "I'm sorry," she said, simply because there was nothing else to say. "Where are the children now?" she asked.

"In different places . . . I have their addresses."

"May I have the addresses? I want to keep in touch with them. Perhaps I'll be able to help them, I am their aunt. Perhaps I could arrange for them to come to America."

Andreas had looked half-disbelieving. "Would you help them?" he asked.

"I promise I'll try," she said, touching Andreas' hand. Then, without being asked, she wrote him a check and handed it to him. He began to cry and burble, and she'd asked him not saying anything, but only to try to pull himself together. Then she had fled, feeling terrible for him, but knowing there was really nothing she could do that she had not already done.

Anna opened her eyes and for a long while looked out the window of the train. Seeing Andreas had shaken her, and reliving their meeting had distressed her all over again. Then, after a time, she managed to set his image aside, and wearily she drifted into sleep as the train moved along. Tomorrow she would sail for America and in seven days she would be in New York and then on her way home to Chicago. Over and over she thought about what she must tell Dorcas, but the more she thought of it, the more her apprehension and hesitancy grew. After a time she forced thoughts of Dorcas and Mattie out of her mind and managed to concentrate only on Jim. How she wished he'd been with her. How she longed for him!

Anna pushed her way through the crowd on deck. It seemed as if every passenger on this ship was crowding at the rail to wave one last good-bye to Germany.

I've said my good-byes, she thought as she finally reached the door that led to the lounge. She shivered; it was cold and damp, and though she seldom drank, she recalled Jim telling her that nothing warmed one as much as Irish whiskey and hot coffee. She sank into a plush chair in the corner. The lounge was empty, but even so the lingering smell of stale cigarette smoke permeated the air.

"May I help you?"

Anna looked up into the waiter's face. "I want some Irish whiskey in coffee . . . can you make that?"

He grinned and nodded. "Irish coffee," he said.

"Yes, Irish coffee."

"And would you like an American newspaper to read? We have last week's *New York Times* and I believe we have the weekend edition of the *Chicago Tribune*."

Anna removed her little pillbox hat and set it down on the table, shaking loose her hair. "I'd like to see the *Trib*."

"One Irish coffee one *Trib* coming up," he responded cheerfully. Anna smiled to herself. He hadn't noticed an accent. He'd taken her for an American, and somehow that thought made her feel good.

In a few moments the waiter returned bearing the paper under his arm and a masterpiece of Irish coffee in the other. "I wasn't expecting anything quite so elegant," Anna said as the young blond waiter put down the drink. It was in a huge goblet and it was topped with mounds of whipped cream and garnished with shaved chocolate.

"Enjoy it, and here's your paper."

Anna took a long sip. Beneath the whipped cream the hot coffee mixed with whiskey fairly steamed up. Jim was right, it was an instant cure for the kind of cold brought on by the penetrating dampness of the ocean.

Anna unfolded the paper and perused the stories on the front page, her eyes coming to an instant halt on the long story headlined "Civil-Rights Lawyer to Be Prosecuted."

Speaking for the state's attorney's office, Jim Parnell today confirmed that prominent Chicago lawyer Alex Webber, now retired, will stand trial for embezzlement.

Christiana Prentice, daughter of the victim, the late Mavis Prentice, charges that Webber took over $25,000 from her widowed mother's trust fund.

"Alex Webber may have been a saint to his clients, but I know him for what he is," Miss Prentice stated.

Jim Parnell, who will try the case, said only that "There can be no favors for anyone. Regardless of Webber's reputation, we are all equal under the law."

Anna let the paper drop to the table. How could Jim prosecute Alex Webber? How could he even think Alex could be guilty? Why hadn't Jim refused this case?

She covered her eyes with her hands and shook her head. Too much had happened all at once . . . all her emotions were at war. And she admitted to feeling helpless . . . no, being helpless. Helpless and angry. There was nothing she could do for days. No. I can send him a telegram, she thought. Then, without further hesitation, Anna stood up and fled the lounge. Yet even as she marched off to find the purser, she knew that she felt miserable.

Anna shook her head, but there was no clearing it of the frustration she felt, of the emotions that fought for supremacy. There was simply no denying the fact that Alex Webber had in every emotional sense become her father. And there was no denying that the man she thought she loved was going to destroy him . . . perhaps even send him to jail. Yet Jim knew her feelings for Alex Webber. How could he do this?

17

Propelled by near-gale-force winds, great slabs of ice washed up on the shore of Lake Michigan. February was the cruelest month, the coldest, the most unrelenting, because in February it seemed as if winter would never end.

Anna's cheeks had smarted with the cold, but now inside the overheated Federal Building her skin flushed with the sudden change of temperature. The liquid in her eyes, which had before felt frozen, now felt like tears. And she sniffed because her nose was suddenly running. All weather-induced miseries, she thought angrily as she pushed the elevator button impatiently.

Oh, damn Jim! Damn him! She'd spent her entire return voyage shifting between anger and unhappiness. She'd tried to plan for this encounter . . . then she'd tried to put it out of her mind.

The door of the elevator opened and a gaggle of warmly dressed workers prepared to brave the wintry streets in search of some greasy lunch counter nearly walked over her in their haste. She met them head-on and shoved herself into the elevator. She punched the button, but the elevator had another journey in mind. It went to the basement even though she had pressed up. Then it stopped again where she had gotten on and immediately filled up with more bundled bodies.

Anna pushed out of the elevator and down the hall to Jim's office. His secretary was gone, and without hesitation she opened the door to his inner office and walked in.

"Ann!" Jim looked up from his desk, then scraped the chair back as he stood up.

Behind her the door swung shut. For a moment Anna stood frozen. In her thoughts she had rehearsed what she would say . . . had to say. Now confronted with his seemingly calm reality, she felt less strident, though no less firm in her conviction that he simply had to drop the case against Alex Webber.

"I got your wire," he said, filling the silence.

"And have you dropped the case?" She looked at him hard.

"Ann, I'm a state prosecutor. You know I can't drop the case."

"Then you should resign! How can you do this to an old friend, a man who is practically my father? How? I don't understand you at all!"

"If I did resign it wouldn't stop the case against Alex Webber."

"But you wouldn't be the one . . . it wouldn't be you."

"Ann, you're a lawyer. You know the rules and you know I have to do this. You're letting your emotions override your professional judgment."

"I care about Alex Webber! I don't *have* a professional judgment where he's concerned. I don't understand how you can . . . can be so stubborn!" Hot tears started to flood her eyes. They were tears of sheer anger and frustration, tears of rage, and yes, tears of helplessness.

"You're in a terrible emotional state," he said softly. But as soon as he'd made the observation, he knew he'd spoken the wrong words. A woman who prided herself on her logic, and normally she had a right to such pride, could only be insulted to be called "emotional."

"Emotional! Of course I'm emotional! This will ruin what's left of Alex's life! He's had a magnificent career . . . he doesn't deserve this. It's untrue! I know these allegations are untrue."

"That's what trials are all about . . . proving the truth," he said, feeling miffed that she wasn't even willing to hear him out.

"You still don't have to be the one. Are you going to resign or not?"

He looked at her and could clearly see the stubborn determination in her lower lip. Well, she had misjudged him, and that made him angry too. "No," he said flatly. "No, I am not going to resign."

Anna pulled the ring off her finger. The tears were now running down her face and she was trembling with weariness and anger. "Here," she said, putting it on the desk. Then she whirled around and practically ran out of his office. Once in the corridor she glanced around, then abandoned the idea of waiting for the elevator. She fled toward the sign marked "Exit," flung open the door, and began the long descent to ground level.

It was two o'clock when Anna arrived home. Dorcas was there to meet her, and over coffee and toast Anna poured out Mattie's story to Dorcas.

Dorcas had gotten up from the table and now she stood by the window apparently looking down on the busy street. But Anna knew Dorcas wasn't really watching what happened below; her eyes were nearly glazed over and she stared almost vacantly as she tried to digest it all and make sense of Anna's revelation.

"I should have told you long ago about my child. Perhaps we'd have figured it out," Anna finished.

Dorcas turned slowly and the look on her face said more than all the words either of them might speak. Normally pale, her face had turned ashen and she trembled uncontrollably as she struggled to a chair. Tears filled her eyes and she covered her face with shaking hands. "I almost told you a thousand times that Mattie was adopted," she sobbed. "Oh, God in heaven, I swear I didn't know you were her mother. I didn't know that was why you went to Germany . . . I . . . Oh, Anna, please, please believe me. I didn't know she was yours."

Anna's own tears ran freely and she got up and walked over to Dorcas, taking Dorcas' small white hands in hers and holding them it tightly. "She's not mine, she's yours. You've been her mother," Anna said softly. "You've loved her, looked after her, and brought her almost to womanhood. I know you didn't know."

Dorcas lifted her eyes. "What are we going to do . . . I mean, should we tell her? We can tell her together if you want."

Anna shook her head. "We should leave things as they are, Dorcas. Mattie is happy and we all have each other. You are her mother, the only mother she knows. I love her, and now I'm free to love her even more. But she's happy and we shouldn't upset that happiness. At least not now. If she needs to know when she's older, when she's an adult, maybe then."

Dorcas reached out and embraced Anna. "You know," she choked, "my own child died two days after she was born. Markus brought me Mattie and I just took her and never asked any questions. I should have asked questions."

"No. You did what came naturally. Oh, Dorcas, you've been a wonderful mother, a perfect mother."

"She's a special child," Dorcas said softly. Then Dorcas paused. "Anna, do you know what happened to her father?"

Anna shook her head. "No. I never saw him after she was born."

"I don't know if I should tell you . . . No, I must. Markus told me Mattie's father was a criminal, that he'd been arrested and that he'd escaped. For a long time I worried he'd come and try to take her away from me . . . but Markus told me he didn't even know about us . . . of course, he never told me the important part . . . that you were her mother. I suppose he only told me about the father in case anyone did come looking for her."

Anna felt a sudden cold chill as she remembered the face she thought she had seen in courtroom . . . Kurt's face.

Dorcas misunderstood the expression of consternation on Anna's face. She pressed her lips together, then squeezed Anna's hands back and pulled her own hand away to wipe the tears off her cheeks. "Perhaps it was all a lie," she said. "Perhaps Markus only wanted to frighten me."

Anna didn't reply. It probably was a lie, and certainly there was nothing to be afraid of here in Chicago. She chastised herself for her moment of silliness. Anna sniffed. "She'll be home from school soon, and if she finds us like this she'll wonder what's wrong with us."

Dorcas forced a smile. "You have to call Jim. He called twice this morning to see when you'd be here."

"I've already seen him," Anna said coldly. "It's over between us."

Dorcas looked up in surprise. "I don't understand."

"He's prosecuting Alex . . . I read about it. I wired him. I saw him first thing and broke it off between us."

"Oh, Anna . . . no. I thought you looked terribly upset when you came in. Now I realize you must have been under a terrible strain—the trip, what you found out, and now what's happened with Jim."

"Dorcas, how could I go on being with him?"

"I don't know. Anna, think about it. Be sure. It is his job, you know . . . what would you do if you were in his position?"

"I'd resign."

"Are you sure?"

"Yes. Yes, I'd resign and he should resign."

"Call Alex Webber, Anna. Talk to him."

Anna looked at Dorcas and nodded.

Dorcas got up. "I'm going to wash my face. By the way, I did go to Milwaukee while you were gone."

Judge Harrison Hogarth was elderly, distinguished, and one of the most highly regarded jurists in the Midwest. His home in Evanston was decorated in elegant good taste, with original oil paintings on the walls, long green velvet draperies at the windows, and rich mahogany furnishings. "Good of you to come," he said, greeting Anna in a dark satin smoking jacket and ushering her to a plush red leather chair in his study.

"Not at all," Anna answered. "I'm seldom summoned to the home of a judge."

He laughed and took a seat in his own chair behind a wide expanse of desk. "I hope you don't mind the study— it's ever so much homier than the living room. "Coffee?" He gestured toward an ornate silver coffee service sitting on a side table.

"Thank you," Anna replied.

The judge got up, poured her a cup of coffee and one

for himself, and then turned around. "Cream and sugar?"

"Yes, please."

He prepared her coffee and swirled it around with a spoon and then handed it to her, taking his to his desk. "I've asked you to come here for a very serious reason," he said, looking at her over the gold-rimmed glasses that rested on his nose. His brow was thoughtfully furrowed.

"About one of my cases?" she queried.

He nodded. "You've developed a fine reputation as an attorney, Miss Bock. You've developed an especially fine reputation on First Amendment cases."

"Thank you. Coming from you, that's a real compliment."

He steepled his fingers and looked at them for a long moment. "You filed an appeal in the case of the six anarchists," he said slowly.

"And you, as federal district judge, heard that appeal."

He nodded. "It was well-argued, but I rejected it."

"And I have appealed to the Supreme Court."

He cleared his throat. "I know."

Anna shifted uneasily in her chair. "I don't honestly think we should discuss this," she said, looking him squarely in the eyes.

He smiled. "I wouldn't admire you if you weren't so proper. I know damn well we shouldn't discuss it, and frankly, we won't. What we will discuss is the fact that the Supreme Court has agreed to hear the case." He grinned. "Well, what do you think?"

Anna looked at him in disbelief. "I think it's exciting," she said, feeling her words something of an understatement. Then her face clouded over. "I do have other commitments right now. I phoned Alex Webber. I'm going out to Oak Park to see him tomorrow. I have to help prove his innocence."

Judge Hogarth nodded. "You, my dear, are about to be the first woman to ever argue a case before the Supreme Court of the United States. I think that should take precedence over all else."

"I have to talk to Alex first."

"Talk to him, but keep the importance of this case in mind."

Anna sat back. "I know it's an awesome responsibility and an opportunity too. I'm certain that I can manage both Alex Webber's defense and the Supreme Court appeal." She listened to the sound of her own voice and wondered if she sounded as confident as she was pretending to be. The truth is, I am distracted, she admitted.

Judge Hogarth rubbed his chin. "I've argued before the court many times. It may be a responsibility, but almost no one remembers the lawyer's name. What they remember, if anything, is the name of the justice who cast the most profound written decision. But your appearance will be different. It's historic. You know, I'm glad it's you."

"Thank you." She tried to smile. "I wouldn't have had this opportunity if you hadn't turned down my appeal."

"Let me assure you, that's not the reason I turned it down. And I do suggest you review my decision, have a careful look. Perhaps you can avoid having the Supreme Court turn you down for the same reason."

"I intend to study your decision very carefully indeed."

"I won't be arguing against you," he said. "I invited you here to tell you that if you want any pointers, well, you can consult me."

"That's very generous of you, your honor."

"Well, mostly the judgment will be made on your written arguments. You get to speak for only thirty minutes—a sort of summation of your written arguments."

"I know. I did some preliminary work on the appeal before I went to Europe."

"Under no circumstances go overtime. In fact, you would do well to try to finish before your time is up."

"Would that give me an edge?"

He rubbed his chin thoughtfully. "I daresay it would."

"I suppose I'll receive official notice in a day or two."

"Yes, it's my understanding that they intend to hear the case very soon."

Anna nodded. "It's very kind of you to tell me."

He laughed again. "Personally, I feel a part of history. I think you'll do well, Ann Bock. Go get 'em!''

"Ah, it's my dragon slayer!" Alex Webber beamed as he tilted the old chair in his office back and looked across at Anna.

The office in the back of his house was as cluttered as his law office in town had always been. His desk was piled high with papers and there were books everywhere. He was the same, crumpled and fleshy in the face, yet he was older and his once-sharp eyes seemed a little dimmer.

"I was in Europe, or I would have come sooner. I'll do anything I can to help, anything."

"You broke your engagement to Jim Parnell. Why did you do that?" he asked sharply, surprising her.

"How could I be engaged to someone who's prosecuting you?"

"You haven't given him a fair hearing."

"I don't want to talk about Jim. I want to talk about you, about this charge. I want to help defend you."

"I have all the defense I need. If you don't want to talk about young Parnell, then talk about the Supreme Court. You're going and you're going to give it your all."

"You must let me help you."

"Anna, if I needed your help I'd take it. I don't. I want you to begin planning for your court appearance and I want you to see Parnell. You're a lawyer and you're being no more fair to him than you think he's being to me."

"I just don't understand how he could—"

"See him and prepare yourself and let me take care of myself, will you?"

Anna looked into his eyes. He was stubborn and determined. She knew the look. Silently she nodded, then added, "But if there is anything . . ."

He laughed. "I'll call you."

Anna hurried home from Oak Park, but it was snowing heavily, and it took her nearly two hours.

"Oh, you look tired and frozen," Dorcas said as she

opened the door. She took Anna's snow-laden coat and hung it up near the heater, while Anna struggled out of her boots.

"Where's Mattie?"

"In bed, I'm afraid. Did you want to talk to her?"

Anna nodded. "No, I want to talk to you first. Dorcas, I've got exciting news. I'm going to Washington in April. The court is going to hear my appeal. I've known for two days . . . but I only found out this afternoon when I'd be going."

Dorcas hugged her. "That's wonderful!"

Anna sighed. "Hardly anything in my life seems wonderful these days. But this is . . . well a light in the gloom. I do have one thing to ask you," Anna said, holding on to Dorcas' hands. "Understand, I don't get to say much, the oral argument is not allowed to be over thirty minutes, it's the written argument that counts. Still, I am the first woman to argue a case before the court. I'd like to take Mattie with me to Washington—I'd like to show her the capital and have her in court when I present the argument and file the appeal."

"Of course you can take her!" Dorcas agreed without hesitation.

"I know Mattie will enjoy Washington . . . and it is an important moment for me," Anna admitted.

"It's grand of you to want to have her there. I understand."

Anna kissed her sister-in-law on the cheek. "Thank you," she said. "Oh, thank you for sharing her with me."

Dorcas rubbed her hands across her apron. "Anna, Jim called again."

"I will call him," she answered. "I don't want to, but I will."

"This," Jim declared with a forced smile, "is a very important month. It comes in like a lion, goes out like a lamb, and in between we have the Ides of March and this, the all-important Irish holiday, Saint Paddy's Day!"

Anna stood stiffly next to Jim in the doorway of O'Hara's on State Street. Huge green balloons hung from the rafters of the low rustic ceiling. The tables were all festooned with green party hats, crackers, whistles, banners, napkins, and even specially dyed carnations.

"A sort of New Year's Eve in green," he continued as he led her to a table by the fireplace.

"If we don't celebrate Saint Paddy's Day, we Irish have trouble all year long—and don't we have enough trouble already? Of course a state's attorney and a prominent lawyer ought not to be in an Irish speakeasy and nightclub, but what the hell, it is a saint's day!"

"You're irreverent," she said coldly.

"And you're beautiful, smart, and, oh, yes, a maker of history."

"Oh, stop! You seem to think this is just another evening out. I only agreed to meet you because I'm ashamed I lost my temper. I haven't changed my mind, I still think you should resign, but Alex seems to think I've been unreasonable."

"You were and are," he answered.

Anna pressed her lips together. "I'm not sure why I'm here."

"This isn't the way I wanted to start out," he said, looking at her hard. Damn. Did she really think he was such an ogre? A wave of stubbornness passed over him. She seemed determined to think the worst of him. Well, if that's what she wanted . . .

Anna sat down.

"You know I love you," he said, looking into her eyes.

She avoided his eyes. "I thought I loved you . . ." She shook her head. "I just don't understand how you can do this to Alex, why you won't resign. Let someone else do it."

"I have a job to do and what I have to do, I'll do in my own way," he said evenly. Her emotions were still all wrapped up in a damn ball and they were clouding her normally practical nature.

"Then I guess things will remain as they are. I can't continue our relationship because you aren't the man I thought you were."

"You're too quick to judge, Ann."

"There's nothing to judge."

He pressed his lips together tightly and she could see his Irish temper in his eyes. "Then that's the way it is. Let's have dinner and make pleasantries. Nothing more, nothing less."

"All right," she agreed, but in fact she wanted to run away.

"So, how's it going?" he asked after a moment. "I know what goes into the preparation of an appeal."

Anna took a sip of water from the goblet on the table. "I'm leaving on the tenth of April, and the court will hear the case on the fifteenth. After that, I'll come home to Chicago. Perhaps I can help Alex then. He's so stubborn. He won't take my help now."

"Maybe he won't need help then," Jim said.

"He won't come to trial before then, will he?" She could hear the apprehension in her own voice.

"No. I intend to give him all the time he needs to put together his defense."

"How helpful of you," she said sarcastically.

He ignored the sarcasm. "I'm a helpful fellow."

Anna didn't look up. Anger and confusion were still fighting inside her. She cursed herself for still wanting him, for still caring. She forced herself to change the subject, to bring up a matter that was far away from their personal and professional problems. "Then maybe you can help me," she said, still avoiding his eyes. "I know the state's attorney's office doesn't have a close relationship with the D.A.'s office, but you still have friends there, don't you?"

"Yup." He grinned. "Want a traffic ticket fixed?"

Anna did not laugh. "No, you know I don't have a car. No, nothing like that. I just wondered if you remembered the case you prosecuted and I defended . . . the case of Margaret Olsen?"

"Hard for a fellow to forget a case he so resoundingly lost," he replied. "Sure, I remember. Why?"

"Well, I had a call the other day from a Sergeant O'Malley. He asked me to come in and talk to him—he indicated it had something to do with that case."

Jim raised his brow. "Well, I know they never closed the file. I requested a reinvestigation after your client was acquitted. You know, to see if they could find the alleged chauffeur. But no, I don't know why they'd want to see you."

"Well, I guess I'll just have to wait till Monday," Anna said as the waiter appeared.

"Two green beers," Jim ordered confidently.

"Green beer?" Anna questioned.

Jim nodded. "In spite of everything, it's still Saint Paddy's Day. Tonight we're going to drink green beer, sing a few sad songs, and eat a good meal." Then he said, lifting the glass to his lips, "We'll bid each other farewell."

Anna looked into his face. In her mind she could feel the strength in his arms, and the heat, energy, and excitement that flowed through her when he held her. She longed for him, but there was no going back. He was prosecuting Alex Webber and it was wrong.

Sergeant O'Malley was a big heavyset man with a ruddy complexion and thick snow-white hair. He ushered Anna into his small office and indicated a chair next to his desk. "Damn windy," he said. "Looks like you blew all the way down Randolph Street."

Anna undid her plaid scarf and slipped off her dark green woolen coat. She was all too aware of her disheveled appearance. Her matching fur-trimmed hat was slightly tilted, and underneath it, her hair was a tangle because her hat had been blown off and she'd only put it back on when she'd come inside. "The wind in March blows the city's dirt away," she observed.

He guffawed loudly and continued to chew on the end of his fat cigar. His desk was a mess of disorganized papers and his ashtray was overflowing. The room smelled of cigars, but then, the whole police station had a strange odor. An odor Anna could only describe as "uniquely institutional."

"I asked you down here, counselor, cause we got an open file in the Pridmore case and there's been a couple of developments since the trial."

"How can I help you?" Anna asked, still mystified.

"Well, we'd like to talk to your client, that Margaret

Olsen, but we don't know where she is, and, well, she was acquitted and so we don't want to summon her or anything.''

"What exactly do you want to talk to her about?" Anna questioned.

"We just want her help . . . we want to see if she recognizes a photo of our suspect."

"I do know where she is," Anna allowed. "This doesn't have anything to do with laying charges against her, does it?"

He shook his head emphatically. "Hell, no! We're convinced she's innocent. It's just a matter of letting her see the photos of the suspect. She might recognize him."

"Is he in custody?"

"Nope. But if he's still in Chicago, and we think he is, we'll find him."

"I'm sure my client will cooperate, but I'd like to come with her."

"Sure, no problem."

Anna looked at him curiously. "Tell me," she asked, "what have you got?"

"A man we suspect was tied to Pridmore—who, by the way, seems to have had a kind of double life. Anyway, this here man is called 'The Professor.' We suspect he killed Pridmore and stole not only his wallet but also a lot of negotiable securities from his safe. We also think this here German Professor may be implicated in the murder of as many as four women. He seems to love them, take their money, then kill them."

"My God," Anna said, surprised that the police had, in the final analysis, done a lot of investigative work.

"Yeah, here's his picture . . . at least the only one we got. Odd-looking fellow, wouldn't you say?"

Sergeant O'Malley handed Anna a yellowed photograph with slightly dog-eared edges. She took it and held it to the light. She stared at it and felt the blood drain from her face. Her hand began to tremble and she shivered. It wasn't a good photograph, but it was good enough. Kurt Stein stared back at her, and a chill went through her . . . a chill, then a shock wave. He *had* been at the trial! She had not imagined his face among the spectators that day! Kurt Stein was in Chicago and he knew who she was! "Mattie . . ." Anna whispered as she thought of Kurt's weird, mad, violent personality. Violence that had quite obviously now manifested itself.

"You okay?" Sergeant O'Malley asked, leaning toward her.

Anna looked up at him, wondering how much, if anything, she should tell him. Then she thought: No. She wouldn't tell him anything yet. She didn't want to see Jim again just yet, but now she had to talk to him. This, she told herself, was old business. No, that wasn't it. She fought to be honest with herself. She was terrified and she needed him. It was as simple as that.

"Ann!" Jim strode out his spacious office in the State Building to greet her. "To what do I owe the pleasure of seeing you midday and during the week!"

He had begun enthusiastically, but Anna watched as the smile faded from his face and was replaced with a look of concern. She knew her own expression must reveal the turmoil of emotions that were flooding over her. "We have to talk," she said urgently.

"Come on in." He opened the door to his office and glanced at his secretary. "Take my calls," he told her.

Even as Jim closed the door, Anna began talking, pouring out what she'd learned from Sergeant O'Malley, telling him about the man she'd seen in court, expressing her fears—her fears for herself, but mostly for her daughter . . . her daughter and Kurt's.

"Oh, I shouldn't be burdening you with all this. I shouldn't have come here in the middle of the day. But you did prosecute this case . . ."

"Of course you should have come." He stood close to her, but he didn't hold her as he wanted to. "I'll go back to O'Malley's with you. You'll have to tell him everything you know about this man. It will help the police to catch him." Then he pulled her back and looked into her face, seeing the terror in her eyes.

"Ann, you've got to pull yourself together. Look, he hasn't come near you. I mean, you defended Margaret

Olsen quite a while back. Be logical: if he intended bothering you—in any way—he would have done so by now.''

Anna looked into his eyes and fought to listen to his calm voice. He *was* right. It had been two years. Still, Kurt was far from normal; he might wait, and he was clearly every bit as dangerous as she had suspected. Did he know where she lived? Another violent chill passed through her as again she thought of Mattie. ''You may be right,'' she said slowly, taking some strength from Jim's calm. ''It's not just me,'' she whispered. ''I'm worried about Mattie. What if he tries to reach her?''

Jim looked at her thoughtfully. ''Look, Ann, you've got an important case coming up. You've got to concentrate all your efforts on your preparation. I'll tell you what . . . I have some influence downtown. I'll see to it that you and Mattie are discreetly watched till you're ready to leave for D.C. I'll even see to it that Dorcas is watched while you and Mattie are gone. Maybe, with luck, we'll catch this guy by the time you get back.''

''I don't want Mattie to know.''

''I promise discretion. How about it?''

Anna nodded, already feeling safer because Jim knew and cared. ''If you think that's best,'' she agreed.

She looked up at him and wished things were not the way they were. A part of her wanted him to hold her, to kiss her passionately; another part of her was still filled with anger and confusion and the conviction that he ought not to prosecute Alex personally.

''It's best for you to have protection,'' he reiterated; then, ''Let's go back downtown to O'Malley's . . . I'd like this guy caught as soon as possible.''

It was as if spring were being carried on the wind. The air smelled fresh and clean, it smelled of earth and of flowers, of bushes and newly blossomed trees. And it was warm for April.

''It's going to be absolutely beautiful in Washington,'' Dorcas said. Then she added, ''You look sensational— feminine as well as businesslike.''

Anna was wearing a pert white hat trimmed with black ribbon and a crisp white suit with a black silk blouse.

She wore black and white spectator shoes to match her hat.

"The cherry blossoms will be in bloom," Mattie added. "I read this is the tenth anniversary of their planting."

"It's the perfect time of year to go to Washington," Anna agreed, wondering if Mattie or Dorcas could hear the sound of relief in her voice. How wonderful to get away from Chicago, she thought. How wonderful not to have thoughts of Kurt nagging at the edges of her mind.

"I'm getting on the train," Mattie announced. "Why don't you come and look at our compartment, Mother?"

Dorcas smiled and took Mattie's hand.

"How long before the train leaves?" Anna asked.

"Thirty minutes," Mattie answered as she turned to climb the iron steps.

"I'm glad you're going to Milwaukee, Dorcas."

"She needs a vacation too," Mattie put in, turning as she paused before the big iron door that led into the car where their compartment was located.

"Feeling confident?" Dorcas queried.

"I never feel really confident. And I have been distracted . . . oh, not all the time, but often enough." Anna stopped short of saying why she'd been distracted. Dorcas would think she meant she was distracted by her breakup with Jim. Even now she thought of him, thought of his last words to her about Kurt. "I don't think you have to worry. I doubt he'll come near you."

"I think you're right. I know that every day it's gotten easier. I know I'm starting to relax, to put him out of my mind."

"Good. I want you to win that appeal."

It had been a crisp conversation, not at all like the conversations they had once had. Yet she could see the longing in his eyes and feel her own weakness, her own desire to be with him. But always the image of Alex Webber stepped between them and she could not find it in her heart to forgive Jim for seemingly accepting this case as "just part of his job." I'd have left the state's attorney's office before I'd do this to an old friend, she thought. Why hadn't Jim left? Why did he continue on?

"Anna, you're lost in thought again." Dorcas jostled her arm.

Anna forced a smile. "I was just thinking of the crowd when we arrived. I was surprised by the photographers in the station . . . my goodness."

"You're a celebrity, Anna. Chicagoans are proud, they like the idea that the first woman lawyer to argue a case before the Supreme Court attended law school here and practices here. Besides, you're also going to be speaking to the League of Women Voters, and that's a big organization here."

Anna felt her cheeks go hot. "I owe it all to Alex Webber," she said softly.

"This is a bit unusual," Alex Webber said. "Rather more than a prosecutor is expected to do."

Jim turned and squinted at Webber. The light in the basement of Alex's house was atrocious, and the dust was even worse. "I'm going to start sneezing again," he warned.

Webber ripped open a large box. "I'm a sloppy man," he said with a deep sigh. "Always been bad with paper, out-and-out sloppy."

"If you say Mavis Prentice gave you permission to take the money, I believe you. But unless we find the release form she signed, I'm the only one who'll believe you."

"No, Anna will believe me too. Nice of you to have the trial date set so far in advance. Gives us time to look for the authorization papers. Aren't you afraid of being accused of conflict of interest?"

"Hell, no. If we find the authorization papers, then I don't have to go to trial. I'll just save the state some money."

"You should have told Anna what you're doing. But you didn't, did you?"

"No. I wanted her to have enough faith in me to come back without my proving I'm a boy scout. Anyway, if we don't find the papers, I'll have to prosecute, won't I?"

"Yes, no question about it. Anyway, if you don't, someone else will. But you should have told her you'd delayed the trial date and you should have told her you've been over here for weeks helping me search. She'd have come back.''

"I want her to come back on her own. I want her to realize I'm not as willing to desert my friends as she thinks.'' He sniffed and then let out a terrible-sounding sneeze.

"I should have told her!'' Alex thundered. "You're Mr. Pride and she's Mrs. Prejudice. And I'm a damned slob who can't find one vital little scrap of paper.''

Jim stopped and looked at Alex. "There are two more boxes here. I'll take this one, you take the other.''

Webber snorted. "Stubborn,'' he muttered.

Kurt Stein slumped into the old, faded overstuffed chair in the corner of his room in the Hotel Metropolis. The Metropolis was a seedy run-down hotel on Marquette, and, he thought as he looked about sullenly, the room was equally dilapidated. The furniture was mismatched and scratched, the bedspread had cigarette burns on it, and there were water marks on the ceiling. His eyes fell on the wall next to the chair. A large brown cockroach lazily crawled out from behind the rusted heater and began an unhurried march up the wallpaper. Kurt watched for a few seconds, then reached out and with the flat of his hand smacked the revolting insect flat, its insides adding yet another stain to the wall. He screwed up his face and wiped his hand on the arm of the chair. Then, leaning back in the chair, he unfolded the evening paper and, as he always did, proceeded to read all of it.

As he turned to page five, in pursuit of the continuation of a story from page one, his eyes fastened on a picture of a familiar face—he held the paper under the light—two familiar faces. One was Anna, dressed to the hilt for travel, and the other was a young girl who stood next to her. They were both standing on the station platform, and behind them the cars of the train formed the picture's background. Kurt held the picture to the light and studied their images. The young girl . . . there was no question in his mind, the young girl was his daughter! She was the spitting image of her mother, and if he had

had any doubt, her apparent age confirmed his opinion. Kurt feasted on their picture for another moment, then turned his attention to the accompanying story.

CHICAGO'S LADY LAWYER
GOES TO WASHINGTON

Chicago attorney Ann Bock is about to make history. She is the first woman ever to be allowed to argue a case before the Supreme Court of the United States. Miss Bock, the attorney representing the Milwaukee Twelve—anarchists convicted several years ago of responsibility in a city-side bombing—will present her appeal on 15 April. In the accompanying photo, Miss Bock and Mattie Bock prepare to leave for Washington. While in Washington, they will stay at the Capitol Hotel, and Miss Bock will speak at the annual meeting of the newly formed League of Women Voters.

"We were fortunate to have been able to arrange this speaking engagement on such short notice," the president of the Washington chapter of the LWV, Mrs. Carrie Broadwick, told our correspondent. "Naturally," she went on, "we want to hear from such a prominent First Amendment lawyer."

Kurt's fist automatically doubled in anger. Anna's father had had him arrested in Germany, and he'd ordered him killed. He'd been forced to flee for his life. And just as he was making it, Anna's defense of that whore Margaret Olsen had caused a two-year police investigation that discovered his involvement with Pridmore as well as his relationship with several women whom he had killed. Anna had been a plague on his life since the day he'd met her! He threw the paper to the floor and got up and stomped across the room. His jacket was hanging on a hook near the bed. He fished in his pocket and pulled out his wallet. He had four hundred left, and it was more than enough to get him out of Chicago and take him to Washington. It was time to leave Chicago anyway, he decided. He'd find new opportunities in Washington—and more important, he could even his score with Anna. Yes, he thought, pressing his lips together, Mattie must mean a lot to her . . . but Mattie was his daughter too, and, he vowed, she would know it soon enough.

Lake Michigan sparkled in the spring sunlight, and on the nearby lawn of the shoreline park, two robins pecked for worms in the soft moist soil.

Dorcas was dressed in a blue suit with a matching cape. Her blond hair hung down to nearly her shoulders, then curved slightly under. It was held in place, in spite of the wind, by a little cloche that matched her suit.

Josef was dressed more casually, in slacks and a tweed jacket. He took Dorcas' arm protectively; then, letting her arm loose, he let his hand slide down her arm so he could hold her hand. "Do you miss being in Chicago when you're here?" he inquired.

Dorcas shook her head. "No. I think I like it here better. It's much quieter."

He let a moment elapse while he pondered his words, then said hesitantly, "How would you feel about moving here?"

Dorcas stopped walking, and he turned to face her. "I mean . . . well, I'd like to marry you. I know I'm older. I know I'm not . . . well, haven't been overly demonstrative, but I care for you, Dorcas. I enjoy your company, I want to be with you."

Dorcas reached up and ran her hand over his ruddy face. He was a big man, and in spite of his age, he was, in her eyes, good-looking. "I want to be with you too," she said softly.

His big hand touched her throat; then awkwardly he bent down and kissed her gently.

It began as a warm, friendly kind of kiss. But as his lips lingered on hers, it grew in intensity and he felt her body close to his, and her hands on his suddenly warm face.

"Friendship turned to fire," she whispered, and he held her close, realizing that he wanted not only her companionship but also her love.

"That *is* exactly what it is," he breathed.

They kissed again and then pulled away from each other reluctantly because a group of giggling children came down the path on their bicycles. They walked hand in hand. Then after a time Josef asked, "Can we marry soon?"

Dorcas smiled. "As soon as you like."

"In a month?"

She nodded. Then, with a slightly mischievous tone in her voice she asked, "How do you feel about children?"

Josef flushed. "I'm a bit old . . ."

Dorcas laughed. "No, no . . . I was wondering how you would feel about the children of my former brother-in-law, Andreas. Anna was thinking of bringing them to America because Andreas asked her to help them. I think they might be better off in Milwaukee with us, rather than in Chicago."

"And Mattie?"

Dorcas again smiled. "Mattie's very mature for her age. She may want to stay with Anna until she finishes school. It's her decision."

Josef squeezed Dorcas' hand. "I think young people around the house would keep me young."

Dorcas kissed his hand and smiled. "Keep *us* young," she responded.

18

"Equal justice under the law is the *raison d'être* of the Supreme Court of the United States," Anna told Mattie as their cab moved slowly toward the Capitol Building, where the Supreme Court met on a regular basis. For years there had been talk of building a new edifice to house the high court, but thus far Congress had not appropriated the funds.

Mattie looked out the window as they traveled toward the Capitol. The cherry trees that lined Pennsylvania Avenue were indeed in bloom. "There's a special feeling to this city," she commented, "a feeling of power and history."

Anna smiled proudly, surprised that Mattie, as young as she was, had experienced the sensation that she herself had felt almost immediately. The buildings that were so familiar in books suddenly had dimension and reality, and with that dimension and reality came a wave of understanding for the ideals represented in the stone and mortar of Washington.

"How will it happen?" Mattie asked, turning to Anna. "I mean, what's the procedure?"

"First the marshal announces the entrance of the justices. Everyone stands for that, and the marshal calls out, 'The Honorable Chief Justice and Associate Justices of the Supreme Court of the United States, *Oyez, oyez*'— that's French for 'Hear ye, Hear ye,' and is used by custom to call the court to order." Anna laughed at her own imitation of the marshal.

Their cab drew to a stop at the bottom of the Capitol steps. Anna inhaled deeply, trying to calm her nerves. "I'm afraid you'll have to wait and experience the rest," she said. "I'll be sitting downstairs. You'll have to go to the gallery."

They climbed out of the cab and Anna paid the driver. Then they climbed the steps, entering the great Rotunda with its 180-foot dome featuring the allegorical fresco painted by Constantino Brumidi. For a long moment Anna looked upward; then she directed Mattie to the gallery and presented herself to the guards, who escorted her into the chamber.

Nervously she smoothed her navy-blue Harris-tweed suit and sat down at a small table assigned to her. Looking up, she felt tiny—dwarfed by the massive chamber itself, but also small because she was so far below the dais where the judges would sit. Gradually the chamber filled up with lawyers, court recorders, and judges from lower courts. The gallery too filled, but Anna spotted Mattie, and just before the marshal appeared, she waved and saw Mattie smile back.

The marshal made his traditional call to order and the nine black-frocked judges filed in, their faces stern. "All persons having business before the Honorable, the Supreme Court of the United States, are admonished to draw near and give their attention, for the court is now sitting! God save the United States and this honorable court!" the marshal shouted out to the absolute silence.

Pomp, circumstance, and ritual all combined to make Anna feel even more humble, yet she forced herself to consider her clients and the possible precedent her case could set. After all was said and done, this court was about justice, and its decisions were reversible only by another Supreme Court decision or a constitutional amendment. Not that she would know the decision right away. It could take months for the court judges to write their decisions. And yet she knew history was being set just by the fact that she was here in this chamber, that she would be the first woman to stand and give a thirty-minute argument. Anna surveyed the bench. Real history, she thought, would be made when a woman sat on that bench beside the men.

The first case was presented and dealt with a Texas law. It was argued by an elderly gray-haired lawyer whose booming voice filled the chamber. Then her case was announced, and Anna stood to present her argument.

Long hours of preparation and rehearsal proved rewarding. Nervous though she was, Anna soon felt at ease, even comfortable, as her argument unfolded. In her first appeal before the Appellate Court, Anna had argued that there could be no crime of thought and that the anarchists had originally been convicted largely because they had in their possession literature advocating violence. This time her appeal centered on due process.

"The Fourth Amendment," she said, her eyes fastened on the justices, "protects against unreasonable search and seizure. The Fourteenth Amendment protects against self-incrimination. My clients were forced, by the authorities, to produce materials which incriminated them, and I argue that this is a violation of their rights under both the Fourth and the Fourteenth amendments. I cite Boyd v. the United States, where this court refused to allow the government to compel an individual to produce papers that might help convict him. This decision combined the protections against self-incrimination and unreasonable seizure."

Anna took a deep breath and glanced at her watch, mindful of the advice that she finish early rather than be reprimanded and called to complete her argument.

"My appeal clearly shows that the alleged inflammatory pamphlets were not in distribution. But rather that the defendants were compelled to hand them over. They were then used to form the basis of the prosecution's contention that these men planned to commit acts of violence. I put it to the honorable court that by so compelling the accused, the authorities denied their rights and violated both the Fourth and Fourteenth amendments."

Upon concluding her argument, Anna sat down and thought that the most unnerving aspect of arguing before the court was the absolute stony silence of the atmosphere in which one argued. There was no immediate reaction, no hint of either success or failure . . . there wasn't even the shuffle of feet or the rippling sound of opinion as it swept the spectators of the courtroom. Her moment of history completed, she glanced up to the gallery. Mattie was smiling broadly, and silently clapped her hands. Anna smiled back, thinking that her daughter's admiration was surely the best reward.

"You were wonderful!" Mattie said, hugging Anna. "I told the guard I was your daughter so he'd put me in the front row. I could hear everything you said and see your face too . . . you were wonderful, Tante Anna."

Anna took Mattie's arm. "Come on, let's go have a celebration lunch before we go back to the hotel and get ready for tonight."

"You must be tired," Mattie suggested.

"I am, but I'm running on nervous energy and I can't rest till it's all over."

"I'm so excited being part of this. Oh, Tante Anna, I can't thank you enough for bringing me. I want to be a lawyer. I want to be just like you."

"Be like yourself, my darling. But I won't discourage you from studying law. Just before I gave my argument, I had this idea . . . maybe it was more of a vision. I was thinking how wonderful it would be if there were a woman chief justice or even a woman associate justice. You know, you could be a lawyer and then you could become a judge."

Mattie squeezed her aunt's arm. "I feel as if I have two mothers," she said enthusiastically. "It's a wonderful feeling."

Anna felt her mouth go a little dry. How often since she had learned the truth had she thought of telling Mattie she was her mother? But how would Mattie deal with it? It was one thing to acknowledge admiration and daydream about it, but to find out the truth would be far less romantic. Yes, she thought, putting it out of her mind, it was better that things remain as they were.

"Do you really think I could become a judge?" Mattie asked.

"You can do whatever you want," Anna replied. "As long as you want to do it badly enough."

* * *

Anna stood by their hotel-room window and looked out on the Capitol at twilight. The day, which had been close to perfect, had faded into a sensational sunset. The Capitol dome, which could be seen from every part of the city, stood out against an ever-darkening purple sky, a sky now accentuated by uneven lines of gold light as the sun sank.

"You look lovely," Mattie said as she stood across the room by the door that led to the bathroom.

Anna was wearing her new brilliant red evening gown. Made of crepe de chine, and based on a design by Paul Caret, it featured gentle folds over the stomach and a flaring skirted train in the back. "I'm almost as nervous about tonight as I was about presenting my appeal to the court," she confessed.

"You were stupendous in court," Mattie said, "and you'll be stupendous tonight."

Anna blushed at the unbridled pride in Mattie's voice. She was impressed and enthusiastic as only a young girl could be, still Anna reveled in her daughter's excitement, love, and admiration. It gave her a deep pleasure, a pleasure, she admitted, that helped make up for all the years between, the years during which Mattie had been lost to her. And Mattie helped her to push Jim from her thoughts. Mattie was a distraction, a wonderful distraction.

Anna ran her hand over her dress nervously. "It's almost time for me to go. I'm sorry I have to leave an hour early for that meeting with the newspaper reporter—are you certain you don't mind following in a cab?"

"It'll give me more time to get ready," Mattie said, glancing at her own dress, which was laid out on the bed. It was of blue taffeta. It had a full skirt and was trimmed in ivory lace.

Anna turned when the phone rang. "Maybe it's the reporter canceling the meeting," she said, lifting the receiver.

"A long-distance call for Miss Ann Bock . . ." the voice crackled over the wire.

"I'm Anna Bock," Anna replied.

"Anna . . . Anna, it's Dorcas, in Milwaukee, can you hear me?"

"Yes, of course. Is something wrong?"

"No, everything is right. Everything! Anna, the charges have been dropped against Alex Webber! The story was in the paper this morning! It was Jim! Jim found the proof of Webber's innocence!"

Anna gripped the phone. Jim had found the evidence? Why hadn't he told her he was doing something . . . that he was trying to prove Alex innocent? "Oh, Dorcas, I don't know what to say. I'm relieved . . . so relieved. But I'm ashamed too."

"It's going to be all right, Anna. I know it is. You're in for a big surprise!"

"What surprise?"

"If I tell you, it won't be a surprise. But I will tell you this: Josef and I are getting married."

"Wonderful! You know how pleased I am."

"I know . . . listen, I have to go. This is costing a fortune. Kiss Mattie for me."

Anna opened her mouth to say good-bye, but the line was disconnected.

She smiled and put the receiver back in its cradle. "It was your mother," she said. "With wonderful news."

Mattie pressed her lips together. "I heard part of it."

"Alex Webber is innocent. Jim found the evidence."

"You love Jim and he loves you. You'll be back together in no time now," Mattie said confidently.

Anna smiled. It was a real smile and she felt suddenly lighthearted. "Somehow I think you're right, but we still have things to talk about."

Then she glanced at her watch. "God, I'm going to be late. I'll have to go downstairs now. I ordered my cab for six and yours for seven. Just ask the doorman . . . he knows you're going on alone. Are you sure it's all right?" Anna asked again.

Mattie giggled. "You fuss more than my mother," she complained jokingly. "Of course it's all right. I go to school every day alone in Chicago—after all, I only have to take a cab from one hotel to another."

Anna picked up her evening bag and her wrap. "I'll
~ you in an hour," she promised. "I'll go directly

from the newspaper office to the dining room of the Willard.''

Mattie came across the room quickly and hugged Anna and kissed her. ''You'll be great, don't worry. I'll be right there, right there at the head table.''

Anna returned Mattie's kiss, then turned and hurriedly left, heading down the long corridor toward the elevator.

Kurt watched the entrance of the Capitol Hotel from the park across the street. He saw Anna as she came out of the double doors, and he watched, a slow smile of satisfaction covering his face, as Anna climbed in the cab and drove away toward the appointment she thought she had made with a reporter from the *Washington Daily World.*

Without further thought of Anna, Kurt crossed the street and walked briskly through the lobby to the elevator. Nothing had been difficult. Using his guise as a reporter, he had found out the name of Anna's hotel from an article in the newspaper. He had, using the same subterfuge, gotten her room number from the desk clerk when he'd phoned to make the appointment.

He reached the spacious elevator, and its ornate brass doors opened silently. He strode in and pushed the button for the fifth floor. In seconds he was standing before Room 510.

Mattie turned toward the door when she heard the light tap, and going to it, asked, ''Who is it?''

''Room Service,'' the male voice replied.

Mattie opened the door a crack, but jumped back as it was pushed open with force.

''Who are you?'' she blurted out, feeling suddenly frightened by the appearance of the wild-eyed man who had forced his way into the room and had now slammed the door.

Kurt did not answer her question, but rather took two long steps toward Mattie. He reached out, and as she was about to scream, he roughly put his hand over her mouth. ''Stop it!'' he muttered gruffly. Then, seeing the expression of terror on her face, he frowned and loosened his grip. "I won't hurt you if you promise not to scream . . . do you promise?"

Shaking, Mattie nodded her head.

Kurt dropped his hand slowly and stared into her face.

Mattie's blue eyes filled with tears, "What do you want?" she managed. "Who are you?"

Kurt continued to study her. She looked like her mother and she appeared to be a bright girl. No, she was his daughter too, and he didn't really intend hurting her. What he wanted was money from Anna . . . and he had decided that Anna should suffer because she had caused him so much difficulty. Still, he was here, and so was his daughter. Anna wouldn't like it if he told the girl who he was, so he decided to do just that.

"I'm your father," he said confidently.

Mattie scowled at him. "You are not. My father was Markus von Bock and he died as a result of inhaling poison gas during the war."

Kurt frowned. She sounded sure of herself. "No," he insisted. "I'm your father and we're going away together. Your mother's doing real well. She'll pay to get you back."

"My mother works in an office. She's not rich. She doesn't have any money."

"Don't play games with me!" Kurt stormed. "Your mother's a well-off lawyer! I know who your mother is."

Mattie shook her head. "That's my aunt. You're insane . . . why are you saying these things?"

"She is not your aunt! Anna is your mother and I am your father. I suppose this man you think was your father was Anna's brother . . . I suppose they adopted you or something."

Mattie stared at him and felt her lip quiver. Could his story be true?

Anna stood in the deserted but well-lit lobby of the *Washington Daily World*. It was all marble and hanging chandeliers. Behind an information desk manned by a uniformed guard there was a bank of elevators that served the offices of the paper above. Below, the great presses turned out the daily papers, which were loaded onto trucks from huge platforms at the back of the building.

Anna stood in front of the guard, scowling at him. "Ken Bayliss," she repeated. "He's a feature writer."

The guard lethargically ran his finger down the page of his registry book. "Nope," he said, looking up. "Nobody here by that name."

"There must be," she insisted. "He called and asked me to meet him here."

The guard sighed. "I'll call the city room, but you'll see. There ain't nobody here with that moniker."

Anna waited, and in a moment the guard handed her the telephone. She held the receiver to her ear and spoke into the phone. "Ken Bayliss," she said, then spelled it slowly.

"Nope, nobody here by that name."

"Are you sure?" Anna said, feeling vaguely annoyed.

"I'm the editor," an equally annoyed voice on the other end of the phone responded.

"Oh, I'm sorry, there must be some mix-up," she allowed. Anna hung up and handed the phone back to the guard. "Sorry," she said, waiting for his "I told you so." But it didn't come, so she went back outside to catch a cab to take her to the Willard.

Mattie sat on the edge of the sofa in the large hotel room she was sharing with Anna. Kurt sat across from her, on the edge of the bed. He seemed to Mattie, who had begun to feel a little calmer, a very odd man indeed. He had hypnotic eyes, eyes she felt were in fact filled with madness, though he seemed to be genuine in his assertion that he didn't intend to hurt her. And it seemed quite clear that he did in fact know or had known Tante Anna. He said he had met her at the University of Berlin. Mattie thought about the answers to the questions she had asked him. The answers to those questions confirmed his knowledge of Anna. But what of his claim to be her father? And could Tante Anna be her real mother? Was there even a possibility that he was telling her the truth?

Kurt suddenly stood up. He glanced at his watch. "Come on," he said. "It's time we got out of here."

Mattie pressed her own lips together. "What if I won't come?" she asked, feeling suddenly a bit braver.

"I told you, cooperate, you won't get hurt."

"If it's true I'm your daughter, why would you hurt me?"

He looked at her hard and Mattie could almost see his black pupils flicker. "I need some money, some leeway. I don't want to hurt you"—he narrowed his eyes—"but I'm a desperate man. I've killed before . . . I've even killed people I liked."

Mattie forced herself not to cry. He was a lunatic, and, she decided, it might be better not to make him angry.

"I'll get my coat," she said slowly.

"I can't understand where she is," Anna said, searching through the faces as they entered the dining room. There were crowds of well-dressed women pushing through the double doors and flooding the lobby of the genteel hotel.

"I'm sure she'll be here," Carrie Broadwick said confidently. She was a square-built woman with gray hair, a strong face, and a short compact body. "Perhaps her cab is caught in traffic. It might even have broken down, you know. Look, you come inside and I'll have someone call the hotel. Please don't worry."

Anna nodded, but she couldn't shake her concern.

Carrie, nonetheless, prodded her forward. "You're first to speak, and I'm just certain that when you finish, you'll look down the table and see her sitting right where she's supposed to be sitting."

Anna relented and allowed Carrie to escort her to the head table. The minutes seemed to pass slowly, but Mattie was nowhere to be seen.

The room filled, and the ladies of the League of Women Voters took their seats, and with a tap on the microphone, the meeting was brought to order.

Carrie rose to introduce Anna, who once more nervously looked down the table. Then a note was passed to her. "No answer at the hotel room, must be on her way."

Anna nodded at the person who had handed her the

note, and shuffled her material together and prepared to approach the podium as Carrie was just finishing her introduction.

"And so, for our first speaker of the evening, I take great pleasure in presenting Ann Bock, the first woman attorney ever to present a case before the Supreme Court of the United States."

The women applauded. Then they stood and applauded.

Anna walked to the podium and laid out her notes. The podium was too far forward for her to see the head table, or even to be able to glance down its length to see if Mattie had arrived.

"I'm pleased and honored to be here among you," Anna began, "and I have chosen to speak to you tonight about the unique position of women and the law. . . ."

Jim Parnell leaned over the desk in the Capitol Hotel and scrawled his name into the register. Anna, he thought happily, would be surprised and perhaps even stunned to see him. He hoped she would also be happy because he had left on a sudden irresistible impulse only four hours after finding the document that cleared Alex Webber. He'd filed a press release and phoned Dorcas. Then he'd caught the early-morning train.

"Room 703," the desk clerk said as he slid a large key on a leather key ring across the counter.

Jim took the key, and the porter took his bag and walked to the elevator. They stood waiting while the great gold dial over the elevator showed it moving slowly to street level.

The doors opened, and Jim looked directly into Mattie's pale face. He opened his mouth in surprise and then saw the tall dark-haired, muscular man standing behind her. He had seen Kurt's picture at the police station and he recognized the tight dark curly hair, the angular face and above all the hypnotic eyes. "Mattie!"

Kurt's hand had been on her shoulder, but Mattie spurted forward. "Jim!" She almost shrieked his name and ran into his arms as if for protection.

Kurt stood stock-still, but only for an instant. "Shit," he muttered, then started to sprint across the lobby.

Jim whirled around. "Stop that man!" he shouted. "Police! Doorman! Stop that man!"

He broke loose from Mattie and ran across the lobby. Old men sitting in heavy leather chairs beneath reading lamps dropped their papers and looked up in shock as the sedate atmosphere was disrupted. A woman with puce hair and a small poodle on a leash screamed as Jim knocked over a table and sent a lamp crashing to the floor. He flung himself forward and hurled himself down, grasping Kurt by the legs and dragging him to the floor in what he knew was his best rugby tackle.

Kurt was well-built, but so was Jim, who had the advantage of being on top. He doubled his fist and brought it down hard, hitting Kurt in the face. Kurt, though stunned, fought back. He managed to pull Jim to the side slightly, and they rolled over and over, legs and arms flailing. Each groaned as they tumbled down six cold, hard marble stairs, knocking over a man with luggage as they went. At the bottom of the stairs, and to the left, a small table stopped their momentum. Jim felt a table leg hit his ribs and saw and heard the brass lamp fall to the marble floor. The luck of the roll brought Kurt out on top. But Kurt's punch was deflected by Jim's left arm. Then Jim's Irish temper fully blossomed and he roared and with all his might threw Kurt off him. Kurt seized the fallen table lamp from the floor and came toward Jim menacingly.

Jim scrambled to his feet and advanced on Kurt, blocking the intended blow with his left hand. He punched Kurt in the jaw with his right. Kurt's head snapped back and his eyes rolled back in his head as he crumpled to the floor. Jim, panting and advancing to hit Kurt again, felt a pair of big hands pull at him from behind, and a policeman stepped in front of him, preventing him from further advancing. His nose bleeding, he turned around and looked into the face of the Washington policeman who held his arm. "My identification . . . is in my pocket," he gasped. "This man is wanted for murder in Illinois and he was trying to abduct that young lady!"

Jim pointed to Mattie, who sat in a chair, tears running down her face.

The policeman turned toward her. "Is that true?"

Mattie nodded, then struggled out of the chair and ran to Jim. "I'm so glad you're here," she sniffed.

The police officer checked Jim's identification. " 'Course, you got no jurisdiction here, Mr. State's Attorney."

"But he stopped a crime in process," the other policeman said. He scratched his head. "You staying here?"

Jim nodded.

"Okay, we'll take this guy in and hold him till we contact Illinois. We'll be back to talk to you later."

Jim nodded and held Mattie close. "Did he hurt you?" he asked.

"No . . . I'm supposed to be at the Willard right this second, Anna's making her speech to the League of Women Voters."

Jim nodded. "We'll call and have a message given to her so she won't worry. C'mon, I've got to clean up." He wiped his nose, which was bleeding slightly.

Mattie looked at him appraisingly. "Yes, you'd better."

Jim ordered the bellboy to take his bag to Mattie's room. "This is where Anna will come," he said, "so this is where we better be."

As soon as they reached the room, and before he cleaned off his face, Jim called the Willard and left a message.

Mattie slumped onto the sofa while Jim went in and cleaned off his face and changed his bloodied shirt. He came out still drying off his face with a big white towel. "You sure you're okay?" he asked, looking at Mattie carefully.

"Yes, he said he didn't want to hurt me," Mattie said, a faraway tone in her voice.

Jim studied her expression. How like Ann she looked! And she was still pale. Clearly the episode had not only frightened her but also raised questions in her mind. She seemed to be a million miles away and lost in thought.

"Do you want to talk?" he asked, gently trying to cajole her back to the present.

Mattie lifted her blue eyes slowly. "Who was he? He said he was my father . . . that Tante Anna was my mother. He knew a lot about her . . . true things, things she's told me. He knows her . . . he said he wanted to hurt her and that he needed money." Mattie suddenly paused, then asked, "And what are you doing here?"

Jim grinned at her and then sat down next to her. "I'm in love with Anna and she's been angry at me. Well, she can't be angry anymore, so I quite suddenly decided to come here and surprise her. I wanted to take you both on to New York with me. I want to marry Anna and we'll need a bridesmaid."

Mattie smiled through her tears and leaned over and hugged him. "I was so scared . . . I was so glad to see you." Then, with troubled interest, "Why did he tell me those things? Are they true?"

Jim looked into her eyes. Anna ought to be the one to tell her . . . Anna or Dorcas. But they weren't here, and even if he denied it or suggested she wait, the answer would be obvious in his nonanswer, in his evasiveness. "It's true," he said softly, covering her hand. "You were taken away from Anna when you were born. She went back to Germany to try to find you and discovered you'd been given to Markus and Dorcas. Dorcas didn't know Anna was your mother." He watched her. It was going to take time to come to terms with the truth, but she didn't seem too terribly shaken, except perhaps by the fact that Kurt was her father. Still, Mattie was strong and intelligent. He could almost see her mind working as he spoke to her. He could only hope she was emotionally as strong as she was intellectually.

"Is he a murderer?" Mattie asked.

Jim nodded. "And emotionally unstable. I don't claim to know a lot about these things, Mattie, but I would guess to be as immoral as Kurt Stein, you'd have to have had a horrible childhood."

"I've had a very good childhood," Mattie said slowly. "Especially the last year." She blinked back tears. "It's better to be loved by two mothers than one," she said, leaning against Jim's shoulder. "It sort of makes up for having a father like that . . . that man."

"You just think of me as your father, Mattie. Or at least as someone you can come to when you need help."

Mattie forced a smile. "I have Josef too—two mothers and two fathers."

Jim squeezed her shoulders. "With luck you might soon have half-sisters and brothers too."

Mattie nodded. "That would be wonderful."

All around the huge dining room of the Willard, waiters stood poised in the wings ready to serve the appetizers when Anna finished.

Anna looked out on the sea of faces. No one looked bored or uninterested. "It is our duty to inform citizens on the actions of their elected representatives; to monitor their voting record and to encourage our elected representatives, from all parties, to pass legislation that will redress the imbalances that exist in the law. Women should be their own masters and not the chattels of men. We need to work toward ample property-settlement laws, toward divorce laws which will protect women left with children. We need to build on our recent victories in child labor legislation and in legislation to protect women workers. At all times we must see our goal clearly. That goal is to make women equal under the law."

There was clapping, and Anna smiled and turned to go back to her seat. Her heart sank as she turned around. The seat where Mattie should have been was still empty.

She moved to her seat and saw the note on her plate marked "Urgent." Carrie was still thanking her, and as she finished, the waiters moved into the room and began to deliver the food. Everyone burst into conversation. Anna quickly unfolded the note and read: "Kurt under arrest. I am at hotel with Mattie. She is all right. Come back as soon as you can. Jim."

"Jim . . ."Anna whispered under her breath. Her heart pounded. Kurt had been in Washington! He was under arrest! But the essential message that Mattie was all right calmed her, and the thought that Jim was waiting elated her. That was the surprise Dorcas had spoken of . . . it was Jim.

Anna fairly burst into the room. She ran to Mattie and embraced her, and even as she held her, she sought Jim's eyes. "I don't know where to begin, but God, I'm so glad to see you," she whispered. "Tell me what happened."

Mattie pulled away and led Anna to the sofa. She explained what had happened in detail while Anna, stunned, listened.

"Oh," she murmured, "oh, what if you hadn't come?" She looked at Jim. "What if you hadn't been standing there when the elevator opened?"

"I don't think he would have hurt me," Mattie said. Then she looked into Anna's eyes. "I know everything . . . he told me, and Jim told me."

Anna's eyes flooded with tears. "Oh, Mattie, I love you so. I thought it would be better if . . ."

Mattie allowed Anna to wrap her in her arms. She put her own arms around Anna's neck and said, "I'll always love Dorcas as much as you . . . it's good to have two mothers."

Anna just sobbed as nervous energy, the strain of the day, the shock of Kurt's arrival and arrest, and the surprise of seeing Jim flooded over her. They sat together, holding each other, crying, and then, after a while, laughing.

"I suppose Dorcas told you about Webber?"

"Yes . . . I should have known you'd try to do something to help him. I should have had more faith in you."

"If the evidence hadn't been found, I would have prosecuted."

"Yes, but you presumed Alex was innocent from the beginning, that you would find the evidence, and the case would never come to trial. I . . . I think I assumed he was guilty and I didn't want you to be the one to prove it. I worked with him for years—I knew there was never enough money. I knew he was lax about details too. I guess I assumed he'd gotten verbal permission and not done the paperwork." Anna looked down and shook her head. "We reversed our roles," she said softly. "You defended, I prosecuted, at least in my own mind."

He smiled gently at her and touched her hair. "So are you going to marry me?"

Anna glanced at Mattie, who nodded her approval.

"Yes, yes, and yes again!" Anna said, letting him kiss her.

"I mean now, this week, as soon as we can," Jim pressed.

"Yes . . . as soon as we can." Anna tilted her head and he kissed her again. It was a long kiss, a kiss of long-felt love, of passion, a kiss filled with promise.